Praise for novels of

SUZANNE BROCKMANN

"With its complicated, complex characters and a sexy
romance seasoned with humor and danger,
Brockmann's latest is absolutely irresistible."
—*Booklist* on *Into the Night*

"Thanks to Suzanne Brockmann's glorious pen,
we all get to revel in heartstopping adventure
and blistering romance."
—*Romantic Times BOOKclub*

"Brockmann's complex characters will
capture the reader's sympathy."
—*Publishers Weekly*

"This irresistible hero will fill your dreams
with sizzling passion…. Absolutely spellbinding."
—*Romantic Times BOOKclub* on *Everyday, Average Jones*

"Ms. Brockmann is a one-of-a-kind storyteller!"
—*Romantic Times BOOKclub*

"[Brockmann] spins an unforgettable, riveting adventure
that is fast-paced and a bit chilling."
—*Library Journal* on *The Unsung Hero*

"A smart, thrilling keeper among so many disposable
stories, this is one to recommend heartily to friends."
—*Publishers Weekly* on *The Defiant Hero*

D1016347

SUZANNE BROCKMANN

Tall, Dark and DANGEROUS

MIRA®

MIRA

ISBN 0-7783-2122-3

TALL, DARK AND DANGEROUS

Copyright © 2005 by MIRA Books.

The publisher acknowledges the copyright holder
of the individual works as follows:

PRINCE JOE
Copyright © 1996 by Suzanne Brockmann.

FOREVER BLUE
Copyright © 1996 by Suzanne Brockmann.

www.MIRABooks.com

Printed in U.S.A.

TABLE OF CONTENTS

PRINCE JOE

ACKNOWLEDGMENTS

My eternal thanks to my wonderful friend Eric Ruben, who called me up one day and said, "Hey, Suz, I just read a great article about navy SEALs. You should check it out." (I did, and the rest, as they say, is history.)

Special thanks to the Prince Joe Project volunteers from the Team Ten list at Yahoogroups.com: Rebecca Chappell and Agnes Brach (Cocaptains), and Julie Cozzens, Miriam Caraway, Gail Reddin, Vanathy Nathan, Kristie Elliott and Julie Fish. Ladies, I salute you. Thanks so much for stepping forward and helping out.

Thanks also to Katherine Lazlo and the many other readers who took the time to e-mail me and set me straight about the correct use of "Your Majesty" and "Your Royal Highness."

Last but not least, thanks to the real teams of SEALs, and to all of the courageous men and women in the U.S. military, who sacrifice so much to keep America the land of the free and the home of the brave.

Any mistakes I've made or liberties I've taken are completely my own.

For Eric Ruben, my swim buddy.

Prologue

Baghdad, January 1991

Friendly fire.

It was called friendly because it came from U.S. bombers and missile launchers, but it sure as hell didn't feel friendly to Navy SEAL Lieutenant Joe Catalanotto, as it fell from the sky like deadly rain. Friendly or not, an American bomb was still a bomb, and it would indiscriminately destroy anything in its path. Anything, or anyone, between the U.S. Air Force bombers and their military targets was in serious danger.

And SEAL Team Ten's seven-man Alpha Squad was definitely between the bombers and their targets. They were deep behind enemy lines, damn near sitting on top of a factory known to manufacture ammunition.

Joe Catalanotto, commander of the Alpha Squad, glanced up from the explosives he and Blue and Cowboy were rigging against the Ustanzian Embassy wall. The city was lit up all around them, fires and explosions hellishly illuminating the night sky. It seemed unnatural, unreal.

Except it was real. Damn, it was *way* real. It was dangerous with a capital *D*. Even if Alpha Squad wasn't hit by friendly fire, Joe and his men ran the risk of bumping into a platoon of enemy soldiers. Hell, if they were captured, commando teams like the SEALs were often treated like spies and executed—after being tortured for information.

But this was their job. This was what Navy SEALs were trained to do. And all of Joe's men in Alpha Squad performed their tasks with clockwork precision and cool confidence. This wasn't the first time they'd had to perform a rescue mission in a hot war zone. And it sure as hell wasn't going to be the last.

Joe started to whistle as he handled the plastic explosives, and Cowboy—otherwise known as Ensign Harlan Jones from Fort Worth, Texas—looked up in disbelief.

"Cat works better when he's whistling," Blue explained to Cowboy over his headset microphone. "Drove me nuts all through training—until I got used to it. You *do* get used to it."

"Terrific," Cowboy muttered, handing Joe part of the fuse. His hands were shaking.

Joe glanced up at the younger man. Cowboy was new to the squad. He was scared, but he was fighting that fear, his jaw tight and his teeth clenched. His hands might be shaking, but the kid was doing his job—he was sticking it out.

Cowboy glared back at Joe, daring him to comment.

So of course, Joe did. "Air raids make you clausty, huh, Jones?" he said. He had to shout to be heard. Sirens were wailing and bells were ringing and anti-aircraft fire was hammering all over Baghdad. And of course there was also the brain-deafening roar of the American bombs that were vaporizing entire city blocks all around them. Yeah, they were in the middle of a damned war.

Cowboy opened his mouth to speak, but Joe didn't let him. "I know how you're feeling," Joe shouted as he put the finishing touches on the explosives that would drill one mother of a hole into the embassy foundation. "Give me a chopper jump into cold water, give me a parachute drop from thirty thousand feet, give me a fourteen-mile swim, hell, give me hand-to-hand with a religious zealot. But this… I gotta tell you, kid, inserting into Baghdad with these hundred-pounders falling through the sky is making me a little clausty myself."

Cowboy snorted. "Clausty?" he said. "You? Shoot, Mr. Cat, if there's anything on earth *you're* afraid of, they haven't invented it yet."

"Working with nukes," Joe said. "That sure as hell gives me the creeps."

"Me, too," Blue chimed in.

The kid wasn't impressed. "You guys know a SEAL who *isn't* freaked out by disarming nuclear weapons, and I'll show you someone too stupid to wear the trident pin."

"All done," Joe said, allowing himself a tight smile of satisfaction. They'd blow this hole open, go in, grab the civilians and be halfway to the extraction point before ten minutes had passed. And it wouldn't be a moment too soon. What he'd told Ensign Jones was true. Jesus, Mary and Joseph, but he hated air raids.

Blue McCoy stood and hand-signaled a message to the rest of the team, in case they'd missed hearing Joe's announcement in the din.

The ground shook as a fifty-pound bomb landed in the neighborhood, and Blue met Joe's eyes and grinned as Cowboy swore a blue streak.

Joe laughed and lit the fuse.

"Thirty seconds," he told Blue, who held up the right number of fingers for the rest of the SEALs to see. The squad scrambled to the other side of the street for cover.

When a bomb is about to go off, Joe thought, there's always a moment, sometimes just a tiny one, when everything seems to slow down and wait. He looked at the familiar faces of his men, and he could see the adrenaline that pumped through them in their eyes, in the set of their mouths and jaws. They were good men, and as always, he was going to do his damnedest to see that they got out of this city alive. Forget alive—he was going to get them out of this hellhole untouched.

Joe didn't need to look at the second hand on his watch. He knew it was coming, despite the fact that time had seemed to slow down and stretch wa-a-a-ay out....

Boom.

It was a big explosion, but Joe barely heard it over the sounds of the other, more powerful explosions happening all over the city.

Before the dust even settled, Blue was on point, leading the way across the war-torn street, alert for snipers and staying low. He went headfirst into the neat little crater they had blown into the side of the Ustanzian Embassy.

Harvard was on radio, and he let air support know they were going in. Joe was willing to bet big money that the air force was too busy to pay Alpha Squad any real attention. But Harvard was doing his job, same as the rest of the SEALs. They were a team. Seven men—seven of the armed forces' best and brightest—trained to work and fight together, to the death if need be.

Joe followed Blue and Bobby into the embassy basement. Cowboy came in after, leaving Harvard and the rest of the team guarding their backsides.

It was darker than hell inside. Joe slipped his night-vision glasses on just in time. He narrowly missed running smack into Bobby's back and damn near breaking his nose on the shotgun the big man wore holstered along his spine.

"Hold up," Bob signaled.

He had his NVs on, too. So did Blue and Cowboy.

They were alone down there, except for the spiders and snakes and whatever else was slithering along the hard dirt floor.

"Damned layout's wrong. There's supposed to be a flight of stairs," Joe heard Blue mutter, and he stepped forward to take a look. Damn, they had a problem here.

Joe pulled the map of the embassy from the front pocket of his vest, even though he'd long since memorized the basement's floor plan. The map in his hands was of an entirely different building than the one they were standing in. It was probably the Ustanzian Embassy in some other city, in some country on the other side of the damned globe. Damn! Someone had really screwed up here.

Blue was watching him, and Joe knew his executive officer was thinking what *he* was thinking. The desk-riding genius responsible for securing the floor plan of this embassy was going to have a very bad day in about a week. Maybe less. Because the commander and XO of SEAL Team Ten's Alpha Squad were going to pay him a little visit.

But right now, they had a problem on their hands.

There were three hallways, leading into darkness. Not a stairway in sight.

"Wesley and Frisco," Blue ordered in his thick Southern drawl. "Get your butts in here, boys. We need split teams. Wes with Bobby. Frisco, stay with Cowboy. I'm with you, Cat."

Swim buddies. Blue had read Joe's mind and done the smartest thing. With the exception of Frisco, who was babysitting the new kid, Cowboy, he'd teamed each man up with the guy he knew best—his swim buddy. In fact, Blue and Joe went back all the way to Hell Week. Guys who do Hell Week together—that excruciating weeklong torturous SEAL endurance test—stay tight. No question about it.

Off they went, night-vision glasses still on, looking like some kind of weird aliens from outer space. Wesley and Bobby went left. Frisco and Cowboy took the right corridor. And Joe, with Blue close behind him, went straight ahead.

They were silent now, and Joe could hear each man's quiet breathing over his headset's earphones. He moved slowly, carefully, checking automatically for booby traps or any hint of movement ahead.

"Supply room," Joe heard Cowboy breathe into his headset's microphone.

"Ditto," Bobby whispered. "We got canned goods and a wine cellar. No movement, no life."

Joe caught sight of the motion the same instant Blue did. Simultaneously, they flicked the safeties of their MP5s down to full fire and dropped into a crouch.

They'd found the stairs going up.

And there, underneath the stairs, scared witless and shaking like a leaf in a hurricane, was the crown prince of Ustanzia, Tedric Cortere, using three of his aides as sandbags.

"Don't shoot," Cortere said in four or five different languages, his hands held high above his head.

Joe straightened, but he kept his weapon raised until he saw all four pairs of hands were empty. Then he pulled his NVs from his face, squinting as his eyes adjusted to the dim red glow of a penlight Blue had pulled from his pocket.

"Good evening, Your Royal Highness," he said. "I am Navy SEAL Lieutenant Joe Catalanotto, and I'm here to get you out."

"Contact," Harvard said into the radio, having heard Joe's royal greeting to the prince via his headset. "We have made contact. Repeat, we have picked up luggage and are heading for home plate."

That was when Joe heard Blue laugh.

"Cat," the XO drawled. "Have you looked at this guy? I mean, Joe, have you really looked?"

A bomb hit about a quarter mile to the east, and Prince Tedric tried to burrow more deeply in among his equally frightened aides.

If the prince had been standing, he would have been about Joe's height, maybe a little shorter.

He was wearing a torn white satin jacket, reminiscent of an Elvis impersonator. The garment was amazingly tacky. It was adorned with gold epaulets, and there was an entire row of medals and ribbons on the chest—for bravery under enemy fire, no doubt. His pants were black, and grimy with soot and dirt.

But it wasn't the prince's taste in clothing that made Joe's mouth drop open. It was the man's face.

Looking at the Crown Prince of Ustanzia was like looking into a mirror. His dark hair was longer than Joe's, but beyond that, the resemblance was uncanny. Dark eyes, big nose, long face, square jaw, heavy cheekbones.

The guy looked exactly like Joe.

Chapter One

All of the major network news cameras were rolling as Tedric Cortere, crown prince of Ustanzia, entered the airport.

A wall of ambassadors, embassy aides and politicians moved forward to greet him, but the prince paused for just a moment, taking the time to smile and wave a greeting to the cameras.

He was following her instructions to the letter. Veronica St. John, professional image and media consultant, allowed herself a sigh of relief. But only a small one, because she knew Tedric Cortere very well, and he was a perfectionist. There was no guarantee that Prince Tedric, the brother of Veronica's prep-school roommate and very best friend in the world, was going to be satisfied with what he saw tonight on the evening news.

Still, he would have every right to be pleased. It was day

one of his United States goodwill tour, and he was looking his best, oozing charm and royal manners, with just enough blue-blooded arrogance thrown in to captivate the royalty-crazed American public. He was remembering to gaze directly into the news cameras. He was keeping his eye movements steady and his chin down. And, heaven be praised, for a man prone to anxiety attacks, he was looking calm and collected for once.

He was giving the news teams exactly what they wanted—a close-up picture of a gracious, charismatic, fairy-tale handsome European prince.

Bachelor. She'd forgotten to add "bachelor" to the list. And if Veronica knew Americans—and she did; it was her business to know Americans—millions of American women would watch the evening news tonight and dream of becoming a princess.

There was nothing like fairy-tale fever among the public to boost relations between two governments. Fairy-tale fever—and the recently discovered oil that lay beneath the parched, gray Ustanzian soil.

But Tedric wasn't the only one playing to the news cameras this morning.

As Veronica watched, United States Senator Sam McKinley flashed his gleaming white teeth in a smile so falsely genuine and so obviously aimed at the reporters, it made her want to laugh.

But she didn't laugh. If she'd learned one thing during her childhood and adolescence as the daughter of an international businessman who moved to a different and often exotic country every year or so, she'd learned that diplomats and high government officials—particularly royalty—take themselves very, *very* seriously.

So, instead of laughing, she bit the insides of her cheeks as she stopped several respectful paces behind the prince, at the head of the crowd of assistants and aides and advisers who were part of his royal entourage.

"Your Highness, on behalf of the United States Government," McKinley drawled in his thick Texas accent, shaking the prince's hand, and dripping with goodwill, "I'd like to welcome you to our country's capital."

"I greet you with the timeless honor and tradition of the Ustanzian flag," Prince Tedric said formally in his faintly British, faintly French accent, "which is woven, as well, into my heart."

It was his standard greeting; nothing special, but it went over quite well with the crowd.

McKinley started in on a longer greeting, and Veronica let her attention wander.

She could see herself in the airport's reflective glass windows, looking cool in her cream-colored suit, her flame-red hair pulled neatly back into a French braid. Tall and slender and serene, her image wavered slightly as a jet plane took off, thundering down the runway.

It was an illusion. Actually, she was giddy with nervous excitement, a condition brought about by the stress of knowing that if Tedric didn't follow her instructions and ended up looking bad on camera, she'd be the one to blame. Sweat trickled down between her shoulder blades, another side effect of the stress she was under. No, she felt neither cool nor serene, regardless of how she looked.

She had been hired because her friend, Princess Wila, knew that Veronica was struggling to get her fledgling consulting business off the ground. Sure, she'd done smaller, less detailed jobs before, but this was the first one in which the stakes were so very high. If Veronica succeeded with Tedric Cortere, word would get out, and she'd have more business than she could handle. *If* she succeeded with Cortere…

But Veronica had also been hired for another reason.

She'd been hired because Wila, concerned about Ustanzia's economy, recognized the importance of this tour. Despite the fact that teaching Wila's brother, the high-strung Prince of Ustanzia, how to appear calm and relaxed while under the watchful eyes of the TV news cameras was Veronica's first major assignment as an image and media consultant, Wila trusted her longtime friend implicitly to get the job done.

"I'm counting on you, Véronique," Wila had said to Veronica over the telephone just last night. She had added with her customary frankness, "This American connection, is too important. Don't let Tedric screw this up."

So far Tedric was doing a good job. He looked good. He sounded good. But it was too early for Veronica to let herself feel truly satisfied. It was her job to make sure that the prince *continued* to look and sound good.

Tedric didn't particularly like his younger sister's best friend, and the feeling was mutual. He was an impatient, short-tempered man, and rather used to getting his own way. *Very* used to getting his own way.

Veronica could only hope he would see today's news reports and recognize the day's success. If he didn't, she'd hear about it, that was for sure.

Veronica knew quite well that over the course of the prince's tour of the United States she was going to earn every single penny of her consultant's fee. Because although Tedric Cortere was princely in looks and appearance, he was also arrogant and spoiled. And demanding. And often irrational. And occasionally, not very nice.

Oh, he knew his social etiquette. He was in his element when it came to pomp and ceremony, parties and other social posturing. He knew all there was to know about clothing and fashion. He could tell Japanese silk from American with a single touch. He was a wine connoisseur and a gourmet. He could ride horses and fence, play polo and water-ski. He hired countless aides and advisers to dance attendance upon him, and provide him with both his most trivial desires and the important information he needed to get by as a representative of his country.

As Veronica watched, Tedric shook the hands of the U.S. officials. He smiled charmingly and she could practically hear the sound of the news cameras zooming in for a close-up.

The prince glanced directly into the camera lenses and let his smile broaden. Spoiled or not, with his trim, athletic body and handsome face, the man was good-looking.

Good-looking? No, Veronica thought. To call him good-looking wasn't accurate. Quite honestly, the prince was gorgeous. He was a piece of art. He had long, thick, dark hair that curled down past his shoulders. His face was long and lean with exotic cheekbones that hinted of his mother's Mediterranean heritage. His eyes were the deepest brown, surrounded by sinfully long lashes. His jaw was square, his nose strong and masculine.

But Veronica had known Tedric since she was fifteen and he was nineteen. Naturally, she'd developed a full-fledged crush on him quite early on, but it hadn't taken her long to realize that the prince was nothing like his cheerful, breezy, lighthearted yet business-minded sister. Tedric was, in fact, quite decidedly dull—and enormously preoccupied with his appearance. He had spent endless amounts of time in front of a mirror, sending Wila and Veronica into spasms of giggles as he combed his hair, flexed his muscles and examined his perfect, white teeth.

Still, Veronica's crush on Prince Tedric hadn't truly crashed and burned until she'd had a conversation with him—and seen that beneath his facade of princely charm and social skills, behind his handsome face and trim body, deep within his dark brown eyes, there was nothing there.

Nothing *she* was interested in, anyway.

Although she had to admit that to this day, her romantic vision of a perfect man was someone tall, dark and handsome. Someone with wide, exotic cheekbones and liquid brown eyes. Someone who looked an awful lot like Crown Prince Tedric, but with a working brain in his head and a heart that loved more than his own reflection in the mirror.

She wasn't looking for a prince. In fact, she wasn't looking, period. She had no time for romance—at least, not until her business started to turn a profit.

As the military band began to play a rousing rendition of the Ustanzian national anthem, Veronica glanced again at their blurry images in the window. A flash of light from the upper-level balcony caught her eye. *That was odd*. She'd been told that airport personnel would be restricting access to the second floor as a security measure.

She turned her head to look up at the balcony and realized with a surge of disbelief that the flash she'd seen was a reflection of light bouncing off the long barrel of a rifle— a rifle aimed directly at Tedric.

"Get down!" Veronica shouted, but her voice was drowned out by the trumpets. The prince couldn't hear her. No one could hear her.

She ran toward Prince Tedric and all of the U.S. dignitaries, well aware that she was running toward, not away from, the danger. A thought flashed crazily through her head—*This was not a man worth dying for*. But she couldn't stand by and let her best friend's brother be killed. Not while she had the power to prevent it.

As a shot rang out, Veronica hit Tedric bone-jarringly hard at waist level and knocked him to the ground. It was a rugby tackle that would have made her brother Jules quite proud.

She bruised her shoulder, tore her nylons and scraped both of her knees when she fell.

But she saved the crown prince of Ustanzia's life.

When Veronica walked into the hotel conference room, it was clear the meeting had been going on for quite some time.

Senator McKinley was sitting at one end of the big oval conference table with his jacket off, his tie loosened, and his shirtsleeves rolled up. Henri Freder, the U.S. ambassador to Ustanzia, sat on one side of him. Another diplomat and several other men whom Veronica didn't recognize sat on the other. Men in dark suits stood at the doors and by the windows, watchful and alert. They were FInCOM agents, Veronica realized, high-tech bodyguards from the Federal Intelligence Commission, sent to protect the prince. But why were they involved? Was Prince Tedric's life still in danger?

Tedric was at the head of the table, surrounded by a dozen aides and advisers. He had a cold drink in front of him, and was lazily drawing designs in the condensation on the glass.

As Veronica entered the room, Tedric stood, and the entire tableful of men followed suit.

"Someone get a seat for Ms. St. John," the prince ordered sharply in his odd accent. "Immediately."

One of the lesser aides quickly stepped away from his own chair and offered it to Veronica.

"Thank you," she said, smiling at the young man.

"Sit down," the prince commanded her, stony-faced, as he returned to his seat. "I have an idea, but it cannot be done without your cooperation."

Veronica gazed steadily at the prince. After she'd tackled him earlier today, he'd been dragged away to safety. She hadn't seen or heard from him since. At the time, he hadn't bothered to thank her for saving his life—and apparently he had no intention of doing so now. She was working for him, therefore she was a servant. He would have expected her to save him. In his mind, there was no need for gratitude.

But she wasn't a servant. In fact, she'd been the maid of honor last year when his sister married Veronica's brother, Jules. Veronica and the prince were practically family, yet Tedric still insisted she address him as "Your Highness."

She sat down, pulling her chair in closer to the table, and the rest of the men sat, too.

"I have a double," the prince announced. "An American. It is my idea for him to take my place throughout the remaining course of the tour, thus ensuring my safety."

Veronica sat forward. "Excuse me, Your Highness," she said. "Please forgive my confusion. Is your safety still an issue?" She looked down the table at Senator McKinley. "Wasn't the gunman captured?"

McKinley ran his tongue over his front teeth before he answered. "I'm afraid not," he finally replied. "And the Federal Intelligence Commission has reason to believe the terrorists will make another attempt on the prince's life during the course of the next few weeks."

"Terrorists?" Veronica repeated, looking from McKinley to the ambassador and finally at Prince Tedric.

"FInCOM has ID'd the shooter," McKinley answered. "He's a well-known triggerman for a South American terrorist organization."

Veronica shook her head. "Why would South American terrorists want to kill the Ustanzian crown prince?"

The ambassador took off his glasses and tiredly rubbed his eyes. "Quite possibly in retaliation for Ustanzia's new alliance with the U.S.," he said.

"FInCOM tells us these particular shooters don't give up easily," McKinley said. "Even with souped-up security, FIn-COM expects they'll try again. What we're looking to do is find a solution to this problem."

Veronica laughed. It slipped out—she couldn't help herself. The solution was so obvious. "Cancel the tour."

"Can't do that," McKinley drawled.

Veronica looked down the other side of the table at Prince Tedric. He, for once, was silent. But he didn't look happy.

"There's too much riding on the publicity from this event," Senator McKinley explained. "You know as well as I do that Ustanzia needs U.S. funding to get their oil wells up and running." The heavyset man leaned back in his chair, tapping the eraser end of a pencil on the mahogany table. "But the prospect of competitively priced oil isn't enough to secure the size funds they need," he continued, dropping the pencil and running his hand through his thinning gray hair. "And quite frankly, current polls show the public's concern for a little-nothing country like Ustanzia— beg pardon, Prince—to be zilch. Hardly anyone knows who the Ustanzians are, and the folks who do know about 'em don't want to give 'em any of their tax dollars, that's for sure as shootin'. Not while there's so much here at home to spend the money on."

Veronica nodded her head. She was well aware of everything he was saying. It was one of Princess Wila's major worries.

"Besides," the senator added, "we can use this opportunity to nab this group of terrorists. And sister, if they're who we think they are, we want 'em. Bad."

"But if you know for a fact that there'll be another assassination attempt…?" Veronica looked down the table at Tedric. "Your Highness, how can you risk placing yourself in such danger?"

Tedric crossed his legs. "I have no intention of placing myself in any danger whatsoever," he said. "In fact, I will remain here, in Washington, in a safe house, until all danger has passed. The tour, however, will continue as planned, with this lookalike fellow taking my place."

Suddenly the prince's earlier words made sense. He'd said he had a double, someone who looked just like him. He'd said this person was an American.

"This man," McKinley asked. "What was his name, sir?"

The prince shrugged—a slow, eloquent gesture. "How should I remember? Joe. Joe Something. He was a soldier. An American soldier."

"'Joe Something,'" McKinley repeated, exchanging a quick, exasperated look with the diplomat on his left. "A soldier named Joe. Should only be about fifteen thousand men in the U.S. armed forces named Joe."

The ambassador on McKinley's right leaned forward. "Your Highness," he said patiently, "when did you meet this man?"

"He was one of the soldiers who assisted in my escape from the embassy in Baghdad," Tedric replied.

"A Navy SEAL," the ambassador murmured to McKinley. "We should have no problem locating him. If I remember correctly, only one seven-man team participated in that rescue mission."

"SEAL?" Veronica asked, sitting up and leaning forward. "What's a SEAL?"

"Part of the Special Operations," Senator McKinley told her. "They're *the* most elite special-operations force in the world. They can operate anywhere—on the sea, in the air and on the land, hence the name, SEALs. If this man who looks so much like the prince really is a SEAL, standing in as the prince's double will be a cakewalk for him."

"He was, however, quite unbearably lower-class," the

prince said prudishly, sweeping some imaginary crumbs from the surface of the table. He looked at Veronica. "That is where you would come in. You will teach this Joe to look and act like a prince. We can delay the tour by—" he frowned down the table at McKinley "—a week, is that what you'd said?"

"Two or three days at the very most, sir." The senator grimaced. "We can announce that you've come down with the flu, try to keep up public interest with reports of your health. But the fact is, after a few days, you'll no longer be news and the story will be dropped. You know what they say: Out of sight, out of mind. We can't let that happen."

Two or three days. Two or three days to turn a rough American sailor—a Navy SEAL, whatever that really meant—into royalty. Who were they kidding?

Senator McKinley picked up the phone to begin tracking down the mysterious Joe.

Prince Tedric was watching Veronica expectantly. "Can you do it?" he asked. "Can you make this Joe into a prince?"

"In two or three *days?*"

Tedric nodded.

"I'd have to work around the clock," Veronica said, thinking aloud. If she agreed to this crazy plan, she would have to be right beside this sailor, this SEAL, every single step of the way. She'd have to coach him continuously, and be ready to catch and correct his every mistake. "And even then, there'd be no guarantee…."

Tedric shrugged, turning back to Ambassador Freder. "She can't do it," he said flatly. "We *will* have to cancel. Arrange a flight back to—"

"I didn't say I couldn't do it," Veronica interrupted, quickly adding, "Your Highness."

The prince turned back to her, one elegant eyebrow raised.

Veronica could hear an echo of Wila's voice. "I'm counting on you, Véronique. This American connection is too important." If this tour were canceled, all of Wila's hopes for the future would evaporate. And Wila's weren't the only hopes that would be dashed. Veronica couldn't let herself forget that little girl waiting at Saint Mary's....

"Well?" Tedric said impatiently.

"All right," Veronica said. "I'll give it a try."

Senator McKinley hung up the phone with a triumphant crash. "I think we've found our man," he announced with a wide smile. "His name's Navy Lieutenant Joseph P.—" he glanced down at a scrap of paper he'd taken some notes on "—Catalanotto. They're faxing me an ID photo right now."

Veronica felt an odd flash of both hot and cold. Good God, what had she just done? What had she just agreed to? What if she couldn't pull it off? What if it couldn't be done?

The fax alarm began to beep. Both the prince and Senator McKinley stood and crossed the spacious suite to where the fax machine was plugged in beneath a set of elegant bay windows.

Veronica stayed in her seat at the table. If this job couldn't be done, she would be letting her best friend down.

"My God," McKinley breathed as the picture was slowly printed out. "It doesn't seem possible."

He tore the fax from the roll of paper and handed it to the prince.

Silently, Tedric stared at the picture. Silently, he walked back across the room and handed the sheet of paper to Veronica.

Except for the fact that the man in the picture was wearing a relaxed pair of military fatigues, with top buttons of the shirt undone and sleeves rolled up to his elbows, except for the fact that the man in the picture had dark, shaggy hair cut just a little below his ears, and the strap of a submachine gun slung over one shoulder, except for the fact that the camera had caught him mid-grin, with good humor and sharp intelligence sparkling in his dark eyes, the man in this picture could very well have been the crown prince of Ustanzia. Or at the very least, he could have been the crown prince's brother.

The crown prince's *better-looking* brother.

He had the same nose, same cheekbones, same well-defined jawline and chin. But his front tooth was chipped. Of course, that was no problem. They could cap a tooth in a matter of hours, couldn't they?

He was bigger than Prince Tedric, this American naval lieutenant. Bigger and taller. Stronger. Rougher edged. Much, *much* more rough-edged, in every way imaginable. Good God, if this picture was any indication, Veronica was going to have to start with the basics with this man. She was going to have to teach him how to sit and stand and walk....

Veronica looked up to find Prince Tedric watching her.

"Something tells me," he said in his elegant accent, "your work is cut out for you."

Across the room, McKinley picked up the phone and dialed. "Yeah," he said into the receiver. "This is Sam McKinley. *Senator* Sam McKinley. I need a Navy SEAL by the name of Lieutenant Joseph—" he consulted his notes "—Catalanotto. Damn, what a mouthful. I need that lieutenant here in Washington, and I need him here yesterday."

Chapter Two

Joe lay on the deck of the rented boat, hands behind his head, watching the clouds. Puffs of blinding white in a crystal blue California sky, they were in a state of constant motion, always changing, never remaining the same.

He liked that.

It reminded him of his life, fluid and full of surprises. He never knew when a cream puff might turn unexpectedly into a ferocious dragon.

But Joe liked it that way. He liked never knowing what was behind the door—the lady or the tiger. And certainly, since he'd been a SEAL, he'd had his share of both.

But today there were neither ladies nor tigers to face. Today he was on leave—shore leave, it was called in the navy. Funny he should spend the one day of shore leave he had this month far from the shore, out on a fishing boat.

Not that he'd spent very much time lately at sea. In fact, in the past few months, he'd been on a naval vessel exactly ninety-six hours. And that had been for training. Some of those training hours he'd spent as an instructor. But some of the time he'd been a student. That was all part of being a Navy SEAL. No matter your rank or experience, you always had to keep learning, keep training, keep on top of the new technology and methodology.

Joe had achieved expert status in nine different fields, but those fields were always changing. Just like those clouds that were floating above him. Just the way he liked it.

Across the deck of the boat, dressed in weekend grunge clothes similar to his own torn fatigues and ragged T-shirt, Harvard and Blue were arguing good-naturedly over who had gotten the most depressing letter from the weekly mail call.

Joe himself hadn't gotten any mail—nothing besides bills, that is. Talk about depressing.

Joe closed his eyes, letting the conversation float over him. He'd known Blue for eight years, Harvard for about six. Their voices—Blue's thick, south-of-the-Mason-Dixon-Line drawl and Harvard's nasal, upper-class-Boston accent—were as familiar to him as breathing.

It still sometimes tickled him that out of their entire seven-man SEAL team, the man that Blue was closest to, after Joe himself, was Daryl Becker, nicknamed Harvard.

Carter "Blue" McCoy and Daryl "Harvard" Becker. The "redneck" rebel and the Ivy League-educated Yankee black man. Both SEALs, both better than the best of the rest. And both aware that there was no such thing as prejudices and prejudgments in the Navy SEALs.

Out across the bay, the blue-green water sparkled and danced in the bright sunshine. Joe took a deep breath, filling his lungs with the sharp salty air.

"Oh, Lord," Blue said, turning to the second page of his letter.

Joe turned toward his friend. "What?"

"Gerry's getting married," Blue said, running his fingers through his sun-bleached blond hair. "To Jenny Lee Beaumont."

Jenny Lee had been Blue's high school girlfriend. She was the only woman Blue had ever talked about—the only one special enough to mention.

Joe exchanged a long look with Harvard.

"Jenny Lee Beaumont, huh?" Joe said.

"That's right." Blue nodded, his face carefully expressionless. "Gerry's gonna marry her. Next July. He wants me to be his best man."

Joe swore softly.

"You win," Harvard conceded. "Your mail was much more depressing than mine."

Joe shook his head, grateful for his own lack of entanglement with a woman. Sure, he'd had girlfriends down through the years, but he'd never met anyone he couldn't walk away from.

Not that he didn't like women, because he did. He certainly did. And the women he usually dated were smart and funny and as quick to shy away from permanent attachments as he was. He would see his current lady friend on occasional weekend leaves, and sometimes in the evenings when he was in town and free.

But never, ever had he kissed a woman good-night—or good-morning, as was usually the case—then gone back to the base and sat around daydreaming about her the way Bob and Wesley had drooled over those college girls they'd met down in San Diego. Or the way Harvard had sighed over that Hawaiian marine biologist they'd met on Guam. What was her name? Rachel. Harvard *still* got that kicked-puppy look in his brown eyes whenever her name came up.

The truth was, Joe had been lucky—he'd never fallen in love. And he was hoping his luck would hold. It would be just fine with him if he went through life without *that* particular experience, thank you very much.

Joe pushed the top off the cooler with one bare toe. He reached into the icy water to pull out a beer, then froze.

He straightened, ears straining, eyes scanning the horizon to the east.

Then he heard it again.

The sound of a distant chopper. He shaded his eyes, looking out toward the California coastline, to where the sound was coming from.

Silently, Harvard and Blue got to their feet, moving to stand next to him. Silently, Harvard handed Joe the binoculars that had been stowed in one of the equipment lockers.

One swift turn of the dial brought the powerful lenses into focus.

The chopper was only a small black dot, but it was growing larger with each passing second. It was undeniably heading directly toward them.

"You guys wearing your pagers?" Joe asked, breaking the silence. He'd taken his own beeper off after it—and he—had gotten doused by a pailful of bait and briny seawater.

Harvard nodded. "Yes, sir." He glanced down at the beeper he wore attached to his belt. "But I'm clear."

"Mine didn't go off, either, Cat," Blue said.

In the binoculars, the black dot took on a distinct outline. It was an army bird, a Black Hawk, UH-60A. Its cruising speed was about one hundred and seventy miles per hour. It was closing in on them, and fast.

"Either of you in any trouble I should know about?" Joe asked.

"No, sir," Harvard said.

"Negative." Blue glanced at Joe. "How 'bout you, Lieutenant?"

Joe shook his head, still watching the helicopter through the binoculars.

"This is weird," Harvard said. "What kind of hurry are they in, they can't page us and have us motor back to the harbor?"

"One damn big hurry," Joe said. God, that Black Hawk could really move. He pulled the binoculars away from his face as the chopper continued to grow larger.

"It's not World War Three," Blue commented, his troubles with Jenny Lee temporarily forgotten. He had to raise his voice to be heard above the approaching helicopter. "If it was World War Three, they wouldn't waste a Hawk on three lousy SEALs."

The chopper circled and then hovered directly above them. The sound of the blades was deafening, and the force of the wind made the little boat pitch and toss. All three men grabbed the railing to keep their footing.

Then a scaling rope was thrown out the open door of the helicopter's cabin. It, too, swayed in the wind from the chopper blades, smacking Joe directly in the chest.

"Lieutenant Joseph P. Catalanotto," a distorted voice announced over a loudspeaker. "Your shore leave is over."

Veronica St. John went into her hotel suite, then leaned wearily back against the closed door.

It was only nine o'clock—early by diplomatic standards. In fact, if things had gone according to schedule today, she would still have been at a reception for Prince Tedric over at the Ustanzian Embassy. But things had gone very much *not* according to schedule, starting with the assassination attempt at the airport.

She'd gotten a call from the president of the United States, officially thanking her, on behalf of the American people, for saving Prince Tedric's life. She hadn't expected that. Too bad. If she'd been expecting the man in the White House to call, she might have been prepared to ask for his assistance in locating the personnel records of this mysterious navy lieutenant who looked so much like the crown prince of Ustanzia.

Nobody, repeat *nobody* she had spoken to had been able to help her find the files she wanted. The Department of Defense sent her to the Navy. The Navy representatives told her that all SEAL records were in the Special Operations Division. The clerk from Special Operations was as clandestine and unhelpful as James Bond's personal assistant might have been. The woman wouldn't even verify that Joseph Catalanotto existed, let alone if the man's personnel files were in the U.S. Special Operations Office.

Frustrated, Veronica had gone back to Senator McKinley, hoping that he could use his clout to get a fax of Catalanotto's files. But even the powerful senator was told that, for security reasons, personnel records for Navy SEALs were never, repeat *never*, sent via facsimile. It had been a major feat just getting them to fax a picture of the lieutenant. If McKinley wanted to see Joseph P. Catalanotto's personnel file, he would need to make a formal request, in writing. After the request was received, it would take a mandatory three days for the files to be censored for his—and Ms. St. John's—level of clearance.

Three *days*.

Veronica wasn't looking to find Lieutenant Catalanotto's deepest, darkest military secrets. All she wanted to know was where the man came from—in which part of the country he'd grown up. She wanted to know his family background, his level of education, his IQ scores and the results of personality and psychological tests done by the armed forces.

She wanted to know, quite frankly, how big an obstacle this Navy SEAL himself was going to be in getting the job done.

So far, she only knew his name, that he looked like a rougher, wilder version of Tedric Cortere, that his shoulders were very broad, that he carried an M60 machine gun as if it were a large loaf of bread, and that he had a nice smile.

She didn't have a clue as to whether she'd be able to fool the American public into thinking he was a European prince. Until she met this man, she couldn't even guess how much work transforming him was going to take. It would be better to try not to think about it.

But if she didn't think about this job looming over her, she would end up thinking about the girl at Saint Mary's Hospital, a little girl named Cindy who had sent the prince a letter nearly four months ago—a letter Veronica had fished out of Tedric's royal wastebasket. In the letter, Cindy—barely even ten years old—had told Prince Tedric that she'd heard he was planning a trip to the United States. She had asked him, if he was going to be in the Washington, D.C., area, to please come and visit her since she was not able to come to see him.

Veronica had ended up going above the prince—directly to King Derrick—and had gotten the visit to Saint Mary's on the official tour calendar.

But now what?

The entire tour would have to be rescheduled and replanned, and Saint Mary's and little Cindy were likely to fall, ignored, between the cracks.

Veronica smiled tightly. Not if *she* had anything to say about it.

With a sigh, she kicked off her shoes.

Lord, but she ached.

Tackling royalty could really wear a person out, she thought, allowing herself a rueful smile. After the assassination attempt, she had run on sheer adrenaline for about six hours straight. After that had worn off, she'd kept herself fueled with coffee—hot, black and strong.

Right now what she needed was a shower and a two-hour nap.

She pulled her nightgown and robe out of the suitcase that she hadn't yet found time to unpack, and tossed them onto the bed as she all but staggered into the bathroom. She closed the door and turned on the shower as she peeled off her suit and the cream-colored blouse she wore underneath. She put a hole in her hose as she took them off, and threw them directly into the wastebasket. It had been a bona fide two-pairs-of-panty-hose day. Her first pair, the ones she'd been wearing at the airport, had been totally destroyed.

Veronica washed herself quickly, knowing that every minute she spent in the shower was a minute less that she'd be able to sleep. And with Lieutenant Joseph P. Catalanotto due to arrive anytime after midnight, she was going to need every second of that nap.

Still, it didn't keep her from singing as she tried to rinse the aches and soreness from her back and shoulders. Singing in the shower was a childhood habit. Then, as now, the moments she spent alone in the shower were among the few bits of time she had to really kick back and let loose. She tested the acoustics of this particular bathroom with a rousing rendition of Mary Chapin Carpenter's latest hit.

She shut off the water, still singing, and toweled herself dry.

Her robe was hanging on the back of the bathroom door, and she reached for it.

And stopped singing, mid-note.

She'd left her robe in the bedroom, on the bed. She hadn't hung it on the door.

"No…you're right. You're *not* alone in here," said a husky male voice from the other side of the bathroom door.

Chapter Three

Veronica's heart nearly stopped beating, and she lunged for the door and turned the lock.

"I figured you didn't know I was in your room," the voice continued as Veronica quickly slipped into her white terrycloth bathrobe. "I also figured you probably wouldn't appreciate coming out of the bathroom with just a towel on—or less. Not with an audience, anyway. So I put your robe on the back of the door."

Veronica tightened the belt and clutched the lapels of the robe more closely together. She took in a deep breath, then let it slowly out. It steadied her and kept her voice from shaking. "Who are you?" she asked.

"Who are *you?*" the voice countered. It was rich, husky, and laced with more than a trace of blue-collar New York. "I was brought here and told to wait, so I waited. I've been hustled from one coast to the other like some Federal Express overnight package, only nobody has any explanations as to why or even *who* I'm waiting to see. I didn't even know my insertion point was the District of Columbia until the jet landed at Andrews. And as long as I'm complaining I might as well tell you that I'm tired, I'm hungry and my shorts have not managed to dry in the past ten hours, a situation that makes me very, very cranky. I would damn near sell my soul to get into that shower that you just stepped out of. Other than that, I'm sure I'm very pleased to meet you."

"Lieutenant Catalanotto?" Veronica asked.

"Bingo," the voice said. "Babe, you just answered your own question."

But had she? "What's your first name?" she asked warily.

"Joe. Joseph."

"Middle name?"

"Paulo," he said.

Veronica swung open the bathroom door.

The first thing she noticed about the man was his size. He was big—taller than Prince Tedric by about two inches and outweighing him in sheer muscle by a good, solid fifty pounds. His dark hair was cut much shorter than Tedric's, and he had at least a two-day growth of beard darkening his face.

He didn't look as exactly like the prince as she'd thought when she saw his photograph, Veronica realized, studying the man's face. On closer inspection, his nose was slightly different—it had been broken, probably more than once. And, if it was possible, this navy lieutenant's cheekbones were even more exotic-looking than Tedric's. His chin was slightly more square, more stubborn than the prince's. And his eyes… As he returned her inquisitive stare, his lids dropped halfway over his remarkable liquid brown eyes, as if he was trying to hide his innermost secrets from her.

But those differences—even the size differences between the two men—were very subtle. They wouldn't be noticed by someone who didn't know Prince Tedric very well. Those differences certainly wouldn't be noticed by the array of ambassadors and diplomats Tedric was scheduled to meet.

"According to the name tag on your suitcase, you've gotta be Veronica St. John, right?" he said, pronouncing her name the American way, as if it were two words, *Saint* and *John*.

"Sinjin," she said distractedly. "You don't say Saint John, you say 'Sinjin.'"

He was looking at her, examining her in much the same way that she'd looked at him. The intensity of his gaze made her feel naked. Which of course, underneath her robe, she was.

But he didn't win any prizes himself for the clothing he was wearing. From the looks of it, his T-shirt had had its sleeves forcibly removed without the aid of scissors, his army fatigues had been cut off into ragged shorts, and on his feet he wore a pair of dirty canvas deck shoes with no socks. He looked as if he hadn't showered in several days, and, Lord help her, he smelled that way, too.

"Dear God," Veronica said aloud, taking in all of the little details she'd missed at first. He wasn't wearing a belt. Instead, a length of fairly thick rope was run through the belt loops in his pants, and tied in some kind of knot at the front. He had a tattoo—a navy anchor—on his left biceps. His fingers were blackened with stains of grease, his fingernails were short and rough—a far cry from Prince Tedric's carefully manicured hands. Lord, if she had to start by teaching this man the basics of personal hygiene, there was no way she'd have him impersonating a prince within her three-day deadline.

"What?" he said with a scowl. Defensiveness tinged his voice and darkened his eyes. "I'm not what you expected?"

She couldn't deny it. She'd expected the lieutenant to

arrive wearing a dress uniform, stiff and starched and perfectly military—and smelling a little more human and a little less like a real-life marine mammal-type seal. Wordlessly, she shook her head no.

Joe gazed silently at the girl. She watched him, too, her eyes so wide and blue against the porcelain paleness of her skin. It was hard for him to tell the color of her hair—it was wet. It clung, damp and dark, to the sides of her head and neck.

Red, he guessed. It was probably some shade of red, maybe even strawberry blond, probably curly. Yet, if there really was a God and He was truly righteous, she would have nondescript straight hair, maybe the color of mud. It didn't seem fair that this girl should have wealth, a powerful job, refined manners, a pair of beautiful blue eyes *and* curly red hair.

Without makeup, her face looked alarmingly young. Her features were delicate, almost fragile. She wasn't particularly pretty, at least not in the conventional sense. But her cheekbones were high, showcasing enormous crystal blue eyes. And her lips were exquisitely shaped, her nose small and elegant.

No, she wasn't pretty. But she was incredibly attractive in a way he couldn't even begin to explain.

The robe she wore was too big for her. It drew attention to her slight frame, accentuating her slender wrists and ankles.

She looked like a kid playing dress up in her mommy's clothes.

Funny, from the cut and style of the business suits that had been neatly packed in her suitcase, Joe had expected this Veronica St. John—or "Sinjin," as she'd pronounced it with her slightly British, extremely monied upper-class accent—to be, well…less young. He'd expected someone in their mid-forties at least, maybe even older. But this girl couldn't be a day over twenty-five. Hell, standing here like this, just out of the shower, still dripping wet, she barely looked sixteen.

"You aren't what I expected, either," Joe said, sitting down on the edge of the bed. "So I guess that makes us even."

He knew he was making her nervous, sitting there like that. He knew she was nervous about him getting the bedspread dirty, nervous about him leaving behind the lingering odor of dead fish—bait from the smelly bucket Blue had knocked over earlier that morning. Hell, he was nervous about it himself.

And damn, but that made him angry. This girl was somehow responsible for dragging him away from his shore leave. She was somehow responsible for the way he'd been rushed across the country without a shower or a change of clothes. Hell, it was probably her fault that he was in this five-star hotel wearing his barnacle-scraping clothes, feeling way out of his league.

He didn't like feeling this way. He didn't like the barely concealed distaste he could see in this rich girl's eyes. He didn't like being reminded that he didn't fit into this opulent world of hers—a world filled with money, power and class.

Not that he *wanted* to fit in. Hell, he wouldn't last more than a few months in a place like this. He preferred his own world—the world of the Navy SEALs, where a man wasn't judged by the size of his wallet, or the price of his education, or the cut of his clothes. In *his* world, a man was judged by his actions, by his perseverance, by his loyalty and stamina. In his world, a man who'd made it into the SEALs was treated with honor and respect—regardless of the way he looked. Or smelled.

He leaned back on the big, fancy, five-star bed, propping himself up on his elbows. "Maybe you could give me some kind of clue as to what I'm doing here, honey," he said, watching her wince at his term of endearment. "I'm pretty damn curious."

The rich girl's eyes widened, and she actually forgot to look disdainful for a few minutes. "Are you trying to tell me that no one's told you *anything?*"

Joe sat up. "That's *exactly* what I'm telling you."

She shook her head. Her hair was starting to dry, and it was definitely curly. "But that's impossible."

"Impossible it ain't, sweetheart," he said. A double wince this time. One for the bad grammar, the other for the "sweetheart." "I'm here in D.C. without the rest of my team, and I don't know why."

Veronica turned abruptly and went into the hotel suite's living room. Joe followed more slowly, leaning against the frame of the door and watching as she sifted through her briefcase.

"You were supposed to be met by—" she pulled a yellow legal pad from her notebook and flipped to a page in the back "—an Admiral Forrest?" She looked up at him almost hopefully.

The navy lieutenant just shrugged, still watching her. Lord, but he was handsome. Despite the layers of dirt and his dark, scowling expression, he was, like Prince Tedric, almost impossibly good-looking. And this man was nearly dripping with an unconscious virility that Tedric didn't even *begin* to possess. He was extremely attractive underneath all that grime—if she were the type who went for that untamed, rough-hewn kind of man.

Which, of course, Veronica wasn't. Dangerous, bad-boy types had never made her heart beat faster. And if her heart seemed to be pounding now, why, that was surely from the scare he'd given her earlier.

No, she was not the type to be attracted by steel-hard biceps and broad shoulders, a rough-looking five o'clock shadow, a tropical tan, a molten-lava smile, and incredible brown bedroom eyes. No. Definitely, positively not.

And if she gave him a second glance, it was only to verify the fact that Lieutenant Joseph P. Catalanotto was *not* going to be mistaken for visiting European royalty.

Not today, anyway.

And not tomorrow. But, for Wila's sake, for her own career, and for little Cindy at Saint Mary's, Veronica was going to see to it that two days from now, Joe would be a prince.

But first things first. And first things definitely included putting her clothes back on, particularly since Lieutenant Catalanotto wasn't attempting to hide the very, *very* male appreciation in his eyes as he looked at her.

"Why don't you help yourself to something to drink," Veronica said, and Joe's gaze flickered across the suite, toward the elaborate bar that was set up on the other side of the room. "Give me a minute to get dressed," she added. "Then I'll try to explain why you're here."

He nodded.

She walked past him, aware that he was still watching right up to the moment she closed the bedroom door behind her.

The man's accent was atrocious. It screamed New York City—blue-collar New York City. But okay. With a little ingenuity, with the right scheduling and planning, Joe wouldn't have to utter a single word.

His posture, though, was an entirely different story. Tedric stood ramrod straight. Lieutenant Catalanotto, on the other hand, slouched continuously. And he walked with a kind of relaxed swagger that was utterly un-princely. How on *earth* was she going to teach him to stand and sit up straight, let alone *walk* in that peculiar, stiff, princely gait that Tedric had perfected?

Veronica pulled fresh underwear and another pair of panty hose—number three for the day—from her suitcase. Her dark blue suit was near the top of the case, so she pulled it on, then slipped her tired feet into a matching pair of pumps. A little bit of makeup, a quick brush through her almost-dry hair...

Gloves would cover his hands, she thought, her mind going a mile a minute. Even if that engine grease didn't wash off, it could be hidden by a pair of gloves. Tedric himself often wore a pair of white gloves. No one would think that was odd.

Joe's hair was an entirely different matter. He wore his hair short, while Tedric's flowed down past his shoulders.

They could get a wig for Joe. Or hair extensions. Yes, hair extensions would be even better, and easier to keep on. Provided Joe would sit still long enough to have them attached...

This was going to work. This was *going* to work.

Taking a deep breath and smoothing down her suit jacket, Veronica opened the door and went back into the living room.

And stopped short.

The living room of her hotel suite was positively crowded.

Senator McKinley, three different Ustanzian ambassadors, an older man wearing a military dress uniform covered with medals, a half-dozen FInCOM security agents, Prince Tedric *and* his entire entourage all stood frozen and staring at Joe Catalanotto, who had risen to his feet in front of the sofa. The tension in the room could have been cut by a knife.

The man in uniform was the only one who spoke. "Nice to see that you dressed for the occasion, Joe," he said with a chuckle.

Joe crossed his arms. "The guys who shanghaied me forgot to bring my wardrobe trunk," he said dryly. Then he smiled. It was a genuine, sincere smile that warmed his face and touched his eyes. "Good to see you, Admiral."

Joe looked around the room, his gaze landing on Prince Tedric's face. Tedric was staring at him as if he were a rat that had made its way into the hotel room from the street below.

Joe's smile faded, and was replaced by another scowl. "Well," he said. "I'll be damned. If it isn't my evil twin."

Veronica laughed. She couldn't help it. It just came bubbling out. She bit down on the inside of her cheek, and all but clamped her hand across her mouth. But no one seemed to notice—no one but Joe, who glanced over at her in surprise.

"Don't you know who you're talking to, young man? This is the crown prince of Ustanzia," Senator McKinley said sternly to Joe.

"Damn straight I know who I'm talking to, Pop," Joe said tightly. "I'm the kind of guy who never forgets a face— particularly when I see it every morning in the mirror. My team of SEALs pulled this bastard's sorry butt out of Baghdad." He turned back to Tedric. "Keeping free and clear of war zones these days, Ted, you lousy bastard?"

Everyone in the room, with the exception of Joe and the still-grinning admiral, drew in a shocked breath. Veronica was amazed that her ears didn't pop from the sudden drop in air pressure.

The crown prince's face turned an interesting shade of royal purple. "How dare you?" he gasped.

Joe seemed to grow at least three feet taller and two feet broader. He took a step or two toward Tedric, and everyone in the room—with the exception of the admiral— drew back.

"How dare *you* put yourself into a situation where my

men had to risk their lives to pull you back out?" Joe all but snarled. "One of my men spent *months* in intensive care because of you, dirtwad. I'll tell you right now, you're damned lucky—*damned* lucky—he didn't die."

The deadly look in Joe's eyes was enough to make even the bravest man quiver with fear. They were *all* lucky that Joe's friend hadn't died, Veronica thought with a shiver, or else they'd be witnessing a murder. And unlike the morning's assassination attempt, she had no doubt that Joe would succeed.

"Mon Dieu," Tedric said, hiding the fact that his hands were shaking by slipping into his native French and turning haughtily to his aides. "This…this…*creature* is far more insolent than I remembered. Obviously we cannot risk sending him into public, masquerading as *me*. He would embarrass my heritage, my entire *country*. Send him back to whatever rock he crawled out from under. There is no other option. Cancel the tour."

On the other side of the room, one of the senator's assistants quickly translated Tedric's French into English, whispering into McKinley's ear.

With a humph, the prince stalked toward the door, taking with him Senator McKinley's hopes for lower-priced oil and Wila's dreams of economic security for her country.

But McKinley moved quickly, and cut Prince Tedric off before he reached the door.

"Your Highness," McKinley said soothingly. "If you're serious about obtaining the funding for the oil wells—"

"He's a monster," Tedric proclaimed loudly in French. McKinley's assistant translated quietly for the senator. "Even Ms. St. John cannot turn such a monster into a prince."

Across the room, Joe watched as Veronica hurried over to the prince and Senator McKinley and began talking in a lowered voice. Turn a monster into a prince, huh? he thought.

"You always did know how to liven up a party, son."

Joe turned to see Admiral Michael "Mac" Forrest smiling at him. He gave the older man a crisp salute.

The admiral's familiar leathery face crinkled into a smile. "Cut the bulldinky, Catalanotto," he said. "Since when did you start saluting? For criminy's sake, son, shake my hand instead."

The admiral's salt-and-pepper hair had gone another shade whiter, but other than that, the older man looked healthy and fit. Joe knew that Mac Forrest, a former SEAL himself, still spent a solid hour each day in PT—physical training—despite the fact that he needed a cane to walk. Ever since Joe first met him, the Admiral's left leg had been shorter than his right, courtesy of the enemy during the Vietnam War.

Mac's handclasp was strong and solid. With his other hand, he clapped Joe on the shoulder.

"It's been nearly a year and you haven't changed the least bit," Admiral Forrest announced after giving Joe a once-over. The older man wrinkled his nose. "Including your clothes. Jumping Jesse, what hole *did* we drag you out of?"

"I was on leave," Joe said with a shrug. "I was helping Blue pull in a major tuna and the bait bucket spilled on me. The boys in the Black Hawk didn't give me a chance to stop at my apartment to take a shower and pick up a change of clothes."

"Yeah." The admiral's blue eyes twinkled. "We were in kind of a hurry to get you out here, in case you didn't notice."

"I noticed," Joe said, crossing his arms. "I take it I'm here to do some kind of favor for him." With his chin, Joe gestured across the room toward Prince Tedric, who was still deep in discussion with Senator McKinley and Veronica.

"Something tells me you're not happy about the idea of doing Tedric Cortere any favors," Mac commented.

"Damn straight," Joe said, adding, "sir. That bastard nearly got Frisco killed. We were extracting from Baghdad with a squad of Iraqi soldiers on our tail. Frisco took a direct hit. The kid nearly bled to death. What's maybe even worse, at least in his eyes, is that his knee was damn near destroyed. Kid's in a wheelchair now, and fighting hard to get out."

Mac Forrest stood quietly, just letting Joe tell the story.

"We'd reached the Baghdad extraction point when Prince Charming over there refused to board the chopper. We finally had to throw him inside. It only gave us about a thirty-second delay, but it was enough to put us into the Iraqi soldiers' firing range, and that's when Frisco was hit. Turns out His Royal Pain-in-the-Butt refused to get into the bird because it wasn't luxurious enough. He nearly got us all killed because the interior of an attack helicopter wasn't painted in the colors of the Ustanzian flag."

Joe looked steadily at the admiral. "So go ahead and reprimand me, Mac," he added. "But be warned—there's nothing you can say that'll make me do any favors for *that* creep."

"I'm not so sure about that, son," Mac said thoughtfully, running his hand across the lower part of his face.

Joe frowned. "What's going on?"

"Have you seen the news lately?" Mac asked.

Joe looked at him for several long moments. "You're kidding, right?"

"Just asking."

"Mac, I've been in a chopper, a transport jet and a jeep tonight. None of them had in-flight entertainment in the form of the evening news," Joe said. "Hell, I haven't even seen a newspaper in the past eighteen hours."

"This morning there was an assassination attempt on Tedric."

Aha. Now it suddenly all made sense. Joe nodded. "Gee, sir," he said. "And I already smell like bait. How appropriate."

Mac chuckled. "You always *were* a smart mouth, Catalanotto."

"So what's the deal?" Joe asked. "Where am I inserting? Ustanzia? Or, oh joy, are we going back to Baghdad?"

Inserting. It was a special operations term for entering—either stealthily or by force—an area of operation.

The admiral perched on the arm of the sofa. "You've already inserted, son," he said. "Here in D.C. is where we want you—for right now. That is, if I can convince you to volunteer for this mission." Briefly, he outlined the plan to have Joe stand in for the crown prince for the remainder of the American tour—at least until the terrorists made another assassination attempt and were apprehended.

"Let me get this straight," Joe said, sitting down on the couch. "I play dress-up in Cortere's clothes—which is the equivalent of painting a giant target on my back, right? And I'm doing this so that the United States will have more *oil?* You've got to do better than that, Mac. And don't start talking about protecting Prince Ted, because I don't give a flying fig whether or not that bastard stays alive long enough to have his royal coffee and doughnut tomorrow morning."

Mac looked across the room, and Joe followed the older man's gaze. Veronica was nodding at Prince Tedric, her face serious. Red. Her hair was dry, and it was definitely red. Of course. It *had* to be red.

"I don't suppose working with Veronica St. John would be an incentive?" Mac said. "I had the opportunity to meet her several weeks ago. She's a real peach of a girl. Rock-solid sense of humor, though you wouldn't necessarily know it to look at her. Pretty, too."

Joe shook his head. "Not my type," he said flatly.

"Mrs. Forrest wasn't my type when I first met her," Mac stated.

Joe stood. "Sorry, Mac. If that's the best you can do, I'm outta here."

"Please," Mac said quietly, putting one hand on Joe's arm. "I'm asking for a personal favor here, Lieutenant. Do this one for me." The admiral looked down at the floor, and when he looked back at Joe, his blue eyes were steely. "Remember that car bomb that took out a busload of American sailors in London three years ago?"

Silently, Joe nodded. Oh, yeah. He remembered. Mac Forrest's nineteen-year-old son had been one of the kids killed in that deadly blast, set off by a terrorist organization called the Cloud of Death.

"My sources over at Intelligence have hinted that the assassins who are gunning for Prince Tedric are the same terrorists who set off that bomb," the admiral said. His voice trembled slightly. "It's Diosdado and his damned Cloud of Death again. I want them, Lieutenant. With your help, I can get them. Without your help…." He shook his head in despair.

Joe nodded. "Sir, you've got your volunteer."

Chapter Four

It was nearly two-thirty in the morning before Veronica left the planning meeting.

All of the power players had been there—Senator McKinley, whose million-dollar smile had long since faded; Henri Freder, the Ustanzian Ambassador; Admiral Forrest, the salty-looking military man Veronica had met several weeks ago at an embassy function in Paris; stern-faced Kevin Laughton, the Federal Intelligence Commission agent in charge of security; and Prince Tedric's four chief aides.

It had been decided that Prince Tedric should be spirited away from the hotel to a safe house where he'd be guarded by FInCOM agents and Ustanzian secret service men. The American sailor, Joe Catalanotto, would simply move into Tedric's suite of rooms on the tenth floor, thus arousing no suspicion among the hotel staff and guests—or even among the prince's own lesser servants and assistants, who would not be told of the switch.

After convincing the prince to give Veronica St. John a

chance to work with the sailor, McKinley had gotten the ball rolling. Prince Tedric was gone, much to everyone's relief.

Veronica and the prince's main staff were working to reschedule the beginning of the tour. The idea was to organize a schedule that would require Joe to have the least amount of contact with diplomats who might recognize that he was not the real prince. And the FInCOM agents put in *their* two cents worth, trying to set up times and places for Joe to appear in public that would provide the assassins with an obvious, clear target without putting Joe in more danger than necessary.

"Where's Catalanotto?" Admiral Forrest kept asking. "He should be here. He should be part of this op's planning team."

"With all due respect, Admiral," Kevin Laughton, the FInCOM chief, finally said, "it's better to leave the strategizing to the experts." Laughton was a tall man, impeccably dressed, with every strand of his light brown hair perfectly in place. His blue eyes were cool, and he kept his emotions carefully hidden behind a poker face.

"In that case, Mr. Laughton," Forrest said tartly, "Catalanotto should definitely be here. And if you paid close attention, sir, you might even learn a thing or two from him."

"From a navy *lieutenant?*"

"Joe Cat is a Navy SEAL, mister," Forrest said.

There was that word again. SEAL.

But Laughton didn't look impressed. He looked put-upon. "I should've known this was going too smoothly," he said tiredly. He turned to Forrest. "I'm sure you're familiar with the expression, Admiral: Too many cooks spoil the broth?"

The admiral fixed the younger man with a decidedly fishlike stare. "This man is going to be your bait," he said. "Can you honestly tell me that if your roles were reversed, you wouldn't want in on the planning stages?"

"Yes," Laughton replied. "I can."

"Bulldinky." Forrest stood. He snapped his fingers and one of his aides appeared. "Get Joe Cat down here," he ordered.

The man fired off a crisp salute. "Yes, sir." He turned sharply and disappeared.

Laughton was fuming. "You can't pull rank on me. I'm FInCOM—"

"Trust me, son," Forrest interrupted, sitting down again and rocking back in his chair. "See these do-hickeys on my uniform? They're not just pretty buttons. They mean when I say 'stop,' you stop. And if you need that order clarified, I'd be more than happy to call Bill and have him explain it to you."

Veronica bit the insides of her cheeks to keep from smiling. By Bill, the admiral was referring to the President. Of the United States. The look on Kevin Laughton's face was not a happy one.

The admiral's young aide returned and stood patiently at attention just behind Forrest's chair. Forrest tipped his head to look up at him, giving him permission to speak with a nod.

"Lieutenant Catalanotto is unable to attend this meeting, sir," the aide said. "He's getting a tooth capped, and…something done with his hair, sir. I think."

"Thank you, son," Forrest said. He stood, pushing his chair back from the conference table. "In that case, I suggest we adjourn and resume in the morning, when Lieutenant Catalanotto can attend."

"But—"

The admiral fixed Laughton with a single look. "Don't make me make that phone call, mister," he said. "I may have phrased it kind of casually, but my suggestion to adjourn *was* an order." He straightened and picked up his cane. "I'm going to give you a little hint, Laughton, a hint that most folks usually learn the first day of basic training. When an officer gives an order, the correct response is, 'Yes, sir. Right away, sir.'"

He glanced around the table, giving Veronica a quick wink before he headed toward the door.

She gathered up her papers and briefcase and followed, catching up with him in the corridor.

"Excuse me, Admiral," she said. "I haven't had time to do any research—I haven't had time to *think*—and I was hoping you could clue me in. What exactly is a *SEAL?*"

Forrest's leathery face crinkled into a smile. "Joe's a SEAL," he said.

Veronica shook her head. "Sir, that's not what I meant."

His smile became a grin. "I know," he said. "You want me to tell you that a Navy SEAL is the toughest, smartest, deadliest warrior in all of the U.S. military. Okay. There you have it. A SEAL is the best of the best, and he's trained to specialize in unconventional warfare." His smile faded, giving his face a stern, craggy cast. "Let me give you an example. Lieutenant Catalanotto took six men and went one hundred miles behind the lines during the first night of Operation Desert Storm in order to rescue Tedric Cortere—who was too stupid to leave Baghdad when he was warned of the coming U.S. attack. Joe Cat and his Alpha Squad—they're part of SEAL Team Ten—went in undetected, among all the bombs that were falling from U.S. planes, and pulled Cortere and three aides out without a single fatality."

Admiral Forrest smiled again as he watched an expression of disbelief flit across Veronica's face.

"How on earth…?" she asked.

"With a raftload of courage," he answered. "And a whole hell of a lot of training and skill. Joe Cat's an expert in explosives, you know, both on land and underwater. And he knows all there is to know about locks and security systems. He's a top-notch mechanic. He understands engines in a way that's almost spiritual. He's also an expert marksman, a sharpshooter with damn near any ordnance he can get his hands on. And that's just the tip of the iceberg, missy. If you want me to continue, then we'd better find a place to sit and get comfortable, because it's going to take a while."

Veronica tried hard to connect everything she'd just heard with the grimy, unkempt, seemingly uneducated man who had appeared in her hotel room. "I see," she finally said.

"No, you don't," Forrest countered, a smile softening his words. "But you will. Best thing to do is go find Joe. And when he talks to you, really listen. You'll know soon enough what being a SEAL means."

Joe sat in the hairdresser's portable chair, looking at himself in the hotel-room mirror.

He looked…different.

A dentist had come in and capped the tooth he'd chipped three years ago while on a training mission and had never had fixed.

Joe had stopped noticing it after a while. He'd had the rough edges filed down the day of the accident, but he'd never had the time or inclination to get the damn thing capped.

The capped tooth wasn't the only thing different about him now. Joe's short dark hair was about six inches longer— and no longer short—thanks to the hair extensions the tired-looking stylist had almost finished attaching.

It was odd, seeing himself with long hair like this.

Joe had grown his hair out before, when he'd had advance warning of covert operations. But he liked wearing his hair short. It wasn't military-regulation short, just a comfortable length that was easy to deal with.

Long hair got in the way. It worked its way into his mouth, hung in his face, and got in his eyes at inopportune moments.

And it made him look like that cowardly idiot, Tedric Cortere.

Which was precisely the point, right now.

God help them, Joe vowed, if they expected him to wear those satin suits with the ruffles and metallic trim, and those garish rings on his fingers. No, God help *him*. This was a job, and if the powers that be wanted him to dress like an idiot, he was going to have to dress like an idiot. Like it or not.

Joe stared into the mirror at the opulence of the hotel room. This place gave him the creeps. He was nervous he might break something or spill something or touch something he wasn't supposed to touch. And his nervousness really annoyed him. Why *should* he be nervous? Why *should* he feel intimidated? It was only a lousy hotel room, for Pete's sake. The only difference between this room and the cheap motel rooms he stayed in when he traveled was that here the TV wasn't chained down. Here there was a phone in the bathroom. And the towels were thick and plentiful. And the carpets were plush and clean. And the wallpaper wasn't stained, and the curtains actually closed all the way, and the furniture wasn't broken and mismatched. Oh yeah, and the price tag for a one-night stay—that was different, too.

Sheesh, this place was as different from the places he usually stayed as night was to day, Joe reminded himself.

But the truth was, he wished he *was* staying at a cheap motel. At least then he could lie on the bed and put his feet up without being afraid he'd ruin the bedspread. At least he wouldn't feel so goddammed out of his league.

But he was stuck here until another assassination attempt was made or until the prince's U.S. tour ended in five weeks.

Five weeks.

Five weeks of feeling out of place. Of being afraid to touch anything.

"Don't touch!" he could still hear his mother say, when as a kid, he went along on her trips to Scarsdale, where she cleaned houses that were ten times the size of their tiny Jersey City apartment. "Don't touch, or you'll hear from your father when we get home."

Except Joe didn't have a father. He had a whole slew of stepfathers and "uncles," but no father. Still, whoever was temporarily playing the part of dear old dad at home would have leaped at any excuse to kick Joe's insolent butt into tomorrow.

Jeez, what was wrong with him? He hadn't thought about *those* "happy" memories in years.

The hotel-room door opened with an almost-inaudible click and Joe tensed. He looked up, turning his head and making the hairdresser sigh melodramatically.

But Joe had been too well-trained to let someone come into the room without giving them the once-over. Not while he was looking more and more like a man who'd been an assassin's target just this morning.

It was only the media consultant. Veronica St. John.

She posed no threat.

Joe turned his head, looking back into the mirror, waiting for the rush of relief, for the relaxation of the tension in his shoulders.

But it never came. Instead of relaxing, he felt as if all of his senses had gone on alert. As if he'd suddenly woken up. It was as if he were about to go into a combat situation. The colors in the wallpaper seemed sharper, clearer. The sounds of the hairdresser behind him seemed louder. And his sense of smell heightened to the point where he caught a whiff of Veronica St. John's subtle perfume from all the way across the room.

"Good God," she said in her crisp, faintly British-accented voice. "You look…amazing."

"Well, thank you, sweetheart. You're not so bad yourself."

She'd moved to where he could see her behind him in the mirror, and he glanced up, briefly meeting her gaze.

Blue eyes. Oh, baby, those eyes were blue. Electric blue. Electric-*shock* blue.

Joe looked up at her again and realized that the current of awareness and attraction that had shot through him had gone through her, as well. She looked as surprised as he felt. Surprised, no doubt, that a guy from his side of the tracks could catch her eye.

Except he didn't look like himself anymore. He looked like Prince Tedric.

It figured.

"I see you had the opportunity to take a shower," she said, no longer meeting his eyes. "Did your clothes get taken down to the laundry?"

"I think so," he said. "They were gone when I got out of the bathroom. I found this hotel robe…. I'd appreciate it if you could ask Admiral Forrest to send over a uniform in the morning. And maybe some socks and shorts…?"

Veronica felt her cheeks start to heat. Lord, what was wrong with her? Since when did the mention of men's underwear make her face turn as red as a schoolgirl's?

Or maybe it wasn't the mention of unmentionables that was making her blush. Maybe it was the thought that this very large, very charismatic, very handsome, and very, *very* dangerous man was sitting here, with absolutely nothing on underneath his white terry-cloth robe.

From the glint in his dark brown eyes, it was clear that he was able to read her mind.

She used every ounce of her British schooling to keep her voice sounding cool and detached. "There's no need, Your Highness," she said. "We go from here to your suite. A tailor will be arriving soon. He'll provide you with all of the clothing you'll need for the course of the next few weeks."

"Whoa," Joe said. "Whoa, whoa! Back up a sec, will ya?"

"A tailor," Veronica repeated. "We'll be meeting with him shortly. I realize it's late, but if we don't get started with—"

"No, no," Joe said. "Before that. Did you just call me 'Your Highness'?"

"I'm done here," the hairdresser said. In a monotone, he quickly ran down a quick list of things Joe could and could not do with the extensions in his hair. "Swim—yes. Shower—yes. Run a comb through your hair—no. You have to be careful to comb only above and below the attachment." He turned to Veronica. "You have my card if you need me again."

"Find Mr. Laughton on your way out," Veronica said as Joe stood and helped the man fold up his portable chair. "He'll see that you get paid."

She watched, waiting until the hairdresser had closed the hotel-room door tightly behind him. Then she turned back to Joe.

"Your Highness," she said again. "And Your Excellency. You'll have to get used to it. This is the way you're going to be addressed."

"Even by you?" Joe stood very still, his arms folded across his chest. It was as if he were afraid to touch anything. But that was ridiculous. From the little information Veronica had gleaned from Admiral Forrest, Joe Catalanotto, or Joe Cat as the admiral had called him, wasn't afraid of *any*thing.

She crossed the room and sat down in one of the easy

chairs by the windows. "Yes, even by me." Veronica gestured for him to sit across from her. "If we intend to pull off this charade—"

"You're right," Joe said, sitting down. "You're absolutely right. We need to go the full distance or the shooters will smell that something's not right." He smiled wryly. "It's just, after years of 'Hey, you!' or 'Yo, paesan!' 'Your Highness' is a little disconcerting."

Veronica's eyebrows moved upward a fraction of an inch. It figured she'd be surprised. She probably thought he didn't know any four-syllable words.

Damn, what *was* it about her? She wasn't pretty, but…at the same time, she *was*. Her hair was gorgeous—the kind of soft curls he loved to run his fingers through. Joe found his eyes drawn to her face, to her delicate, almost-pointed nose, and her beautifully shaped lips. And those eyes…

His gaze slid lower, to the dark blue blazer that covered her shoulders, tapering down to her slender waist. She wore a matching navy skirt that ended a few inches above her knees, yet still managed to scream of propriety. Her politely crossed legs were something else entirely. Not even the sturdy pumps she wore on her feet could hide the fact that her legs were long and graceful and sexy as hell—the kind of legs a man dreams about. *This* man, anyway.

Joe knew that she was well aware he was studying her. But she had turned away, pretending to look for something in her briefcase, purposely ignoring the attraction he knew was mutual.

And then the phone rang—a sudden shrill noise that broke the quiet.

"Excuse me for a moment, please," Veronica said, gracefully standing and crossing the room to answer it.

"Hello?" she said, glancing back at Joe. As she watched, he leaned his head back and closed his eyes.

Thank goodness. He couldn't undress her any further with eyes that were closed. And with his eyes closed, she didn't have to be afraid that the warmth that spread throughout her entire body at his unmasked interest would somehow show. Heaven help her if this man got the idea that he could make her heart beat harder with a single look. She had enough to worry about without having to fight off some sailor's amorous advances.

"The tailor has arrived," one of Tedric's aides told her. "May I ask how much longer you'll be?"

"We'll be up shortly," Veronica said. "Please arrange to have coffee available. And something to eat. Doughnuts. Chocolate ones." Lt. Joe Catalanotto looked the chocolate-doughnut type. They could all certainly use some extra sugar to keep them awake.

She hung up the phone and crossed back to Joe. His head was still back, and his eyes were closed. He'd slumped down in the chair as if he had no bones in his entire body.

He was totally, absolutely and quite soundly asleep.

Veronica sat down across from him and leaned forward, studying his face. He'd shaved and somehow managed to get all of the grease and dirt off in the shower. Even his hands were free of grime. His hair was clean and now, with the extensions, quite long. To the average eye, he might have looked quite a bit like Prince Tedric, but Veronica knew better.

Tedric had never been—and never would be—this handsome.

There was an edge to Joe Catalanotto's good looks. A sharpness, a definition, an honesty that Tedric didn't have. There was something vibrant about Joe. He was so very alive, so vital, as if he took each moment and lived it to its very fullest. Veronica had never met anyone quite like him before.

Imagine taking a squad of seven men deep behind enemy lines, she thought, with bombs falling, no less. Imagine having the courage and the confidence to risk not just one's own life, but six other lives, as well. And then imagine actually *enjoying* the danger.

Veronica thought of the men she knew, the men she was used to working with. They tended to be so very...careful. Not that they weren't risk takers—oftentimes they were. But the risks they took were financial or psychological, never physical. Not a single one would ever put himself into any real physical danger. A paper cut was the worst they could expect, and *that* usually required a great deal of hand-holding.

Most men looked softer, less imposing when asleep, but not Joe. His body may have been relaxed, but his jaw was tightly clenched, his lips pulled back in what was almost a snarl. Underneath his lids, his eyes jerked back and forth in REM sleep.

He slept ferociously, almost as if these five minutes of rest were all he'd get for the next few days.

It was strange. It was very strange. And it was stranger still when Veronica sighed.

It wasn't a particularly weighty sigh, just a little one, really. Not even very loud.

Still, Joe's eyes flew open and he sat up straight. He was instantly alert, without a hint of fatigue on his lean face.

He took a sip directly from a can of soda that was sitting on the glass-topped end table and looked at Veronica steadily, as if he hadn't been fast asleep mere seconds earlier. "Time for the tailor?" he said.

She was fascinated. "How do you do that?" she asked, leaning forward slightly, searching his eyes for any sign of grogginess. "Wake up so quickly, I mean."

Joe blinked and then smiled, clearly surprised at her interest. His smile was genuine, reaching his eyes and making the laugh lines around them deepen. Lord, he was even more attractive when he smiled that way. Veronica found herself smiling back, hypnotized by the warmth of his eyes.

"Training." He leaned back in his chair and watched her. "SEALs take classes to study sleep patterns. We learn to catch catnaps whenever we can."

"Really?" Joe could see the amusement in her eyes, the barely restrained laughter curving the corners of her mouth. Her natural expression was a smile, he realized. But she'd taught herself to put on that serious, businesslike facade she wore most of the time. "Classes to learn how to sleep and wake up?" she asked, letting a laugh slip out.

Was she laughing *at* him or *with* him? He honestly couldn't tell, and he felt his own smile fade. Damn, what was it about this particular girl that he found so intimidating? With any other woman, he'd assume the joke was shared, and he'd feel glad that he was making her smile. But *this* one…

There was attraction in her eyes, all right. Genuine animal attraction. He saw it there every time she glanced in his direction. But there was also wariness. Maybe even fear. She didn't want to be attracted to him.

She probably didn't think he was good enough for her.

Damn it, he was a Navy SEAL. There was nobody better. If she wanted to ignore the fire that was ready to ignite between them, then so be it. Her loss.

He would find plenty of women to distract him during this way-too-simple operation, and—

With a hiss of silk, she crossed her long legs. Joe had to look away.

Her loss. It was her loss. Except every cell in his body was screaming that the loss was *his*.

Okay. So he'd seduce her. He'd ply her with wine—no,

make that expensive champagne—and he'd wait until the heat he saw in her eyes started to burn out of control. It would be that easy. And then... Oh, baby. It didn't take much to imagine his hands in her soft red hair, then sweeping up underneath the delicate silk of her blouse, finding the soft, sweet fullness of her breasts. He could picture one of those sexy legs wrapped around one of his legs, as she pressed herself tightly against him, her fingers reaching for the buckle of his belt as he plundered her beautiful mouth with his tongue and...

Sure, it might be that easy.

But then again, it might not.

He had no reason on earth to believe that a woman like this one would want anything to do with him. From the way she dressed and acted, Joe was willing to bet big bucks that she wouldn't want any kind of permanent thing with a guy like him.

Veronica St. John—"Sinjin," she pronounced it with that richer-than-God accent—could probably trace her bloodline back to Henry the Eighth. And Joe, he didn't even know who the hell his father was. And wouldn't *that* just make dicey dinner conversation. *"Catalanotto... Italian name, isn't it? Where exactly is your father from, Lieutenant?"*

"Well, gee, I don't know, Ronnie." He wondered if anyone had ever called her Ronnie, probably not. *"Mom says he was some sailor in port for a day or two. Catalanotto is her name. And where she came from is anyone's guess. So is it really any wonder Mom drank as much as she did?"*

Yeah, that would go over *real* well.

But he wasn't talking about marriage here. He wasn't talking about much more than quenching that sharp thirst he felt whenever he looked into Veronica St. John's eyes. He was talking about one night, maybe two or three or four, depending on how long this operation lasted. He was talking short-term fling, hot affair—not a lot of conversation required.

It was true, he didn't have a lot of experience with debutantes, but hell, her money and power were only on the surface. Peel the outer trappings away, and Veronica St. John was a woman. And Joe knew women. He knew what they liked, how to catch their eye, how to make them smile.

Usually women came to him. It had been a long while since he'd actively pursued one.

This could be fun.

"We trained to learn how to drop instantly into rapid-eye-movement sleep," Joe said, evenly meeting the crystal blueness of Veronica's eyes. "It comes in handy in a combat situation, or a covert op where there may be only brief stretches of time safe enough to catch some rest. It's kept more than one SEAL alive on more than one occasion."

"What else do SEALs learn how to do?" Veronica asked.

Oh, baby, what you don't know…

"You name it, honey," Joe said, "we can do it."

"My name," she declared in her cool English accent, sitting back in her chair and gazing at him steadily, "is Veronica St. John. Not honey. Not babe. Veronica. St. John. Please refrain from using terms of endearment. I don't care for them."

She was trying to look as chilly as her words sounded, but Joe saw heat when he looked into her eyes. She was trying to hide it, but it was back there. He knew, with a sudden odd certainty, that when they made love, it was going to be a near religious experience. Not *if* they made love, *When*. It *was* going to happen.

"It's a habit that's gonna be hard to break," he said.

Veronica stood, briefcase in hand. "I'm sure you have a number of habits that will be a challenge to break," she said. "So I suggest we not keep the tailor waiting a minute longer. We have plenty of work to do before we can get some sleep."

But Joe didn't move. "So what am I supposed to call you?" he asked. "Ronnie?"

Veronica looked up to find a glint of mischief in his dark eyes. He knew perfectly well that calling her "Ronnie" would not suit. He was smiling, and she was struck by the even whiteness of his teeth. He may have chipped one at one time, but the others were straight and well taken care of.

"I think Ms. St. John will do quite well, thank you," she said. "That *is* how the prince addresses me."

"I see," Joe murmured, clearly amused.

"Shall we?" she prompted.

"Oh, yes, please," Joe said overenthusiastically, then tried to look disappointed. "Oh…you mean shall we *leave?* I thought you meant…" But he was only pretending that he misunderstood. He couldn't keep a smile from slipping out.

Veronica shook her head in exasperation. "Two days, Lieutenant," she said. "We have two days to create a miracle, and you're wasting time with sophomoric humor."

Joe stood, stretching his arms above his head. His feet and legs were bare underneath his robe. So was the rest of him, but Veronica was determined not to think about that.

"I thought you were going to call me 'Your Highness.'"

"Two days, *Your Highness*," Veronica repeated.

"Two days is a breeze, Ronnie," he said. "And I've decided if I'm the prince I can call you whatever I want, and I want to call you Ronnie."

"No, you most certainly will not!"

"Why the hell not? I'm the prince," Joe said. "It's your choice—Ronnie or Honey. I don't care."

"My Lord, you're almost as incorrigible as Tedric," Veronica sputtered.

"'My Lord,'" Joe mused. "Yeah, you can call me that. Although I prefer 'Your All-Powerful Mightiness.' Hey, while

I'm making royal decrees, why don't you go ahead and give the serfs a day off."

He was laughing at her. He was teasing her, and enjoying watching her squirm.

"You know, this is going to be a vacation for me, Ron," he added. "Two days of prep is a cakewalk."

Veronica laughed in disbelief. How *dare* he…? "Two days," she said. "You're going to have to completely relearn how to walk and talk and stand and sit and *eat*. Not to mention memorizing all the names and faces of the aides and ambassadors and government officials that the prince is acquainted with. And don't forget all the rules and protocols you'll have to learn, all of the Ustanzian customs and traditions…"

Joe spread his hands and shrugged. "How hard could it be? Give me a videotape of Tedric and half an hour, and you'll think I'm the same guy," he said. "I've gone on far tougher missions with way less prep time. Two days—forty-eight hours—is a luxury, sweetheart."

How could he think that? Veronica was so stressed out by the rapidly approaching deadline she could barely breathe.

"*Less* than forty-eight hours," she told him sharply. "You have to sleep some of that time."

"Sleep?" Joe smiled. "I just did."

Chapter Five

"And never, *ever* open the door yourself," Veronica said. "Always wait for someone—a servant—to do it for you."

Joe gazed at her across the top of his mug as he sat on the other side of the conference table in Tedric's royal suite. "Never?" he said. He took a sip of coffee, still watching her, his dark eyes mysterious, unreadable. "Old Ted never opens the door for anyone?"

"If he were with a king or a queen, he might open the door," Veronica said, glancing down at her notes. And away from those eyes. "But I doubt you'll be running into any such personages on *this* tour."

"What does Ted do when he's all alone?" Joe started to put his mug down on the richly polished oak tabletop, but stopped as if he were afraid to mar the wood. He pulled one of Veronica's file folders closer and set his mug down on top of the stiff manila. "Just stand there until a servant comes along to open the door? That could be a real drag if he's in a rush to use the head." He rested his chin in the palm of his hand, elbow on the table, as he continued to gaze at her.

"Your Highness, an Ustanzian prince never rests his elbows on the top of a table," Veronica said with forced patience.

Joe smiled and didn't move. He just watched her with half-closed bedroom eyes that exuded sexuality. They'd been working together all night, and not once had he let her forget that she was a woman and he was a man. "I'm not a Ustanzian prince," he said. "Yet."

Veronica folded her hands neatly on top of her notes. "And it's not called a 'head,'" she said. "Not john, not toilet, not bathroom. It's a water closet. W.C. We went through this already, remember, Your Highness?"

"How about I call it the Little Prince's Room?" Joe asked.

Veronica laughed despite her growing sense of doom. Or maybe because of it. What was she going to do about Joe Catalanotto's thick New Jersey accent? And what was she going to do about the fact that this man didn't, for even one single second, take *any*thing they were doing seriously?

And to further frustrate her, she was ready to drop from exhaustion, while he looked ready to run laps.

"My mother's name is Maria. She was an Italian countess before she met my father. My father is King Derrick the Fourth, *his* father was Derrick the Third," Joe recited. "I was born in the capital city on January 7, 1961…. You know, this would be a whole lot easier on both of us if you would just hand me your file on this guy, and give me a videotape so I can see firsthand the way he walks and stands and…"

"Excuse me, Lieutenant." A FInCOM agent by the name of West stood politely to one side.

Joe looked up, an instant Naval Officer. He sat straighter and even looked as if he was paying attention. Now, why couldn't Veronica get him to take *her* that seriously?

"At Admiral Forrest's request, Mr. Laughton requires

your consultation, sir, in planning the scheduling of the tour, and the strategy for your protection," West continued. "That is, if you wish to have any input."

Joe stood. "Damn straight I do," he said. "Your security stinks. Fortunately those terrorists took the night off, or I'd already be dead."

West stiffened. "The security we've provided has been top level—"

"What I'm saying is your so-called top-level security isn't good enough, pal," Joe countered. He looked back at Veronica. "What do you say you go take a nap, Ronnie, and we meet back at..." He glanced at his watch. "How's eleven-hundred hours? Just over two hours."

But Veronica stood, shaking her head. She wanted desperately to sleep, but unless she attended this meeting, the visit to Saint Mary's would be removed from the tour schedule. She spoke directly to the FInCOM agent. "I'd like to have some input in this meeting, too, Mr. West," she said coolly. "I'm sure Mr. Laughton—or Admiral Forrest—won't mind if I sit in."

Joe shrugged. "Suit yourself."

"Princes don't shrug, Your Highness," Veronica reminded him as they followed West out into the corridor and toward the conference room.

Joe rolled his eyes.

"And princes don't roll their eyes," she said.

"Sheesh," he muttered.

"They don't swear, either, Your Highness," Veronica told him. "Not even those thinly veiled words you Americans use in place of the truly nasty ones."

"So you're *not* an American," Joe said, walking backward so he could look at her. "Mac Forrest must've been mistaken. He told me, despite your fancy accent, that you were."

Joe had talked about her with Admiral Forrest. Veronica felt a warm flash of pleasure that she instantly tried to squelch. So what if Joe had talked with the admiral about her. *She'd* talked to the admiral about Joe, simply to get some perspective on whom she'd be dealing with, who she'd be working closely with for the next few weeks.

"Oh, I'm American," Veronica said. "I even say a full variety of those aforementioned nasty words upon occasion."

Joe laughed. He had a nice laugh, rich and full. It made her want to smile. "That I won't believe until I hear it."

"Well, you won't hear it, Your Highness. It wouldn't be polite or proper."

Her shoe caught in the thick carpeting, and she stumbled slightly. Joe caught and held her arm, stopping to make sure she had her balance.

Veronica looked really beat. She looked ready to fall on her face—which she just about did. Joe could feel the warmth of her arm, even through the sleeve of her jacket and blouse. He didn't want to let her go, so he didn't. They stood there in the hotel corridor, and FInCOM Agent West waited impatiently nearby.

Joe was playing with fire. He knew that he was playing with fire. But, hell. He was a demolitions expert. He was used to handling materials that could blow sky-high at any time.

Veronica looked down at his hand still on her arm, then lifted enormous blue eyes to his.

"I'm quite all right, Your Highness," she said in that Julie Andrews accent.

"You're tired as hell," he countered bluntly. "Go get some sleep."

"Believe it or not, I do have some information of importance to add to this scheduling meeting," she said hotly, the crystal of her eyes turning suddenly to blue flame. "I'd truly appreciate it if you'd unhand me so we could continue on our way, Your Highness."

"Wait," Joe said. "Don't tell me. A prince never offers a helping hand, is that it? A prince lets a lady fall on her face, right?"

"A prince doesn't take advantage of a lady's misfortune," Veronica said tightly. "You helped me—thank you. Now let me go. Please. Your Excellency."

Joe laughed. This time it was a low, dangerous sound. His hand tightened on her arm and he drew her even closer to him, so that their noses almost touched, so that Veronica could feel his body heat through the thin cotton shirt and dark slacks the tailor had left him with after the early-morning fitting.

"Babe, if you think this is taking advantage, you've never been taken advantage of." He lowered his voice and dropped his head down so he was speaking directly into her ear. "If you want, I'll demonstrate the differences. With pleasure."

She could feel the warmth of his breath on her neck as he waited for her to react. He was expecting her to run, screaming, away from him. He was expecting her to be outraged, upset, angry, offended.

But all she could think about was how utterly delicious he smelled.

What would he say, what would he do if she moved her head a fraction of an inch to the right and pressed her cheek against the roughness of his chin. What would he do if she lifted her head to whisper into *his* ear, "Oh, yes"?

It wouldn't be the response he was expecting, that was certain.

But the truth was, this wasn't about sex, it was about power. Veronica had played hardball with the big boys long enough to know that.

It wasn't that he wasn't interested—he'd made that more than clear in the way he'd looked at her all night long. But

Veronica was willing to bet that right now Joe was bluffing. And while she wasn't going to call his bluff, she was going to let him know that merely because he was bigger and stronger than she, that didn't mean he'd automatically win.

So she lifted her head and, keeping her voice cool, almost chilly, said, "One would think that a Navy SEAL might be aware of the dangers of standing too long in a public corridor, considering someone out there wants Tedric—whom, by the way, you look quite a bit like these days—dead."

Joe laughed.

Not exactly the response *she* was expecting after her verbal attack. Another man might have been annoyed that his bluff hadn't worked. Another man might have pouted or glowered. Joe laughed.

"I don't know, Ron," he said, letting her go. His dark eyes were genuinely amused, but there was something else there, too. Could it possibly be respect? "You sound so...proper, but I don't think you really are, are you? I think it's all an act. I think you go home from work, and you take off the Margaret Thatcher costume, and let down your hair and put on some little black sequined number with stiletto heels, and you go out and mambo in some Latin nightclub until dawn."

Veronica crossed her arms. "You forgot my gigolo," she said crisply. "I go pick up my current gigolo and then *we* mambo till dawn."

"Let me know when there's an opening, honey," Joe said. "I'd love to apply for the job."

All humor had gone from his eyes. He was dead serious. Veronica turned away, afraid he'd see just from looking at her how appealing she found the thought of dancing with him until dawn, their bodies clasped together, moving to the pulsing beat of Latin drums.

"We'd best not keep Mr. Laughton waiting," she said. "Your Excellency."

"Damn," Joe said. "Margaret Thatcher's back."

"Sorry to disappoint you," Veronica murmured as they went into the secret-service agents' suite. "But she never left."

"Saint Mary's, right here in Washington," Veronica said from her seat next to Joe at the big conference table. "Someone keeps taking Saint Mary's off the schedule."

"It's unnecessary," Kevin Laughton said in his flat, almost-bored-sounding Midwestern accent.

"I disagree." Veronica spoke softly but firmly.

"Look, Ronnie," Senator McKinley said, and Veronica briefly shut her eyes. Lord, but Joe Catalanotto had all of them calling her Ronnie now. "Maybe you don't understand this, dear, but Saint Mary's doesn't do us any good. The building is too small, too well protected, and too difficult for the assassins to penetrate. Besides, it's not a public event. The assassins are going to want news coverage. They're going to want to make sure millions of people are watching when they kill the prince. Besides, there's no clear targeting area going into and out of the structure. It's a waste of our time."

"This visit's been scheduled for months," Veronica said quietly. "It's been scheduled since the Ustanzian secretary of press announced Prince Tedric's American tour. I think we can take one hour from one day to fulfill a promise the prince made."

Henri Freder, the Ustanzian ambassador to the United States, shifted in his seat. "Surely Prince Tedric can visit this Saint Mary's at the end of the tour, after the Alaskan cruise, on his way back home."

"That will be too late," Veronica said.

"Cruise?" Joe repeated. "If the assassins haven't been apprehended before the cruise to Alaska is scheduled, there's no way in hell we're getting on that loveboat." He looked around the table. "A cruise ship's too isolated. It's a natural target for tangos."

He smiled at their blank expressions. "Tangos," Joe repeated. "T's. Terrorists. The bad guys with guns."

Ah. There was understanding all around.

"Unless, of course, we're ready and waiting for 'em," Joe continued. "And maybe that's not such a bad idea. Replace the ship's personnel and passenger list with platoons of SEALs and—"

"No way," Laughton said. "FInCOM is handling this. It isn't some military operation. SEALs have no place in it."

"Terrorists are involved," Joe countered. "SEAL Team Ten has had extensive counterterrorist training. My men are prepared for—"

"War," Laughton finished for him. "Your men are prepared and trained for *war*. This is not a war, Lieutenant."

Joe pointed to the cellular phone on the table in front of Laughton. "Then you'd better call the terrorists. Call the Cloud of Death, call up Diosdado. Call him up and tell him that this is not a war. Because *he* sure as hell thinks it's one."

"Please," Veronica interjected. "Before we continue, may we all agree to keep Saint Mary's on the schedule?"

McKinley frowned down at the papers in front of him. "I see from the previous list that there weren't going to be any media present at the event at Saint Mary's."

"Not all of the events scheduled were for the benefit of the news cameras, Senator," Veronica said evenly. She glanced around the table. "Gentlemen. This rescheduling means hours and hours of extra work for all of us. I'm trying my best to cooperate, as I'm sure you are, too. But I happen to know that this appearance at Saint Mary's was of utmost importance to Prince Tedric." She widened her eyes innocently. "If necessary, I'll ring up the prince and ask for *his* input and—"

"No need to do that," Senator McKinley said hastily.

Getting self-centered Prince Tedric in on this scheduling nightmare was the last thing *any*one wanted, Veronica included. His so-called "input" would slow this process down to a crawl. But she was prepared to do whatever she had to do to keep the visit to Saint Mary's on the schedule.

McKinley looked around the table. "I think we can keep Saint Mary's on the list." There was a murmur of agreement.

Joe watched Veronica. Her red curls were up in some kind of feminine arrangement on the top of her head. With her delicate features and innocent blue eyes, she looked every inch the demure, cool English lady; and again, Joe was struck by the feeling that her outward appearance was only an act. She wasn't demure *or* cool, and if his gut feelings were right, she could probably outmanipulate the entire tableful of them. Hell, she just had. But she'd done it so subtly that no one was even aware they'd been manipulated.

"About the Alaskan cruise," Senator McKinley said.

"That's not until later in the tour." Joe leaned back in his chair. "Let's keep it off the public schedule for now. We don't want the T's—terrorists—choosing that opportunity above everything else. We want 'em to strike early on. But still, we can start making arrangements with the SEAL teams, start getting 'em prepped for a potential operation aboard ship."

"No SEALs," Kevin Laughton said tersely.

Joe gave the FInCOM agent a disbelieving look. "You *want* high casualties? Is that your goal here?"

"Of course not—"

"We're all on the same team, pal," Joe said. "We all work for the U.S. Government. Just because I'm Navy and you're Fink—"

"No SEALs." Laughton turned to an aide. "Release this schedule to the news media ASAP, keeping the cruise information off the list." He stood. "My men will start scouting each of these sites."

Joe stood up, too. "You should start right here in this hotel," he said. "If you're serious about making the royal suite secure, you're understaffed. And the sliding door to the balcony in the bedroom doesn't lock. What kind of security is that?"

Laughton stared at him. "You're on the *tenth* floor."

"Terrorists sometimes know how to climb," Joe said.

"I can assure you you're quite safe," Laughton said.

"And I can assure you that I'm not. If security stays as is, if Diosdado and his gang decide to come into this hotel to rid the world of Prince Tedric, then I'm as good as dead."

"I can understand your concern," Laughton said. "But—"

"Then you won't have any objection to bringing the rest of my Alpha Squad out here," Joe interrupted. "You're obviously undermanned, and I'd feel a whole hell of a lot better if—"

"No," Laughton said. "Absolutely not. A squad of Navy SEALs? Utter chaos. My men won't stand for it. I won't have it."

"I'm going to be standing around, wearing a damned shooting target on my chest," Joe retorted. "I want my own guys nearby, watching my back, plugging the holes in FInCOM's security net. I can tell you right now, they won't get in your boys' way."

"No," Laughton said again. "*I'm* in charge of security, and I say *no*. This meeting is adjourned."

Joe watched the FInCOM chief leave the room, then glanced up to find Veronica's eyes on him.

"I guess we're going to have to do this the hard way," he said.

* * *

The man known only as Diosdado looked up from his desk as Salustiano Vargas was shown into the room.

"Ah, old friend," Vargas greeted him with relief. "Why did your men not say it was you they were bringing me to see?"

Diosdado was silent, just looking at the other man as he thoughtfully stroked his beard.

Vargas threw himself down into a chair across from the desk and casually stretched his legs out in front of him. "It has been too long, no?" he said. "What have you been up to, man?"

"Not as much as you have, apparently." Diosdado smiled, but it was a mere shadow of his normally wide, toothy grin.

Vargas's own smile was twisted. "Eh, you heard about that, huh?" His smile turned to a scowl. "I would have drilled the bastard through the heart if that damned woman hadn't pushed him out of the way."

Diosdado stood. "You are lucky—very, *very* lucky—that your bullet missed Tedric Cortere," he said harshly.

Vargas stared at him in surprise. "But—"

"If you had kept in touch, you would have been aware of what I have spent *months* planning." Diosdado didn't raise his voice when he was angry. He lowered it. Right now, it was very, *very* quiet.

Vargas opened his mouth to speak, to protest, but he wisely shut it tightly instead.

"The Cloud of Death intended to take Cortere hostage," Diosdado said. "Intends," he corrected himself. "We still intend to take him." He began to pace—a halting, shuffling process as he dragged his bad leg behind him. "Of course, now that you have intervened, the prince's security has been strengthened. FInCOM is involved, and my contacts tell me that the U.S. Navy is even playing some part in Cortere's protection."

Vargas stared at him.

"So what," Diosdado continued, turning to face Salusti-ano Vargas, "do you suggest we do to bring this high level of security and protection back to where it was before you fouled things up?"

Vargas swallowed, knowing what the other man was going to tell him, and knowing that he wasn't going to like what he heard.

"They are all waiting for another assassination attempt," Diosdado said. "Until they *get* another assassination at-tempt, security will be too tight. Do you know what you are going to do, my old friend Salustiano?"

Vargas knew. He knew, and he didn't like it. "Diosdado," he said. "Please. We're friends. I saved your *life*—"

"You will go back," Diosdado said very, very softly, "and you will make another attempt on the prince's life. You will fail, and you will be apprehended. Dead or alive—your choice."

Vargas sat in silence as Diosdado limped, shuffling, from the room.

"Tell me what it is about Navy SEALs that makes Kevin Laughton so upset, Your Highness," Veronica said as she and Joe were delivered safely back to Prince Tedric's hotel suite. "Why doesn't he want your Alpha Squad around?"

"He knows his guys would give him problems if my guys were brought in to do their job," Joe said. "It's a slap in the face. It implies I don't think FInCOM can get the job done."

"But obviously, you don't think they can."

Joe shook his head and sat down heavily in one of the plush easy chairs in the royal living room. "I think they're probably top-notch at mid-level protection," he said. "But my life's on the line here, and the bad guys aren't street punks or crazy people with guns. They're professionals. Di-

osdado runs a top-notch military organization. He's a formidable opponent. He could get through this kind of security without blinking. But he couldn't get through the
Alpha Squad. I *know* my SEALs are the best of the best.
SEAL Team Ten is elite, and the Alpha Squad is made up
of the best men in Team Ten. I want them here, even if I
have to step on some toes or offend some FInCOM agents.
The end result is I stay alive. Are you following me?"

Veronica nodded, sitting down on the sofa and resting
her briefcase on a long wooden coffee table.

The sofa felt so comfortable, so soft. It would be so easy
to let her head fall back and her eyes close....

"Maybe we should take a break," Joe said. "You can barely
keep your eyes open."

"No, there's so much more you need to learn," Veronica
said. She made herself sit up straight. If *he* could stay awake,
she could, too. "The history of Ustanzia. The names of Ustanzian officials." She pulled a file from her briefcase and
opened it. "I have fifty-seven pictures of people you will
come into contact with, Your Highness. I need you to memorize these faces and names, and—Lord, if there were only
another way to do this."

"Earphone," Joe said, flipping through the file.

"Excuse me?"

He looked up at her. "I wear a concealed earphone," he
said. "And you have a mic. We set up a video camera so that
you can see and hear everything I'm doing while you're
some safe distance away—maybe even out in a surveillance
truck. When someone comes up to shake my hand, you feed
me his name and title and any other pertinent info I might
need." He flipped through the photos and handed them
back to Veronica. "Pick out the top ten and I'll look 'em
over. The others I don't need to know."

Veronica fixed him with a look, suddenly feeling extremely awake. What did he mean, the others he didn't need to know? "All fifty-seven of these people are diplomats Tedric knows quite well. You could run into any one of these people at any time during the course of this tour," she said. "The original file had over three hundred faces and names."

Joe shook his head. "I don't have time to memorize faces and names," he said. "With the high-tech equipment we have access to—"

"*You* don't have time?" Veronica repeated, eyebrows lifted. "We're *all* running out of time, Lieutenant. It's *my* task to prepare you. Let me decide what there is and isn't time for."

Joe leaned forward. "Look, Ronnie, no offense, but I'm used to preparing for an operation at my own speed," he said. "I appreciate everything you're trying to do, but in all honesty, the way that Ted walks and talks is the least of my concerns. I've got this security thing to straighten out and—"

"That's Kevin Laughton's job," she interrupted. "Not yours."

"But it's my ass that's on the line," he said flatly. "FIn-COM's going to change their security plans, or this operation is not going to happen."

Veronica tapped her fingernails on the legal pad she was holding. "And if you don't look and act enough like Prince Tedric," she said tartly, "this operation is not going to happen, either."

"Get me a tape," Joe countered. "Get me a videotape and an audiotape of the guy, and I promise you, I *swear* to you, I will look and act and sound exactly like Ted."

Veronica's teeth were clenched tightly together in annoyance. "Details," she said tightly. "How will you learn the details? Assuming, of course, that you are able to miraculously transform yourself into European royalty simply by viewing a videotape?"

"Write 'em down," Joe said without hesitation. "I retain written information better, anyway." The telephone rang and he paused briefly, listening while West answered it. "Lieutenant, it's for you," the FInCOM agent said.

Joe reached for the extension. "Yo. Catalanotto here."

Yo. The man answered the phone with "Yo" and Veronica was supposed to believe he'd be able to pass himself off as the prince, with little or no instruction from her?

"Mac," Joe said into the telephone. It was Admiral Forrest on the other end. "Great. Thanks for calling me back. What's the word on getting Alpha Squad out here?"

How did a lieutenant get away with calling an admiral by his first name, anyway? Veronica had heard that Forrest had been a SEAL himself at one time in his long navy career. And from what little she knew about SEALs so far, she suspected they were unconventional in more than just their warfare tactics.

Joe's jaw was tight and the muscles in the side of his face were working as he listened to Forrest speak. He swore sharply, not bothering to try to disguise his bad language. As Veronica watched, he rubbed his forehead—the first sign he'd given all day that he was weary.

"FInCOM has raised hell before," he said. "That hasn't stopped us in the past." There was a pause and he added hotly, "Their security is lax, sir. Damn, you know that as well as I do." Another pause. "I was hoping I wouldn't have to do that."

Joe glanced up and into Veronica's watching eyes. She looked away, suddenly self-conscious about the fact that she was openly eavesdropping. As she shuffled through the file of photographs, she was aware of his gaze still on her.

"Before you go, sir," he said into the telephone. "I need another favor. I need audio- and videotapes of Tedric sent to my room ASAP."

Veronica looked up at that, and directly into Joe's eyes. "Thanks, Admiral," he said and hung up the phone. "He'll have 'em sent right over," he said to Veronica as he stood.

He looked as if he were about to leave, to go somewhere. But she didn't even get a chance to question him.

"FInCOM's having a briefing about the tour locations here in D.C.," Joe said. "I need to be there."

"But—"

"Why don't you take a nap?" Joe said. He looked at his watch, and Veronica automatically glanced at hers. It was nearly five o'clock in the evening. "We'll meet back here at twenty-one hundred hours."

Veronica quickly counted on her fingers. Nine o'clock. "No," she said, standing. "That's too long. I can give you an hour break, but—"

"This briefing's important," Joe said. "It'll be over at twenty-hundred, but I'll need an extra hour."

Veronica shook her head in exasperation. "Kevin Laughton doesn't even *want* you there," she said. "You'll spend the entire time arguing—"

"Damn straight, I'm going to argue," Joe said. "If FInCOM insists on assuming the tangos are going to mosey on up to the front door and ring the bell before they strike, then I've got to be there, arguing to keep the back door protected."

Joe was already heading toward the door. West and Freeman scrambled to their feet, following him.

"Put those details you were talking about in writing," Joe suggested. "I'll see you in a few hours."

Veronica all but stamped her foot. "You're supposed to be working with me," she said. "You can't just…leave…."

But he was gone.

Veronica threw her pad and pen onto the table in frustration. Time was running out.

Chapter Six

Veronica woke up from her nap at seven-thirty, still exhausted but too worried to sleep. *How* was Joe going to learn to act like Prince Tedric if he wouldn't give her any time to properly teach him?

She'd made lists and more lists of details and information Joe had no way of knowing—things like, the prince was right-handed. That was normally not a problem, except she'd noticed that Joe was a lefty. She'd written down trivial information such as the fact that Tedric always twirled the signet ring he wore on his right hand when he was thinking.

Veronica got up from the table and started to pace, alternately worried, frustrated and angry with Joe. Who in blazes actually *cared* what Tedric did with his jewelry? Who, truly, would notice? And why was she making lists of details when basic things such as Tedric's walk and ramrod-straight posture were being ignored?

Restless, Veronica pawed through the clothes in her suitcase, searching for a pair of bike shorts and her exercise bra. It was time to try to release some of this nervous energy. She dug down farther and found her favorite tape. Smiling grimly, she crossed to the expensive stereo system built into the wall and put the tape into the tape deck. She pushed Play and music came on. She cranked the volume.

The tape contained an assorted collection of her favorite songs—loud, fast songs with pulsating beats. It was good music, familiar music, *loud* music.

Her sneakers were on the floor of the closet near the bathroom. As Veronica sat on the floor to slip them onto her feet and tie them tightly, she let the music wash over her. Already she felt better.

She scrambled up and into the center of the living room, pushing the furniture back and away, clearing the floor, giving herself some space to move.

With the furniture out of the way, Veronica started slowly, stretching out her tired muscles. When she was properly warmed up, she closed her eyes and let the music embrace her.

And then she began to dance.

Halfway through the tape, it came to her—the answer to her frustration and impotent anger. She had been hired to teach Joe to act like the prince. With his cooperation, the task was formidable. Without his cooperation, it was impossible. If he failed to cooperate, she would have to threaten to withdraw.

Yes, that was exactly what she had to do. At nine o'clock, when she went down the hall to the royal suite, she would march right up to Joe and look him in the eye and—

A man wearing all black was standing just inside her balcony doorway, leaning against the wall, watching her dance.

Veronica leaped backward, her body reacting to the unannounced presence of a large intruder before her brain registered the fact that it was Joe Catalanotto.

Heart pounding, chest heaving, she tried to catch her breath as she stared at him. How in God's name had *Joe* gotten into her room?

Joe stared, too, caught in the ocean-blueness of Veronica's eyes as the music pounded around them. She looked frightened, like a wild animal, uncertain whether to freeze or flee.

Turning suddenly, she reached for the stereo and switched the music off. The silence was abrupt and jarring.

Her red curls swung and bounced around her shoulders as she turned rapidly back to look at him again. "What are you doing here?" she asked.

"Proving a point," he replied. His voice sounded strained and hoarse to his own ears. There was no mystery as to why that was. Seeing her like this had made his blood pressure rise, as well as other things.

"I don't understand," she said, her eyes narrowing as she studied his face, searching for an answer. "How did you get in? My door was locked."

Joe gestured to the sliding door that led to the balcony. "No, it wasn't. In fact, it was open. Warm night. If you breathe deeply, you can almost smell the cherry blossoms."

Veronica was staring at him, struggling to reconcile his words with the truth as she knew it. This room was on the tenth floor. Ten stories up, off the ground. Visitors didn't simply stroll in through the balcony door.

Joe couldn't keep his gaze from sliding down her body. Man, she was one hot package. In those skintight purple-and-turquoise patterned shorts and that tight, black, racer-backed top that exposed a firm, creamy midriff, with all those beautiful red curls loose around her pale shoulders, she looked positively steamy. She was slender, but not skinny as he'd thought. Her waist was small, her stomach flat, flaring out to softly curving hips and a firm, round rear end. Her legs were incredible, but he'd already known that. Still, in those tight shorts, her shapely legs seemed to go on and on and on forever, leading his eyes to her derriere. Her breasts were full, every curve, every detail intimately outlined by the stretchy fabric of her top.

And, God, the way she'd been dancing when he'd first climbed onto the balcony had exuded a raw sensuality, a barely contained passion. He'd been right about her. She *had* been hiding something underneath those boxy, conservative suits and that cool, distant attitude. Who would have guessed she would spend her personal time dancing like some vision on MTV?

She was still breathing hard from dancing. Or maybe—and more likely—she was breathing hard from the sudden shock he'd given her. He'd actually been standing inside the balcony door for about ten minutes before she looked up. He'd been in no hurry to interrupt. He could have stayed there, quite happily, and watched her dance all night.

Well, maybe not *all* night…

Veronica took a step back, away from him, as if she could see his every thought in his eyes. Her own eyes were very wide and incredibly, brilliantly blue. "You came in…from the *balcony?*"

Joe nodded and held something out to her. It was a flower, Veronica realized. He was holding a rather tired and bruised purple-and-gold pansy, its petals curled up for the night. She'd seen flowers just like it growing in flower beds outside the hotel.

"First I climbed down to the ground and got this," Joe said, his husky voice soft and seductive, warmly intimate. "It's proof I was actually there."

He was still holding the flower out to her, but Veronica couldn't move, her mind barely registering the words he spoke. A black band was across his forehead, holding his long hair in place. He was wearing black pants and a long-sleeved black turtleneck, with some kind of equipment vest over it, even though the spring night *was* quite warm. Oddly enough, his feet were bare. He wasn't smiling, and his face looked harsh and unforgiving. And dangerous. Very, *very* dangerous.

Veronica gazed at him, her heart in her throat. As he stepped closer and pressed the flower into her hand, she was pulled into the depths of his eyes. The fire she saw there became molten. His mouth was hard and hungry as his gaze raked her body.

And then his meaning cut through.

He'd climbed *down* to the *ground...? And* back up again? Ten *stories?*

"You climbed up the outside of the hotel and no one stopped you?" Veronica looked down at the flower, hoping he wouldn't notice the trembling in her voice.

He crossed to the sliding door and pulled the curtain shut. Was that for safety's sake, or for privacy? Veronica wondered as she turned away. She was afraid he might see his unconcealed desire echoed in her own eyes.

Desire? What was wrong with her? It was true, Joe Catalanotto was outrageously good-looking. But despite his obvious physical attributes, he was rude, tactless and disrespectful, rough in his manners and appearance. In fact, he was about as far from being a prince as any man she'd ever known. They'd barely even exchanged a civil conversation. All they did was fight. So why on earth could she think of nothing but the touch of his hands on her skin, his lips on hers, his body...?

"No one saw me climbing down *or* up," Joe said, his voice surrounding her like soft, rich velvet. "There are no guards posted on this side of the building. The FInCOM agents don't see the balcony for what it is—a back door. An accessible and obvious back door."

"It's so far from the ground," she countered in disbelief.

"It was an easy climb. Under an hour."

Under an hour. *This* is what he'd been doing with his time, Veronica realized suddenly. He should have been working with *her*, learning how to act like Tedric, and instead he was climbing up and down the outside of the hotel like some misguided superhero. Anger flooded through her.

Joe took a step forward, closing the small gap between them. The urge to touch her hair, to skim the softness of her cheek with his knuckle, was overpowering.

This was *not* the scenario he'd imagined when he'd climbed up the side of the hotel and onto her balcony. He'd expected to find Veronica hard at work, scribbling furiously away on the legal pad she always carried, or typing frantically into her laptop computer. He'd expected her to be wearing something that hid her curves and disguised her femininity. He'd expected her hair to be pinned up off her neck. He'd expected her to look up at him, gasping in startled surprise, as he walked into the room.

And, yeah, he'd expected her to be impressed when he told her he'd scaled the side of the hotel in order to prove that FInCOM's security stank.

Instead, finally over her initial shock at seeing him there, Veronica folded her arms across her delicious-looking breasts and glared at him. "I can't *believe* this," she said. "I'm supposed to be teaching you how to fool the bloody world into thinking you're Prince Tedric and you're off playing commando games and climbing ten stories up the outside of this hotel?"

"I'm not a commando, I'm a SEAL," Joe said, feeling his own temper rise. "There's a difference. And I'm not playing games. FInCOM's security stinks."

"The President of the United States hasn't had any qualms about FInCOM's ability to protect *him*," Veronica said tersely.

"The President of the United States is followed around by fifteen Finks, ready to jump into the line of fire and take a bullet for him if necessary," Joe countered. He broke away, pulling off the headband and running his fingers through his sweat-dampened hair. "Look, Ronnie, I didn't come here to fight with you."

"Is that supposed to be an apology?"

It wasn't, and she knew it as well as he did. "No."

Veronica laughed in disbelief at his blunt candor. "No," she repeated. "Of course not. Silly me. Whatever could I have been thinking?"

"I can't apologize," Joe said tightly. "Because I haven't done anything wrong."

"You've wasted time," Veronica told him. "My time. Maybe you don't understand, but we now have less than twenty-four hours to make this charade work."

"I'm well aware of the time we have left," Joe said. "I've looked at those videotapes Mac Forrest sent over. This is *not* going to be hard. In fact, it's going to be a piece of cake. I can pose as the prince, no problem. You've gotta relax and trust me." He turned and picked up the telephone from one of the end tables Veronica had pushed aside to clear the living-room floor of furniture. "I need you to make a phone call for me, okay?"

Veronica took the receiver from his hand and hung the phone back up. "No," she said, icily. "I need *you* to stop being so bloody patronizing, to stop patting my hand and telling me to relax. I need *you* to take me seriously for one damned minute."

Joe laughed. He couldn't help himself. She was standing there, looking like some kind of hot, steamed-up-windows dream, yet sounding, even in anger, as if she was trying to freeze him to death.

"Ah, you find this funny, do you?" Her eyes were blue ice. "I assure you, Lieutenant, you can't do this without me, and I am very close to walking out the bloody door."

She was madder than hell, and Joe knew the one thing he *shouldn't* do was keep laughing. But damned if he couldn't stop. "Ronnie," he said, pretending he was coughing instead of laughing. Still, he couldn't hide his smile. "Ronnie, Ronnie, I *do* take you seriously, honey. Honest."

Her hands were on her hips now, her mouth slightly open in disbelief. "You are *such* a…a jerk!" she said. "Tell me, is your real intention to…to…foul this up so royally that you won't have to place yourself in danger by posing as the prince?"

Joe's smile was wiped instantly off his face, and Veronica knew with deadly certainty that she'd gone too far.

He took a step toward her, and she took a step back, away from him. He was very tall, very broad and *very* angry.

"I *volunteered* for this job, babe," he told her, biting off each word. "I'm not here for my health, or for a paycheck, or for fame and fortune or for whatever the hell *you're* here for. And I'm sure as hell *not* here to be some kind of lousy martyr. If I end up taking a bullet for Prince Tedric, it's going to be despite the fact that I've done everything humanly possible to prevent it. Not because some pencil-pushing agency like FInCOM let the ball drop on standard security procedures years ago."

Veronica was silent. What could she possibly say? He was right. If security wasn't tight enough, he could very well be killed. She couldn't fault him for wanting to be sure of his own safety. And she didn't want to feel this odd jolt of fear and worry she felt, thinking about all of the opportunities the terrorists would have to train their gunsights on Joe's head. He was brave to have volunteered for this mission—particularly since she knew he had no love for Tedric Cortere. She shouldn't have implied otherwise.

"I'm sorry," Veronica murmured. She looked down at the carpet, unable to meet his eyes.

"And as for taking you seriously…" Joe reached out and with one finger underneath her chin, he lifted her head so that she was forced to look up into his eyes. "You're wrong. I take you *very* seriously."

The connection was there between them—instant and hot. The look in Joe's eyes was mesmerizing. It erased everything, *everything* between them—all the angry words and mistrust, all the frustration and misunderstandings—and left only this basic, almost primitive attraction, this simplest of equations. Man plus woman.

It would be so easy to simply give in. Veronica felt her body sway toward him as if pulled by the tides, ancient and unquestioning. All she had to do was let go, and there would be only desire, consuming and overpowering. It would surround them, possess them. It would take them on a flight to paradise.

But that flight was a round trip. When it ended, when they lay spent and exhausted, they'd be right here—right back where they'd started.

And then reality would return. Veronica would be embarrassed at having been intimate with a man she barely knew. Joe would no doubt be smug.

And they would have wasted yet another hour or two of their precious preparation time.

Joe was obviously thinking along the exact same lines. He ran his thumb lightly across her lips. "What do you think, Ronnie?" he asked, his voice husky. "Do you think we could stop after just one kiss?"

Veronica pulled away, her heart pounding even harder.

If he kissed her, she would be lost. "Don't be foolish," she said, working hard to keep her voice from shaking.

"When I make love to you," he said, his voice low and dangerous and *very* certain, "I'm going to take my sweet time."

She turned to face him with a bravado she didn't quite feel. *"When?"* she said. "Of all the macho, he-man audacity! Not *if*, but *when* I make love to you…. Don't hold your breath, Lieutenant, because it's not going to happen."

He smiled a very small, very infuriating smile and let his eyes wander down her body. "Yes, it is."

"Ever hear the expression 'cold day in hell'?" Veronica asked sweetly. She crossed the room toward her suitcase, found a sweatshirt and pulled it over her head. She was still perspiring and was still much too warm, but she would have done damn near anything to cover herself from the heat of his gaze.

He picked up the telephone again. "Look, Ronnie, I need you to call my room and ask to speak to me."

"But you're not there."

"That's the point," he said. "The boys from FInCOM think I'm napping, nestled all snug in my bed. It's time to shake them up."

Careful to keep her distance, careful not to let their fingers touch, Veronica took the phone from Joe and dialed the number for the royal suite. West picked up the phone.

"This is Ms. St. John," she said. "I need to speak to Lieutenant Catalanotto."

"I'm sorry, ma'am," West replied. "He's asleep."

"This is urgent, Mr. West," she said, glancing up at Joe, who nodded encouragingly. "Please wake him."

"Hang on."

There was silence on the other end, and then shouting, as if from a distance. Veronica met Joe's eyes again. "I think they're shaken up," she said.

"Hang up," he said, and she dropped the receiver into the cradle.

He picked up the phone then, and dialed. "Do you have a pair of sweats or some jeans to pull on over those shorts?" he asked Veronica.

"Yes," she said. "Why?"

"Because in about thirty seconds, fifty FInCOM agents are going to be pounding on your door— Hello? Yeah. Kevin Laughton, please." Joe covered the mouthpiece with his hand and looked at Veronica who was standing, staring at him. "Better hurry." He uncovered the phone. "Yeah, I'm still here."

Veronica scrambled for her suitcase, yanking out the one pair of blue jeans she'd packed for this trip.

"He is?" she heard Joe say into the telephone. "Well, maybe you should interrupt him."

She kicked off her sneakers and pulled the jeans on, hopping into them one leg at a time.

"Why don't you tell him Joe Catalanotto's on the line. Catalanotto." He sighed in exasperation. "Just say Joe Cat, okay? He'll know who I am."

Veronica pulled the jeans up and over her hips, aware that Joe was watching her dress. She buttoned the waistband and drew up the zipper, not daring to look in his direction. *When I make love to you…* Not if, *when*. As if their intimate joining were already a given—indisputable and destined to take place.

"Yo, Laughton," Joe said into the telephone. "How's it going, pal?" He laughed. "Yeah, I thought I'd give you a little firsthand demonstration, and identify FInCOM's security weak spots. How do you like it so far?" He pulled the receiver away from his ear. "That good, huh? Yeah, I went for a little walk down in the gardens." He met Veronica's eyes and grinned, clearly amused. "Yeah, I was struck by the beauty of the flowers, so I brought one with me up to Ms. St. John's room to share with her, and—"

He looked at the receiver, suddenly gone dead in his hands, and then at Veronica.

"I guess they're on their way," he said.

Chapter Seven

"I need more coffee," Veronica said. How could Joe be so *awake?* She hadn't seen him yawn even once as they'd worked through the night. "I think my laryngitis idea might work—after all, we've been giving the news media reports that Prince Tedric is ill. You wouldn't have to speak and—"

"You know, I'm not a half-bad mimic," Joe insisted. "If I work on it more, I can do a decent imitation of Prince Tedric."

Veronica closed her eyes. "No offense, Joe, but I seriously doubt you can imitate Tedric's accent just from listening to a tape," she said. "We have better things to do with your time."

Joe stood and Veronica opened her eyes, gazing up at him.

"I'm getting you that coffee," he said. "You're slipping. You just called me 'Joe.'"

"Forgive me, Your Highness," she murmured.

But he didn't smile. He just looked down at her, the expression in his eyes unreadable. "I like Joe better," he finally said.

"This isn't going to work, is it?" she asked quietly. She met his eyes steadily, ready to accept defeat.

Except he wasn't defeated. Not by any means. He'd been watching videotapes and listening to audiotapes of Prince Tedric in all of his spare moments. It was true that he hadn't had all that many spare moments, but he was well on his way to understanding the way Tedric moved and spoke.

"I can do this," Joe said. "Hell, I look just like the guy. Every time I catch my reflection and see my hair this way, I see Ted looking back at me and it scares me to death. If it can fool *me*, it can fool everyone else. The tailor's delivering the clothes he's altered sometime tomorrow. It'll be easier for me to pretend I'm Tedric if I'm dressed for the part."

Veronica gave him a wan smile. Still, it *was* a smile. She was so tired, she could barely keep her eyes open. She'd changed out of her jeans and back into her professional clothes hours ago. Her hair was up off her shoulders once again. "We've got to work on Tedric's walk. He's got this rather peculiar, rolling gait that—"

"He walks like he's got a fireplace poker in his pants," Joe interrupted her.

Veronica's musical laughter echoed throughout the quiet room. One of the FInCOM agents glanced up from his position guarding the balcony entrance.

"Yes," she said to Joe. "You're right. He does. Although I doubt anyone's described it quite that way before."

"I can walk that way," Joe said. He stood, and as Veronica watched, he marched stiffly across the room. "See?" He turned back to look at her.

She had her face in her hands and her shoulders were shaking, and Joe was positive for one heart-stopping moment that she was crying. He started toward her, and knelt in front of her and— She was laughing. She was laughing so hard, tears were rolling down her face.

"Hey," Joe said, faintly insulted. "It wasn't *that* bad."

She tried to answer, but could get no words out. Instead, she just waved her hand futilely at him and kept on laughing.

Her laughter was infectious, and before long, Joe started to chuckle and then laugh, too.

"Do it again," she gasped, and he stood and walked, like Prince Tedric, across the room and back.

Veronica laughed even harder, doubling over on the couch.

The FInCOM agent was watching them both as if they were crazy or hysterical—which probably wasn't that far from the truth.

Veronica wiped at her face, trying to catch her breath. "Oh, Lord," she said. "Oh, God, I haven't laughed this hard in years." Her eyelashes were wet with her tears of laughter, and her eyes sparkled as, still giggling, she looked up at Joe. "I don't suppose I can talk you into doing that again?"

"No way," Joe said, grinning back at her. "I draw the line at being humiliated more than twice in a row."

"I wasn't laughing at you," she said, but her giggles intensified. "Yes, I was," she corrected herself. "I *was* laughing at you. I'm so sorry. You must think I'm frightfully rude." She covered her mouth with her hand, but still couldn't stop laughing—at least not entirely.

"I think I only looked funny because I'm not dressed like the prince," Joe argued. "I think if I were wearing some sequined suit and walking that way, you wouldn't be able to tell the two of us apart."

"And *I* think," Veronica said. "*I* think...I think it's hopeless. I think it's time to give up." Her eyes suddenly welled with real tears, and all traces of her laughter vanished. "Oh, *damn...*" She turned away, but she could neither stop nor hide her sudden flow of tears.

She heard Joe's voice, murmuring a command to the FInCOM agents, and then she felt him sit next to her on the sofa.

"Hey," he said softly. "Hey, come on, Veronica. It's not that bad."

She felt his arms go around her and she stiffened only slightly before giving in. She let him pull her back against his chest, let him tuck her head in to his shoulder. He was so warm, so solid. And he smelled so wonderfully good...

He just held her, rocking slightly, and let her cry. He didn't try to stop her. He just held her.

Veronica was getting his shirt wet, but she couldn't seem to stop, and he didn't seem to mind. She could feel his hand in her hair, gently stroking, calming, soothing.

When he spoke, his voice was quiet. She could hear it rumble slightly in his chest.

"You know, this guy we're after?" Joe said. "The terrorist? His name's Diosdado. One name. Kind of like Cher or Madonna, but not so much fun. Still, I bet he's as much of a celebrity in Peru, where he's from. He's the leader of an organization with a name that roughly translates as 'The Cloud of Death.' He and a friend of his—a man named Salustiano Vargas—have claimed responsibility for more than twelve hundred deaths. Diosdado's signature was on the bomb that blew up that passenger flight from London to New York three years ago. Two hundred and fifty-four people died. Remember that one?"

Veronica nodded. She most certainly did. The plane had gone down halfway across the Atlantic. There were no survivors. Her tears slowed as she listened to him talk.

"Diosdado and his pal Vargas took out an entire busload of U.S. sailors that same year," Joe said. "Thirty-two kids—

the oldest was twenty-one years old." He was quiet for a moment. "Mac Forrest's son was on that bus."

Veronica closed her eyes. "Oh, God…"

"Johnny Forrest. He was a good kid. Smart, too. He looked like Mac. Same smile, same easygoing attitude, same tenacity. I met him when he was eight. He was the little brother I never had." Joe's voice was husky with emotion. He cleared his throat. "He was nineteen when Diosdado blew him to pieces."

Joe fell silent, just stroking Veronica's hair. He cleared his throat again, but when he spoke, his voice was still tight. "Those two bombings put Diosdado and The Cloud of Death onto the Most Wanted list. Intel dug deep and came up with a number of interesting facts. Diosdado had a last name, and it was Perez. He was born in 1951, the youngest son in a wealthy family. His name means, literally, 'God's gift.'" Joe laughed a short burst of disgusted air. "He wasn't God's gift to Mac Forrest, or any of the other families of those dead sailors. Intel also found out that the sonuvabitch had a faction of his group right here in D.C. But when the CIA went to investigate, something went wrong. It turned into a firefight, and when it was over, three agents and ten members of The Cloud of Death were dead. Seven more terrorists were taken prisoner, but Diosdado and Salustiano Vargas were gone. The two men we'd wanted the most got away. They went deep underground. Rumor was Diosdado had been shot and badly hurt. He was quiet for years—no sign of him at all—until a few days ago, when apparently Vargas took a shot at Prince Tedric."

Joe was quiet again for another moment. "So there it is," he said. "The reason we can't just quit. The reason this operation *is* going to work. We're going to stop those bastards for good, one way or another."

Veronica wiped her face with the back of her hand. She

couldn't remember the last time she'd cried like this. It must have been the stress getting to her. The stress and the fatigue. Still, to burst into tears like that and…

She sat up, pulling away from Joe and glancing around the room, alarmed, her cheeks flushing with embarrassment. She'd lost it. She'd absolutely lost it—and right in front of Joe and all those FInCOM agents. But the FInCOM agents were gone.

"They're outside the door," Joe said, correctly reading her thoughts. "I figured you'd appreciate the privacy."

"Thank you," Veronica murmured.

She was blushing, and the tip of her nose was pink from crying. She looked exhausted and fragile. Joe wanted to wrap her back in his arms and hold her close. He wanted to hold her as she closed her eyes and fell asleep. He wanted to keep her warm and safe from harm, and to convince her that everything was going to be all right.

She glanced at him, embarrassment lighting her crystal blue eyes. "I'm sorry," she said. "I didn't mean to—"

"You're tired." He gave her an easy excuse and a gentle smile.

They were alone. They were alone in the room. As Joe held her gaze, he knew she was aware of that, too.

Her hair was starting to come free from its restraints, and strands curled around her face.

He couldn't stop himself from reaching out and lightly brushing the last of her tears from her cheek. Her skin was so soft and warm. She didn't flinch, didn't pull away, didn't even move. She just gazed at him, her eyes blue and wide and so damned innocent.

Joe couldn't remember ever wanting to kiss a woman more in his entire life. Slowly, so slowly, he leaned forward, searching her eyes for any protest, alert for any sign that he was taking this moment of truce too far.

Her eyes flickered and he saw her desire. She wanted him to kiss her, too. But he also saw doubt and a flash of fear. She was afraid.

Afraid of what? Of him? Of herself? Or maybe she was afraid that the overwhelming attraction they both felt would ignite in a violent, nearly unstoppable explosion of need.

Joe almost pulled back.

But then her lips parted slightly, and he couldn't resist. He wanted a taste—just a taste—of her sweetness.

So he kissed her. Slowly, gently pressing his lips to hers.

A rush of desire hit him low in the gut and it took every ounce of control to keep from giving in to his need and pulling her hard into his arms, kissing her savagely, and running his hands along the curves of her body. Instead, he made himself slow down.

Gently, so gently, he ran his tongue across her lips, slowly gaining passage to the softness of her mouth. He closed his eyes, forcing himself to move still more slowly, even slower now. She tasted of strawberries and coffee—an enticing combination of flavors. He caressed her tongue with his own and when she responded, when she opened her mouth to him, granting him access and deepening their kiss, he felt dizzy with pleasure.

This was, absolutely, the sweetest kiss he'd ever shared.

Slowly, still slowly, he explored the warmth of her mouth, the softness of her lips. He touched only her mouth with his, and the side of her face with the tips of his fingers. She wasn't locked in his arms, their bodies weren't pressed tightly together. Still, with this gentle, purest of kisses, she had the power to make his blood surge through his veins, to make his heart pound in a wild, frantic rhythm.

He wanted her desperately. His body was straining to become joined with hers. And yet...

This kiss was enough. It was exhilarating, and it made

him feel incredibly happy. Happy in a way he'd never been even while making love to the other women he'd had relationships with—women he'd been attracted to and slept with, but hadn't particularly cared for.

He felt a tightness in his chest, a weight of emotion he'd never felt before as, beneath his fingers, Veronica trembled.

He pulled back then, and she looked away, unable to meet his eyes.

"Well," she said. "My word."

"Yeah," Joe agreed. He hadn't intended to whisper, but he couldn't seem to speak any louder.

"That was…unexpected."

He couldn't entirely agree. He'd been expecting to kiss her ever since their eyes first met and the raw attraction sparked between them. What was unexpected was this odd sense of caring, this emotional noose that had somehow curled itself around his chest. It was faintly uncomfortable, and it hadn't disappeared even when he'd ended their kiss.

She glanced at him. "Maybe we should get back to work."

Joe shook his head. "No," he said. "I need a break, and you do, too." He stood, holding out his hand to her. "Come on, I'll walk you to your room. You can take a nap. I'll meet you back here in a few hours."

Veronica didn't take his hand. She simply gazed up at him. "Come on," he said again. "Cut yourself some slack."

But she shook her head. "There's no time."

He gently touched her hair. "Yes, there is. There's definitely time for an hour of shut-eye," he said. "Trust me, Ronnie, you're gonna need it to concentrate."

Joe could see indecision on her face. "How about forty minutes?" he added. "Forty winks. You can crash right here on the couch. I'll order some coffee and wake you up at—" he glanced at his watch "—oh-six-twenty."

Slowly she nodded. "All right."

He bent down and briefly brushed her lips with his. "Sleep tight," he said.

She stopped him, touching the side of his face. "You're so sweet," she said, surprise in her voice.

He had to laugh. He'd been called a lot of things in his life, and "sweet" wasn't one of them. "Oh, no, I'm not."

Veronica's lips curved into a smile. "I didn't mean that to be an insult." Her smile faded and she looked away, suddenly awkward. "Joe, I have to be honest with you," she said quietly. "I think that kiss…was a mistake. I'm so tired, and I wasn't thinking clearly and, well, I hope you don't think that I… Well, right now it's not… We're not… It's a *mistake*. Don't you think?"

Joe straightened. The noose around his chest was so damn tight he could hardly breathe. A mistake. Veronica thought kissing him had been a mistake. He shook his head slowly, hiding his disappointment behind a tight smile. "No, and I'm sorry *you* think that," he replied. "I thought maybe we had something there."

"Something?" Veronica echoed, glancing up at him.

This time it was Joe who looked away. He sat down next to her on the couch, suddenly tired. How could he explain what he meant, when he didn't even know himself? Damn, he'd already said too much. What if she thought by "something" he meant he was falling in love with her?

He pushed his hair back with one hand and glanced at Veronica.

Yeah, she wanted him to fall in love with her about as much as she wanted a hole in the head. In the space of a heartbeat, he could picture her dismay, picture her imagining the restraining order she'd have to get to keep him away from her. He was rough and uncultured, blue-collar through and through. *She* hung out with royalty. It would be embarrassing and inconvenient for her to have some crazy, rough-edged, lovesick sailor following her around.

Gazing into her eyes, he could see her trepidation.

So he gave her a cocky smile and prayed that she couldn't somehow sense the tightness in his chest. "I thought we had something great between us," he said, leaning forward and putting his hand on her thigh.

Veronica moved back on the couch, away from him. His hand fell aside.

"Ah, yes," she said. "Sex. Exactly what I thought you meant."

Joe stood. "Too bad."

She glanced at him but didn't meet his gaze for more than a fraction of a second. "Yes, it is."

He turned away, heading for the bedroom and his bed. Maybe some sleep would make this pressure in his chest lighten up or—please, God—even make it go away.

"Please, don't forget to wake me," Veronica called.

"Right," he said shortly and closed the door behind him.

The knock on the door came quickly, no less than five minutes after Joe had called room service for coffee. Man, he thought, people really hopped to it when they thought a guy had blue blood.

West and the other FInCOM agent, Freeman, both drew their guns, motioning for Joe to move away from the door. It was an odd sensation. He was the one who usually did the protecting.

The door opened, and it was the room-service waiter. West and Freeman handed Joe two steaming mugs of fragrant coffee. Joe carried them to the coffee table and set them down.

Veronica was still asleep. She'd slid down on the couch so that her head was resting on the seat cushion. She clutched a legal pad to her chest.

She looked incredibly beautiful. Her skin was so smooth and soft looking, it was all he could do not to reach out with one knuckle to touch her cheek.

Veronica St. John.

Who would have guessed he would have a thing for a prim-and-proper society girl named Veronica St. John? "Sinjin," for Pete's sake.

But she wasn't interested in him. That incredible, perfect kiss they'd shared had been "a mistake."

Like *hell* it had.

Joe had had to force himself to fall asleep. Only his extensive training had kept him from lying on the bed, staring at the ceiling and expending his energy by playing their kiss over and over and over again in his mind. He'd spent enough time doing that while he was in the shower, after he woke up. Each time he played that kiss over in his head, he tried to figure out what he'd done wrong, and each time, he came up blank. Finally he'd had to admit it—he'd done nothing wrong. That kiss had been perfect, not a mistake.

Now all he had to do was convince Veronica of that fact.

Yeah, right. She was stubborn as hell. He'd have a better chance of convincing the Mississippi River to flow north.

The hell of it was, Joe found himself actually *liking* the girl, trying to make her smile. He wanted to get another look behind her so-very-proper British facade. Except he wasn't sure exactly where the facade ended and the real girl began. So far, he'd seen two very conflicting images—Veronica in her prim-and-proper work clothes, and Veronica dressed down to dance. He was willing to bet that the real woman was hidden somewhere in the middle. He was also willing to bet that she would never willingly reveal her true self. Especially not to *him*.

Joe had more than just a suspicion that Veronica considered him substandard. He was the son of a servant, while she was a daughter of the ruling class. If she had a relationship with him, it would be a lark, a kick. She'd be slumming.

Slumming.

God, it was an ugly word. But, so what? So she'd be slumming. Big deal. What was he going to do if she approached him? Was he going to turn her down? Yeah, right. Like hell he'd turn her down.

He could just picture the scenario.

Veronica knocks on his door in the middle of the night and he says, "Sorry, babe, I'm not into being used by curious debutantes who want a peek at the way the lower half lives and loves."

Yeah, right.

If she knocked on his door, he'd fling it open wide. Let her go slumming. Just let him be the one she was slumming with.

Veronica stirred slightly, shifting to get more comfortable on the couch, and the legal pad she'd been holding fell out of her arms. Joe moved quickly and caught it before it hit the floor.

Her hair was starting to come undone, and soft red wisps curled around her face. Her lips were slightly parted. They were so soft and delicate and delicious. He knew that firsthand.

It didn't take much to imagine her lifting those exquisite lips to his for another perfect kiss—for a deep, demanding, soulful kiss that would rapidly escalate into more. *Way* more.

And then what?

Then they'd be lovers until she got tired of him, or he got tired of her. It would be no different from any of the other relationships he'd had.

But so far, everything about this *was* different. Veronica St. John wasn't some woman he'd met in a bar. She hadn't approached him, handed him the keys to her car or her motel room and asked if he was busy for the next twenty-four hours. She hadn't even approached him at all.

She wasn't his type. She was too high-strung, too uptight.

But something he'd seen in her eyes promised a paradise the likes of which he'd never known. Hell, it was a paradise he was probably better off never knowing.

Because what if he never got tired of her?

There it was. Right out in the open. The big, ugly question he'd been trying to avoid. What if this noose that had tightened around his chest never went away?

But that would never happen, right?

He couldn't let Veronica's wealth and high-class manners throw him off. She was just a woman. All those differences he'd imagined were just that—imagined.

So how come he was standing there like an idiot, staring at the girl? Why was he too damned chicken to touch her, to wake her up, to see her sleepy blue eyes gazing up at him?

The answer was clear—because even if the impossible happened, and Joe actually did something as idiotically stupid as fall in love with Veronica St. John, she would never, not in a million years, fall in love with him. Sure, she might find him amusing for a few weeks or even months, but eventually she'd come to her senses and trade him in for a more expensive model.

And somehow the thought of that stung. Even now. Even though there was absolutely nothing between them. Nothing, that is, but one perfect kiss and its promise of paradise.

"Yo, Ronnie," Joe said, hoping she'd wake up without him touching her. But she didn't stir.

He bent down and spoke directly into her ear. "Coffee's here. Time to wake up."

Nothing.

He touched her shoulder, shaking her very slightly.

Nothing.

He shook her harder, and she stirred, but her eyes stayed tightly shut.

"Go away," she mumbled.

Joe pulled her up into a sitting position. Her head lolled against the back of the couch. "Come on, babe," he said. "If I don't wake you up, you're going to be madder than hell at me." He gently touched the side of her face. "Come on, Ronnie. Look at me. Open your eyes."

She opened them. They were astonishingly blue and very sleepy. "Be a dear, Jules, and ring the office. Tell them I'll be a few hours late. I'm bushed. Out too late last night." She smiled and blew a kiss into the air near his face. "Thanks, luv." Then she tucked her perfect knees primly up underneath her skirt, put her head back down on the seat cushions and tightly closed her eyes.

Jules?

Who the hell was Jules?

"Come on, Veronica," Joe said almost desperately. He had no right to want to hog-tie this Jules, whoever the hell he was. No right at all. "You wanted me to wake you up. Besides, you can't sleep on the couch. You'll wake up with one hell of a backache."

She didn't open her eyes again, didn't sigh, didn't move.

She was fast asleep, and not likely to wake up until she was good and ready.

Gritting his teeth, Joe picked Veronica up and carried her into the bedroom. He set her gently down on the bed, trying to ignore the way she fit so perfectly in his arms. For half a second, he actually considered climbing in under the covers next to her. But he didn't have time. He had work to do. Besides, when he got in bed with Veronica St. John, it was going to be at her invitation.

Joe took off her remaining shoe and put it on the floor, then covered her with the blankets.

She didn't move, didn't wake up again. He didn't give in to the desire to smooth her hair back from her face. He just stared down at her for another brief moment, knowing that the smart thing to do would be to stay far, far away from this woman. He knew that she was trouble, the likes of which he'd never known.

He turned away, needing a stiff drink. He settled for black coffee and set to work.

Chapter Eight

Veronica sat bolt upright in the bed.

Dear Lord in heaven, she wasn't supposed to be asleep, she was supposed to be working and—

What time was it?

Her watch read twelve twenty-four. Oh, no, she'd lost the entire morning. But she must have been exhausted. She couldn't even remember coming back here to her own room and—

Oh, Lord! She realized she wasn't in her own room. She was in the prince's bedroom, in the prince's bed. No, not the prince's. *Joe's. Joe's* bed.

With a dizzying flash, Veronica remembered Joe pulling her into his arms and kissing her so slowly, so sensuously that every bone in her body seemed to melt. He had rid them of their clothes like a seasoned professional and...

But...she was still dressed. Right down to her hose, which were twisted and uncomfortable. She'd only *dreamed* about

Joe Catalanotto and his seductive eyes and surprisingly gentle hands.

The kiss had been real, though; and achingly, shockingly tender. It figured. Joe would know exactly how to kiss her to make her the most vulnerable, to affect her in the strongest possible way.

She'd expected him to kiss her almost roughly—an echo of the sexual hunger she'd seen in his eyes. She could have handled that. She would have known what to say and do.

Instead, Joe had given her a kiss that was more gentle than passionate, although the passion had been there, indeed. But Veronica was still surprised by the restraint he'd shown, by the sweetness of his mouth against hers, by the slow, lingering sensuality of his lips. She could very well have kissed him that way until the end of time.

Time. Lord! She'd wasted so much *time*.

Veronica swung her legs out of bed.

She'd *told* Joe to wake her up. Obviously, he hadn't. Instead of waking her, he'd carried her here, into his bedroom.

She found one of her shoes on the floor, and searched to no avail for the other. Perfect. One shoe off and one shoe on, having slept away most of the day, her dignity in shreds, she'd have to go out into the living room where the FInCOM agents were parked. She'd have to endure their knowing smirks.

She was a wimp. She'd fallen asleep—and stayed asleep for *hours*—while on the job.

And Joe...Joe hadn't kept his promise to wake her up.

She'd been starting to...like him. She'd been attracted from the start, but this was different. She actually, genuinely *liked* him, despite the fact that he came from an entirely different world, despite the fact that they seemed to argue almost constantly. She even liked him despite the fact that he clearly wanted to make their relationship sexual.

Despite all that, she'd thought he had been starting to like her, too.

Her disappointment flashed quickly into anger. How *dare* he just let her sleep the day away? The *bastard*...

Veronica fumed as she tucked her blouse back into the top of her skirt and straightened her jacket, thankful her suit was permanent-press and wrinkle-proof.

Her hair wasn't quite so easy to fix, but she was determined not to emerge from the bedroom with it down and flowing around her shoulders. It was bad enough that she'd been sleeping in Joe's bed. She didn't want it to look as if he'd been in there with her.

Finally, she took a deep breath and, single shoe in her hand and head held high, she went into the living room.

If the FInCOM agents smirked condescendingly, Veronica refused to notice. All she knew was, Joe was not in the room. Good thing, or she might have lost even more of her dignity by throwing her shoe directly at his head.

"Good afternoon, gentlemen," she said briskly to West and Freeman as she gathered up her briefcase. Ah, good. There was her missing shoe, on the floor in front of the sofa. She slipped them both onto her feet. "Might I ask where the lieutenant has gone?"

"He's up in the exercise room," one of them answered.

"Thanks so very much," Veronica said and breezed out the door.

Joe had already run seven miles on the treadmill when Veronica walked into the hotel's luxuriously equipped exercise room. She looked a whole lot better. She'd showered and changed her clothes. But glory hallelujah, instead of putting on another of those Margaret Thatcher suits, she was wearing a plain blue dress. It was nothing fancy, obviously designed to deemphasize her femininity, yet somehow, on Veronica, it hugged her slender figure and made her look like a million bucks. Her shoes were still on the clunky side, but oh, baby, those legs…

Joe wiped a trickle of sweat that ran down the side of his face. When had it gotten so hot in here?

But her greeting to him was anything but warm.

"I'd like to have a word with you," Veronica said icily, without even a hello to start. "At your convenience, of course."

"Did you have a good nap?" Joe asked.

"Will you be much longer?" she asked, staring somewhere off to his left.

That good, huh? Something had ticked her off, and Joe was willing to bet that that something was him. He'd let her sleep. Correction—he'd been unable to wake her up. It wasn't his fault, but now he was going to pay.

"Can you give me five more minutes?" he countered. "I like to do ten miles without stopping."

Joe wasn't even out of breath. Veronica could see from the computerized numbers lit up on the treadmill's controls, that he'd already run nine miles. But he didn't sound winded.

He was sweating, though. His shorts were soaking wet. He wasn't wearing a shirt, and his smooth, tanned skin was slick as his muscles worked. And, dear Lord, he had so *many* muscles. Beautifully sculpted, perfect muscles. He was gorgeous.

He was watching her in the floor-to-ceiling mirrors that covered the walls of the exercise room. Veronica leaned against the wall near the door and tried not to look at Joe, but everywhere she turned, she saw his reflection. She found herself staring in fascination at the rippling muscles in his back and thighs and arms, and then she started thinking about their kiss. Their fabulous, heart-stoppingly romantic kiss. Despite his nonchalant attitude, that kiss had been laced with tenderness and laden with emotion. It was unlike any kiss she'd experienced *ever* before.

Veronica had been well aware that Joe had been holding back when he kissed her that way. She'd felt his restraint and the power of his control. She had seen the heat of desire in his eyes and known he wanted more than just a simple, gentle kiss.

Veronica couldn't forget how he'd searched her eyes as he'd leaned toward her and…

Excellent. Here she was, standing there reliving Joe's kiss while staring at his perfect buttocks. Veronica glanced up to find his amused dark eyes watching her watch his rear end. No doubt he could read her mind. Of course the fact that she'd been nearly drooling made it all the easier for him to know what she'd been thinking.

She might as well give in, Veronica admitted to herself. She might as well sleep with the man and get it over with. After all, he was so bloody positive that it was going to happen. And after their kiss, despite her best intentions, all Veronica could think about was "When was he going to kiss her again?" Except he hadn't woken her up, which meant that he probably didn't even *like* her, and now *she* was mad as hell at him. Yes, kissing him *had* been a royal mistake. Although at the time, when she'd said those words, she'd meant another kind of mistake entirely. She'd meant their timing had been wrong. She'd meant it had been a mistake to add a romantic distraction to all of the other distractions already driving her half mad.

Then, of course, he'd said what *he'd* said, and…

The fact that Joe saw their growing relationship as one based purely on sex only added to Veronica's confusion. She knew that a man like Joe Catalanotto, a man accustomed to intrigue and high adventure, would never have any kind of long-term interest in a woman who worked her hardest to be steady and responsible and, well, quite frankly, *boring*. And even if that wasn't the case, even if by some miracle Joe fell madly and permanently in love with her, how on earth would she handle his leaving on dangerous, top-secret missions? How could she simply wave goodbye, knowing she might never again see him alive?

No, thank you very much.

So maybe this pure sex thing didn't add to her confusion. Maybe it simplified things. Maybe it took it all down to the simplest, most basic level.

Lord knew, she *was* wildly attracted to him. And so what if she was watching him?

Veronica met Joe's gaze almost defiantly, her chin held high. One couldn't have a body like that and expect people *not* to look. And watching Joe run was like watching a dancer. He was graceful and surefooted, his motion fluid and effortless. She wondered if he could dance. She wondered—not for the first time—what it would feel like to be held in his arms, dancing with him.

As Veronica watched, Joe focused on his running, increasing his speed, his arms and legs churning, pumping. The treadmill was starting to whine, and just when Veronica was sure Joe was going to start to slow, when she was positive he couldn't keep up the pace a moment longer, he went even faster.

His teeth were clenched, his face a picture of concentration and stamina. He looked like something savage, something wild. An untamed man-creature from the distant past. A ferocious, barbaric warrior come to shake up the civility of Veronica's carefully polite twentieth-century world.

"Hoo-yah!" someone called out, and Joe's face broke into a wide smile as he looked up at three men, standing near the weight machine in the corner of the room. As quickly as his smile appeared, the barbarian was gone.

Odd, Veronica hadn't noticed the other men before this. She'd been aware of the FInCOM agents lurking near her, but not these three men dressed in workout clothes. They seemed to know Joe. SEALs, Veronica guessed. They had to be the men Joe had asked Admiral Forrest to send.

Joe slowed at last, returning the treadmill to a walking speed as he caught his breath. He stepped off and grabbed a towel, using it to mop his face as he came toward Veronica.

"What's up?"

Joe was steaming. There was literally visible heat rising from his smooth, powerful shoulders. He stopped about six feet away from her, clearly not wanting to offend her by standing too close.

His friends came and surrounded him, and Veronica was momentarily silenced by three additional pairs of eyes appraising her with frank male appreciation. Joe's eyes alone were difficult enough to handle.

Joe glanced at the other men. "Get lost," he said. "This is a private conversation."

"Not anymore," said one of them with a Western twang. He was almost as tall as Joe, but probably weighed forty pounds less. He held out his hand to Veronica. "I'm Cowboy, ma'am."

She shook Cowboy's hand, and he held on to hers far longer than necessary, until Joe gave him a dark look.

"All right, quick introductions," Joe said. "Lieutenant McCoy, my XO—executive officer—and Chief Becker and Ensign Jones. Also known as Blue, Harvard and Cowboy. Miss Veronica St. John. For you illiterates, it's spelled Saint and John, two words, but pronounced *Sinjin*. She's Prince Tedric's media consultant, and she's on the scheduling team for this op."

Lt. Blue McCoy looked to be about Joe's age—somewhere in his early thirties. He was shorter and smaller than the other men, with the build of a long-distance runner and the blue eyes, wavy, thick blond hair and handsome face of a Hollywood star.

Harvard—Chief Becker—was a large black man with steady, intelligent brown eyes and a smoothly shaven head. Cowboy's hair was even longer than Blue McCoy's, and he wore it pulled back into a ponytail at the nape of his neck. His eyes were green and sparkling, and his smile boyishly winsome. He looked like Kevin Costner's younger brother, and he knew it. He kept winking at her.

"Pleased to meet you," Veronica said, shaking hands with both Blue and Harvard. She was afraid if she offered Cowboy her hand again, she might never get it back.

"The pleasure's all ours, ma'am," Cowboy said. "I love what you've done with the captain's hair."

"Captain?" Veronica looked at Joe. "I thought you were a Lieutenant."

"It's a term of endearment, ma'am," Blue said. He, too, had a thick accent, but his was from the Deep South. "Cat's in command, so sometimes he gets called Captain."

"It's better than some of the other things they call me," Joe said.

Cat.

Admiral Forrest had also called Joe by that nickname. Cat. It fit. As Joe ran on the treadmill, he looked like a giant cat, so graceful and fluid. The nickname, while really just a shortened form of Catalanotto, wasn't too far off.

"Okay, great," Joe said. "We've made nice. Now you boys get lost. Finish your PT, and let the grown-ups talk."

Lt. McCoy took the other two men by the arms and pulled them toward weight-lifting equipment. Harvard began to bench-press heavy-looking weights while Cowboy spotted him, one eye still on Joe and Veronica.

"Now let's try this one more time," Joe said with a smile. "What's up? You look like you want to court-martial me."

"Only if the punishment for mutiny is still execution," Veronica said, smiling tightly.

Joe looped his towel around his neck. "Mutiny," he said. "That's a serious charge—especially considering I did my damnedest to wake you up."

Veronica crossed her arms. "Oh, and I suppose your 'damnedest' included putting me in a nice soft bed, where I'd be sure to sleep away most of the day?" she said. She glanced around, at both the FInCOM agents and the other SEALs, and lowered her voice. "I might *also* point out that it was hardly proper for *me* to sleep in *your* bed. It surely looked bad, and it implied…certain things."

"Whoa, Ronnie." Joe shook his head. "That wasn't my intention. I thought you'd be more comfortable, that's all. I wasn't trying to—"

"I'm an unmarried woman, Lieutenant," Veronica interrupted. "Regardless of what you intended, it is not in my best interests to take a nap in any man's bed."

Joe laughed. "I think maybe you're overreacting just a *teeny* little bit. This isn't the 1890s. I don't see how your reputation could be tarnished simply from napping in my bed. If I were in there with you, it'd be an entirely different matter. But if you want to know the truth, I'd be willing to bet no one even noticed where you were sleeping this morning, or even that you were asleep. And if they did, that's their problem."

"No, it's *my* problem," Veronica said sharply, her temper flaring. "Tell me, Lieutenant, are there many women in the SEALs?"

"No," Joe said. "There're none. We don't allow women in the units."

"Aha," Veronica retorted. "In other words, you're not familiar with sexual discrimination, because your organization is based on sexual discrimination. That's just perfect."

"Look, if you want to preach feminism, fine," Joe said, his patience disintegrating, "but do me a favor—hand me a pamphlet to read on the subject and be done with it. Right now, I'm going to take a shower."

By now they had the full, unconcealed attention of the three other SEALs and the FInCOM agents, but Veronica was long past caring. She was angry—angry that he had let her sleep, angry that he was so macho, angry that he had kissed her—and particularly angry that she had liked his kiss so damn much.

She blocked Joe's way, stabbing at his broad chest with one finger. "Don't you *dare* run away from me, Lieutenant," she said, her voice rising with each word. "You're operating in *my* world now, and I will not have you jeopardizing my career through your own *stupid* ignorance."

He flinched as if she'd slapped him in the face and turned away, but not before she saw the flash of hurt in his eyes. Hurt that was rapidly replaced by anger.

"Jesus, Mary and Joseph," Joe said through clenched teeth. "I was only trying to be nice. I thought sleeping on the couch would screw up your back, but forget it. From now on, I won't bother, okay? From now on, we'll go by the book."

He pushed past her and went into the locker room. The FInCOM agents and the three other SEALs followed, leaving Veronica alone in the exercise room. Her reflection gazed back at her from all angles.

Perfect. She'd handled that just perfectly.

Veronica had come down here to find out why he'd let

her sleep so long, and wound up in a fierce argument about sexual discrimination and her pristine reputation. That wasn't the real issue at all. It had just been something to shout about, because Lord knew she couldn't walk up to him and shout that his kiss had turned her entire world upside down and now she was totally, utterly and quite thoroughly off-balance.

Instead, she had called him names. *Stupid. Ignorant.* Words that had clearly cut deep, despite the fact that he was anything but stupid and far from ignorant.

What Veronica had done was take out all her anger and frustration on the man.

But if anyone was to blame here, it was herself. After all, she was the one foolish enough to have fallen asleep in the first place.

"Hey, Cat!" Cowboy called loudly as he showered in the locker room. "Tell me more about fair Veronica 'Sinjin.'"

"There's nothing to tell," Joe answered evenly. He glanced up to find Blue watching him.

Damn. Blue could read his mind. Joe's connection to Blue was so tight, there were few thoughts that appeared in Joe's head that Blue wasn't instantly aware of. But what would Blue make of the thoughts Joe was having right now? What would he make of the sick, nauseous feeling Joe had in the pit of his stomach?

Stupid. Ignorant.

Well, that about summed it all up, didn't it? Joe certainly knew now exactly what Veronica St. John thought of him, didn't he? He certainly knew why she'd thought that kiss was a mistake.

Cowboy shut off the water. Dripping, he came out of the stall and into the room. "You sure there's nothing you can tell us about Veronica, Cat? Oh, come on, buddy, I can think of a thing or two," he said, taking a towel from a pile of clean ones and giving himself a perfunctory swipe. "Like, are you and she doing the nightly naked two-step?"

"No," Joe replied flatly, pulling on his pants.

"You planning on it?" Cowboy asked. He slipped into one of the plush hotel robes that were hanging on the wall.

"Back off, Jones," Blue said warningly.

"No." Joe answered Cowboy tersely as he yanked his T-shirt over his head and thrust his arms into the sleeves of his shirt.

"Cool," Cowboy said. "Then you don't mind if I give her a try—"

Joe spun and grabbed the younger man by the lapels of his robe, slamming him up against a row of metal lockers with a crash. "Stay the hell away from her," he snapped. He let go of Cowboy, and turned to include Blue and Harvard in his glare. "All of you. Is that clear?"

He didn't wait for an answer. He turned and stalked out of the room, slamming the door behind him.

The noise echoed as Cowboy stared at Harvard and Blue.

"Shoot," he finally said. "Anybody have any idea what the hell's going on?"

Chapter Nine

Room service arrived at the royal suite before Joe did.

"Set it out on the table, please," Veronica instructed the waiter.

She'd ordered a full-course meal, from appetizers to dessert, complete with three different wines.

This afternoon's lesson was food—or more precisely, *eating* food. There was a hundred-dollar-a-plate charity luncheon in Boston, Massachusetts, that had been left on the prince's tour schedule. Both the location and the visibility of the event were right for a possible assassination attempt, but it was more than a hi-and-bye appearance. It would involve more than Joe's ability to stand and wave as if he were Prince Tedric.

The hotel-suite door opened, and Joe came inside, followed by three FInCOM agents. His shirt was unbuttoned, revealing his T-shirt underneath, and he met Veronica's eyes only briefly before turning to the laden dining table. It was quite clear that he was still upset with her.

"What's this?" he asked.

"This is practice for the Boston charity luncheon," Veronica replied. "I hope you're hungry."

Joe stared at the table. It was loaded with dishes covered with plate-warmers. It was set for two, with a full array of cutlery and three different wineglasses at each setting. What, didn't Miss High-and-Mighty think he knew how to eat with a fork? Didn't she know he dined with admirals and four-star generals at the Officers' Club?

Stupid. Ignorant.

Joe nodded slowly, wishing he was still pissed off, wishing he was still nursing the slow burn he'd felt upstairs in the exercise room. But he wasn't. He was too tired to be angry now. He was too tired to feel anything but disappointment and hurt. Damn, it made him feel so vulnerable.

The room-service waiter was standing next to the table, looking down his snotty nose at Joe's unbuttoned shirt. Gee, maybe the waiter and Veronica had had a good laugh about Joe before he'd arrived.

"This is unnecessary," he said, turning back to look at Veronica. Man, she looked pretty in that blue dress. Her hair was tied back with some kind of ribbon, and— Forget about her, he told himself harshly. She was just some rich girl who'd made it more than clear that they lived in two different worlds, and there was no crossing the border. He was stupid and ignorant, and kissing him had been a mistake. "Believe it or not, I already know which fork is for the salad and which fork is for the dessert. It might come as a shock to you, but I also know how to use a napkin and drink from a glass."

Veronica actually looked surprised, her blue eyes growing even wider. "Oh," she said. "No. No, I knew that. That's not what this is." She let a nervous laugh escape. "You actually thought *I* thought I'd need to teach you how to eat?"

Joe was not amused. "Yeah."

My God, he was serious. He was standing there, his powerful arms folded across his broad chest, staring at her with those mystifying dark eyes. Veronica remembered that flash of hurt in Joe's eyes when they'd argued in the exercise room. What had she said? She'd called him stupid and ignorant. Oh, Lord. She *still* couldn't believe those words had come out of her mouth.

"I'm so sorry," she said.

His eyes narrowed slightly, as if he couldn't believe what he was hearing.

"I owe you an apology," Veronica explained. "I was very angry this afternoon, and I said some things I didn't mean. The truth is, I was frustrated and angry with myself. *I* was the one who fell asleep. It was all my fault, and I tried to take it out on you. I shouldn't have. I *am* sorry."

Joe looked at the waiter and then at the FInCOM agents who were sitting on the sofa, listening to every word. He crossed to the door and opened it invitingly. "You guys mind stepping outside for a sec?"

The FInCOM agents looked at each other and shrugged. Rising to their feet, they crossed to the door and filed out into the corridor. Joe turned to the waiter. "You, too, pal." He gestured toward the open door. "Take a hike."

He waited until the waiter was outside, then closed the door tightly and crossed back to Veronica. "You know, these guys *will* give you privacy if you ask for it," he said.

She nodded. "I know," she said. She lifted her chin slightly, steadily meeting his gaze. "It's just…I was rude to you in public, I felt I should apologize to you in public, too."

Joe nodded, too. "Okay," he said. "Yeah. That sounds fair." He looked at her, and there was something very close to admiration in his eyes. "That sounds really fair."

Veronica felt her own eyes flood with tears. Oh, damn,

she was going to cry. If she started to cry, she was going to feel once more just how gentle Joe's hard-as-steel arms could be. And Lord, she didn't want to be reminded of that. "I *am* sorry," she said, blinking back the tears.

Oh, *damn*, Veronica was going to cry, Joe thought as he took a step toward her, then stopped himself. No, she was trying hard to hide it. It was better if he played along, if he pretended he didn't notice. But, man, the sight of those blue eyes swimming in tears made his chest ache, reminding him of this morning, when he'd held her in his arms. Reminding him of that unbelievable kiss...

Veronica forced a smile and held out her hand to him. "Still friends?" she asked.

Friends, huh? Joe had never had a friend before that he wanted to pull into his arms and kiss the living daylights out of. As he gazed into her eyes, the attraction between them seemed to crackle and snap, like some living thing.

Veronica was okay. She was a decent person—the fact that she'd apologized proved that. But she came from miles on the other side of the railroad tracks. If their relationship became intimate, she'd still be slumming. And *he'd* be...

He'd be dreaming about her every night for the rest of his life.

Joe let go of Veronica's hand as if he'd been stung. Jesus, Mary and Joseph, where had *that* thought come from...?

"Are you all right?" The concern in her eyes was genuine.

Joe stuffed his hands in his pockets. "Yeah. Sorry. I guess I'm... After we do this dining thing, I'm going to take another short nap."

"A three-minute nap this time?" Veronica asked. "Or maybe you'll splurge, and sleep for five whole minutes...?"

Joe smiled, and she gave him an answering smile. Their gazes met and held. And held and held and held.

With another woman, Joe would have closed the gap between them. With another woman, Joe would have taken two short steps and brought them face to face. He would have brushed those stray flame-colored curls from the side of her beautiful face, then lifted her chin and lowered his mouth to meet hers.

He had tasted her lips before. He knew how amazing kissing Veronica could be.

But she wasn't another woman. She was Veronica St. John. And she'd already made it clear that sex wasn't on their agenda. Hell, if a kiss was a mistake, then making love would be an error of unbelievable magnitude. And the truth was, Joe didn't want to face that kind of rejection.

So Joe didn't move. He just gazed at her.

"Well," she said, slightly breathlessly, "perhaps we should get to work."

But she didn't cross toward the dining table, she just gazed up at him, as if she, too, were caught in some kind of force field and unable to move.

Veronica was beautiful. And rich. And smart. But more than just book smart. She was people smart, too. Joe had seen her manipulate a tableful of high-ranking officials. She couldn't have done that on an Ivy League diploma alone.

He didn't know the first thing about her, Joe realized. He didn't know where she came from, or how she'd gotten here, to Washington, D.C. He didn't know how she'd come to work for the crown prince of Ustanzia. He didn't know why she'd remained, even after the assassination attempt, when most civilians would have headed for the hills and safety.

"What's your angle?" Joe asked.

Veronica blinked. "Excuse me?"

He reworded the question. "Why are you here? I mean, I'm here to help catch Diosdado, but what are *you* getting out of this?"

She looked out the window at the afternoon view of the capital city. When she glanced back at Joe, her smile was rueful. "Beats me," she said. "I'm not getting paid nearly half enough, although it could be argued that working for royalty is a solid career boost. Of course, it all depends on whether we can successfully pass you off as Prince Tedric."

She sank down onto the couch and looked up at him, elbow on her knee, chin in her hand. "We have less than six hours before the committee makes a decision." She shook her head and laughed humorlessly. "Instead of becoming more like Tedric, you seem more different from him than when we started. I look at you, Joe, and you don't even *look* like the prince anymore."

Joe smiled as he sat next to her on the couch. "Lucky for us, most people won't look beneath the surface. They'll expect to see Ted, so…they'll see Ted."

"I *need* this thing to work," Veronica said, smoothing her skirt over her knees. "If this doesn't work…"

"Why?" Joe asked. "Mortgage payment coming due on the castle?"

Veronica turned and looked at him. "Very funny."

"Sorry."

"You don't really want to hear this."

Joe was watching her, studying her face. His dark eyes were fathomless, and as mysterious as the deepest ocean. "Yes, I do."

"Tedric's sister has been my best friend since boarding school," Veronica said. "Even though Tedric is unconcerned with Ustanzia's financial state, Wila has been working hard to make her country more solvent. It matters to her—so it matters to me." She smiled. "When oil was discovered, Wila actually did cartwheels right across the Capital lawn. I thought poor Jules was going to have a heart attack. But then she found out how much it would cost to drill. She's counting on getting U.S. aid."

Jules.

Be a dear, Jules, and ring the office. Veronica had murmured those words in her sleep, and since then, Joe had been wondering, not without a sliver of jealousy, exactly who this Jules was.

"Who's Jules?" Joe asked.

"Jules," Veronica repeated. "My brother. He conveniently married my best friend. It's quite cozy, really, and very sweet. They're expecting a baby any moment."

Her brother. Jules was her brother. Why did that make Joe feel so damned good? He and Veronica were going to be friends, nothing more, so why should *he* care whether Jules was her brother or her lover or her pet monkey?

But he *did* care, damn it.

Joe leaned forward. "So that's why Wila didn't come on this tour instead of Brain-dead Ted? Because she's pregnant?"

Veronica tried not to smile, but failed. "Don't call Prince Tedric that," she said.

He smiled at her, struck by the way her eyes were the exact shade of blue as her dress. "You know, you look pretty in blue."

Her smile vanished and she stood. "We should really get started," she said, crossing to the dining table. "The food's getting cold."

Joe didn't move. "So where did you and Jules grow up? London?"

Veronica turned to look back at him. "No," she replied. "At first we traveled with our parents, and when we were old enough, we went away to school. The closest thing we had to a permanent home was Huntsgate Manor, where our Great-Aunt Rosamond lived."

"Huntsgate Manor," Joe mused. "It sounds like something out of a fairy tale."

Veronica's eyes grew dreamy and out of focus as she gazed out the window. "It was so wonderful. This big, old, moldy, ancient house with gardens and grounds that went on forever and ever and ever." She looked up at Joe with a spark of humor in her eyes. "Not really," she added. "I think the property is only about four or five acres, but when we were little, it seemed to go to the edge of the world and back."

Night and day, Joe thought. Their two upbringings were as different as night and day. He wondered what she would do, how she would react if she knew about the rock he'd crawled out from under.

Veronica laughed, embarrassed. "I don't know why I just told you all that," she said. "It's hardly interesting."

But it *was* interesting. It was fascinating. As fascinating as those gigantic houses he'd gone into with his mother, the houses that she'd cleaned when he was a kid. Veronica's words were another porthole to that same world of "Look but don't touch." It was fascinating. And depressing as hell. Veronica had been raised like a little princess. No doubt she'd only be content to spend her life "happily ever after," with a prince.

And he sure as hell didn't fit *that* bill.

Except, what was he doing, thinking about things like happily ever after?

"How about you, Joe?" she asked, interrupting his thoughts. "Where did you grow up?"

"Near New York City. We really should get to work," he said, half hoping she'd let the subject of his childhood drop—and half hoping that she wouldn't.

She wouldn't. "New York City," she said. "I've never lived there, I've only visited. I remember the first time I was there as a child. It all seemed to be lights and music and Broadway plays and marvelous food and…*people*, people everywhere."

"I didn't see any plays on Broadway," Joe said dryly. "Although when I was ten, I snuck out of the house at night and hung around the theater district, trying to spot celebrities. I'd get their autograph and then sell it, make a quick buck."

"Your parents probably *loved* that," Veronica said. "A ten-year-old, all alone in New York City…?"

"My mother was usually too drunk to notice I was gone," Joe said. "And even if she had, she wouldn't have given a damn."

Veronica looked away from him, down at the floor. "Oh," she said.

"Yeah," Joe said. "Oh."

She fiddled with her hair for a moment, and then she surprised him. She looked up and directly into his eyes and smiled—a smile not without sorrow for the boy he'd once been. "I guess that's where you learned to be so self-reliant. And self-confident."

"Self-reliant, maybe. But I grew up with everyone always telling me I wasn't good enough," Joe said. "No, that's not true. Not everyone. Not Frank O'Riley." He shook his head and laughed. "He was this mean old guy who lived in this grungy basement apartment in one of the tenements over by the river. He had a wooden leg and a glass eye and his arms were covered with tattoos and all the kids were scared sh— Scared to death of him. Except me, because I was the toughest, coolest kid in the neighborhood—at least among the under-twelve set.

"O'Riley had this garden—really just a patch of land. It couldn't have been more than twelve by four feet. He always had something growing—flowers, vegetables—it was always something. So I went in there, over his rusty fence, just to prove I wasn't scared of the old man.

"I'd been planning to trample his flowers, but once I got into the garden, I couldn't do it," Joe said. "They were just too damn pretty. All those colors. Shades I'd never even imagined. Instead, I sat down and just looked at them.

"Old Frank came out and told me he'd loaded his gun and was ready to shoot me in my sorry butt, but since I was obviously another nature lover, he'd brought me a glass of lemonade instead."

Why was he telling her this? Blue was the only person he'd ever mentioned Frank O'Riley to, and never in such detail. Joe's friendship with Old Man O'Riley was the single good memory he carried from his childhood. Chief Frank O'Riley, U.S.N., retired, and his barely habitable basement apartment had been Joe's refuge, his escape when life at home became unbearable.

And suddenly he knew why he was telling Veronica about Frank, his one childhood friend, his single positive role model. He wanted this woman to know where he came from, who he really was. And he wanted to see her reaction; see whether she would recognize the importance old Frank had played in his life, or whether she would shrug it off, uncaring, uninterested.

"Frank was a sailor," Joe told Veronica. "Tough as nails, and with one hell of a foul mouth. He could swear like no one I've ever known. He fought in the Pacific in World War Two, as a frogman, one of the early members of the UDTs, the underwater demolition teams that later became the SEALs. He was rough and crude, but he never turned me away from his door. I helped him pull weeds in his garden in return for the stories he told."

Veronica was listening intently, so he went on.

"When everyone else I knew told me I was going to end up in jail or worse, Frank O'Riley told me I was destined to become a Navy SEAL—because both they and I were the best of the best."

"He was right," Veronica murmured. "He must be very, *very* proud of you."

"He's dead," Joe said. He watched her eyes fill with compassion, and the noose around his chest grew tighter. He was in big trouble here. "He died when I was fifteen."

"Oh, no," she whispered.

"Frank had one hell of a powerful spirit," Joe continued, resisting the urge to pull her into his arms and comfort her because *his* friend had died more than fifteen years ago. "Wherever I went and whatever I did for the three years after he died, he was there, whispering into my ear, keeping me in line, reminding me about those Navy SEALs that he'd admired so much. On the day I turned eighteen, I walked into that navy recruitment office and I could almost feel his sigh of relief."

He smiled at her and Veronica smiled back, gazing into his eyes. Again, time seemed to stand totally still. Again, it was the perfect opportunity to kiss her, and again, Joe didn't allow himself to move.

"I'm glad you've forgiven me, Joe," she said quietly.

"Hey, what happened to 'Your Highness'?" Joe asked, trying desperately to return to a more lighthearted, teasing tone. She was getting serious on him. Serious meant being honest, and in all honesty, Joe did *not* want to be friends with this woman. He wanted to be lovers. He was *dying* to be her lover. He wanted to touch her in ways she'd never been touched before. He wanted to hear her cry out his name and—

Veronica looked surprised. "I've forgotten to call you that, haven't I?"

"You've been calling me Joe lately," he said. "Which is fine—I like it better. I was just curious."

"You're nothing like the real prince," she said honestly.

"I'm not sure if that's a compliment or an insult."

She smiled. "Believe me, it's a compliment."

"Yeah, that's what I thought," Joe said. "But I wasn't sure exactly where *you* stood."

"Prince Tedric…isn't very nice," Veronica said diplomatically.

"He's a coward and a flaming idiot," Joe stated flatly.

"I guess you don't like him very much, either."

"Understatement of the year, Ronnie. If I end up taking a bullet for him, I'm gonna be really upset." He smiled grimly. "That is, if you can be upset and dead at the same time."

Veronica stared at Joe. If he ended up taking a bullet…

For the first time, the reality of what Joe was doing hit her squarely in the stomach. He was risking his life to catch a terrorist. While Tedric spent the next few weeks in the comfort of a safe house, Joe would be out in public. Joe would be the target of the terrorists' guns.

What if something went wrong? What if the terrorists succeeded, and killed Joe? After all, they'd already managed to kill hundreds and hundreds of people.

Joe suddenly looked so tired. Were his thoughts following the same path? Was he afraid he'd be killed, too? But then he glanced up at Veronica and tried to smile.

"Mind if we skip lunch?" he asked. "Or just postpone it for a half hour?"

Veronica nodded. "We can postpone it," she said.

Joe stood, heading toward the bedroom. "Great, I've gotta crash. I'll see you in about thirty minutes, okay?"

"Do you want me to wake you?" she asked.

Joe shook his head, no. "Thanks, but…"

Oh, baby, he could just imagine her coming into his darkened bedroom to wake him up. He could just imagine coming out of a deep REM sleep to see that face, those eyes looking down at him. He could imagine reaching for her, pulling her down on top of him, covering her mouth with his....

"No, thanks," he said again, reaching up with one hand to loosen the tight muscles in his neck and shoulders. "I'll set the alarm."

Veronica watched as he closed the bedroom door behind him.

They were running out of time. Despite his reassurances, Veronica didn't believe that Joe could pull it off.

But those weren't the only doubts she was having.

Posing as Prince Tedric could very easily get Joe killed.

Were they doing the right thing? Was catching these terrorists worth risking a man's life? Was it fair to ask Joe to take those risks when Tedric so very clearly wouldn't?

But out of all those doubts, Veronica knew one thing for certain. She did not want Lieutenant Joe Catalanotto to die.

Chapter Ten

Veronica was ready nearly thirty minutes before the meeting was set to start.

She checked herself in the mirror for the seven thousandth time. Her jacket and skirt were a dark olive green. Her silk blouse was the same color, but a subtle shade lighter. The color was a perfect contrast for her flaming-red hair, but the suit was boxy and the jacket cut to hide her curves.

Joe would call it a Margaret Thatcher suit. And he was right. It made her look no-nonsense and reliable, dependable and businesslike.

So, all right, it wasn't the height of fashion. But she was sending out a clear message to the world. *Veronica St. John could get the job done*.

Except, in a few minutes, Veronica was going to have to walk out the hotel-room door and head down the corridor to the private conference room attached to Senator McKinley's suite. She was going to go into the meeting and sit down at the table without the slightest clue whether or not she had actually gotten this particular job done.

She honestly didn't know whether or not she'd been able to pull off the task of turning Joe Catalanotto into a dead ringer for Prince Tedric.

Dead ringer. What a horrible expression. And if the security team of FInCOM agents didn't protect Joe, that's exactly what he'd be. Dead. Joe, with his dancing eyes and wide, infectious smile… All it would take was one bullet and he would be a thing of the past, a memory.

Veronica turned from the mirror and began to pace.

She'd worked with Joe all afternoon, going over and over rules and protocols and Ustanzian history. She had shown him the strange way Prince Tedric held a spoon and the odd habit the prince had of leaving behind at least one bite of every food on his plate when eating.

She had tried to show Joe again how to walk, how to stand, how to hold his head at a royal angle. Just when she thought that maybe, just *maybe* he might be getting it, he'd slouch or shrug or lean against the wall. Or make a joke and flash her one of those five-thousand-watt smiles that were so different from any facial expression Prince Tedric had ever worn.

"Don't worry, Ronnie. This is not a problem," he'd said in his atrocious New Jersey accent. "I'll get it. When the time comes, I'll do it right."

But Veronica wasn't sure what she should be worrying about. Was she worried Joe wouldn't be able to pass for Prince Tedric, or was she worried that he *would?*

If Joe looked and acted like the prince, then he'd be at risk. And damn it, why should Joe have to risk his life? Why not let the prince risk his *own* life? After all, Prince Tedric was the one the terrorists wanted to kill.

Veronica had actually brought up her concerns to Joe before they'd parted to get ready for this meeting. He'd laughed when she'd said she thought it might be for the best if he couldn't pass for Tedric—it was too dangerous.

"I've been in dangerous situations before," Joe had told her. "And this one doesn't even come close." He'd told her about the plans and preparations he was arranging with both Kevin Laughton's FInCOM agents and the SEALs from his Alpha Squad. He'd told her he'd wear a bulletproof vest at all times. He'd told her that wherever he went, there would be shielded areas where he could easily drop to cover. He'd reminded her that this operation had minuscule risks compared to most other ops he'd been on.

All Veronica knew was, the better she came to know Joe, the more she worried about his safety. Frankly, this situation scared her to death. And if this *wasn't* dangerous, she didn't want to know what dangerous meant.

But danger was part of Joe's life. Danger was what he did best. No wonder he wasn't married. What kind of woman would put up with a husband who risked his life as a matter of course?

Not Veronica, that was for sure.

Although it wasn't as if Joe Catalanotto had dropped to his knees and begged her to marry him, was it? And he wasn't likely to, either. Despite the incredible kiss they'd shared, a man like Joe, a man used to living on the edge, wasn't very likely to be interested in anything long-term or permanent. *Permanent* probably wasn't even in his vocabulary.

Veronica shook her head, amazed at the course her thoughts had taken. *Permanent* wasn't in *her* vocabulary, either. At least not right now. And certainly not when attached to the words *relationship* and *Joe Catalanotto*. At least fifty percent of the time, the man *infuriated* her. Of course, the rest of the time he made her laugh, or he touched her with his gentle sweetness, or he burned her with that look in his eyes that promised a sexual experience the likes of which she'd never known before.

Either Veronica was fighting with Joe, or fighting the urge to throw herself into his arms.

There'd been one or two...or three or so times—certainly no more than six or eight, at any rate—this afternoon, when Veronica had found herself smiling foolishly into Joe's deep brown eyes, marveling at the length of his eyelashes, and finding her gaze drawn to his straight, white teeth and his rather elegantly shaped lips.

In all honesty, once or twice, Veronica had actually thought about kissing Joe again. Well, maybe more than once or twice.

So, all right, she admitted to herself. He *was* rather unbearably handsome. And funny. Yes, he was undeniably funny. He always knew exactly what to say to make her damn near choke with laughter on her tea. He was blunt and to the point. Often tactless at times—most of the time. But he was always honest. It was refreshing. And despite his rough language and unrefined speech, Joe was clearly intelligent. He hadn't had the best of educations, that much was true, but he seemed well-read and certainly able to think on his own, which was more than Veronica could say for Prince Tedric.

So, okay. Maybe now that she and Joe had had a chance to really talk, maybe now he didn't infuriate her fifty percent of the time. Maybe he only infuriated her, say, twenty percent of the time. But spending twenty percent of her time angry or annoyed or worrying about him was still too much—even for the kind of casual, sexual relationship Joe wanted.

Obviously, Veronica had to continue to keep her distance. Squaring her shoulders, she resolved to do precisely that. She'd stay far, far away from Joe Catalanotto. No more kisses. No more lingering looks. No more long talks about her personal life. From now on, her relationship with Joe would be strictly business.

Still a few minutes early, Veronica took her purse and briefcase and locked her hotel room door behind her. Down at the end of the corridor, she could see FInCOM agents standing outside the royal suite where Joe was getting dressed. More agents were farther down the hall, outside the conference room.

The conference-room door was ajar, so Veronica went in.

This was it. Tonight they would decide whether or not they could successfully pass a Navy SEAL off on the American public as Prince Tedric of Ustanzia.

If the answer was yes, Veronica's friend Wila would be one step closer to getting her American funding, and Joe would be one step closer to catching Diosdado, the terrorist.

She sat down at the empty oval conference table and crossed her legs.

If the answer was no, Joe would return to wherever it was Navy SEALs went between missions, and Veronica would sleep easier at night, knowing that assassins weren't trying to end his life.

Except, if Joe wasn't on *this* mission, he'd probably be on some other, what he considered *truly* dangerous mission. So really, whatever happened, Veronica was going to end up worrying, wasn't she?

Veronica frowned. She was certainly expending a bit of energy thinking about a man she had decided most definitely to stay away from.

Besides, after this meeting, she probably wasn't ever going to see Joe Catalanotto again. And the pang of remorse she felt was *surely* only because she'd failed at her assignment. It wouldn't be long before Veronica had trouble remembering Joe's name. And he certainly wouldn't give *her* a second thought.

Senator McKinley came into the room, followed by his aides and the Ustanzian ambassador and *his* aides. Both men nodded a greeting, but Veronica's attention was pulled away by a young woman taking orders for coffee or tea.

"Earl Grey," Veronica murmured, smiling her thanks.

When she looked up, Kevin Laughton and some of his FInCOM security team had come into the room, along with Admiral Forrest.

The older man caught Veronica's eye and winked a hello. He came around the oval table and pulled out the seat next to hers. "Where's Joe?" he asked.

Veronica shook her head, glancing around the room again. Even in a crowd like this, Joe would have stood out. He was bigger than most men, taller and broader. Unless he was crawling across the rug on his hands and knees, he hadn't yet arrived.

"Still getting changed, I guess," she said to Mac Forrest.

"How's the transformation going?" Forrest asked. "You got him eating lady fingers with his pinky sticking out yet?"

Veronica snorted and gave him a disbelieving look.

"It's going *that* well, huh? Hmm." The admiral didn't seem disappointed. In fact, he gave her a downright cheerful smile. "He'll get it. Did he tell you, he's a pretty darn good mimic? He's got a real ear for language, Joe Cat does."

An ear for language? With his thick accent? Oh, come on…. Veronica didn't want to offend the admiral by rolling her eyes—at least not outwardly.

"Joe's a good man," Forrest told her. "A little too intense sometimes, but that's what makes him a good commander. You win his loyalty, and he'll be loyal to the end. He demands loyalty in return—and gets it. His men would follow him to hell and back." He chuckled. "And they have, on more than one occasion."

Veronica turned toward him. "Joe doesn't think this operation is dangerous," she said. "If that's true, what exactly *is* dangerous?"

"To a SEAL?" Forrest mused. "Let's see…. Breaking into a hostile high-security military installation to track down a pilfered nuclear warhead might be considered dangerous."

"*Might* be?"

"Depends on the location of the military installation, and how well-trained that hostile military organization actually is," he said. "Another dangerous op might be to make a HAHO jump from a plane—"

"A what?"

"HAHO," Forrest repeated. "A high-altitude high-opening parachute jump. It's when you get the green light to jump from the plane at about thirty thousand feet—way up high where the bad guys can't hear the sound of your airplane approaching. You yank the cord, the chute opens and you and your squad parasail silently to the landing zone. And maybe, when you get there, you rescue fifteen hostages—all children—from a bunch of tangos who wouldn't bat an eye over spilling the blood of innocent kids. And maybe before you can pull the kids out of there, the op goes from covert to full firefight. So you rock and roll with your HK, knowing that your body is the only thing shielding a nine-year-old from the enemy's bullets."

Veronica frowned. "Would you mind repeating that last bit in English? Before you can pull the kids out of there…what?"

Forrest grinned, a twinkle in his blue eyes. "The terrorists become aware of your presence and open fire. You've got an instant battlefield—a full firefight. You return fire with your HK—your submachine gun—scared to death because there's a tiny little girl standing directly behind you."

Veronica nodded. "I thought that was what you said." She studied Admiral Forrest's weathered face. "Are these actual operations you're describing or merely hypothetical scenarios?"

"That's classified information," the old man said. "Of course, you're a smart girl. You can probably figure out they wouldn't be classified if they were hypothetical, right?"

Veronica was silent, digesting all he had said.

"Heads up, missy," Forrest whispered. "Looks like this meeting's about to start."

"Let's get this show on the road," Senator McKinley said, his voice cutting above the other conversations from his seat at the head of the table. "Where the hell is Catalanotto?"

McKinley was looking directly at Veronica, as were most of the other people at the table. They honestly expected her to provide them with an answer.

"He said he'd be here," she said calmly. "He'll be here." She glanced at her watch. "He's only a few minutes late."

Just then, West, one of the FInCOM agents, stepped through the door. "Crown Prince Tedric of Ustanzia," he announced.

Aha. *That* was why Joe was late. He was coming to this meeting dressed in the prince's clothes. The tailor had dropped off several large garment bags late this afternoon. No doubt Joe had wanted to wear one of the resplendent suits to make him look more like Tedric.

Any minute now he'd saunter into the room, wearing a garish sequined jacket and a sheepish grin.

But West stepped back and a figure appeared in the doorway.

He was dressed in gleaming white pants and a short white jacket that clung to his broad shoulders and ended at his waist. There were no sequins in sight, but plenty of medals covered his chest, along with a row of golden buttons decorated with the royal Ustanzian shield. The shield also glittered from the bejeweled ring he wore on his right hand. His gleaming black hair was combed directly back from his face.

It was Joe. It had to be Joe, didn't it?

Veronica searched his eyes, looking for the now quite-familiar differences between Joe's and Prince Tedric's faces. But with his shoulders back, his head held at that haughty angle, and no sign of a smile curving his lips, Veronica wasn't sure exactly *who* was standing in the doorway.

And then he spoke. "I greet you with the timeless honor and tradition of the Ustanzian flag," he said in the prince's unmistakable faintly British, faintly French accent, "which is woven, as well, into my heart." ·

Chapter Eleven

Nobody moved.

Everyone stared at Prince Tedric. It *was* Prince Tedric, not Joe. That voice, that accent… Except, what was the real prince doing here, away from the safety of his secure room on the other side of town? It didn't make sense. And his shoulders seemed so broad….

As Veronica watched, the prince took several steps into the room with his peculiar, stiff royal gait. He walked like he had a fireplace poker in his pants, as Joe had so inelegantly described. Veronica fought the urge to giggle. This had to be the prince, indeed. About half-a-dozen dark-suited FInCOM agents followed him inside, and one of them closed the door tightly behind them.

One royal eyebrow lifted a fraction of an inch at the people still sitting at the conference table, and the Ustanzian ambassador scrambled to his feet.

"Your Highness!" he said. "I didn't realize you'd be attending…."

McKinley stood, too. The rest of the table followed suit. Still, as Veronica rose to her feet, she stared. This man wasn't Joe. Or was it? Tedric had never seemed so tall, so imposing. But this couldn't be Joe. That voice had been Tedric's. And that walk. And that haughty look.

The prince's gaze swept around the table. His eyes passed over Veronica without the slightest hint of familiarity, without the tiniest bit of recognition or warmth. He looked through her, not at her. No, it wasn't Joe. Joe would have winked or smiled. And yet...

He held out a hand decorated with a huge gold and jeweled ring for the Ustanzian ambassador to bow over.

Senator McKinley cleared his throat. "Your Excellency," he said. "It was dangerous for you to come here. I should have been informed." He glanced at his chief aide and hissed, "Why wasn't I informed?"

The prince affixed the senator with a very displeased stare. "I am not used to asking permission to leave my room," he said.

He was the prince. Veronica tried to tell herself that she was now convinced of that fact, yet doubt lingered.

"But, Your Highness," Kevin Laughton chimed in. "It's just not safe." He looked over at the FInCOM agents who had arrived with the prince. "I *must* be told of any movement." He looked more closely at the men and a funny look crossed his face. Veronica tried to follow his gaze, to see what he saw, but he quickly looked back at the prince, his face once again expressionless.

"If there was something you needed," Henri Freder, the Ustanzian ambassador, interjected, "all you had to do was ask, Your Highness. We will provide you with all your requests, I can assure you."

"Sit, please, sit. Sit, sit," the prince said impatiently.

Everyone sat. Except the prince. He stood pointedly next to Senator McKinley's seat at the head of the table.

Rather belatedly, McKinley realized his mistake. He hastily stood and offered the prince his chair, moving around to one of the empty seats on the side of the oval table.

On the other side of the room, one of the FInCOM agents coughed. When Veronica glanced at him, he gave her a quick wink. It was Cowboy—one of the SEALs from Joe's Alpha Squad. At least, she thought it was. She did a double take, but when she looked again, he was gone.

She turned and stared at the man who was settling himself in the now vacant chair at the head of the table. "I'll need something to write on and a pen," he announced to no one in particular. "And a glass of water."

Had she imagined Cowboy standing there? Was this really Joe, or was it Prince Tedric? Veronica honestly did not know.

Around her, all of the aides and assistants were scrambling. One of them provided the prince with a smooth white pad of paper, another with a plastic ballpoint pen that the prince simply looked at in disdain. Yes, he had to be the real prince. No one could possibly imitate that disgusted look, could they? Another assistant produced a gold-plated fountain pen, which the prince took with a nod, and yet another presented him with a tall, ice-filled glass of water.

"Thank you," he said, and Veronica sat up.

Thank you? Those words weren't in Tedric's vocabulary. At least, Veronica had never heard him say them before.

Senator McKinley was giving the prince a detailed report on all that had been done over the past several days, and on the changes to the scheduled tour.

Veronica stared down the table at the man now sitting at its head. Prince Tedric never said thank-you. This man was Joe. It *had* to be Joe. But…he didn't look or act or sound *anything* like the Joe she was starting to know so well.

The prince took a sip of his water, removed the cap from his pen.

This would prove it. Joe was left-handed; the prince only used his right.

The prince took the pen in his right hand and jotted a quick note on his pad of paper.

Oh, my God, it wasn't Joe. It was the prince. Unless...

As the senator continued to talk, the prince tore the piece of paper from the pad and folded it neatly in half. He glanced over his shoulder and one of the aides was instantly behind him. He handed the aide the piece of paper and whispered a few words into the young man's ear before turning back to Senator McKinley.

Veronica watched as the aide came around the table, directly toward her. The young man handed her the folded piece of paper.

"From Prince Tedric," the aide whispered almost soundlessly in her ear.

She glanced down the table toward the prince, but he wasn't paying her the slightest attention. He was absently twisting his ring as he listened to McKinley.

Why would Prince Tedric write *her* a note?

Hardly daring to breathe, she unfolded the paper.

"Hey, Ronnie," she read, printed in big, childish block letters. "How'm I doing? Love, Prince Joe."

Veronica laughed. Aloud. McKinley stopped talking midsentence. The entire table turned and looked at her. Including Joe, who gave her a withering look, identical to those she'd received from Prince Tedric in the past. "It's Joe," she said.

Nobody understood. They all just stared at her as if she'd gone mad—except Kevin Laughton, who was nodding, a small smile on his face, and Admiral Forrest, who was rocking back in his seat and chuckling.

Veronica gestured down toward the head of the table, toward Joe. "This is not Prince Tedric," she explained. "It's Lieutenant Catalanotto. Gentlemen, he's fooled us all."

Everyone started talking all at once.

The prince's haughty expression turned into a slow, friendly smile as he gazed down the table at Veronica. His cold eyes turned warm. Oh, yes, this was definitely Joe.

"You're amazing," she mouthed to him. She knew he wouldn't be able to hear her over the din, but she had no doubt he could read her lips. She wouldn't be surprised to find there was nothing Joe Catalanotto couldn't do, and do well.

He shrugged. "I'm a SEAL," he mouthed back, as if that explained everything.

"I knew it was the lieutenant," Veronica heard Kevin Laughton say. "But only because I knew three of the men who came in with him weren't on my staff."

"I knew it was him, too," Senator McKinley's loud voice boomed. "I was waiting to see when y'all would catch on."

Still, Veronica gazed into Joe's dark eyes. "Why didn't you tell me?" she silently asked.

"I did," he answered.

And he was right. He *had* told her. "Don't worry, I'll get it," he'd said. "I'm a pretty good mimic."

Pretty good?

Veronica laughed. He was *amazing*.

Joe smiled back at her as everyone around them continued to talk at once. But they might have been alone in this room, for all the attention she paid anyone else.

That was admiration he could see in Veronica's blue eyes. Admiration and respect. She wasn't trying to hide it. She was sending him a message with her eyes as clear as the one she'd sent with her lips.

Joe could also see traces of the attraction she was never

really able to conceal. It was always back there, lurking, waiting patiently for the moment when her defenses were down, waiting for her to temporarily forget that he wasn't a regular of the country-club set.

And, God, he was waiting, too.

Except she wasn't going to forget. It was only at times like this, when they were safely across the room from each other, that Veronica gazed into his eyes. It was only when she was safely out of reach that she let him drown in the swirling ocean-blueness of her eyes.

It didn't take much to imagine what being Veronica St. John's lover would be like, to see her with her red curls tumbled down her back, dressed only in the skimpiest of satin and lace, desire turning her sea-colored eyes to blue flames. As Joe gazed into her eyes, he felt himself going under for the third and final time.

He wanted her so desperately, he was nearly dizzy with desire. Somehow, some way, he was going to change her mind, break through that flimsy wall she'd thrown up between them.

Admiral Forrest raised his voice to be heard over the noise. "I think this meeting can be adjourned," he said. "We can announce to the press that Prince Tedric's tour will resume as of oh-eight-hundred hours tomorrow. Are we in agreement?"

Veronica reluctantly pulled her eyes away from the molten lava of Joe's gaze. Her heart was pounding. Good Lord, the way that man looked at her! If they had been alone, he would have kissed her again. Or if he hadn't, maybe *she* would have kissed *him!*

Lord save her from herself.

She shuffled the papers in front of her, attempting to regain her equilibrium as the room slowly cleared.

Senator McKinley shook her hand briefly, commending her on a job well-done before he rushed off to another appointment.

Veronica could feel Joe's eyes still on her as he stood and talked to Admiral Forrest. The FInCOM men tried to escort them out of the room, but Joe hung back, clearly waiting for her.

Taking a deep breath, she gathered her briefcase and went to join them.

Joe was looking down at the ring on his hand. "Did you know this ring is worth more than a new car?" he mused. "And did you know old Ted has about twenty of 'em?"

Mac Forrest grinned at Veronica, slapping Joe on the back one more time as they walked down the hotel corridor. "You couldn't tell it was Joe, could you?" Forrest asked her.

Veronica glanced up at Joe. She wasn't prepared for the jolt of warmth and energy that surrounded her as she met his dark eyes. He was smiling at her, and she found herself smiling foolishly back, until she realized the Admiral had asked her a question. She tore her eyes away.

"No, sir, I couldn't," she answered hoping that she didn't sound as breathless as she felt. "Except..."

"What?" Joe asked.

She looked up at him, bracing herself before meeting his hypnotizing eyes again. "You said 'Thank you,'" she replied. "Tedric wouldn't dream of thanking a servant."

"Well, maybe ol' Ted's been reading up on the American version of Miss Manners," Joe said. "Because for the next five weeks, he's going to be saying 'thank you' to all the lowly servants. And maybe even 'please,' every now and then."

"That's fine with me. I think everyone should say thank-you. I think it's rude not to," Veronica said.

"The equipment you ordered is coming in late tonight," Admiral Forrest said to Joe. "It'll be ready for tomorrow."

"We leave the hotel at oh-eight-hundred?" Joe asked.

Veronica dug into her briefcase and checked the schedule. "That's right," she said. "There're a number of public appearances—just visual things—a chance for the news reporters to get footage of you climbing in and out of limousines and waving. Tomorrow night there's an optional embassy function, if you feel up to it. There *will* be people there who know Tedric quite well, though. You'll have to be ready to recognize them."

"Can *you* recognize them?" Joe asked.

"Well, yes," Veronica said. "Of course. But—"

"Then I'm ready," he said with a grin.

"We've ordered a surveillance van," Admiral Forrest said to her. "You'll have the seat of honor at the main mike. Joe will wear an earphone and a microphone so the communication can go both ways. He'll hear you and you'll hear him. *And* we'll have miniature video cameras set up, so you'll be able to see both Joe *and* from Joe's point of view."

They stopped outside the royal suite, waiting while West went inside to make a quick security sweep. "All clear," he said, coming back out. The entire group moved into the room.

Admiral Forrest clasped Joe's hand again. "Good job, son." He nodded at Veronica. "You, too, missy." He glanced at his watch. "I've got to make some status reports." As Mac turned to leave, he shook his finger at Joe. "No more unauthorized field trips down the outside of the building," he admonished. "No more games." He turned to the other SEALs, Blue, Cowboy and Harvard, who were standing by the door with the FInCOM agents. "You're on the same side as security now," he said to them. "You make sure Lieutenant Catalanotto stays secure. Have I made myself clear?"

"I gave them liberty tonight, Admiral," Joe interjected. "I figured—"

"You figured wrong," Forrest said. "As of thirty minutes ago, this operation has started."

Cowboy clearly wasn't happy about that.

The admiral opened the door to the hallway. "As a matter of fact, I need to see this security team in the corridor, pronto."

"But, sir—" Cowboy started.

"That was an order, Ensign," Forrest barked.

Still, the three SEALs didn't move until Joe gave them an almost-imperceptible nod.

The door closed behind them and the room was suddenly silent.

"What was *that* about?" Veronica asked Joe, suddenly aware of how close they were standing, of how delicious he smelled, of how he managed to make even that ridiculous white jacket look good.

He gave her one of his familiar sheepish smiles as he sat on the arm of the sofa. "I think Mac's realized that Diosdado could get lucky and take me out," he said. "He doesn't want to lose the commanding officer of the Alpha Squad."

"He doesn't want to lose a friend," Veronica corrected him.

"He's not going to," Joe said. "I have no intention of dying." It was a fact. His quiet statement combined with the certainty in his eyes and on his face convinced Veronica that it was, indeed, a fact. He looked hard and invincible, and quite possibly immortal.

But he wasn't immortal. He was human. He was flesh and blood, and starting tomorrow morning, he was going to be a target. When he stepped out the hotel door dressed as Prince Tedric, there could be an assassin's gun trained on him.

By tomorrow at this time, Joe could very well have been shot. He could be seriously injured. Or worse. He could be dead.

Permanently dead.

Joe might be able to disregard the danger, but Veronica couldn't. He was going to be out in public with a security team that wasn't up to par. Sure, the odds were better now that the three SEALs from the Alpha Squad had joined FInCOM's team, but there were no guarantees.

Veronica was going to be safely tucked away in some surveillance vehicle where, if the terrorists *did* get through the security force, she'd have a front-row seat to watch Joe die.

He was sitting there watching her, and she was struck by his casual bravery, his unassuming heroism. He was doing this for Admiral Forrest, for the admiral's dead son, and for all of the other U.S. sailors who'd been killed at Diosdado's hands. And for all the people, sailors and civilians, who would be hurt or killed by the terrorists if they were not stopped here and now.

Yes, there was a chance that he might die. But in Joe's eyes, it was obviously a risk worth taking if it meant they'd catch these killers. But what a tremendous risk, an incredible sacrifice. He'd be risking his life, his precious, irreplaceable life. It was the most he could possibly give. And to Joe, it was also the least he could do.

"Has anyone bothered to thank you for what you're doing?" Veronica asked, her throat feeling unnaturally tight as she gazed into Joe's eyes.

He shrugged, a loose casual move, echoed in his easygoing smile. "If it all works out, I'll probably get the Ustanzian Medal of Honor." He glanced down at the rows of Prince Tedric's medals on his chest and made a face. "Considering Ted's got four, I'm not sure I want one," he added. "Even if I can talk 'em out of giving me one, there'll be some kind of ceremony, and I'll have to smile for the cameras and shake Ted's sweaty hand."

"And if it doesn't work out…?" Her voice trembled.

He shrugged and his smile became a grin. "Then I won't have to shake Ted's hand, right?"

"Joe."

He stood up. "Ronnie," he said, mimicking her intensity. "Lighten up, all right?"

But she couldn't. How could she lighten up when tomorrow he might very well be dead? Veronica glanced around the room, aware once again that they were alone. They were alone, and she might never have another chance to hold him in her arms.

Despite her resolve to stay away from Joe, Veronica stepped toward him, closing the gap between them, slipping her arms around his waist and holding him tightly, resting her head against his shoulder.

He was shocked. She'd seen the surprise in his eyes. She still felt it in the stiffness and tension in his entire body. Never in a million years had he expected her to put her arms around him.

As she started to pull back, she lifted her head and she could see a vulnerability deep in his eyes, a flash of almost childlike wonder. But it was gone so quickly, she was left wondering if she hadn't imagined it.

He almost didn't react. *Almost* didn't. But before she pulled away, he encircled her with his arms, holding her gently but quite firmly in place. He sighed very softly as he allowed his body to relax against hers.

Joe couldn't make himself release her. Veronica was in his arms, and he was damned if he was going to let her go. She fit next to him so perfectly, they might have been made for each other. She was soft in all the right places, and firm in all the others. Holding her like this was heaven.

Veronica stared up at him, her ocean blue eyes wide.

There were few things he wanted right this moment as much as he wanted to kiss her. He wanted to plunder her soft, sweet mouth with his tongue. To kiss her deeply, savagely, until she clung to him, dizzy from desire. He wanted to sweep her into his arms and carry her into the bedroom, where he'd undress her with his teeth and kiss every inch of her smooth, supple body before driving himself into her sweet, welcoming warmth.

He felt nearly delirious just thinking about it—the sheer bliss. And it would start with one small kiss...

He slowly lowered his head to kiss her.

Veronica gazed up into his eyes, transfixed, lips slightly parted.

He was a fraction of a second from paradise, and...she turned her head.

Joe's mouth landed on her cheek as she quickly pulled free of his arms.

Frustration made every muscle in his body tighten. *Damn* it. What had just happened here? Hell, *she'd* made the first move. She was the one who'd put her arms around him. And then...

"Veronica," he said, reaching for her.

But she stepped away from him, out of reach, as the door opened and the FInCOM agents and SEALs came back inside.

"I gotta run, Cat," Admiral Forrest called out, waving briefly through the open door. "We'll talk tomorrow. Be good."

"Well," Veronica said, her voice intentionally light as she collected her briefcase. "I'll see you in the morning, Lieutenant."

That was it? She was going to not kiss him and then just walk away?

She wouldn't meet his eyes as she made a beeline for the door, and short of running after her and tackling her, there was little that Joe could do to stop her.

"Thanks again," Veronica added, and she was out the door.

"Walk her to her room," Joe ordered West, suddenly afraid for her, walking alone in the hotel corridor, even the short distance to her own room.

The man nodded and followed Veronica, closing the door behind him.

"Thanks again?" Cowboy echoed her departing words. He wiggled his eyebrows suggestively at Joe. "Something happen in here we should know about?"

Joe shot him one long look. "Stop," he said.

Cowboy started to say something else, but wisely kept his mouth shut.

Thanks again.

Veronica's words echoed in Joe's head. *Thanks again.*

She had been thanking him. Of course. When she had put her arms around him, she wasn't giving in to the attraction that simmered between them. No way. She was *thanking* him. She was being the generous aristocrat thanking the lowly servant. Damn, he was *such* a fool.

Joe had to sit down.

"Everything all right, Cat?" Blue asked softly in his gentle Southern accent.

Joe stood again and headed for the bedroom. "Fine," he answered shortly, keeping his head turned away so his friend wouldn't see the hurt he knew was showing in his eyes.

Chapter Twelve

When the embassy party started at nine—twenty-one-hundred hours according to Joe—Veronica was feeling an old pro at handling the equipment in the surveillance van.

She wore a lightweight wireless headset with an attached microphone positioned directly under her lips. Joe could hear every word she spoke through a miniature receiver hidden in his right ear. And Veronica could hear him quite clearly, too. His wireless mike was disguised as a pin he wore in the lapel of his jacket.

She could see Joe, too, on a TV screen built into the side panel of the van. Another screen showed a different angle—Joe's point of view. Both views were courtesy of miniaturized video cameras discreetly held by several FInCOM agents. So far, Veronica hadn't had much use for the TV screen that showed the world from Joe's eyes. It would come in handy tonight, though.

The three SEALs from Alpha Squad were also wearing microphones and earphones patched into the same frequency that Veronica and Joe were using. It was easy to tell Blue's, Cowboy's and Harvard's voices apart, and of course, she would recognize Joe's voice anywhere.

More often than not, the SEALs used some kind of abbreviated lingo, using phrases like "LZ" and "recon" and "sneak and peek." They talked about the "T's" or "tangos," which Veronica knew to mean terrorists. But for every word she recognized, they used four others whose meanings were mysterious. It was like listening to another language.

Throughout the day, Veronica had reminded Joe when to bow and when to wave, when to ignore the news cameras, and when to look directly into their lenses and smile. She'd warned him when his smile became a bit too broad— too Joe-like—and he'd adjusted instantly in order to seem more like the real prince.

The high-tech equipment made the process infinitely easier than any other job she'd ever done.

What she was never going to get used to, however, was the slightly sick feeling in the pit of her stomach as she watched Joe on the video cameras and wondered when the assassins were going to strike.

"Okay," came the word from Kevin Laughton, who was also in the surveillance van. "The limo is approaching the embassy."

"Got it," West said over the van's speakers. "I see them coming up the drive." FInCOM was using a different frequency for their radio communication. Joe's earphone had been modified to maintain a direct link with them, too. If someone—SEAL or Fink—so much as breathed a warning, he wanted to hear it.

"Check, check," Veronica heard Joe say into his mike. "Am I on?"

"We're reading you," Laughton said. "Do you copy?"

"Gotcha," Joe said. "Ronnie, you with me?"

"I'm here," Veronica said, purposely keeping her voice low and calm. Her heart was beating a mile a minute at the thought of Joe walking into the Ustanzian Embassy and actually relying on her for the information he needed to pull off his masquerade as Prince Tedric. And if *she* was on edge, he must be incredibly nervous. He not only had to think about successfully portraying Tedric, but he also had to worry about not getting killed.

"Cameras are on," a FInCOM agent's voice reported. "Surveillance van, do you have picture?"

"Roger that, FInCOM," Veronica said, and Joe laughed, just as she'd known he would.

"What, are you getting into this?" he asked her.

"Absolutely," she said smoothly. "I don't know the last time I've so looked forward to an embassy party. I get to sit out here in comfort instead of tippy-toeing around all those dignitaries and celebrities, eating overcooked hors d'oeuvres and smiling until my face hurts."

Joe leaned across the limousine, closer to the camera. "Overcooked hors d'oeuvres?" he said, making a face. *"That's* what I have to look forward to here?"

"Ready to open the limo doors," West's voice announced. "Everyone in position?"

"Joe, be careful," Veronica murmured quickly.

He touched his ear briefly, giving her the signal that he heard her. She saw something flicker in his eyes before he looked away from the video camera.

What was he thinking? Was he thinking of last night, of the way he'd almost kissed her? He *would* have kissed her again, and she probably would have kissed him, too, if she hadn't heard the hotel-room door start to open.

Probably? Definitely—despite her better judgment. She should be grateful they had been interrupted when they were. She *knew* she was grateful that she'd heard the sound of the doorknob turning. How awful would it have been to have three FInCOM agents, three SEALs and one navy admiral open the door to find her locked in Joe's embrace.

Joe had been oddly distant this morning—no doubt a direct result of her rapid flight from his hotel room last night. Veronica felt guilty about running away. But if she'd stayed, and if he'd pursued her, she would have ended up in his arms again. And, quite probably, she would have ended up in his bed.

She had thought maybe a little time and a little distance would take the edge off the attraction she felt for this man. But when she had walked out of her room this morning, Joe had been dressed in one of Tedric's least flashy dark suits and was already waiting with the FInCOM agents in the corridor. She'd looked at him, their eyes had met, and that attraction had sparked again.

No, time and distance had done nothing. She'd wanted to kiss Joe as much this morning as she had wanted to kiss him last night. Maybe even more so.

The security team had led him down the hallway to the elevators and she'd followed a step or two behind. Once downstairs, they'd gone immediately to work.

Admiral Forrest had explained the array of equipment in the van, and Joe had stared unsmiling into the cameras as the screens and relays were checked and double-checked. She'd talked to him over her headset, and although his replies had started out terse and to the point, over the course of the long day, he'd warmed up to his usual self, with his usual sardonic humor.

"Doors are opening," West announced now, and the pictures on the TV screens jumped as the agents holding the cameras scrambled out of the limo.

The paparazzi's flashbulbs went off crazily as Joe stepped out of the long white car, and Veronica held her breath. If someone was going to shoot him, it would happen now, as he was walking from the car to the embassy. Inside the building, security was very tight. He would still be in some danger, but not half as much as out here in the open.

The FInCOM agents surrounded him and hustled him inside, one of them roughly pushing Joe's head down, out of target range.

"Well, *that* was fun," Veronica heard Joe say as the embassy doors closed behind them. "Warn me next time you decide to put me in a half nelson, would you, guys?"

"We're inside," West's voice said.

On Veronica's video screen, the Ustanzian ambassador approached Joe, followed by an entourage of guests and celebrities. Joe instantly snapped into character, shoulders back, expression haughty.

"Henri Freder, Ustanzian ambassador to the United States," Veronica told Joe. "He knows who you are. He was at the meeting last night, and he's available to help you."

"Your Highness." Freder gave Joe a sweeping bow. "It is with great pleasure that I welcome you to the Ustanzian Embassy."

Joe nodded in return, just a very slight inclination of his head. Veronica smiled. Joe had Tedric's royal attitude down cold.

"The man to Freder's left is Marshall Owen," Veronica said to Joe, calling up additional background on Owen on the computer. "Owen's a businessman from...Atlanta, Georgia, who owns quite a bit of real estate in Europe, Ustanzia included. He's a friend of your father's. You've only met him three or four times—once in Paris. You played racketball. You won, but he probably threw the game. Shake his hand and address him as 'Mr. Owen'—Daddy owes him quite a bit of money."

On-screen, Joe shook Marshall Owen's hand. "Mr.

Owen," he said in Tedric's unmistakable accent. "A pleasure to see you again, sir. Will you be in town long? Perhaps
you can come to the hotel for a visit? There are racketball
courts next to the weight room, I believe."

"Excellent," Veronica murmured.

With this equipment and Joe's ability to mimic, it was
going to be—what was that expression of Joe's?—a piece
of cake.

Joe sat on the couch in the royal suite, drinking beer from
the bottle and trying to depressurize.

There was a soft knock on the hotel-room door, and
West moved to answer it, opening it only slightly. The FIn-
COM agent opened it wider and Veronica slipped inside.

She smiled when she saw Joe. "You were great today."

He felt his face relaxing as he smiled back at her. "You
weren't so shabby yourself." He started to stand, but she
waved him back into his seat. "Want a beer? Or something
to eat? We could order up…?"

Jesus, Mary and Joseph, could he sound any more eager
for her company?

She shook her head, still smiling at him. "No, thank
you," she said. "I really just wanted to stop in and tell you
what a good job you did."

Joe had tried to keep his distance all day long. He'd
tried to act cool and disinterested. Tried. Jesus, Mary and
Joseph, after last night, after he realized Veronica had only
put her arms around him as a gesture of thanks, he should
have had no problem staying away from her. He should
have known better. Even after she'd apologized for her
angry outburst, for calling him stupid and ignorant, he
should have known that just because she'd apologized for
saying those things, it didn't mean that she didn't think
they were true.

Veronica had told him that she wanted to be friends— yeah, probably the way she would befriend a stray dog.

But all day long, he'd found himself playing to the hidden video cameras, knowing she was watching him, enjoying the sound of her voice speaking so intimately into his ear.

It didn't matter that they were dozens, sometimes even hundreds of yards apart. Veronica was his main link to the surveillance van. Hers was the voice Joe heard most often over his miniaturized earphone. He had to depend on her and trust her implicitly when she gave him information and instructions. Whether she knew it or not, their relationship *had* become an intimate one.

And Joe suspected that she knew it.

He was staring at her again, he realized. Her eyes were so blue and wide as she gazed back at him.

He looked away first. Who was he kidding? What was he trying to do? Weren't two rejections enough? What did he want, three for three?

"It's getting late," he said gruffly, wanting her either in his arms or gone.

"Well," she said, clearly flustered. "I'm sorry. I'm…" She shook her head and fished for a moment in her briefcase. "Here is tomorrow's schedule," she added, handing him a sheet of paper. "Good night, then." She moved gracefully toward the door.

"Saint Mary's," Joe said aloud, his eyes catching the name halfway down the schedule.

Veronica stopped and turned back toward him. "Yes, that's right," she said. "I meant to ask you to wear something… special."

"What? My giant chicken suit?"

She laughed. "Not exactly what I had in mind."

"Then maybe you should be more specific."

"Blue jacket, red sash, black pants," Veronica instructed.

"I think of it as Tedric's Prince Charming outfit. Didn't you get fitted for something like that?"

"I did and I'll wear it tomorrow." Joe bowed. "Your wish is my command."

Chapter Thirteen

Veronica rode to Saint Mary's in the limousine with Joe.

He was wearing the Prince Charming-like suit she'd asked him to wear, and he looked almost ridiculously handsome.

"This is going to be a difficult one," she said, doing some last-minute work on her laptop computer.

"Are you kidding?" Joe said. "No media, no fanfare—how hard could it be?"

"I'm going in with you this time," Veronica said, as if she hadn't heard him.

"Oh, no, you're not," he countered. "I don't want you within ten feet of me."

She looked up from her computer screen. "There's no danger," she said. "Saint Mary's wasn't on the schedule we released to the press."

"There's always danger," Joe insisted. "There's always a possibility that we're being followed."

Veronica looked out the rear window. Three other limos, plus the surveillance van, were trailing behind them.

"Goodness gracious," she said in mock surprise. "You're right! We're being followed by three *very* suspicious-looking limousines and—"

"Knock off the comedy routine, St. John," Joe muttered. "You're not going in there, and that's final."

"You don't want me to get hurt." Veronica closed her computer and slid it back into its carrying case. "That's so sweet."

"That's me," Joe said. "Prince Sweetie-Pie."

"But I *need* to go in."

"Ronnie—"

"Saint Mary's is a hospice, Joe," Veronica said quietly. "For children with cancer."

Joe was silent.

"There's a little girl named Cindy Kaye who is staying at Saint Mary's," she continued, her voice low and even. "She wrote a letter to Tedric, asking him to stop and visit her during his tour of the United States. She'd like to meet a real prince before—well—before she dies." She cleared her throat. "Cindy has an inoperable brain tumor. She's been writing to Tedric for months—not that he bothers to read the letters. But I've read them. Every single one. She's incredibly bright and charming. And she's going to die in a matter of weeks."

Joe made a low, pain-filled sound. He rubbed his forehead with one hand, shielding his eyes from her view.

"I spoke to her mother on the phone this morning," Veronica said. "Apparently Cindy's taken a turn for the worse. She's been practicing her curtsy for months, but as of last night, she's..." She cleared her throat again. "The tumor's affecting more and more of her motor functions, and she's now unable to get out of bed."

Joe swore, long and loud, as the limo pulled up outside the hospice.

It was a clean, white building, with lots of windows, and beautiful flowers growing in the neatly tended gardens outside. There was a statue of the Madonna, also gleaming white, in among the flowers. It was lovely to look at, so peaceful and serene. But inside… Inside were children, all dying of cancer.

"What am I supposed to say to a kid who's dying?" Joe asked, his voice hoarse.

"I don't know," Veronica admitted. "I'll come with you—"

"No way." Joe shook his head.

"Joe—"

"I said, *no*. I'm *not* risking your life, goddammit!"

Veronica put her hand on his arm and waited until he looked up at her. "Some things are worth the risk."

Cindy Kaye was tiny, so skinny and frail. She looked more like a malnourished six-year-old than the ten-year-old Veronica knew her to be. Her long brown hair was clean and she wore a pink ribbon in it. She was lying on top of her bedspread, wearing a frilly pink dress with lots of flounces and lace. Her legs, covered in white tights, looked like two slender sticks. She wore white ballet slippers on her narrow feet.

The little girl's brown eyes filled with tears, tears that spilled down her cheeks, as Joe came into the room and gave her his most royal of bows.

"Milady," he said in Tedric's unmistakable accent. He approached Cindy and the vast array of tubes and IVs and medical equipment that surrounded her without the slightest hesitation. He sat on the edge of Cindy's bed and lifted her skeletal hand to his lips. "It is a great honor to meet you at last. Your letters have brought great joy and sunshine to my life."

"I wanted to curtsy for you," Cindy said. Her voice was trembling, her speech slurred.

"When my sister, the Princess Wila, was twelve," Joe said, leaning forward as if he were sharing a secret with her, "she injured her back and neck in a skiing accident, and was confined to her bed, much the way you are now. Our great-aunt, the Duchess of Milan, taught her the proper social etiquette for such a situation. The duchess taught her the 'eyelid curtsy.'"

Cindy waited silently for him to continue.

"Close your eyes," Joe commanded the little girl, "count to three, then open them."

Cindy did just that.

"Excellent," Joe said. "You must have royal blood in your veins to be able to do the eyelid curtsy so elegantly your very first time."

Cindy shook her head, the corners of her mouth finally curving upward.

"No royal blood? I don't believe it," Joe said, smiling back at her. "Your dress is very beautiful, Cindy."

"I picked it out just for you," she said.

Joe had to lean close to understand. He looked up to meet the eyes of the woman seated beside the bed—Cindy's mother. She gave him such a sweet, sorrowful, thankful smile, he had to look away. Her daughter, her precious, beautiful daughter, was dying. Joe had always believed he was a strong man, but he wasn't sure he would have the strength to sit by the bedside of his own dying child, day after day, hiding all his frustration and helplessness and deep, burning anger, offering only comforting smiles and peaceful, quiet, reassuring love.

He felt some of that frustration and rage form a tornado inside him, making his stomach churn. Somehow, he kept smiling. "I'm honored," he said to Cindy.

"Do you speak Ustanzian?" Cindy asked.

Joe shook his head. "In Ustanzia we speak French," he said.

"Je parle un peu français," Cindy said, her words almost unrecognizable.

Oh, God, thought Veronica. Now what?

"Très bien," Joe said smoothly. "Very good."

Veronica relaxed. Joe knew a bit of French, too. Thank goodness. That might have been a real disaster. Imagine the child's disappointment to find that her prince was an imposter...

"I would love to see your country," Cindy said, in her stilted schoolgirl French.

Oh, dear. Veronica stood. "Cindy, I'm sure Prince Tedric would love for you to see his country, too, but he should really practice his English, now that he's visiting America."

Joe looked up at her. "It's all right," he murmured, then turned back to Cindy. "I know a way you can see my country," Joe replied in perfect French. His accent was impeccable—he spoke like a native Parisian. "Close your eyes, and I will tell you all about my beautiful Ustanzia, and you will see it as if you are there."

Veronica's mouth was hanging open. Joe spoke *French?* *Joe* spoke *French?* She pulled her mouth shut and listened in silence as he described Ustanzia's mountains and valleys and plains in almost poetic language—both in French and English, as he translated the too-difficult words for the little girl.

"It sounds wonderful," Cindy said with a sigh.

"It is," Joe replied. He smiled again. "Do you know some people in my country also speak Russian?" He then repeated his question in flawless Russian.

Veronica had to sit down. Russian? What *other* languages did he speak? Or maybe she should wonder what languages *didn't* he speak...

"Do you speak Russian?" Joe asked the little girl.

She shook her head.

"Say '*da*,'" Joe said.

"*Da*," she said.

"That's Russian for 'yes,'" he told her, and smiled—a big, wide, warm Joe smile, not one of Tedric's pinched smiles. "Now you speak Russian."

"*Da*," she said again, with a brilliant smile in return.

A FInCOM agent appeared in the doorway. When Joe looked up, the man touched his watch.

"I have to go now," Joe said. "I'm sorry I can't stay longer."

"That's okay," Cindy said, but once again her eyes filled with tears.

Joe felt his heart clench. He'd been there, visiting Cindy, for only thirty minutes. When they'd set up the schedule for the tour, McKinley had wanted to allot only five minutes for Saint Mary's, but Veronica had been adamant that they take a full half hour. But now, even a half hour didn't seem long enough.

"I'm so glad I got to meet you," Joe said, leaning forward to kiss her on the forehead as he stood.

"Your Highness…?"

"Yes, milady?"

"I heard on the news that there are lots of kids hungry in Ustanzia right now," Cindy said, laboring over the words.

Joe nodded seriously. "Yes," he said. "That news report was right. My family is trying to fix that."

"I don't like it when kids are hungry," she said.

"I don't either," Joe said, his voice husky. The tornado inside him was growing again. How could this child think of others' troubles and pain, when her own pain was so great?

"Why don't you share your food with them?" Cindy said.

"It's not always that easy," Joe said. But she already knew that. Surely she, of all people, knew that.

"It should be," she said.

He nodded. "You're right. It should be."

She closed her eyes briefly—an eyelid curtsy.

Joe bowed. What could he say now? Stay well? That would be little more than a cruel joke. I'll see you soon? An untruth. Both he and the child knew they would never meet again. His rage and frustration swelled up into his throat, making it difficult to speak. "Goodbye, Cindy," he managed to say, then moved toward the door.

"I love you, Prince," Cindy said.

Joe stopped, and turned back to her, fighting hard to smile. "Thank you," he said. "I'll treasure this day, Cindy—always—and carry you forever in my heart."

The little girl smiled, made happy by such a small thing, such a small pleasure.

Somehow Joe kept the smile on his face until he was outside the room. Somehow he managed to walk down the hall without putting his fist through a wall. Somehow he managed to keep walking—until the burning rage in his stomach and throat and behind his eyes grew too intense, and his feet wouldn't carry him another step forward.

He turned toward the wall—the same wall he hadn't put his fist through—and leaned his arms against it, burying his face in the crook of his elbow, hoping, *praying* that the pain that was burning him would soon let up.

But why should it? The pain Cindy was in wasn't going to let up. She was going to die, probably in a matter of days. The injustice of it all was like a knee to his groin. Bile filled his mouth and he wanted to shake his fist at the sky and curse the God who could let this happen.

"Joe."

Ronnie was there, then. Leading him down the hall, she pulled him into the semiprivacy of a tiny chapel. Warm and soft, she put her arms around him and held him tightly.

"Oh, God," he said, fighting the hot rush of tears to his eyes. "Oh, *God!*"

"I know," she said. "I know. But you were so good. You made her smile. You made her *happy.*"

Joe pulled back to look at Veronica. Light filtered in through the stained-glass windows, glowing red and blue and gold on the tile floor. "I'm not even a real prince," he said harshly. "It was all just a lie."

Veronica shook her head. "Tedric would've disappointed her horribly," she said. "You've given her something good to dream about."

Joe laughed, but it came out sounding more like a sob. He stared up at the crucifix on the wall behind the altar. "Yeah, but for how long?"

"For as long as she needs good dreams," Veronica said quietly.

Joe felt his eyes fill with tears again. He tried to blink them back, but one or two escaped, rolling down his face. He was crying. God, he hadn't cried since he was fifteen years old. Embarrassed, he wiped at his face with the back of one hand. "This is why you insisted that Saint Mary's stay on the schedule," he said gruffly. "*You're* really the one responsible for making that little girl happy."

"I think it was teamwork," Veronica said, smiling at him through her own tears.

He'd never seen her look more beautiful. Nearly everything she'd done up to this point, he realized, she'd done for the sake of one little dying girl. Sure, she wanted to help catch the terrorists. And she wanted to help her friend, the princess of Ustanzia. But what *really* had driven her to make sure Joe could pass as Prince Tedric, was the little sick kid back in that bed.

He knew that as sure as he knew his heart was beating. The noose around Joe's chest drew so tight, for one heart-stopping moment he was sure he'd never be able to breathe again. But then something snapped—not the noose, but something in his head—and a little voice said, "You're in love with this woman, you flaming idiot," and he knew it was true.

She was wonderful. And he was *crazy* in love with her.

Her smile faded and there was only warmth in her eyes, warmth and that ever-present flame of desire. She moved back into his arms, and lifted her mouth to his and…

God, he was kissing her. He was actually kissing her.

He took her lips hungrily, pulling her lithe body closer to him. He wanted to inhale her, devour her, become one with her. He kissed her again and again, his tongue sweeping fiercely past any pretense of civility, as he savagely claimed her mouth.

He could feel her arms around his neck, feel her pressing herself even tighter against him as she kissed him with equal abandon.

It was so right. It was so utterly, perfectly right. This woman, his arms around her, their two hearts beating—pounding—in unison. Two souls intertwined. Two minds so different, yet alike.

Joe knew with sudden frightening clarity what he'd been fighting and denying to himself for days now.

He wanted.

Ronnie St. John.

Permanently.

As in "till death do us part."

He wanted to make love to her, to possess her, to own her heart as completely as she owned his. He wanted to see her eyes widen in pleasure, hear her cry his name as he filled her, totally, absolutely, in a perfect act of total and binding love.

For the first time in his life, Joe understood the concept

of happily ever after. It was a promise he'd never allowed himself before, an impossible rank he'd never thought to achieve.

But it was right there, staring him in the face whenever Veronica walked into the room. It was in the way she stood, the way she tilted her head very slightly as she listened to him talk, the way she tried so ineffectually to tuck her wild curls back up into her bun, the way her blue eyes danced as she laughed. And it was in the way she was kissing him, as if she, too, wanted to wrap her gorgeous mile-long legs around his waist and feel him inside her forever and ever and ever and *ever*.

But then, as suddenly as the kiss had started, it stopped.

Veronica pulled away, as if she suddenly realized that they were standing in the middle of the hospice chapel, surrounded by stained glass and soothing dark wood and candles, with a FInCOM agent watching them from the doorway. A nun knelt quietly before the altar. They'd been standing there, kissing, in front of a *nun*, for crying out loud....

Veronica's cheeks flushed pink as Joe looked into her eyes, trying to see what she was thinking. Was this just another "mistake"? Or was this simply a more emotional thank-you? Or was it more than that? Please, God, he wanted it to be more. He wanted it to mean she was feeling all of the things that he felt. But they weren't alone, and he couldn't ask. He couldn't even speak. All he could do was hope.

She looked away from him, the expression in her eyes unreadable as she murmured an apology.

An apology. Mistakes and accidents required apologies.

Joe's heart sank as the FInCOM agents quickly led them both back to the waiting limos. And when Kevin Laughton hustled Veronica into a different limousine and she didn't even glance in Joe's direction before getting inside, his heart shattered.

He had his answer. That kiss had been another mistake.

Joe was quiet on the charter flight to Boston. Even his friends from the Alpha Squad knew enough to stay away from him.

Veronica slipped into the seat next to his, and he glanced up, his eyes wary.

"Are you all right?" she asked quietly.

He smiled tightly. "Why wouldn't I be all right?"

Veronica wasn't sure how to answer that question. Because you just spent time with a dying child. Because you talked to her and you didn't try to pretend that she had a future, that she wasn't dying. Because it hurts like hell to know that there's nothing you or anyone else can do for that little girl, except make her smile a few more times....

And because you kissed me as if your world were crumbling beneath your very feet, and when I pulled away, you looked at me as if I were ripping the heart from your chest....

Joe shook his head. "You know, that's the problem when big, mean guys like me show we actually have a soul," he complained. "Everyone gets all worried, like, he lost it once, now he's gonna burst into tears every time someone says 'Boo.' Well, forget about it. I'm fine."

Veronica nodded, not daring to comment, certainly not daring to mention the kiss. Not yet. They sat for a moment in silence, and then she turned back to look at him. "I had no idea you spoke French," she said, tackling a much safer subject, hoping he'd be the one to bring up the topic of the kiss they'd shared. "*And* Russian?"

Joe shrugged. "I'm a language specialist," he said, shortly. "It's no big deal."

"How many languages do you speak?"

"Eight," he said.

"Eight," Veronica repeated. The way he said it, it was nothing. She spoke English and French and a very small bit of Spanish, and *that* hadn't been nothing. In fact, it had been a great deal of work.

"Someone in the team has to be able to communicate with the locals," he said, as if that explained everything. His SEAL Team needed him to speak eight different languages, so he'd learned eight different languages.

"What else do you specialize in?" she asked.

Joe shrugged. "The usual SEAL tricks."

"Balancing beach balls on your nose and barking like a dog?"

He finally smiled. "Not quite," he said.

"I assume some kind of swimming is involved," Veronica said. "Or else you wouldn't be called SEALs."

"Yeah, swimming," he said. "And scuba diving. Skydiving. Parasailing." He started ticking the list off on his fingers. "Explosives, underwater and on land. Weapons and other high-tech war toys. Martial arts and some less conventional hand-to-hand techniques. Computers. Locks. Alarm systems. And so on."

"Admiral Forrest said you were a sharpshooter," Veronica said. "An expert marksman."

"Everyone in SEAL Team Ten is," he replied, shrugging it off.

"Besides languages, what else do *you* specialize in?" Veronica asked.

He gazed at her for several long seconds. "I know a little more than the other guys when it comes to the high-tech war toys," he finally said. "I'm also a classified expert in jungle, desert and arctic survival. You know about the languages and my…ability to mimic. Comes in handy at times.

I can fly any type of aircraft, from a chopper to a Stealth."
He smiled, but it lacked the wattage of his usual grins.
"Hell, I could probably handle the space shuttle if I had to.
And I'm an expert mechanic. I could fix it if it breaks.
There's some other stuff that you don't want to know, and
some that I can't tell you."

Veronica nodded slowly. Admiral Forrest had told her
much of this before, but she hadn't believed it. She probably still wouldn't believe it if she hadn't heard Joe speaking
perfect French. He could do all those incredible things, superhuman things, and yet it was his humanity—his compassion and kindness for a dying child—that had moved her
the most. Moved her profoundly.

She looked down at her hands, folded nervously in her
lap. "Joe, about this morning," she started to say.

"It's okay, Ronnie. You can forget about it," he interrupted, knowing that she was talking about their kiss. His
eyes were guarded as he glanced at her again. He looked
away, out the window of the jet. "It was…something we
both needed right then. But, it…didn't mean anything,
and I know you're not going to let it happen again. No more
mistakes, right? So we don't need to talk about it. In fact,
I'd rather *not* talk about it."

"But…"

"Please," he said, turning to look at her again.

It didn't mean anything. His words suddenly penetrated,
and Veronica stared at him, her mouth slightly open. She
closed her mouth, and looked back down at her hands.

She sat there in silence, afraid to move, afraid to breathe,
afraid to *think*, because she was afraid of what she'd feel.

It didn't mean anything.

That kiss had been more than a kiss. It had been an ex-
change of emotions, a joining of souls. It had been filled
with feelings she didn't want to feel, powerful feelings for

a man who scared her more than she wanted to admit. A man who specialized in making war. A man who risked his life as a matter of course. A man she'd tried to keep her distance from. Tried and failed.

She'd kissed him. In *public*. And he thought it didn't *mean* anything?

The seat-belt light flashed on, and the pilot's voice came over the loudspeaker.

"We're approaching Boston. Please return to your seats."

Joe stared out the window as if he'd never seen Boston before, as if the aerial view was infinitely more interesting than anything he could see inside the jet.

Veronica forced her voice to sound even and controlled. "We'll be arriving in Boston in a few minutes," she said. Joe lifted his head in acknowledgment, but still didn't look in her direction. "From the airport, it's only about a fifteen-minute drive downtown to the hotel where the charity luncheon is being held. Your speech will be on a TelePrompTer. It'll be brief and all you'll have to do is read it.

"This evening, there's a private party on Beacon Hill," she said, wishing she felt as cool and detached as she sounded. Wishing she didn't feel like crying. *It didn't mean anything*. "The host and hostess are friends of Wila's. And mine. So I won't be in the surveillance van tonight."

He turned and frowned at her, his dark eyes piercing. "What? Why not?"

"Ambassador Freder will be in the van," Veronica said, purposely not meeting the intensity of Joe's gaze. "I'll be attending my friends' party. There'll be virtually no risk for you. Consider this another one of Tedric's obligations that couldn't be gotten out of."

She could feel him watching her, giving her a long, measuring look. "There's never no risk," he said. "I'd feel much better if you were in the van."

"We won't stay long," she said, glancing up at him.

"Just long enough to get shot, maybe, huh?" Joe said. He forced a smile. "Relax, Ronnie, I was kidding."

"I don't think getting shot is ever funny," Veronica said tightly.

"Sorry," he said. God, she was strung as tight as he was. Probably the tension from worrying about his reaction to this morning's kiss. No doubt the relief hadn't set in yet.

Sitting next to her like this was torture. Joe jerked his thumb toward the window. "It's been a while since I've been in New England," he said. "Mind if I...?"

Veronica shook her head. "No, that's... Go right ahead and..."

He'd already turned to look out the window.

She'd been dismissed.

Rather than stare at the back of Joe's head, agonizing over his impersonal words, Veronica ignored the seat-belt sign and stood, moving toward the front of the plane where there were several empty seats.

It didn't mean anything.

Maybe not to Joe, but that kiss *had* meant something to Veronica.

It meant *she'd* been a real fool.

Chapter Fourteen

Salustiano Vargas, the former right hand of the man known by most of the world only as Diosdado, stared at the telephone in his cheap motel room as it rang. It was hotter than hell in there and the air conditioner chugged away to no avail.

He had told no one, *no one*, where he would be staying. Still, he knew damn well who was on the other end of the line. There was nowhere he could run where Diosdado couldn't find him.

He picked it up after the seventeenth ring, unable to stand it any longer. "Yes?"

Diosdado said only one word. "When?"

"Soon," Vargas replied, closing his eyes. "You have my word."

"Good." The line was cut without a goodbye.

Vargas sat in the heat for several moments, not moving. It truly *was* hotter than hell in this cheap room.

When he stood, it took him only a few minutes to pack

up his things. He carried his suitcase to his rented car and headed across town—toward a fancy, expensive resort. He couldn't afford to stay there, but he would put it on his credit card. He wanted luxury. He wanted clean sheets, a firm bed. He wanted room service and a view of a sparkling swimming pool with young girls lounging around it. He wanted the cool, sweet, fresh air of a fancy hotel room.

He didn't want hell. He'd be there soon enough.

As the applause died down, Joe smiled in the direction of the TV news cameras. "Good afternoon," he said. "It is an honor and a pleasure to be here today."

Veronica couldn't concentrate on his words. All her attention was on Blue and Cowboy and Harvard's voices as they kept a constant lookout for danger.

This was the perfect setting for an assassination attempt. There were TV cameras here from every network, including cable news, and the event was political—a hundred-dollars-a-plate fund-raiser for a well-known senator's reelection campaign.

But if the terrorists were going to try to shoot the prince—Joe—they hadn't set up in any of the obvious vantage points. If they were here, they were in with the crowd, sitting in the rows of banquet tables.

FInCOM agents were everywhere. Veronica could see them on her video screens, their eyes sweeping the crowd, watchful for any sign of danger or trouble.

Please, Lord, protect Joe and keep him safe—

There was a sudden commotion at one of the tables in the back, and Veronica's heart lodged in her throat.

She could hear the SEALs shouting and see the FInCOM agents running, all converging on one table, and one man.

"I have my rights!" the man was shouting as he was wrestled to the floor. "I've done nothing wrong! I'm a Vietnam veteran and I want to know—"

Noise erupted as people tried to get away from the commotion, and the FInCOM agents tried to get the man out of the room. And Joe… Joe was still standing at the podium, watching. Why didn't he get down, out of harm's way?

"Joe," Veronica said into her microphone. "Take cover!" But he didn't move.

"Joe!" she said again. "Damn it, get down!"

He wasn't listening. He was watching as the man was dragged toward the door.

"Wait," he said sharply, his commanding voice echoing over the PA system, cutting through hubbub, through the sound of eight hundred voices all talking at once. "I said, *wait!*"

Blue froze. They all froze—the FInCOM agents and their prisoner, looking up toward Joe. A hush fell over the crowd.

"Is he armed?" Joe asked, more quietly now.

Blue shook his head. "No, sir."

"I only wanted to ask a question, Your Highness," the man called out, his voice ringing clearly across the room.

Veronica sat on the edge of her seat, watching. She could see the TV cameras catching every bit of the drama.

"He only wanted to ask a question," Joe repeated mildly. He turned to Kevin Laughton, who now stood on the stage next to him. "Has it become illegal in this country to ask a question?"

"No, sir," Laughton said. "But—"

Joe turned pointedly away from Laughton. "He would like to ask a question," he said to the watching crowd, "and I would like to *hear* his question, if the rest of you don't mind…?"

Someone started to clap, and after a brief smattering of applause, Joe bowed his head to the man.

"The question I wanted to ask you, Prince Tedric," the man said in his clear voice, "and the question I want to ask *all* of you," he added, addressing the entire crowd, "is how can you sit here in good conscience, spending so much money for one meal, when right next door a homeless shelter and soup kitchen for Vietnam veterans is about to be shut down from lack of funding?"

It was so quiet in the room, a pin could have been heard falling on the floor.

Joe didn't answer at first. He let the question sit, filling the air, surrounding all the luncheon guests.

"What is your name?" Joe asked the man.

"Tony Pope, sir," the man said. "Sergeant Tony Pope, U.S. Marines, retired."

"You served in Vietnam, Sergeant?" Joe asked.

Pope nodded. "Yes, sir."

Joe looked at Blue and the FInCOM agents who were still holding Pope's arms. "I think you can release him," he said. "I think we've determined he's not out for blood."

"Thank you, sir." Pope straightened his jacket and tie.

He was a good-looking man, Veronica realized, with a neatly trimmed goatee and mustache. His suit was well-tailored, if rather worn and fraying in spots. He held himself proudly, standing tall, with his shoulders back and head high.

"Do you run this homeless shelter, Sergeant Pope?" Joe asked.

"Yes, sir," Pope replied. "The Boylston Street Shelter. For ten years, sir." His mouth tightened. "We've had some tough times, but never like this. The few grants we had left ran out, and it'll be six months before we stand a chance of getting any additional funding. And now the city says we need to make repairs to the facility by the end of the month—Friday—or our site's condemned. We barely have enough cash to feed our residents, let alone make the kind of repairs they're demanding. To be bluntly honest, sir, the Vietnam vets that live at Boylston Street Shelter are getting screwed—again."

"How many men use your facility?" Joe asked quietly.

"Daily we average around two hundred and fifty," the man replied. "These are men who have nowhere else to go—no food, no place but the street to sleep."

Joe was silent.

"Our yearly overhead cost is twenty thousand dollars," Tony Pope said. He looked around the room. "That's what two hundred of you are paying right now, for one *single* meal."

"Is the Boylston Street Shelter serving lunch today?" Joe asked.

"Today and every day," Pope said. "Until they nail our doors shut."

"Do you mind if I come take a look?" Joe asked.

If Pope was surprised, he hid it well. "I'd be honored."

"No way," Veronica heard Kevin Laughton say vehemently. "Absolutely no way."

"Joe, what are you doing?" she asked. "You can't leave the building, it's not safe."

But Joe had already jumped down, off the stage, and was striding between the tables, toward Sgt. Tony Pope, U.S.M.C., retired.

As Veronica watched, Pope led Joe—surrounded by FIn-COM agents and his three SEALs—out of the room. The TV news cameras and reporters scrambled after them.

The shelter was, quite literally, right next door to the hotel. Once inside, Pope gave Joe—and the camera crews—a tour of his modest facility, from the cafeteria to the kitchen. He pointed out the holes in the roof and the other parts of the building that needed repairs. He introduced Joe to many of the longtime residents and workers.

Joe addressed them by rank, even the grungiest, rag-clad

winos, and spoke to them all with the utmost respect and courtesy.

And as Joe was leaving, he slipped the jeweled ring from his finger and handed it to Tony Pope. "Fix your roof," he said.

Tears sprang to the older man's eyes. "Your Highness," he said. "You've already given us so much." He gestured to the TV cameras. "The publicity alone is priceless."

"You need some quick cash, and I have one ring too many," Joe said. "The solution is so obvious. So simple." He smiled into the TV news cameras. "Just like my friend Cindy says.'"

"Oh, Joe, that ring's not yours to give away," Veronica breathed, knowing that she would pay for the ring herself, if she had to.

The final scene in the evening news report showed all of the men in the Boylston Street Shelter sharply saluting Prince Tedric as he left the building.

"Sergeant Tony Pope asks that contributions be sent directly to the Boylston Street Shelter," the news anchor said, "at 994—"

The phone rang, and Veronica pushed the Mute button as she answered it.

"Did you see it?" It was Henri Freder, the Ustanzian ambassador. "Did you see the news? It's not just a local story, it's being run nationally, *and* by the cable network."

"I saw it," Veronica said.

"Gold," Freder said. "Pure, solid gold."

"I know that ring was valuable, sir," Veronica started to say. "But—"

"Not the ring," Freder enthused. "Prince Tedric's image! Absolutely golden! He is America's newest hero. Everyone *loves* him. We couldn't have done it better if we'd tried. I've got to go, my other phone is ringing—"

Veronica stared at the disconnected telephone and slowly hung up the receiver. Everyone loved Prince Tedric—who was really a sailor named Joe, and not a real prince at all.

Or was he?

He was more of a prince than Tedric had ever been.

Now, because of Joe, everyone loved Prince Tedric. Except Veronica. She was falling in love with a prince named Joe.

Veronica had two hours to rest before the party. She lay down on the bed and stared at the ceiling, trying not to let the words Joe had spoken on the plane echo in her mind.

The kiss they'd shared. *It didn't mean anything.*

She was in love with a man who had told her, on more than one occasion, that the best she could hope for with him was a casual sexual relationship. He'd told her that the kisses they'd shared meant nothing to him.

He *did* desire her, though.

Veronica knew that from looking into his eyes. She knew it, too, from the way he'd kissed her in the chapel at Saint Mary's. If they'd been alone, it wouldn't have taken much for that one, single kiss to escalate into lovemaking.

But he didn't love her.

So now what? Was she going to just sit around loving Joe from a distance until the terrorists were caught, until he went back to SEAL Team Ten's temporary base in California? Or was she going to do something foolish, like make love to the man, stupidly hoping that the physical act would magically make him fall in love with her, too?

It would never happen. He would have all he'd ever wanted from her—sex. And she would have a broken heart.

A single tear slid down the side of her face and lodged rather uncomfortably in her ear. Perfect. She was now one-hundred-percent pitiable and pathetic.

The telephone rang, and Veronica rolled over and looked at it. She contemplated letting the front desk take a message, but after three rings, she finally picked it up. She wasn't going to get any sleep anyway.

"Veronica St. John," she said on a sigh.

"Hey."

It was Joe.

Veronica sat up, hastily wiping the moisture from her face, as if he would somehow be able to tell she'd been crying. She hadn't expected the caller to be Joe. Not in a million years. Not after their dreadful conversation on the plane.

"Are you awake?" he asked.

"I am now," she said.

"Oh, damn," he said, concern tingeing his voice. "Did I really wake you?"

"No, no," she said. "I was just... No."

"Well, I won't take too much of your time," Joe said. His husky voice sounded slightly stiff and unnatural. "I just wanted to tell you that if you get any flak about me giving away that ring of Tedric's—"

"It's all right," Veronica interrupted. "The ambassador called and—"

"I just wanted to let you know that I'll pay for it," Joe said. "I don't know what I was thinking—giving away something that didn't belong to me. But—"

"It's all taken care of," Veronica said.

"It is?"

"Your popularity rating is apparently through the roof," she told him. "I think the Ustanzian ambassador is considering having you knighted or perhaps made into a saint."

Joe laughed. "I can see it now. Joe, the patron saint of celebrity impersonators."

"Don't you mean, the patron saint of dying children and

struggling causes?" Veronica said softly. "You know, Joe, you never fail to surprise me."

"That makes two of us," he muttered.

"What?"

"Nothing. I should go—.""

"You really are softhearted, aren't you?" Veronica asked.

"Honey, I'm not soft anywhere." She could almost see him bristle.

"I didn't mean that as an insult," she said.

"Look, I just have a problem with the way this country treats war veterans, all right?" he said. "I'm tired of seeing good men, soldiers and sailors who risked their lives fighting for this country, being forced to live in the lousy gutter."

Veronica pushed her hair from her face, suddenly understanding. This was personal. This had something to do with that old sailor Joe had known when he was a child. What was his name…? "Frank O'Riley," she said, hardly realizing she'd spoken aloud.

Joe was silent for several long seconds. "Yeah," he finally said. "Old Man O'Riley went on a binge and lost his job. Got himself evicted. It damn near killed him to think of losing his garden, and he sobered up, but it was too late. No one helped him. He was a war hero, and he was out on the street in the goddammed middle of the goddammed winter."

"And because of that, he died," Veronica guessed correctly.

"He caught pneumonia." Joe's voice was curiously flat, and she knew by his lack of inflection and emotion that Frank O'Riley's death *still* hurt him deeply.

"I'm sorry," Veronica murmured.

Joe was quiet again for a moment. Then he sighed. "What I don't get, is how the hell our armed forces can send our guys to fight a war without really preparing them. And if we *are* going to send out these…*kids*, then we shouldn't be so damned surprised when they come home and fall apart. And then—and this is *real* genius—we try to sweep the pieces under the rug so no one will see. Nice move, huh?"

"Those are pretty tough words for someone who specializes in making war," Veronica said.

"I'm not suggesting we demilitarize," Joe said. "I think that would be a mistake. No, I just think the government should take responsibility for the veterans."

"But if there were no wars, there'd be no veterans. If we spent money on diplomatic relations rather than guns and—"

"Right," Joe said. "But there are enough bad guys in the world that wouldn't hesitate to step forward and kick some butt if our country couldn't defend itself. I mean, sure we could hand out flowers and love beads, but we'd get back a round of machine-gun fire in our gut. There are some mean bastards out there, Ronnie, and they don't want to play nice. We need to be as tough and as mean as they are."

"And that's where *you* come in," Veronica said. "Mr. Tough and Mean. Ready to fight whatever war pops up."

"I'm a fighter," Joe stated quietly. "I've been prepared for war my entire life." He laughed softly, his voice suddenly so intimate and low in her ear. "It's the other surprises in life that knock me over."

"You are so utterly un-knock-overable." Veronica wished the same were true of herself.

"You're wrong," Joe countered. "The past few days, I can barely remember what solid ground feels like."

Veronica was quiet. She could hear Joe breathing on the other end of the phone line, three doors down the hotel corridor. "Cindy?" she asked softly. He didn't say a word. "I'm sorry," she added. "I should have prepared you more for—"

"Not Cindy," he said. "I mean, going to see her *was* tough, but…I was talking about you."

Veronica felt all the air leave her lungs. "Me?" She couldn't speak in more than a whisper.

"God, would you look at the time? I gotta go."

"Joe, what—"

"No, Ronnie, I don't know why I said that. I'm just asking for trouble and—" He broke off, swearing softly.

"But—"

"Do yourself a favor tonight, babe," Joe said brusquely. "Stay the hell away from me, okay?"

The phone line was disconnected with a click.

Veronica sat on the bed for a long time, holding the receiver against her chest. Was it possible…? Could it be…? Did Joe think *she* was the one who didn't want any kind of relationship?

What was it that he'd said on the plane…? About the kiss they'd shared… *It didn't mean anything, and I know you're not going to let it happen again.*

You're not going to let it happen again.

Not *we. You.* Meaning Veronica. Meaning…what? That she was the one who was preventing their relationship from growing?

The telephone began to emit a series of piercing tones, and Veronica quickly dropped the receiver into the cradle.

If Joe really thought she didn't want a relationship with him, then she was going to have to set him straight.

Veronica stood and crossed to the closet, her nap forgotten. She looked quickly through her clothes, glancing only briefly at the rather staid dress she'd intended to wear to the party tonight. That dress wouldn't do. It wouldn't do at all….

Chapter Fifteen

Joe stood in the marble-tiled front hallway of Armand and Talandra Perrault's enormous Beacon Hill town house, chatting easily in French with the couple who were the host and hostess of tonight's party.

Armand Perrault was a charming and gracious silver-haired Frenchman who'd retired a millionaire from his import-export business. His wife, Talandra, was a tall, beautiful young black woman with a rich, infectious laugh.

Talandra had known Veronica from college. Apparently they'd been roommates and good friends. They'd even gone on vacations together—that was how Talandra had met Wila Cortere, Joe's supposed sister.

God, at times like this, Joe felt like such a liar.

"Where *is* Véronique, Your Highness?" Talandra asked him.

He fought the temptation to shrug. "She wasn't ready to leave the hotel when I was," he said instead in Tedric's royal accent. "I'm sure she'll be here soon."

Ambassador Freder was in the surveillance van, sitting in Veronica's seat, ready to provide names and facts and any other information Joe might need.

Damn, how he wished it was Veronica whispering in his ear. Even though this party was not public and therefore technically a low risk, Joe was on edge. He *liked* knowing that Veronica was safely tucked away in the van, out of danger. Tonight, he was going to spend all of his time wondering where she was, and praying that she was safe.

Damn, he hated not knowing where she was. Where *was* that other limousine?

"May I get you another glass of champagne?" Talandra asked.

Joe shook his head. "No, thank you."

He could feel Talandra's dark brown eyes studying him. "You're not as Wila and Véronique described you," she said.

"No?" Joe's gaze strayed back to the front door as several FInCOM agents pulled it open.

Please, God, let it be her...

The woman who came in the door was a redhead, but there was no way on God's earth it could be Veronica, wearing a dress that exposed so much skin and—

Hot *damn!*

It *was* her. It *was* Veronica.

Over his earphone, Joe could hear Cowboy. "Whoo-ee, boss, babe alert at eleven o'clock!"

Sweet God! Veronica looked...out of this world. The dress she was wearing was black and long, made of a soft silky fabric that clung to her every curve. Two triangles of black barely covered her breasts, and were held up by two thin strips of fabric that crossed her shoulders and met between her shoulder blades, at the cutaway back of the dress. There was a slit up the side of the skirt, all the way up to the top of her thigh, that revealed flashes of her incredible legs. Her shoes were black, with high, narrow heels that were a polar opposite to the clunky-heeled pumps she normally wore.

She was wearing her hair up, piled almost haphazardly on top of her head, with stray curls exploding around her face.

"Tell me, Your Excellency, does Véronique know how you feel?" Talandra whispered into his ear.

Startled, he glanced at her. "Excuse me?"

She just smiled knowingly and crossed the room toward Veronica.

"Yeah, Your Mightiness," Harvard said over Joe's earphone as Joe watched Veronica greet her old friend with a warm hug and kiss. "You might want to keep that royal tongue *inside* your royal mouth, do you copy that?"

Joe couldn't see Cowboy or Harvard, but he knew that wherever they were, they could see him. But what exactly did they see? And what had Talandra seen in his face that made her make that very personal comment?

Was he *that* transparent? Or was this just the way being in love was? Was it impossible to hide? And if so, could Veronica see it just as easily? If so, he was in big trouble here.

Veronica turned her head, about to glance in his direction, and he abruptly turned away. He'd have to stay far, far away from her. He'd already revealed way too much this afternoon, when he'd talked to her on the phone. And damn it, he was trying hard *not* to be in love with her. How tough could it be? After all, he'd spent nearly his entire life not in love with Veronica. It shouldn't be too difficult to get back to that state.

What was love, anyway, but a mutated form of lust? And he'd easily walked away from women he'd lusted after before. Why, then, did his legs feel as if they were caught in molasses when he tried to walk away from Veronica?

Because love *wasn't* lust, and love *wasn't* something a

man could turn off and on like a faucet. *And* he was crazy in love with this woman, no matter that he tried to convince himself otherwise.

And God, if she found out, her gentle pity would kill him.

"Hell, boss," Cowboy said. "She's heading straight toward you, and you're running *away?*"

"You've got it backward, Cat," Harvard chimed in. "A woman like that walks in your direction, you stand very, *very* still."

Blue's south-of-the-Mason-Dixon-Line accent made his voice sound gentle over Joe's earphone, but his words were anything but. "You boys gonna enjoy explaining to Admiral Forrest how you got Joe Cat killed while you were watchin' women instead of watchin' for T's?"

Cowboy and Harvard were noticeably silent as Joe moved around the corner into an enormous room with a hardwood floor.

It was the ballroom—not that he'd ever been in a ballroom in a private house before. But it was pretty damn unmistakable. A jazz trio was playing in one corner, the furniture was placed around the edges of the room and people were out in the middle of the floor, dancing. This had to be the ballroom. It sure as hell wasn't the bathroom or the kitchen.

Joe headed for a small bar set up in the far corner, across from the band. The bartender greeted him with a bow.

"Your Highness," the young man said. "What can I get for you?"

Whiskey, straight up. "Better make it a ginger ale," Joe said instead. "Easy on the ice."

"I'll have the same," said a familiar voice behind him. It was Veronica.

Joe didn't want to turn around. Looking at her from a distance had been hard enough. Up close, that dress just might have the power to do him in.

He closed his eyes briefly, imagining himself falling to his knees in front of her, begging her to…what? To marry him? Yeah, right. Dream on, Catalanotto.

He forced a smile and made himself turn. "Ms. St. John," he said, greeting her formally.

She smiled up at him. Light gleamed off her reddish gold hair, and her eyes seemed to sparkle and dance. She was unbelievably beautiful. Joe couldn't imagine that at one time he'd thought her less than gorgeous.

She lifted her hand, and he took it automatically, bringing it halfway to his lips before he realized what he was doing. God Almighty, all those hands he'd pretended to kiss over the past few days… But this time, he wasn't going to have to pretend. He brought Veronica's hand to his mouth and brushed his lips lightly across her delicate knuckles.

He heard her soft intake of breath, and when he glanced up, he could see that her smile had faded. Her blue eyes were enormous, but she didn't pull her hand away.

Joe stood there, like an idiot, staring into eyes the color of the Caribbean Sea. Her gaze flickered down to his lips and then farther, to the pin he wore in his lapel—the pin that concealed the microphone that would broadcast everything they said to the surveillance truck, the FInCOM agents and the SEALs.

Joe heard only silence over his earphone, and he knew they were all listening. All of them. Listening intently.

"How are you, Your Highness?" Veronica asked, her voice cool and controlled.

Joe found his own voice. "I'm well, thanks," he said. Damn, he sounded hoarse, and not an awful lot like Prince Tedric. He cleared his throat, then moistened his dry lips, and realized that Veronica's eyes followed the movement of his tongue. God, was it possible that she wanted to kiss him…?

Her eyes met his, and something flamed—something

hot, something molten, something that seared him to his very soul, something that made his already dry mouth turn into something resembling the floor of Death Valley.

Veronica gently disengaged her hand from his and reached to take one of the glasses of ginger ale from the bar. "Have you met my friend Talandra?" she asked him.

"Yeah," Joe said, catching himself and correcting himself by saying, "Yes. Yes, I have." He concentrated on doing the Ustanzian accent. But as he watched, she took a delicate sip of her soda and all he could think about were her lips. And the soft curves of her creamy skin, and of her breasts, exposed by the fabulous design of that dress. "She seems…nice."

Their eyes met, and again, he was hit by a wave of heat so powerful it nearly knocked him over.

Veronica nodded politely. "Yes, she is."

What kind of game was this?

She turned to watch the dancers, and her arm brushed against his. She smiled an apology and moved slightly away. But when it happened again, Joe knew damn well it was no accident. At least he hoped it was no accident. His pulse began to race with the implications.

"I love to dance," she said, glancing at him.

Oh yeah, he knew that. He'd seen her dance. It hadn't been like this—all stiff and polite and formal. When she'd danced, she'd moved with a sensuality and abandon that would've shocked the hell out of half of the people in this room.

Veronica tucked her hand into the crook of his elbow, and Joe's heart began to pound.

She was coming on to him.

Not in any way that the video cameras and microphones could pick up, but she *was* coming on to him. It all made sense. The dress, the shoes, the fire she was letting him see in her eyes…

He couldn't figure out why the sudden change of heart.

Joe opened his mouth to speak, but quickly shut it. What could he ask her? What could he say? Certainly nothing that he wanted broadcast over the entire security network.

Instead, he put his hand over hers, covering her cool fingers with his. He gently stroked her smooth skin with his thumb.

Veronica turned to look up at him, and Joe could see her desire in her eyes. No doubt about it—she was letting him see it. She wanted him, and she wanted him to know it.

She smiled then—a beautiful, tremulous smile that brought his heart up into his throat. He wanted to kiss her so badly, he had to clench his teeth to keep from leaning toward her and caressing her lips with his own.

"Your Highness," she said very softly, as if she couldn't find the air to do more than whisper, "may I have this dance?"

He could have her in his arms, right here, right now. Damn, wouldn't that be heaven?

But then, from across the room, came an earsplitting crash.

Joe reacted, pulling Veronica into his arms and shielding her with his body. What the hell was he thinking? What was he doing, standing here next to her like this, as if he weren't the target of assassins? She was close enough so that bullets meant for him could end her life in the beat of a heart.

"It's all right, Cat." He heard Blue's voice over his earphone. "It's cool. Someone dropped a glass. We do not have a situation. Repeat, there is *no* situation."

Joe pulled Veronica in even closer for a second, closing his eyes and pressing her tightly against him before he released her. Adrenaline was flooding his system and his entire body seemed to vibrate. Jesus, Mary and Joseph, he'd never been so scared....

Veronica touched his arm. "I guess we're all on edge," she said with a small smile. "Are you all right?"

Joe looked wound tighter than a drum. There was a wildness in his eyes she'd never seen before and his hand actually trembled as he pushed his hair back, off his face.

"No," he said curtly, not bothering to disguise his voice with Tedric's odd accent. "No, I'm not all right. Ronnie, I need you to stay the hell away from me."

Veronica felt her smile fade. "I thought we were going to...dance."

Joe let out a short burst of exasperated air. "No way," he said. "Absolutely not. No dancing."

She looked down at the floor. "I see."

As Joe watched, Veronica turned and started to walk away, unable to disguise the flash of hurt in her eyes. My God. She thought he was rejecting her. He tried to catch her arm, to stop her, but she was moving faster now.

"No, you *don't* see," he called after her in a low voice.

But she didn't stop walking. Joe started to follow.

Damn! Short of breaking into a sprint, there was no way he could catch her. And although shouting "Yo, Ronnie!" was something Joe Catalanotto might not have hesitated to do even at a posh society party, Prince Tedric was not prone to raising his voice in public.

When Joe rounded the corner into the front hall, Veronica was nowhere in sight. Damn! Double damn! How could he follow her if he didn't know where she went?

He headed toward the living room and the spacious kitchen beyond, hearing the unmistakable sound of Talandra's laughter from that direction.

But Talandra stood near a large stone fireplace, sipping champagne and talking with a group of elegantly dressed women—none of whom were Veronica. "Oh, here's the prince now," Talandra said, smiling at Joe.

There was nothing he could do but go and greet the group of ladies as Talandra made introductions.

"Code Red," came Cowboy's voice, loud and clear over Joe's earphone. "We have an open window on the third floor! Repeat, open window, third floor. Possible break-in. Joe, get the *hell* out of here. Double time! This is not a drill. Repeat. This is *not* a drill!"

Everything switched into slow motion.

Joe had to get out of here. He had to get away from these ladies—God help them all if a terrorist burst into the room firing a submachine gun.

"Get down!" he shouted at the women. "Get to cover!"

Talandra was the first to react. Of course, she'd probably been warned about an assassination attempt. She led the entire group of ladies down a hallway to the back of the house.

God, all it would take was one man and one weapon and— Jesus, Mary and Joseph! Ronnie was somewhere in this house.

"Blue, where's Ronnie?" Joe said into his mike, heading for the kitchen door as he pulled out the sidearm he kept hidden under his jacket. FInCOM had ordered he remain unarmed. He'd smiled and said nothing. He was damn glad now that he'd ignored that order. If someone was going to start shooting at him, damn it, he was going to shoot back. "Blue, I need you to find Ronnie!"

"I don't see her, Cat," his XO reported, his gentle drawl replaced by a staccato stream of nearly accentless words. "But I'm looking. Get your own butt under cover!"

"Not till I know she's safe," Joe retorted as he burst through the kitchen door. A man in a chef's hat looked up at him in shock, his eyes glued to the weapon. "Get down," Joe ordered him. "Or get out. We've got trouble."

The chef scurried for the back door.

A new voice came over the earphone. It was Kevin Laughton, the FInCOM chief. "Veronica St. John's already in a limo, heading back to the hotel. Proceed to the emergency escape vehicle, Lieutenant," he ordered.

"Double-check that info, Alpha Squad," Joe said as he pushed open the pantry door, hard, and went inside, sidearm first. The small storage room was empty.

"Information verified," Harvard's calm voice reported. "Ronnie has left the building. Suggest you do the same, Cat."

Joe was filled with relief. Ronnie was safe. The relief mingled with adrenaline and made him almost light-headed.

"Kitchen's empty and clear," he announced over his mike.

"Move it out, Cat," Cowboy said. "We got this situation under control."

"Are you kidding?" Joe said into his microphone, pushing the door to the living room open an inch. "And leave all the fun to you guys?"

Joe could see about ten FInCOM agents heading toward him. He swore under his breath and stepped back as they came through the door. They surrounded him instantly. West and Freeman were on either side of him, shielding him with their own bodies as they moved him toward the back door.

There was a car idling outside the kitchen, waiting for exactly this type of emergency. The car door was thrown open, and West climbed into the back seat first, pulling Joe behind him. Freeman followed, and before the door was even closed, the driver took off, peeling out down the narrow alleyway and onto the dark city streets.

West and Freeman were breathing hard as they both holstered their weapons. They watched without much surprise as Joe rested his own on his lap.

"You're not supposed to be carrying," West commented.

"Kevin Laughton would throw a hissy fit if he knew," Freeman said. "'Course, he doesn't have to know."

"Imagine Kevin's shock," Joe said, "if he knew that I've got another in my boot and a knife hidden in my belt."

"And probably another weapon hidden somewhere else that you're not telling us about," West said blandly.

"Probably," Joe agreed.

The car was moving faster now, catching green lights at all of the intersections as it headed downtown. Joe took out his earphone—they were out of range. He leaned forward and asked the driver, "Any word on the radio? What's happening back there? Any action?" He hated running away from his squad like this.

The driver shook his head. "The word is it's mostly all clear," he said. "It's an alleged false alarm. One of the party guests claims she opened the window in the third-floor bathroom because she was feeling faint."

Joe sat back in his seat. False alarm. He took a deep breath, trying to clear the nervous energy from his system. His guys were safe. Ronnie was safe. *He* was safe. He holstered his weapon and looked from Freeman to West. "You know, I had no idea you guys were willing to lay it on the line for me."

West looked out one window, Freeman looked out the other. "Just doing our job, sir," West said, sounding bored.

Joe knew better. It was odd, sitting here between two relative strangers—strangers who would have died for him today if they'd had to. It was odd, knowing that they cared.

With a sudden flash, Joe remembered a pair of crystal blue eyes looking at him with enough heat to ignite a rocket engine.

West and Freeman weren't the only ones who cared.

Veronica St. John cared, too.

Chapter Sixteen

Veronica stood at the window, looking out over downtown Boston. With all the city lights reflected in the Charles River, it was lovely. She could see the Esplanade and the Hatch Shell, where the Boston Pops played free concerts in the summer. She could see Back Bay and the Boston Common. And somewhere, down there, hidden by the trees of the common was Beacon Hill, where Talandra lived, and where there was a party going on right this very moment—without her.

She took another sip of her rum and cola, feeling the sweet warmth of the rum spreading through her.

Well, *she'd* certainly made a fool of herself tonight. Again. Veronica could see her wavery reflection in the window. She looked like someone else in this dress. Someone seductive and sexy. Someone who could snap her fingers and have dozens of men come running. Someone who wouldn't give a damn if some sailor didn't want her near him.

She laughed aloud at her foolishness, but her laughter

sounded harsh in the empty hotel suite. She'd gone to this party with every intention of seducing Joe Catalanotto. She'd planned it so perfectly. She'd wear this incredible dress. He would be stunned. They'd dance. She'd dance really close. He would be even more stunned. He would follow her back to the hotel. She'd ask him into her room under the pretense of briefing him for tomorrow. But he'd know better. He'd ask the FInCOM agents to wait outside, and once the hotel-room door closed, he would pull her into his arms and...

It was perfect—except that she'd forgotten one small detail. Her plan would work only if Joe wanted her, too.

She had thought she'd seen desire in his eyes when he looked at her tonight, but obviously, she'd been mistaken.

Veronica took another sip of her drink and turned from the window, unable to bear the silence another minute.

There was a radio attached to the television, and she turned it on. It was set to a soft-rock station—not her favorite kind of music, but she didn't care. Just as long as there was *something* to fill the deadly silence.

She knew she ought to change out of her dress. It was only helping to remind her what a total imbecile she'd been. She looked at herself again in the mirror that hung on the hotel-room wall. The dress was practically indecent. The silky fabric clung to her breasts, broadcasting the fact that she was wearing no bra, and the cut of the dress showed off all kinds of cleavage and skin and curves. Good grief, she might as well have gone topless. *Whatever had possessed her to buy this dress, anyway?* It was like wearing a nightgown in public.

Veronica stared at herself in the mirror. She knew why she had bought the dress. It was to be an unspoken message to Joe. *Here I am. I'm all yours. Come and sweep me off my feet.*

To which he'd responded quite clearly. *Stay the hell away from me*.

She sighed, fighting the tears ready to spring into her eyes. She should change into something more sensible—her flannel nightie, perhaps—instead of standing here, feeling sorry for herself. She wasn't here, in Boston, to be either sexy or romantic. She was here to do her job. She wasn't looking for sex or romance or even friendship, with Joe Catalanotto. She was simply looking to get a job done well. Period, the end.

"You are such a bloody liar," Veronica said aloud to her reflection, her voice thick with disgust.

"You're not talking to me, I hope."

Veronica spun around, nearly spilling her rum and cola down the front of her dress.

Joe.

He was standing no more than three feet away from her, leaning against the wall next to the mirror. He stepped forward and took the drink from her hand.

Veronica's heart was pounding. "What are you doing here?" she gasped. "How did you get in?"

There was no balcony this time. And she was *positive* that the room's single door had been securely locked. But of course, he *had* told her he was an expert at picking locks.

Joe just smiled.

He was still wearing his party clothes. He wore a navy blue military-style jacket that buttoned up both sides of his chest and ended at his trim waist. His pants were made of a khaki-colored fabric that looked soft to the touch. They fit him like a second skin, clinging to his muscular thighs and perfect derriere. They were tucked into a pair of shiny black, knee-high boots. He wore a red sash around his waist, and the splash of color completed the princely picture.

He looked devastatingly, heart-breakingly handsome.

Veronica's stomach flip-flopped. Lord, the way he was smiling at her... But whatever he was doing here, it wasn't personal, she told herself. Joe had made it clear at the party that he wanted her to stay away from him.

As she watched, he set her drink down on the end table next to the sofa and crossed to the windows. He pulled the curtains shut. "I've been wearing my bull's-eye long enough for one day," he said.

Veronica glanced at her watch. It was only nine-thirty. "The Perraults' party was supposed to last until midnight or one o'clock," she said, unable to keep her surprise from sounding in her voice. "You were supposed to stay until at *least* eleven."

Joe shrugged. "We had a little incident."

Veronica took an involuntary step forward, fear propelling her toward him. An *incident?* "Are you all right?"

"It was a false alarm," he said with another of his easy smiles.

He was standing in front of her, relaxed and smiling, absolutely at ease—or so he wanted her to believe. But she knew better. Beneath his feigned calm, he was tense and tight and ready to burst at the seams. He was upset—or he'd been upset.

"Tell me what happened," she said quietly.

He shook his head, no. "I came to get my dance."

She didn't understand. His words didn't seem to make sense. "Your...what?" She looked around the room. This was the first time he'd been in her room at the Boston hotel—how could he have left something behind?

"You asked me to dance," Joe said.

All at once, Veronica understood. He'd come here, to her room, to *dance* with her. She felt her face flush with embarrassment. "You don't have to do this," she said tightly. "I suppose I got a little silly, and—"

"When I told you to stay away from me—"

"It's okay that you didn't want—"

"I didn't want to dance with you, because you're not wearing a bulletproof vest under that dress," Joe said.

Veronica glanced down at her barely covered chest and felt her blush grow even stronger. "Well," she said, trying to sound brisk and businesslike. "Obviously not."

Joe laughed, and she looked up, startled, into the warmth of his eyes.

"God, Ron," he said, holding her gaze. "I didn't even get a chance to tell you how...perfect you look tonight." The warmth turned to pure fire. "You're *gorgeous*," he whispered, moving closer to her, one step at a time.

Veronica closed her eyes. She didn't have the strength to back away. "Don't, Joe," she said quietly.

"You think I didn't *want* to dance with you at that party?" Joe asked. He didn't give her a chance to answer. He touched her, gently cupping her shoulders, and her eyes opened. He slid his hands down to her elbows in the sweetest of caresses. "Lady, tonight I would have sold my soul for one kiss, let alone a chance to hold you in my arms." Gently, he pulled her even closer, clasping her hand in a dance hold. "Like this."

Slowly, he began to dance with her, moving in time to the soft ballad playing over the radio.

Veronica was trapped. She was caught both by his powerful arms and by the heat in his eyes. Her heart was pounding. She'd wanted him to touch her, to hold her, to dance with her, but not this way. Not because he pitied her...

"But I would've sold *my* soul. Not yours." Joe's voice was a husky whisper in her ear as he pulled her even closer. "Never yours, baby. I wasn't about to risk your life for a dance."

Veronica felt her pounding heart miss a beat. What was

he saying? She pulled back to look into his eyes, searching for answers.

"You were in danger just standing next to me," Joe explained. "I should've told you to get lost the minute you walked into that room."

Was he saying that he hadn't wanted to dance with her because he feared for her safety? Dear Lord, if so, then she'd misunderstood his sharp words of warning for a brush-off, for a rejection. When in reality...

"I don't know what I was thinking," Joe said, then shook his head.

In reality, maybe he'd wanted her as badly as she'd wanted him. Veronica felt a burst of hope and happiness so intense, she almost laughed out loud.

"Hell, I *wasn't* thinking," Joe added. "I was... I don't know what I was."

"Stunned?" Veronica supplied. She could smile again, and she smiled almost shyly up at him.

Joe's slow smile turned into a grin. "Yeah. You bet. 'Stunned' about says it all. When you walked into the party, I was totally blown away. And I was thinking with a part of my anatomy that has nothing to do with my brain."

Veronica had to laugh at that. "Oh, really?"

"Yeah," Joe said. His smile grew softer, his eyes gentler. "My heart."

And then he kissed her.

She saw it coming. She saw him lean toward her, felt him lift her chin to meet his mouth. She knew he was going to kiss her. She expected it—she wanted it. But still, the softness of his lips took her by surprise, and the sweetness of his mouth on hers took her breath away.

It was dizzying. The earth seemed to lose all its gravity as he pulled her even closer to him, as he slowly, sensuously, languidly explored her lips with his, as she opened her mouth to him, deepening the kiss.

And still they danced, the thin wool covering his thighs brushing the silk of her dress. The softness of her stomach pressed intimately against the hardness of his unmistakable desire. Her breasts were tight against his powerful chest.

It was heaven. Giving in to her passion, giving up trying to fight it was such an enormous relief. Maybe this was a mistake, but Veronica wasn't going to think about it any-more. At least not right now, not tonight. She was simply going to kiss Joe Catalanotto, and dance with him, and savor every last moment. Every delicious, wonderful, mag-nificent second.

"Yo, Ronnie?" Joe whispered, breaking the kiss.

"Yo, Joe?" she said, still breathless.

He laughed. And kissed her again.

This time it was hotter, harder, stronger. It was still as sweet, but it was laced with a volcanic heat. Veronica knew without a doubt that tonight she was in for the time of her life.

Joe pulled back, breathing hard. "Whoa," he said, free-ing one hand to push his hair back, out of his face. He closed his eyes briefly, took in a deep breath then forced it quickly out. "Ronnie, if you want me to leave, I should go now, because if—"

"I don't want you to leave."

He looked into her eyes. *Really* looked. As if he were searching for the answers to the mysteries of the universe.

Veronica could see his sharp intelligence, his raw, al-most brutal strength, and his gentle tenderness all mixed together in his beautiful deep brown eyes.

"Are you sure?" he asked, his voice a ragged whisper.

Veronica smiled. And kissed him. Lord knew, she'd found the answers to all of her questions in *his* eyes.

"Unh," he said, as she swept her tongue fiercely into his mouth. And then his hands were in her hair, on her throat, on her breasts. He was touching her everywhere, as if he wanted to feel all of her at once and didn't know where to start. But then his hands slid down her back to her derriere, pressing her hips tightly against him, holding her in place as he slanted his head and kissed her even harder.

She opened her legs, taking advantage of the slit up the side of her dress, and she rubbed the inside of her thigh against his. His hand caught her leg, and he pressed her still closer to him.

Joe's mouth slid down to her neck as his hand cupped her breast. The roughness of his callused fingers rasped against the silk as he stroked the hard bud of her nipple.

"Oh, man," Joe breathed between kisses, as he slipped his hand under the fabric of her top, and touched her, really touched her, with nothing between his fingers and her flesh. "For how many days have I been *dying* to touch you like this?"

Veronica's fingers fumbled with the buttons of his jacket. "Probably the same number of days *I've* been dying for you to touch me like that."

He lifted his head, looking into her eyes. "Really?" His gaze was so intense, so serious. "Maybe it was love at first sight, huh?"

Veronica felt her own smile fade as her pulse kicked into overtime. "Love?" she whispered, hardly daring to hope that this incredible man could possibly love her, too.

Joe looked away, down at his hand still cupping her breast. "Love...lust... Whatever." He shrugged and kissed her again.

Veronica tried to hide her disappointment. *Whatever.* Well, all right. "Whatever" was better than not being desired. "Whatever" was what she'd been expecting—what he'd told her to expect from him right from the start.

But she didn't want to think about that now. She didn't want to think about anything but the way he was making her feel as he kissed and caressed her.

Joe pulled back then, and looked into her eyes. Slowly he slid the dress's narrow strap off her right shoulder. As it fell away, the silk covering her breast fell away, too.

And still he gazed into her eyes.

Veronica felt the coolness of the air as it touched her skin. And then she felt Joe, as he lightly ran one finger across the tip of her breast. She felt her body tighten, felt her nipples grow more taut, even more fully aroused.

He held her gaze longer than she would have believed possible before his eyes dropped down to caress the bareness of her breast.

"God," he breathed, moistening his lips with the tip of his tongue. "You're so beautiful."

They were frozen in place as if time had somehow stopped. But time hadn't stopped. Her heart was still beating, and with every beat, every surge of blood through her veins, Veronica wanted him even more.

But still he didn't touch her; at least, no more than another of those light-as-a-feather brushes with one finger. And she wanted him to touch her. She wanted him, so very badly, to touch her.

"If you don't touch me, I'm going to *scream*," she said from between clenched teeth.

Joe's smile turned hot. "Is that a threat or a promise?" he asked.

"Both," she said, lost in the heat of his eyes. She was begging now. "Touch me."

"Where?" he asked, his voice hoarse. "How?"

"My breast, your mouth," she said. "Now. *Please*."

He didn't hesitate. He brought his mouth to her breast and swept his tongue across her sensitive nipple. Veronica cried out, and he drew her into his mouth, pulling hard.

She reached for him, pushing his jacket off his shoulders. The buttons on his shirt were so tiny, so difficult to unfasten. But she wanted his shirt off. She wanted to run her hands against all those incredible muscles in his chest and shoulders and arms. She wanted to feel the satiny smoothness of his skin beneath her fingers.

She could hear her voice moaning her pleasure as Joe suckled and kissed her again and again.

But then he lifted his head and, stopping only to kiss her deeply on the mouth, he gazed into her eyes again. "What else do you want?" he demanded. "Tell me what you want."

"I want this bloody shirt off you," she said, still worrying the buttons.

He reached up with both hands and pulled. Buttons flew everywhere, but the shirt was open. He yanked it off his arms.

Veronica touched his smooth, tanned muscles with the palms of her hands, closing her eyes at the sensation, running her fingers through the curly dark hair on his chest. Oh, yes. He was so beautiful, so solid.

"Tell me what you want," Joe said again. "Come on, Ronnie, tell me where you want me to touch you."

She opened her eyes. "I want you to touch every single inch of me with every single inch of you. I want you and me on that bed in the other room. I want to feel you between my legs, Joe—"

Joe picked her up. He simply swept her effortlessly into his arms and carried her into the bedroom.

Veronica had her hands on the button of his pants before he yanked back the bedcover and laid her on the clean white sheets.

As she unfastened his sash, he found the zipper in the back of her dress. As he peeled her dress down toward her hips, she unzipped his pants and pushed them over his incredible rear end.

Her dress landed with a hiss of silk on the carpet and Joe pulled back, nearly burning her with his eyes as he took her in, lying propped up on her elbows on the bed, wearing only her black lace panties and a pair of thigh-high stockings. Lord, when he looked at her like that, with that fire in his eyes, she felt like the sexiest woman in the world.

She sat up, taking the last of the pins from her hair.

Slowly, he pushed off his shoes and stepped out of his trousers, still watching her.

Veronica was watching him, too. She rolled first one and then the other stocking from her legs as she let herself look at Joe. He was wearing only a pair of white briefs. She'd seen him in running shorts before, shorts that were nearly as brief, that exposed almost as much of his magnificent body. But this time she really let herself look.

His shoulders were broad and solid as rock. His arms were powerful and so very big. She couldn't have even begun to span his biceps with both of her hands, although she wanted rather desperately to try. His chest was wide and covered with thick dark hair. His muscles were clearly defined, and they rippled sensually when he so much as breathed. His stomach was a washboard of ridges and valleys, his hips narrow, his legs as strong as steel.

Yes, when she'd seen him run, although she'd tried not to look, she'd managed to memorize his body in amazing, precise detail, down to the scars on his shoulder and left leg, and the anchor tattoo on his arm.

But tonight there *were* some differences. She let her eyes linger on the enormous bulge straining the front of his briefs.

Veronica looked up to find Joe watching her, a small smile playing across his lips.

"Part of me wants to stand here and just look at you all night," he said.

She glanced down at his arousal, then smiled into his eyes. "Another part of you won't be very happy if you do that."

"Damn straight," he said with a laugh.

"Do I really have to beg you to come over here?" Veronica asked.

"No."

And then he was next to her on the bed and she was in his arms, and Lord, he was kissing her, touching her, running his hands across her body, filling her mouth with his tongue, tangling her legs with his.

It was ecstasy. Veronica had never felt anything remotely like it before. It was the sweetest, purest, most powerful passion she had ever known.

This was love, she thought. This incredible whirlwind of emotions and heightened sensations was love. It carried her higher, to an intellectual and emotional plane she'd never before imagined, and at the same time, it stripped her bare of every ounce of civility she had, leaving her ruled by ferocious passion, enslaved by the burning needs of her body.

She touched him, reaching down between their bodies to press the palm of her hand against his hardness, and when he cried out, she heard herself answer—the primitive call and response between a savage animal and his equally savage mate.

His hands were everywhere and his mouth was everywhere else. His fingers dipped down inside the lace of her panties, and he moaned as he felt her wet heat.

"Yes," Veronica said. It was the only word she seemed able to form with her lips. "Yes."

She tugged at his briefs, pulling him free from their confines, moaning her pleasure at the sensation of him in her hands. He was silky smooth and so hard, and oh…

He sat up, pulling away from her to slide her panties down and off. She sat up, too, following him, kneeling next to him on the bed, reaching for him, unwilling to let him go.

Joe groaned. "Ronnie, baby, I got to get a condom on."

He turned to reach for his pants, now crumpled on the floor, but Veronica was faster. She opened the drawer of the bedside table and took out a small foil package—one of the condoms she'd bought just hours ago when she'd bought the dress. She'd put them in the drawer in hopes of using them precisely this way with precisely this man.

"Whoa," Joe said as she pressed it into his hand. He was surprised that she was prepared. "I guess it's stupid *not* to be ready for anything these days, huh?"

He was just holding the little package, looking at her.

Good Lord, did he actually think she kept these things on hand all the time? Was he imagining a steady stream of male visitors to her room? Veronica took it from him and tore it open. "I bought it for you. For you and me," she said, somehow finding her voice in her need to explain. "I was hoping we'd make love tonight."

She saw the understanding in his eyes. She'd bought it because she'd wanted to make love—to *him*.

Veronica touched him, covering him with her fingers, gazing from that most intimate part of him, to the small ring of latex in her hand. "I'm not sure exactly how this is supposed to work," she said. "It doesn't really look as if it's going to fit, does it?"

She gazed into the heat of his eyes as he took the condom from her. "It'll fit," he said.

"Are you sure?" she asked, her smile turning devilish.

"Maybe I should have bought the extra-large Navy SEAL size."

Joe laughed as he quickly and rather expertly sheathed himself. "Flattery will get you *everything*."

Veronica encircled his neck with her arms, brushing the hard tips of her breasts against his solid chest and her soft stomach against his arousal. "I don't want everything," she breathed into his ear. "I think I already told you precisely what I want."

He kissed her—a long, sweet, slow, deep kiss that made her bones melt and her muscles feel like jelly. Still kissing her, he pulled her onto his lap, so that she was straddling his thighs. Then, taking her hips in his hands, he slowly, so slowly, lifted her up, above him.

Veronica pulled back from Joe's kiss, her eyes open. He began to lower her down, on top of him, and as the very tip of him parted her most intimately, he opened his own eyes, meeting her gaze.

Slowly, impossibly slowly, a fraction of an inch at a time, he lowered her onto him, staring all the while into her eyes.

The muscles in his powerful arms were taut, but the sweat on his upper lip wasn't from physical exertion. He lifted her slowly back up, off him, and then brought her down again, so that he was barely inside her, setting a deliberate and leisurely teasing rhythm.

Veronica moaned. She wanted more. She wanted *all* of him. She tried to shift her weight, to bring herself down more fully on top of him, but his strong arms held her firmly in place. Her moan changed to a cry of pleasure as his mouth latched on to her breast, but still he didn't release her hips.

"Please," she cried, the words ripped from her throat. "Joe, please! I want more!"

He covered her mouth with his, kissing her fiercely as he

arched his body up and pushed her hips down and filled her completely, absolutely, incredibly.

The sound she heard herself make was almost inhuman as he plunged into her, filling her again and again and again. The rhythm was frantic, feverish, and Veronica threw back her head, delirious from the sweet sensations exploding inside her as she found her release. Arrows of pleasure shot through her—straight to her heart.

Joe's fingers stabbed through her hair as he called out her name and she clung to his neck and shoulders. She rode his explosive release, letting his passion carry her higher, even higher, loving the way he held her as if he were never going to let her go.

And then it was over. Joe sank back on the bed, pulling her down along with him.

Veronica could feel his heart beating, hear him breathing, feel his arms still tightly around her. She waited, hoping he would be the first to speak.

But he didn't speak. The silence stretched on and on and on, and through it, Veronica died a thousand times. He was regretting their lovemaking. He was trying to figure out a way to get out of her room with the least amount of embarrassment. He was worrying about the rest of the tour, wondering if she was going to chase after him like a lovesick fool and…

He sighed. And stretched. And nuzzled the side of her face. Veronica turned toward him and he met her lips in a slow, lingering kiss.

"When can we do this again?" he asked, his voice husky in the quiet. He brushed her hair back so he could see her face.

His eyes were half-closed, but she could see traces of the ever-present flame still burning.

He *didn't* regret what they'd just done. How could he, if

he already wanted to know when they'd make love again? She smiled, suddenly feeling ridiculously, foolishly happy. His answering smile was sleepy, and very, *very* content.

"You gonna answer my question?" he asked. His eyes opened slightly wider for a second. "Or is that smile my answer?"

Veronica slowly trailed her fingers down his arm, watching as they followed the contours of his muscles. "Are you in any hurry to leave?" she asked.

His arms tightened around her. "Nope."

"Good."

"Yeah."

Veronica glanced up at him and saw he was watching her. He smiled again, laughing softly as she met his eyes.

"What?" she asked.

"You really want to know?"

She nodded, making a face at him. "Of course. You look at me and laugh. I should say I'd want to know what you were thinking."

"Well, I was thinking, who would've guessed that proper Ms. Veronica St. John is a real screamer in bed."

Veronica laughed, feeling her cheeks heat. "But I'm not," she protested. "I mean, I *don't*... I mean, I never have before.... Made all that...noise, I mean."

"I loved it," Joe said. "And I love it even more, knowing that I'm the only one who makes you do it." His words were teasing, but his eyes were serious. "It's an incredible turn-on, baby." His voice got lower, softer, more intense. "*You're* an incredible turn-on."

"You're embarrassing me," she admitted, pressing her warm cheeks against his shoulder.

"Perfect," he replied, with his wonderful, husky laugh. "I also love it when you blush."

Veronica closed her eyes. He loved what she did, he

loved when she blushed. What she would have given to hear him say that he loved *her*.

"You know what would absolutely kill me?" Joe asked, his voice still low and very, very sexy.

Oh, dear Lord, she could feel him growing inside her. She felt her body respond, felt her pulse start to quicken.

"If you danced for me," Joe said, answering his own question.

Veronica closed her eyes, imagining the nuclear heat that would be generated in the room if she danced for Joe— and only for Joe. She could imagine discarding various articles of clothing until she moved in time to music clad only in the tiniest black panties and the fire from his eyes....

Veronica blushed again. Could she really dance for him that way? Without laughing or feeling foolish?

Joe hugged her tighter. "No pressure," he said quietly. "I only want you to dance for me if you want to. It's just a fantasy, that's all. I thought I'd share it with you. No big deal. Two out of three's not bad."

Veronica lifted her head. "Two out of three...?"

"Fantasies that have come true," Joe said. He smiled. "The first one was making love to you. The second one was making love to you twice in the same night."

"But..."

Joe kissed her sweetly. Then he made his second fantasy come true.

Chapter Seventeen

Chicago, Dallas and Houston were a blur. During the day and sometimes in the evening, Veronica sat in the surveillance van, feeding information to Joe via his earphone, praying that the man she loved wasn't about to be killed in front of her very eyes.

Joe would look into the hidden, miniaturized video cameras and smile—a sweet, hot, secret smile meant only for her.

At night, Joe came to her room. How he got out from under the watchful eyes of the FInCOM agents, Veronica never knew. How he got into her room was also a mystery. She never heard him. She would just look up, and he'd be there, smiling at her, heat in his eyes.

In Dallas, he came carrying barbecued chicken, corn on the cob and a six-pack of beer. He was wearing jeans and T-shirt and an old baseball cap backward on his head. He wouldn't tell her where he got the food and beer, but she had the feeling he'd climbed down the outside of the building to the street below and walked a few blocks over to a restaurant.

They had a picnic on her living-room floor, and made love before they'd finished eating, right there on the rug in front of the sofa.

He always stayed until dawn, holding her close. They sometimes talked all night, sometimes slept, always woke up to make love again. But as the sun began to rise, he would vanish.

Then in Albuquerque, there was another "incident," as Joe called them. Veronica sat in the van, her heart in her throat after one of the FInCOM agents thought he saw a man with a concealed weapon in the crowd outside the TV station where "Tedric" had been interviewed.

The SEALs and the FInCOM agents had leapt into action, ready to protect Joe. They'd hustled him into the limousine and to safety, but Veronica was shaken.

She sat in her hotel room, fighting tears, praying Joe would arrive soon, praying his quicksilver smile would make her forget about the danger he was in, day in and day out, as he stood in for the real prince. But she had to remember that he was no stranger to dangerous situations. His entire life was filled with danger and risk. Even if he survived these particular assassins, it would only be a matter of time before he'd be facing some new danger, some other perhaps-even-more-deadly risk.

How could she let herself love a man who could die—violently—at any given moment?

"Yo, Ronnie."

Veronica turned around.

Joe. There he was, still dressed in his shiny white jacket and dark blue pants, his hair slicked back from his face. He looked tired, but he smiled at her, and she burst into tears.

He came across the room so quickly, she didn't see him move. Pulling her into his arms, he held her tightly.

"Hey," he said. "Hey."

Embarrassed, she tried to pull away, but he wouldn't let her go.

"I'm sorry," she said. "Joe, I'm sorry. I just…"

Joe lifted her chin and kissed her gently on the mouth.

"I'm all right," he told her, knowing, the way he always did, exactly what she was thinking. "I'm fine. Everything's okay."

"For right now," she said, looking up into the mysterious midnight depths of his eyes, wiping the tears from her face with the heel of her hand.

"Yeah," he said, catching a tear that hung on her eyelashes with one finger. "For right now."

"And tomorrow?" she asked. "What about tomorrow?" She knew she shouldn't say the words, but they were right on the tip of her tongue and she couldn't hold them back.

He gently ran his hand through her hair again and again as he gazed down into her eyes. "You really that worried about me?" he asked, as if he couldn't quite believe her concern.

"I was scared today," Veronica admitted. She felt her eyes well with tears again and she tried to blink them back.

"Don't be scared," Joe told her. "Blue and the other guys aren't going to let anything happen to me."

Nice words and a nice thought, but Blue and Cowboy and Harvard weren't superhuman. They were human, and there was no guarantee one of them wouldn't make a very human mistake.

Tomorrow at this time, Joe could very well be dead.

Tomorrow, or next week or next year…

Reaching up, Veronica pulled his head down and kissed him. She kissed him hard, almost savagely, and he responded instantly, pulling her against his body, lowering his hands to press her hips closer to him.

She found the buckle of his belt and started to unfasten it, and he lifted her up and carried her into the bedroom.

Veronica pulled him tightly to her and closed her eyes, trying to shut out her fears. With the touch of his hands, with his mouth and his body against hers, tomorrow didn't exist. There was only here and only now. Only ecstasy.

But when morning dawned, and Joe crept out of bed trying not to wake her, Veronica still hadn't slept. She watched him dress, then closed her eyes as he kissed her gently on the lips.

And then he was gone.

It was not beyond the realm of possibility that he could be gone forever.

Phoenix, Arizona.

The April sunshine was blazing hot, reflecting off the streets, heating the air and making it difficult to breathe.

Inside the protection of the limousine parked on the street in front of the brand-new Arizona Theatre and Center for the Arts building, Joe was cool and comfortable.

But he was glad for the sunglasses he wore. Even with them on, even with the tinted glass of the limo, Joe squinted in the brightness as he sat up to get a better look at the morning's location.

A broad set of shallow steps led to a central courtyard. It was flat and wide and surrounded by a series of marble benches placed strategically in the shade of flowering trees. The lobby of the theater was directly behind the courtyard, and the Center for the Arts offices surrounded it on the other two sides.

There was a stage in the courtyard, set up in the shade of the theater. That was where Joe—as Tedric—would go for the theater's dedication ceremony.

People were already milling around, trying to stay cool in the shade, fanning themselves with copies of the arts center's events schedule.

Joe could hear Veronica over his earphone as she sat in the surveillance van.

"Please test your microphones, Alpha Squad," she said.

Blue, Cowboy and Harvard all checked in.

"Lieutenant Catalanotto?" she said, her voice brisk and businesslike.

"Yo, Ronnie, and how are you this fine morning?" Joe said, even though he'd spent the night with her, even though he'd left her room mere hours earlier and knew *exactly* how well she was.

"A simple check would be sufficient," she murmured. "Cameras?"

Joe grinned into the miniaturized video camera that the FInCOM agent sitting across from him was carrying. God forbid someone should find out about the incredible steamy nights they spent together—the high-class media consultant and the sailor from a lousy part of New Jersey. Veronica always played it so cool in public, often addressing him as "Lieutenant Catalanotto," or "Your Highness."

Actually, they'd never talked about whether or not she wanted their relationship to go public. Joe had just assumed she didn't, and had taken precautions to protect her.

Of course, Blue and Cowboy and Harvard knew where Joe went every night. They had to know. Without their help, it would have been too damned hard to get out from under the FInCOM agents' eyes. But aside from the ribbing he endured when the four SEALs were alone, Joe knew his three friends would never tell a soul. They were SEALs. They knew how to keep a secret.

And as far as Joe was concerned, Veronica St. John was the best-kept secret *he'd* ever known.

She'd been upset last night. That incident in Albuquerque had really shaken her up. She'd actually *cried* because she'd been so afraid for him. For *him*. And the way she'd made love to him…as if the world were coming to an end. Oh, man. That had been powerful.

Joe had thought at first that maybe, just maybe, the impossible had happened and Veronica had fallen in love with him. Why else would she have been so upset? But even though he'd tried to bring up the subject of her concerns for his safety later in the night, she hadn't wanted to talk.

All she'd wanted was for him to hold her. And then make love to her again.

Joe smiled at the irony. He falls in love for the first time in his life, and for the first time in his life, *he's* the one who wants to talk. Yeah, it was true. He had been in bed with a gorgeous, incredibly sexy woman, and what he wanted desperately was to *talk* after they made love. But all *she* wanted was more high-energy sex.

Of course, Joe reminded himself, he sure had suffered, making Veronica happy last night. Oh, yeah. Life should *always* be so tough.

Joe closed his eyes briefly, remembering the smoothness of her skin, the softness of her breasts, the sweetness of surrounding himself in her heat, the hot pleasure in her beautiful, bluer-than-the-ocean eyes, the curve of her lips as she smiled up at him, the sound of her ragged cry as he took her with him, over the edge…

Joe opened his eyes, taking a deep breath and letting it quickly out. Oh, *yeah*. He was going out in public in about thirty seconds. Somehow he seriously doubted that old Ted would appreciate Joe pretending to be the prince with a raging and quite obvious royal hard-on for all the world to see. And he had a job to do, to boot. It was time to go.

Joe climbed from the limo and felt the sudden rush of heat. It was like opening an oven door. Welcome to Phoenix, Arizona.

As the FInCOM agents hustled him across the courtyard,

Joe tried to bring himself back to the business at hand. Daydreaming about his lover was good and fine and—

Lover.

Veronica St. John was his lover.

For the past four amazing days and incredible nights, Veronica St. John had been his *lover*.

The word conjured up her mysterious smile, the devilish light in her eyes that promised pleasures the likes of which he'd never known before, the softness of her sighs, the feel of her fingers in his hair, their legs intertwined, bodies slippery with soap as they kissed in the hotel's oversize bathtub....

But...

Did she think of him as her lover? Did she ever even consider the word *love* when she thought about him?

God, what he would give to hear her say that she loved him.

Damn, he was distracted today. He forced himself to look again at the buildings. *Pay attention*, he ordered himself. *Hell of a lot of good it'll do you to realize you're in love with this woman and then get yourself killed.*

Joe looked around him. The roofs of the office buildings were lower than the theater roof. They were the perfect height and distance from the stage—perfect, that is, for a sniper to shoot from. Of course, the office windows—if they could be opened—wouldn't be a bad choice for a shooter, either.

Joe snapped instantly alert, instantly on the job.

Damn, the Arizona Theatre and Center for the Arts dedication ceremony was the ideal setup for an assassination attempt. The crowd. The TV news cameras. The three buildings, forming a square U, with the courtyard between them. The glare from the sun. The heat making everyone tired and lazy.

"This is it," Joe murmured.

"You bet, Cat," Blue's voice came over his earphone. "If I were a tango, I'd pick this one."

"What?" Veronica asked from her seat in the surveillance truck. "What was that you said?"

The FInCOM agents were hurrying Joe to the relative safety of the theater lobby. Once inside, he couldn't answer Veronica, because the governor of Arizona was shaking his hand.

"It's a real honor, Your Excellency," the governor said with his trademark big, wide, white-toothed smile. "I can't tell you how much it means to the people of Arizona to have you here, at the dedication of this very important theater and arts center."

"Dear Lord," Joe heard Veronica say over his earphone. Then there was silence. When she spoke again, her voice was deceptively calm. Joe knew damn well that her calm was only an act. "Joe, you think that the terrorists are going to be here, don't you? Today. Right now."

Joe couldn't answer. Ronnie had to know that he couldn't answer. She could see him on her video screen. He was standing in a crowd of government officials. She could hear the governor still talking.

Joe smiled at something the lieutenant governor said, but his mind was focused on the voices of his men from the Alpha Squad—and the woman—his lover—sitting inside the surveillance van.

"Damn it, Joe," Veronica said, her voice breaking and her calm cracked. "Shake your head. Yes or no. Is there going to be an assassination attempt here this afternoon?"

Inside the surveillance van, Veronica held her breath, her eyes riveted to the video monitor in front of her. Joe looked directly into the camera, his dark eyes intense—and filled with excitement. He nodded once. Yes.

Dear God. Veronica took a deep breath, trying to steady

herself. As she watched, the governor of Arizona said something, and the entire group of men and women surrounding Joe laughed—Joe included.

Dear God. She'd actually seen *excitement* in Joe's eyes. He was excited because something was finally going to happen. He was ready. And willing. Willing to risk his *life*...

Her mouth felt dry. She tried to moisten her lips with her tongue, but it didn't help.

Dear God, don't let him die. "Joe," she said, but then couldn't speak.

He touched his ear, the sign that he had heard her.

She could hear Blue's unmistakable accent, and the voices of Cowboy and Harvard as the three men tried to outguess the assassin.

Cowboy was on the roof of the theater with high-powered binoculars and a long-range, high-powered rifle of his own. He did a visual sweep of the two lower roofs, reporting in continuously. No one was up there. No one was *still* up there.

"Windows in the offices don't open," Kevin Laughton said, from his seat next to Veronica. "Repeat, windows do *not* open."

"I'm watching 'em anyway," Cowboy said.

"You're wasting time," Laughton said. "And manpower. We could use you down in the crowd."

"The hell I'm wasting time," Cowboy muttered. "And if you think this shooter's going to be standing in the crowd, you're dumber than the average Fink."

On-screen, Joe was still talking to the governor and his aides. "The theater and these arts buildings are very beautiful," he said. "All these windows—it's quite impressive, really. Do they open?"

"The windows?" the governor asked. "Oh, no. No, these buildings are all climate controlled, of course."

"Ah," Joe said in Tedric's funny accent. "So if someone

inside absolutely needed some fresh air, they'd have to have a glass cutter, yes?"

The governor looked slightly taken aback, but then he laughed. "Well, yes," he said. "I suppose so."

"Roger that, Mr. Cat," Cowboy said. "My thoughts exactly. Court-martial me if you have to, FInCOM, but I'm watching those windows."

"Okay," Veronica heard Blue say. "They're coming out to the stage. Let's be ready. You, too, Cat."

"Shall we go to the stage?" the governor asked Joe.

Joe nodded. "I'm ready," he said with a smile.

He was so calm. He was walking out there to be a target, and he was *smiling*. Veronica could barely breathe.

Two of the FInCOM agents opened the doors that led to the courtyard. Outside, a band began to play.

"Joe," Veronica said again. Dear Lord, if she didn't tell him now, she might never get another chance....

He touched his ear again. He heard her.

"Joe, I have to tell you...I love you."

Joe stepped outside into the sunshine, and the heat and brightness exploded around him. But it wasn't all from the sun. In fact, most of it was coming from inside him, from the center of his chest, from his very heart.

She loved him. Ronnie *loved* him.

He laughed. Ronnie loved *him*. And she'd just announced it to everyone who was working on this operation.

"Hell, Ronnie, don't go telling him that *now*," Blue's scolding voice sounded over Joe's earphone. "Cat's gotta concentrate. Come on, Joe, keep your eyes open."

"I'm sorry," Veronica said. She sounded so small, so lost.

Joe touched his ear, trying to tell her that he'd heard her, wishing there was a way he could say he loved her, too. He touched his chest, his heart, with one hand, hoping that she'd see and understand his silent message.

And then he climbed the stairs to the stage.

"Come on, Cat," Blue's voice said. "Stop grinning like a damn fool and get to work."

Work.

His training clicked in, and Joe was instantly focused. Damn, with this warm sensation in his heart, he was better than focused. Veronica loved him, and he was damn near superhuman.

He checked the stage to make sure the cover zones were where FInCOM had said they would be.

The podium was reinforced, and it would act as a shield—provided, of course, that the shooter didn't have armor-piercing bullets. Down behind the back of the stage was also shielded. There was a flimsy metal railing to keep people from falling off the platform, but that could be jumped over easily. The stage was only about eight feet from the ground.

Joe scanned the crowd. About six hundred people. Five different TV cameras, some of them rolling live for the twelve o'clock news. He knew with an uncanny certainty that the assassin wouldn't fire until he stepped up to the podium.

"Roof is *still* clear," Cowboy announced. "No movement at the windows. Shoot, FInCOM, maybe you better keep watching that crowd. I got nothing yet."

Joe sat in a folding chair as the governor approached the podium.

"We're going to make this dedication ceremony as quick as possible," the governor said, "so we can get inside that air-conditioned lobby and have some lemonade."

The crowd applauded.

Veronica's heart was in her throat. Joe was sitting there, just *sitting* there, as if there weren't any threat to his life.

"Without further ado," the governor continued, "I'd

like to introduce our special guest, Crown Prince Tedric of Ustanzia."

The sound of the crowd's applause masked the continuous comments of the SEALs and the FInCOM agents. On Veronica's video screen, Joe stood, raising both hands to quiet the crowd.

"Thank you," he said into the microphone. "Thank you very much. It's an honor to be here today."

"I still got zip on either roof," Cowboy said. "No movement near the windows, either. I'm starting to think these tangos don't know a good setup when they see—"

A shot rang out.

One of the big glass windows in the front of the theater shattered into a million pieces.

The crowd screamed and scattered.

"Joe!" Veronica gripped the table in front of her, leaning closer to the screen, praying harder than she'd ever prayed in her life.

He was gone, she couldn't see him. Had he ducked behind the podium, or fallen, struck by the bullet?

On her headphones, she could hear all three SEALs reporting in, all talking at once. The roofs were still clear, no shooter visible at the windows.

Beside her, Kevin Laughton had rocketed out of his seat. "What do you mean, you don't know where that came from?" he was shouting over the chaos. "A shot was fired— it had to come from *somewhere!*"

"Do we need an ambulance?" another voice asked. "Repeat, is medical assistance needed?"

Another shot, another broken window.

"God damn," Laughton said. "Where the *hell* is he shooting from?"

Joe heard the second shot, felt the impact of the bullet as it hit the stage, and knew. The assassin was *behind* him.

Inside the theater. And with all of the shielding facing out, away from the theater, Joe was a Goddamn sitting duck. It was amazing he was still alive. That second shot should have killed him.

It should have, but it hadn't. The son of a bitch had missed.

Joe dove off the stage headfirst, weapon drawn, shouting instructions to his men and to the FInCOM agents who were surrounding him. Cowboy was on the roof of the theater, for God's sake. They could cut the shooter off, nail the bastard.

Inside the surveillance van, the video monitors went blank. Power was gone. Lord, what was happening out there? Veronica had heard Joe's voice. He was alive, thank God. He hadn't been killed. Yet.

The gunman was inside the theater. Upper balcony, above the lobby, came the reports. The back door was surrounded, they had the assassin cornered.

Veronica stood, pushing past Kevin Laughton and opening the door of the van. She could see the theater, see the two shattered windows. She could see the FInCOM agents crouched near the front of the theater. She could see three figures, scaling the outside of the theater, climbing up to the roof.

God in heaven, it was Joe and two of his SEALs.

Veronica lowered her mouthpiece into place. She hadn't wanted to speak before this, afraid she'd only add to the confusion, but this…

"Joe, what are you doing?" she said into the microphone. "You're the *target!* You're supposed to get to safety!"

"We need radio silence," Blue's voice commanded. "Right now. Except for reports of tango's location."

"Joe!" Veronica cried.

One of the FInCOM agents leaned out the van door. "I

can't cut this line," he said to Veronica, "so unless you're quiet, I'm going to have to take your headset."

Veronica shut her mouth, watching as a tiny figure—Cowboy—helped Joe and the rest of his team up onto the theater roof.

Up on the roof, Joe looked around. There was one door, leading to stairs that would take them down.

You all right? Cowboy hand-signaled to Joe.

Fine, he signaled back.

The gunman surely had a radio, and was probably monitoring their spoken conversation. From this point on, the SEALs would communicate only with hand signals and sign language. No use tipping the gunman off by letting him know they were coming.

Harvard had an extra HK submachine gun, and he handed it to Joe with a tight smile.

Another shot rang out.

"Agent down," came West's voice over Joe's earphone. "Oh, man, we need a medic!"

"T's location stable," said another voice. "Holding steady in the lobby balcony."

"Get that injured man out of the line of fire," Laughton commanded.

"He's dead," West reported, his normally dispassionate voice shaken. "Freeman's dead. The bastard plugged him through the eye. The sonuvabitch—"

Let's go, Joe signaled to his men. *I'm on point.*

Blue gestured to himself. He wanted to lead the way instead. But Joe shook his head.

Soundlessly he opened the door and started down the stairs.

Another shot.

More chaos. Another agent was hit with unerring accuracy.

"Stay down," Laughton ordered his men. "This guy's a sharpshooter and he's here for the long haul. Let's get our own shooters in position."

Silently, with deadly stealth, fingers on the triggers of their submachine guns, the SEALs moved down the stairs.

Veronica paced. She hadn't heard Joe's voice in many long minutes. She could no longer see any movement on the roof.

"One of the cameras is back on," someone said from inside the surveillance van, and she went back in to see.

Sure enough, the video camera that had been dropped and left on the stage had come back to life. It now showed a sideways and somewhat foggy picture of the theater lobby. Behind the reflections in the remaining glass windows, Veronica could see the shadowy shape of the assassin on the upper balcony.

It was quiet. No one was moving. No one was talking. Then...

"FInCOM shooters, hold your fire." It was Joe's voice, loud and clear, over the radio.

Veronica felt herself sway, and she groped for her seat. Joe and his SEALs were somewhere near the gunman—in range of the FInCOM agent's guns. Please, God, keep him safe, she prayed.

A door burst open. She heard it more than she saw it on the shadowy video screen.

The gunman turned, firing a machine gun rather than his rifle. But there was no one there.

Another door opened, on the other side of the balcony, but the gunman had already moved. Using some sort of rope, he swung himself over the edge and down to the first floor.

Veronica saw Joe before the gunman did.

He was standing in the lobby, gun aimed at the man scurrying down the rope. She knew it was Joe from his gleaming white jacket. The three other SEALs were dressed in dull brown.

"Hold it right there, pal," she heard Joe say over her headphones. "We can end this game one of two ways. We can either take you out of here in a body bag, or you can drop your weapons right now and we'll all live to see tomorrow."

The gunman was frozen, unmoving, halfway down the rope as he stared at Joe.

Then he moved. But he didn't drop his gun, he brought it up, fast, aimed directly toward Joe's head.

The sound of gunfire over the radio was deafening.

The gunman jumped to the ground—or did he fall? Who had been hit? And where was Joe…?

"Joe!" Veronica couldn't keep silent another second as she leaned closer to the blurry screen.

"Do you need medical assistance?" a voice asked over the headphones.

"Alpha Squad, check in," Blue's voice ordered. "McCoy."

"Becker."

"Jones."

"Catalanotto," Joe's familiar, husky voice said. "We're all clear. No need of a medic, FInCOM."

Veronica closed her eyes and rested her head on her arms on the tabletop.

"This stupid sonuvabitch just made himself a martyr for the cause," Joe's voice said into her ear.

Joe was alive. It was all over, and Joe was alive.

This time.

Chapter Eighteen

It was after nine o'clock in the evening—twenty-one hundred hours—before Veronica's phone rang.

She'd been busy all afternoon and evening with meetings and debriefings. She'd worked with Ambassador Freder and Senator McKinley, scheduling the remainder of Prince Tedric's tour. A report had come in from FIn-COM that made them all breathe easier. The assassin had been ID'd as Salustiano Vargas—Diosdado's former right-hand man. *Former.* Apparently the two terrorists had parted ways, and Vargas was no longer connected with the Cloud of Death. He had been acting on his own. Why? No one seemed to know. At least not yet. At any rate, Vargas was dead. *He'd* be giving them no answers.

But now that the assassin was no longer a threat, the ambassador and senator wanted to get the tour back on track. Tedric was flying in from the District of Columbia. He would meet them all in Seattle in the morning, where they would board a cruise ship to Alaska. They would finish the tour with a flourish.

Security would return to near normal. Two or three FIn-COM agents would remain, but everyone else, including the SEALs—including Joe—would go home.

At dinnertime, Veronica had searched for Joe, but was told he was in high-level security debriefings. She returned to her room to pack, but couldn't stop thinking. *What if he didn't get finished before morning?* Sometimes those meetings went on all night. What if she didn't see him before she had to leave…?

But then, at nine o'clock, the phone rang. Veronica closed her eyes, then picked it up. "Hello?"

"Yo, Ronnie."

"Joe." *Where are you? When will you be here?* She clamped her mouth tightly shut over those words. She didn't own him. She may have given her feelings away this morning when she'd told him—and the entire world—that she loved him, but she could stake no claim on his time or his life.

"Have you had dinner yet?" he asked.

"No, I was…" *Waiting for you.* "I wasn't hungry."

"Think you'll be hungry in about twenty minutes?" he asked.

"Hungry for what?" She tried to make her voice sound light, teasing, but her heart felt heavy. No matter how she approached this relationship, the conclusion she kept coming to was that it wasn't going to work out. Tomorrow they were both heading in different directions, and that would be it. All that was left was tonight. She'd been so worried earlier that she wasn't going to get to spend this final night with Joe. But now she couldn't help but think that it might be easier to simply say goodbye over the phone.

"Ow," he said, laughter in his voice. "You kill me, lady. But I meant are you hungry for *food.* Like, you and me—

the real me, no disguises—going out somewhere for dinner."
He paused. "In public. Like to a restaurant." He paused
again, then laughed. "God, am I smooth, or what? I'm trying to ask you out to dinner, Ron. What do ya say?"

He didn't give her time to answer. "I'm still downtown,"
he continued, "but I can catch a cab and make it up to the
hotel in about fifteen or twenty minutes. Wear that black
dress, okay? We'll go up to Camelback Mountain. Mac says
there's a great restaurant at the resort there. There's a band
and dancing, and a terrific view of the city."

"But—"

"Oh, yes. There's a cab pulling up, right outside. Gotta
run, babe. Get dressed—I'll be right there."

"But I don't want to go out. It's our last night—maybe
forever—and I want to spend it alone with you," Veronica
said to the dead phone line.

She slowly hung up the phone.

She had one more night with Joe. One more night to last
the rest of her life. One more night to burn her imprint permanently into his memory.

Hmm.

Veronica picked up the phone and dialed room service.
Joe wanted dinner and dancing and a view of the city? The
view from this room wasn't too shabby. And the four-star
restaurant in this hotel delivered food to the rooms. As for
dancing…

Holding the telephone in one hand, Veronica crossed to
the stereo that was attached to the entertainment center.
Yes, there was a tape deck. She smiled.

For the first time, Joe actually knocked on her door rather
than picking the lock and letting himself in.

With the long skirt of her black silk dress shushing about
her legs, Veronica crossed to the hotel-room door and flung

it open and herself into his arms. "Lord, I've waited all day to do this," she said. "You scared me to death this morning."

Having his arms around her felt so good. And when his lips met hers, she felt herself start to melt and she wrapped her own arms more tightly around his neck. Her fingers laced through his hair and—

Veronica pulled back.

His long hair was gone. Joe had cut his hair. Short. *Really* short. She looked at him, really *looked* at him for the first time since she'd opened her hotel-suite door. He was wearing a naval dress uniform. It was dark blue with rows and rows and *rows* of medals and ribbons on his left breast. He wore a white hat on his head, and he took it off, holding it almost awkwardly in his hands. His dark eyes were slightly sheepish as he watched her take in his haircut. His hair had been buzz cut around his ears and at the back. The top and front were slightly longer—just long enough so that a lock of dark hair fell forward over his forehead.

He smiled ruefully. "The barber went a little overboard," he said. "I don't usually wear it quite this short and..." He closed his eyes, shaking his head. "Damn, you hate it."

Veronica touched his arm, shaking her own head. "No," she said. "No, I don't *hate* it...." But she didn't like it, either. Not that he looked bad. In fact, he didn't. If anything, his short cut made his lean face more handsome than ever. But it also made him look harder, tougher, unforgiving— dangerous on an entirely new level. He looked like exactly what he was—a highly trained, highly competent special- forces officer. She couldn't help but be reminded that he was a man who risked his life as a matter of course. And *that* was what Veronica didn't like. "It suits you," she told him.

He searched her eyes, and whatever he saw there seemed to satisfy him. "Good."

"You look...wonderful," Veronica said honestly.

"So do you." His eyes flared with that familiar heat as he ran them down and then back up her body.

"This is the way I thought you were going to look—before we met," she said.

A brief shadow flickered across his face. "Yeah, well, I guess I oughta tell you, I can count on my fingers and toes the times I've worn this dress uniform. What you saw when we met is closer to the truth. I usually wear fatigues or jeans. And if I've been working with engines, they're usually covered with grease or dirt."

Why was he telling her this? It seemed almost like a warning. He seemed so serious, Veronica felt compelled to make things lighter. "Are you saying this because you want me to do your laundry?" she teased.

Joe gave her one of his quicksilver grins. Yes, seeing him smile that way, his teeth so very white against his lean, tanned face, Veronica could say that this new haircut definitely suited him. "You *want* to do my laundry?" he countered.

The casual question suddenly seemed to carry more meaning, as Joe watched her intently. His dark eyes were sharp, almost piercing as he waited for an answer.

Veronica laughed, trying to hide her sudden nervousness. Why were they talking about *laundry?* "I don't do my *own* laundry," she said with a shrug. "When do I have time?"

She stepped back, opening the door wider to let him in. "We're standing in the hall," she added. "Won't you come in?"

Joe hesitated. "Maybe we should just go...."

She smiled. "Think if you come inside we'll never leave?"

He touched the side of her face. "I don't just think it, baby, I *know* it."

She kissed the palm of his hand. "Would that be so terrible?" she whispered, gazing up into the midnight depths of his eyes.

"No." He stepped inside the room, closing the door behind him.

Veronica was nervous. Joe could see that she was nervous as she moved out of his grasp and into the room and—

The table was set and covered with a very grand-looking room-service dinner. And the rest of the room… Veronica had pushed all the furniture out of the center of the living room.

She'd done that before. Back in D.C. Back when he'd climbed up to the balcony and gone in her sliding-glass door and…

Joe looked up to find her watching him. She moistened her lips nervously and smiled. "Dinner and dancing," she explained. "I made room, so that we could dance."

"We?"

Veronica blushed, but she held his gaze. "So I can dance for you," she correctly herself softly. "Although, at some point you *will* dance with me, too. But maybe we should have dinner first."

The fragrant smell of gourmet food filled the air. Joe knew that he hadn't eaten since lunchtime. He also knew that dinner was the very last thing he wanted right now. Veronica was going to dance for him. She was going to dance the way he'd seen her dance when he'd climbed up to her room. Only this time, she would know right from the start that he was watching. "Maybe we should have dinner later," he said huskily.

As he watched, she crossed to the window and closed the curtains. God, his heart was pounding as if he'd just run a three-minute mile. He could feel his blood surging hotly through his veins with each pulsing beat. She was really going to do this. She knew he wanted her to—he'd asked her to dance for him. But he'd never thought she'd actually do it. He thought he'd asked for too much.

Veronica smiled at him as she crossed back to the dinner table and took a bottle of beer from a small bottle cooler. She opened it, poured it into a glass and carried it to him.

"Thanks," Joe said as she handed him both the glass and the bottle.

"Why don't you sit down?" Veronica murmured, and with a whisper of silk, she moved back to the other side of the room.

Sit down. Yeah, right. Sit down. As Joe lowered himself into a chair, Veronica crossed to the stereo and slipped a tape into the deck.

Joe knew what her dancing meant to her. She'd told him that it was private and intensely personal. It was a way to let off steam, to unwind, to really relax. And she was going to share it with him now. She was going to let her personal, private pleasure become *his* pleasure.

The fire that was shooting through his veins reached his heart and exploded. Veronica St. John had told him she loved him today. And tonight, by sharing herself with him this way, she was showing him just how much.

The music started—softly, slowly—and Ronnie stood in the middle of the room, head back, eyes closed, arms at her sides. God, she was beautiful. And she was his. All his. Forever, if he had anything to say about it. And he did. He had a lot to say about it. Hell, he could write a book on the subject.

The music changed with a sudden burst of volume, and Veronica brought her hands up sharply, into the air.

And then she began to move.

She was graceful, fluid, and her dress seemed an extension of her body, moving with her. Her eyes were still closed, but then she opened them and looked directly at Joe.

She blushed, and his heart burned even hotter. She was such a contradiction. The slightest thing could make her blush—until passion overcame her. And when that happened, she was amazingly uninhibited. Joe had never had a lover like Veronica St. John. One moment she was seemingly prim and proper, and the next she was wild, giving him pleasure in ways he'd only dreamed of, and telling him— quite specifically, in no uncertain terms—exactly what he could and should do to please her.

As Joe watched, Veronica closed her eyes again, and again the music changed, the rhythm getting stronger, faster, more insistent. Her dancing, too, became less careful, less contained. Her movements were freer, broader, more powerful.

More passionate.

She reached up with both hands and with one swift motion, removed the pins that were holding her hair. It tumbled down around her shoulders, an avalanche of red gold curls.

Joe's mouth was dry, and he took a sip of the beer she'd given him.

Veronica kicked off her high heels, and, as Joe watched, she *became* the music. She moved to the funky, bluesy instrumental piece, visually capturing every nuance, every musical phrase with her body.

Her body.

They hadn't been lovers for long, but Joe already knew every inch of Veronica's beautiful body intimately. But seeing her body in motion this way was an entirely new experience. Her dress barely restrained her breasts and they moved with and against the forces of gravity. The black silk slid across her abdomen and thighs, allowing glimpses of the firm muscles and flesh underneath when occasionally it clung for a second or two.

Veronica made a twisting, writhing motion that was pure sex, pure abandon.

The long skirt of her dress was no longer moving with her—it was getting in her way.

This time when she opened her eyes and looked at Joe, she didn't blush. She smiled—a sweet, hot, sexy smile—and reached behind her for the zipper of her dress. In less than a heartbeat, the dress pooled around her feet, and she was naked—save for a pair of black silk panties. She kicked the dress aside, still dancing, still moving and spinning.

A thong. She was wearing thong panties, black silk against her skin so creamy and white.

And still she danced.

For him.

I've died, Joe thought, *and gone to heaven.*

She moved closer to him, smiling at the look he knew damn well was on his face. He was hypnotized. Stupefied. Totally overcome. And extremely aroused.

Still moving, she held out her hands to him. "Dance with me."

It was not an invitation he needed to hear twice. He set his beer on the nearest end table and rose to his feet. And then, God, she was in his arms, moving with him and against him to that bluesy melody.

Her skin was so smooth, so silky beneath his hands. He touched her everywhere. Her softly rounded bottom, her full breasts, her flat stomach, her long, willowy arms. He was still in his uniform and she was nearly naked, and he had never, *never* been so turned on in his entire life. They were dancing so close, their legs were intertwined. He could feel the heat between her legs against his thigh. She could surely feel his arousal—she pressed against him, her slow, sexy movement driving him crazy, and the sight of her, nearly naked in his arms, making him throb with need.

"Ronnie…"

Somehow she knew that he'd had nearly all he could take. She lifted her mouth to his and kissed him. Joe heard himself groan. He couldn't get enough of her.

He felt her fingers unbuckling his belt and swiftly unfastening his pants. And then he was in her hands. It was good, but it wasn't good enough.

"Ronnie, I need—"

"I know."

She covered him with a condom she'd procured from God-knew-where, and slipped out of her panties as she kissed him again.

"Lift me up," Veronica murmured.

"Yes," he breathed. She wrapped her arms around his neck and her legs around his waist as he ensheathed himself in her wonderful, smooth heat. "Oh, baby…"

She moved on top of him, against him, with him. She was in his arms, in his heart, in his very soul. This passionate, fiery woman, who could be blazing hot one moment and gently sweet the next, this woman with the sharp sense of humor and quiet touch that hid a will of steel—a will that was ruled by the kindest heart he'd ever known—this was the one woman he'd been waiting for all his life. All the love he'd made, all the women he'd known before, had meant nothing to him. No one had moved him. No one had even come close to holding him. He'd always been able to close the door and walk away from a woman without looking back.

But there was no way he'd ever be able to walk away from Veronica. Not without leaving his heart behind—ripped from his chest.

He clung to her, holding her as tightly as she held him, plunging himself deeply into her again and again.

He loved her. He wanted to tell her, but the words—those three simple little words—didn't come easily. The truth was, saying them scared him to death. Now, wasn't that funny? He was a SEAL. He'd faced platoons of enemy soldiers, he'd looked death in the teeth without batting an eye more times than he could count, yet the thought of uttering one very simple sentence made him sweat.

Ronnie's fingers were in his hair. Her mouth was covering his face and lips with kisses.

"Joe," she breathed, "Joe. I want more—" He moved, backing her up against the wall to anchor her in place, and she tipped back her head. "Yes…"

Her release was incredible. She cried out as he drove himself into her, giving her all she'd asked for. Her arms tightened around his neck, her fingers clutched him.

"I love you," Veronica cried. "Oh, Joe, I love you!"

Her words pushed him over the edge. She loved him. She really did. He exploded in a blinding white burst of pleasure so exquisite, so pure that the world seem to disintegrate around him.

Baby, I love you, too.

Chapter Nineteen

Joe slowly became aware of his surroundings.

Ronnie's head was resting on his shoulder, her breath warm against his neck. His own forehead leaned against the wall. And his knees were damned shaky.

He could feel Veronica's heart beating, hear her soft sigh.

He didn't want to move. He'd never made love quite like this in his life, and he didn't want it to end. Of course, it had ended, but as long as they stayed right here, in this same position, these remarkable feelings could linger on.

It was, needless to say, incredibly exhilarating. His future looked so different, so much brighter, with Ronnie in the picture. For the first time in his life, Joe found himself actually considering the possibility of having children. Not for a good long time, of course. He wanted Ronnie all to himself for years and years and *years*. But down the road, making a baby, creating a new life would be exciting in a way he'd never imagined before. Fifty percent him and fifty percent her, with two hundred percent of their love…

The jeweler's box he carried in his pocket dug into his ribs and Joe had to laugh. He hadn't even asked Ronnie to marry him yet, and here he was, practically naming their kids.

"You didn't have to say that, you know," she whispered.

She lifted her head and lowered herself to the floor. The spell was broken. Or was it? Joe still felt an incredible warmth in his chest. He used to think it felt like a noose, he realized, but now it was a good feeling, a warmth surrounding his heart, giving him an amazing sense of peace and belonging.

"Didn't have to say what?" he asked.

Veronica moved away from him slightly, giving him room to adjust his clothes. She was still naked, but she seemed unaware of that as she gazed at him, concern darkening her blue eyes.

"You didn't have to say that you love me, too," she said.

Joe froze, hands stilled on the buckle of his belt. Had he actually spoken those words out loud?

"I'd rather that you be honest with me," she continued. "Don't say things you don't mean. Please?"

Veronica turned away, unable to continue looking into Joe's eyes, unable to keep up the brave front. But, bloody hell, here she'd just spoken of being honest…. "The truth is, Joe," she said, her voice shaking slightly, "I'm going to miss you terribly when you're gone, and—"

Joe drew her into his arms, moving with her so they sat on the sofa, Veronica on his lap. "Who says I'm going anywhere?" he asked softly, smoothing her hair back from her face and kissing her gently on the lips.

Veronica felt her eyes fill with tears. Damn! She blinked them back. "Tomorrow I'm flying to Seattle and you're—"

He interrupted her with another gentle kiss. "And who says when I said…what I said, that I wasn't being honest?"

He ran his free hand down the curve of her hip and back up again, then cupped her breast. It was impossible not to touch her.

"You love me." Her disbelief was evident in her voice.

"Is that really so hard to believe?"

Veronica touched the side of his face. "You're so sweet," she said. At the mock flare of indignation in his eyes, she added quickly, "I know you don't think so, but you *are*. You're incredibly *kind*, Joe. And I know you have…feelings for me, but you don't have to pretend that they're more than—" She stared down in silence at the small black velvet box Joe pulled from his pocket and held out to her. "What's this?"

"Open it," he said. His face looked so serious, so hard. His eyes were so intense.

"I'm afraid to."

Joe smiled, and it softened his face. "It's not a grenade," he said. "Just open it, Ron, will ya?"

Slowly, she took it from him. It was small and square and black and furry. It looked an awful lot like a jeweler's box. What was he giving her? She couldn't even begin to imagine the possibilities. Her heart was pounding, she realized. She took a deep breath to steady herself. Then, gazing into Joe's beautiful eyes, looking for some sort of clue as to what was inside, she opened the box.

She glanced down and her heart stopped. It was a ring. It was an enormous, beautiful, glittering diamond ring.

"Marry me," Joe said huskily.

"Dear Lord!" Veronica breathed.

As she stared up into his eyes, her expression of shock made Joe smile. "I guess you weren't expecting this, huh?"

She shook her head.

"Neither was I," he told her honestly. "But that ring's not pretend, Ronnie. And neither is what I feel. I…you know…love you—" God, he'd said it and he wasn't struck by lightning. "And I want to make this thing we have permanent. You follow?"

She was silent. Her eyes were as large as dinner plates as she gazed at him. She was still naked, and he couldn't have kept from touching her, from stroking her soft skin, if his life depended on it. She was lovely, and he was already uncomfortably aroused again. God, he'd just had the best sex of his life, and already he wanted her again. He couldn't get enough of her. He never would.

But why wouldn't she answer? Why wouldn't she tell him that she wanted to marry him, too?

"Say something, baby." Joe tried to disguise his insecurity, but knew that he'd failed miserably. It showed in his eyes, in his voice. "The suspense is killing me. Tell me what you think. Good idea? Bad idea? Have I gone crazy, here?"

Veronica was dumbfounded. Joe Catalanotto—Lt. Joe Catalanotto of the U.S. Navy SEALs—wanted to *marry* her. He'd meant it when he'd said that he loved her. He loved her. He *loved* her, and dear Lord, she should be ecstatic. She should be hearing wedding bells and picturing herself in a gorgeous white wedding dress, walking down the aisle of a church to meet this man at the altar. The one man that she truly loved.

But she couldn't picture herself at a wedding. She could only see herself at a funeral. *Joe's* funeral.

"When…" she started, then cleared her throat. She shivered slightly, suddenly aware of the chill of the air-conditioning against her bare skin. Joe ran his hand up and down her arm, trying to warm her. "When are you planning to retire?"

He stared at her blankly. "What?"

"From the SEALs," she explained. "When are you going to retire from active duty?"

Veronica could see that he didn't get how this pertained to his wedding proposal, but he shrugged and answered her anyway. "Not for a long time," he said. "I don't know. Not for another fifteen years. Twenty if I can manage it."

Her heart sank. Fifteen or twenty years. Two decades of watching the man she loved leave on countless high-risk missions. Two decades of not knowing whether or not he would return. Two decades of sheer *hell*. If he lived that long…

"I'm career navy, Ronnie," Joe said quietly. "I know I'm no prince, but I *am* an officer and—"

"You *are* a prince." Veronica kissed him swiftly on the lips. "I've never met anyone even half as princely as you are."

He was embarrassed. So of course, he tried to turn it into a joke. "Well, damn," he said. "All the naked women tell me that whenever I get them on my lap."

Veronica had to smile. "I *am* naked," she said. "Aren't I?"

"I noticed," he said, lightly touching her breast.

"Do you want me to put on some clothes?"

"I was thinking more along the lines that I should get rid of mine," Joe murmured, bringing his lips to where his hand had just been. But he only kissed her gently before lifting his head again. "Try it on."

The ring. He meant the ring.

She knew she shouldn't. She had no idea what her answer was going to be. She was so utterly, totally torn.

Still, Veronica took the ring from the box and slipped it onto her left hand. It was a little bit too large.

"Say the word, and we can get it sized," Joe said. "Or, if you want, you can pick out something different…."

Veronica looked at the ring's simple, elegant setting through a haze of tears. "This is so beautiful," she said. "I wouldn't want anything else."

"When I saw it," Joe said quietly, "I knew it belonged to

you." He lifted her chin up toward him. "Hey. Hey, are you crying?"

Veronica nodded her head, yes, and he drew her even closer to him. He pulled her mouth to his and kissed her sweetly. She wanted so very much to tell him, "Yes, I'll marry you." But she wanted to go to bed every night with him beside her. And she wanted to wake up every morning knowing that he was going to be there again the next night. She didn't want a Navy SEAL, she wanted a regular, normal man.

But maybe if she asked, he'd leave the SEALs. Lord knows, he could do damn near anything, get any kind of job he wanted. He was an expert in so many different fields. He could work as a translator. Or he could work as a mechanic, she didn't care. Let him get covered with engine grease every day. She'd learn to do the bloody laundry if that's what it took. She just wanted to know that he would be safe. And alive.

But Veronica knew she couldn't ask him to leave the SEALs. And even if she *did* ask him, she knew that he wouldn't quit. Not for her. Not for anything. She'd seen him at work. He loved the risk, lived for the danger.

"Please, Joe," she whispered. "Make love to me again."

He stood, holding her in his arms, and carried her into the bedroom.

Veronica wanted desperately to marry Joe. But Joe was already married—to the Navy SEALs.

As Veronica slept, curled up next to him in the bed, Joe stared at the ceiling.

She hadn't said yes.

He'd asked her to marry him, and she'd asked him a bunch of questions in return, but she hadn't said yes.

She hadn't said no, either. But she'd taken off the ring

and put it back in the box. She gave him some excuse about how she was afraid it was going to fall off. She was afraid she was going to lose it.

But if Ronnie had given *him* any kind of ring that meant that she wanted him forever, that she loved him "till death do us part," Joe would damn sure be wearing it, regardless of the size.

It was entirely possible that he was heading full steam ahead into an emotional train wreck. It was entirely possible that although Veronica had said that she loved him, she didn't love him enough to want "forever." Hell, it was entirely possible that although she had said she loved him, she didn't love him at all.

But no. He had to believe that she loved him. He'd seen it in her eyes, felt it in her touch. She *did* love him. The sixty-four-thousand-dollar question was, how much?

Across the room, from the chair where he'd thrown his clothes, his pocket pager shrilled.

Joe extracted himself from the bed, trying not to wake Veronica, but as he moved swiftly across the room, she stirred and sat up.

"What was *that?*" she asked.

"My pager," he said. "I'm sorry. I've got to make a phone call."

Veronica leaned forward and snapped on the light, squinting at him in the sudden brightness. As she watched, he sat back down on the edge of the bed, running his fingers through his short hair before he picked up the telephone. He quickly dialed—a number he had memorized.

"Yeah," he said into the phone. "Catalanotto." There was a pause. "I'm still in Phoenix." Another pause. "Yeah. Yeah, I understand." He glanced back at Veronica, his face serious. "Give me three minutes, and I'll call right back." Another pause. He smiled. "Right. Thanks."

He dropped the receiver into the cradle and faced Veronica.

"I can get a week's leave, if I want it," he said bluntly. "But I need to know right now if I should take it. And I don't want to take it if you can't spend the time with me. Do you know what I'm saying?"

Veronica glanced at the clock. "You get called at four-thirty in the morning about whether or not you want *leave?*" she asked in dismay.

Joe shook his head. "No," he replied. "I get called and ordered to report to the base at Little Creek. There's some kind of emergency. They're calling in all of SEAL Team Ten, including the Alpha Squad."

Veronica felt faint. "What kind of emergency?"

"I don't know," he said. "But even if I *did* know, I couldn't say."

"If we were married, could you tell me?"

Joe smiled ruefully. "No, baby. Not even then."

"So you just pack up and leave," Veronica said tightly, "and maybe you'll come back?"

He reached for her. "I'll always come back. You gotta believe that."

She sat up, moving out of reach, keeping her back to him so that he couldn't see the look on her face. This was her worst nightmare, coming true. This was what she didn't want to spend the next twenty years doing. This fear, this emptiness was exactly what she didn't want to spend the next two decades feeling.

"I either have to officially take leave, or go check in with the rest of the team. What do you think?" he asked again. "Can you get time off, too?"

Veronica shook her head. "No." Funny, her voice sounded so cool and in control. "No, I'm sorry, but I have to be on the cruise ship with Prince Tedric, starting tomorrow."

She could feel his eyes on the back of her head. She sensed his hesitation before he turned back to the telephone.

He picked it up and dialed. "Yeah, it's Joe Cat again. I'm in."

Veronica closed her eyes. He was in. But in for what? Something that was going to get him killed? She couldn't stand it. Not knowing where he was going, what he'd be doing, was awful. She wanted to *scream*....

"Right," he said into the phone. "I'll be ready."

He hung up the phone, and she felt the mattress shift as he stood.

"I have to take a quick shower," he said. "There's a car coming in ten minutes."

Veronica spun around to face him. "Ten *minutes!*"

"That's how it works, Ronnie. I get a call, I have to leave. Right away. Sometimes we get preparation time, but usually not. Let me take a shower—we can talk while I'm getting dressed."

Veronica felt numb. This wasn't her worst nightmare. This fear she felt deep in her stomach was beyond anything she'd ever imagined. She wanted to tell him, *beg* him to take the leave. She would quit her job if she had to. She would do anything, *anything* to keep him from going on that unnamed, unidentified, probably deadly emergency mission.

And then what? she wondered as she heard the sound of the shower. She stood and slipped into her robe, suddenly feeling terribly chilled. She would lose her job, her reputation, her *pride*, for one measly week of Joe's company. But after that week of leave was up, he would be gone. He'd go where duty called, when duty called, no matter the danger or risk. Sooner or later it would happen. Sooner or later— and probably sooner—he was going to kiss her goodbye, leaving her with her heart in her throat. He would leave her alone, watching the clock, waiting, praying for him to return. Alive. And he wouldn't come back.

Veronica couldn't stand it. She wouldn't be able to stand it.

The water shut off, and several moments later Joe came out of the bathroom, toweling himself dry. She watched silently as he slipped on his briefs and then his pants.

"So," he said, rubbing his hair with the towel one last time, glancing over at her. "Tell me when you'll be done with the Ustanzian tour. I'll try to arrange leave."

"It won't be for another two or three weeks," Veronica said. "After the cruise, we'll be heading back to D.C., and then to Ustanzia from there. By then, Wila will have had the baby, and—" She broke off, turning away from him. Why were they having this seemingly normal-sounding conversation, when every cell in her body was screaming for her to hold him— hold him and never let go? But she couldn't hold him. A car was coming in five minutes to take him away, maybe forever.

"Okay," Joe was saying. She could hear him slipping his arms into his jacket and buttoning it closed. "What do you say I meet you in Ustanzia? Just let me know the exact dates and—"

Veronica shook her head. "I don't think that's a good idea."

"Okay," he said again, very quietly. "What *is* a good idea, Ronnie? You tell me."

He wasn't moving now. Veronica knew even without looking that he was standing there, his lean face unsmiling, his dark eyes intense as he watched her, waiting for her to move, to speak, to do something, *anything*.

"I don't have any good ideas."

"You don't want to marry me." It wasn't a question, it was a statement.

Veronica didn't move, didn't say anything. What could she possibly say?

Joe laughed—a brief burst of air that had nothing to do with humor. "Hell, from the way it sounds, you don't even want to *see* me again."

She turned toward him, but she wasn't prepared for the chill that was in his eyes.

"Boy, did I have *you* pegged wrong," he said.

"You don't understand," Veronica tried to explain.. "I can't live the way you want me to live. I can't take it, Joe."

He turned away, and she moved forward, stopping him with a hand on his arm. "We come from such different worlds," she said. His world was filled with danger and violence and the ever-present risk of death. Why couldn't he see the differences between them? "I can't just…pretend to fit into your world, because I know I won't. And I know you won't fit into mine. You can't change any more than I can, and—"

Joe pulled away. His head was spinning. Different worlds. Different classes was more like it. God, he should have known better. What was he thinking? How could he have thought a woman like Veronica St. John—a wealthy, high-class, gentrified lady—would want more from him than a short, steamy affair?

He'd been right—she'd been slumming.

That was all this was to her.

She had been slumming. She had been checking out how the lower class lived. She had been having sex with a blue-collar man. Officer or not, that was what Joe was, what he would always be. That was where he came from.

Veronica was getting her hands dirty, and Joe, he'd gone and fallen in love. God, he was a royal idiot, a horse's ass.

He took the ring box from where it still sat on the bedside table and dropped it into his pocket. Damned if he was going to let her walk away with a ring that had put a serious dent into his life savings.

"Try to understand," Veronica said, her eyes swimming with tears. She stood in front of the door, blocking his exit. "I love you, but…I can't marry you."

And all at once Joe *did* understand. She may have been slumming—at first. But she'd fallen in love with him, too. Still, that love wasn't enough to overcome the differences between their two "worlds" as she called it.

He should walk away. He *knew* he should walk away. But instead he touched her face and brushed his thumb across her beautiful lips. And then he did something he'd never done before. He begged.

"Please, Ronnie," Joe said softly. "This thing between us…it's pretty powerful. Please, baby, can't we try to work this out?"

Veronica stared up into Joe's eyes, and for a second, she almost believed that they could.

But then his pager beeped again, and the fear was back. Joe had to go. Now. Reality hit her hard and she felt sick to her stomach. She turned and moved away from the door.

"That's your answer, huh?" he said quietly.

Veronica kept her back to him. She couldn't speak. And she couldn't bear to watch him leave.

She heard him open the bedroom door. She heard him walk through the hotel suite. And she heard him stop, heard him hesitate before he opened the door to the corridor.

"I thought you were tougher than this, Ron," he said, a catch in his voice.

The door clicked quietly as it closed behind him.

Chapter Twenty

The guys in Alpha Squad were avoiding Joe. They were keeping their distance—and it was little wonder, considering the black mood he was in.

The "emergency" calling them all back to Little Creek had been no more than an exercise in preparedness—a time test by the powers that be. The top brass were checking to see exactly how long it would take SEAL Team Ten to get back to their home base in Virginia, from their scattered temporary locations around California and the Southwest.

Blue was the only man who ignored Joe's bad mood and stayed nearby as they completed the paperwork on the exercise and on the Ustanzian tour operation. Blue didn't say a word, but Joe knew his executive officer was ready to lend a sympathetic ear, or even a shoulder to cry on if he needed it.

Early that evening, before they left the administration office, there was a phone call for Joe. From Seattle.

Blue was there, and he met Joe's eyes as the call was announced. There was only one person in Seattle who could possibly be calling Joe.

Veronica St. John.

Why was she calling him?

Maybe she'd changed her mind.

Blue turned away, sympathy in his eyes. Damn it, Joe thought. Were his feelings, his hope for the impossible *that* transparent?

There was no real privacy in the office, and Joe had to take the call at an administrator's desk, with the man sitting not three feet away from him.

"Catalanotto," he said into the phone, staring out the window.

"Joe?" It *was* Veronica. And she sounded surprised to hear his voice. "Oh, Lord, I didn't think I'd actually get through to you. I thought…I thought I'd be able to leave a message with your voice mail or…something."

Terrific. She didn't actually want to speak to him. Then why the hell had she called? "You want me to hang up?" he asked. "You can call back and leave a message."

"Well, no," she said. "No, of course not. Don't be silly. I just…didn't think you'd be there. I thought you'd be…shooting bad guys…or something."

Joe smiled despite the ache in his chest. "No," he said. "*Yesterday* I shot the bad guy. Today I'm doing the paperwork about it."

"I thought…"

"Yes…?"

"Aren't you shipping out or…something?"

"No," Joe said. "It was an exercise. The brass wanted to see how fast SEAL Team Ten could get our butts back to Little Creek. They do that sometimes. Supposedly it keeps us on our toes."

"I'm glad," she said.

"I'm not," he stated flatly. "I was hoping they were sending us down to South America. We're *still* no closer to nailing Diosdado. I was looking forward to tracking him down and having it out with him once and for all."

"Oh," she said very softly. And then she was silent.

Joe counted to five very slowly, then he said, "Veronica? You still there?"

"Yes," she replied, and he could almost see her shake her head to get herself back on track. But when she spoke, her voice was no less tentative. "I'm sorry, I…um, I was calling to pass on some news I received this afternoon. Mrs. Kaye called from Washington, D.C. Cindy died this morning at Saint Mary's."

Joe closed his eyes and swore.

"Mrs. Kaye wanted to thank you again," Veronica continued, her voice shaking. She was crying. Joe knew just from the way her voice sounded that she was crying. God, his arms ached to hold her. "She wanted to thank both of us, for your visit. It meant a lot to Cindy."

Joe held tightly to the phone, fighting to ignore the six pairs of curious eyes and ears in the room.

Veronica took a deep breath, and he could picture her wiping her eyes and face, adjusting her hair. "I just thought you'd want to know," she said. She took another breath. "I have to run. The cruise ship sails in less than an hour."

"Thanks for calling to tell me, Veronica," Joe said.

There was another silence. Then she said, "Joe?"

"Yeah."

"I'm sorry," she said falteringly. "About…you and me. About it not working out. I didn't mean to hurt you."

Joe couldn't talk about it. How could he stand here in the middle of all these people and talk about the fact that his heart had been stomped into a million tiny pieces? And even if he could, how could he admit it to her—the woman responsible for all the pain?

"Was there something else you wanted?" he asked, his voice tight and overly polite.

"You sound so… Are you…are you all right?"

"Yeah," he lied. "I'm great. I'm getting on with my life, okay? Now, if you'll excuse me, I'll get back to it, all right?"

Joe hung up the phone without waiting to see if she said goodbye. He turned and walked away, past Blue, past the guard at the front desk. He walked out of the building and down the road, heading toward the empty parade grounds. He sat in the grass at the edge of the field and held his head in his hands.

And for the second time in his adult life, Joe Catalanotto cried.

Standing at the pay phone, Veronica dissolved into tears.

She hadn't expected to speak to Joe. She hadn't expected to hear his familiar voice. It was such a relief to know that he wasn't risking his life—at least not today.

But he'd sounded so stilted, so cold, so unfriendly. He'd called her Veronica, not Ronnie, as if she were some stranger he didn't know. He was getting on with his life, he'd said. He clearly wasn't going to waste any time worrying about what might have been.

That was the way she wanted it, wasn't it? So why did she feel so awful?

Did she actually *want* Joe Catalanotto carrying a torch for her? Did she *want* him to be hurt? Did she *want* his heart to be broken?

Or maybe she was afraid that by turning him down, she'd done the wrong thing, made the wrong choice.

Veronica didn't know. She honestly didn't know.

The only thing she was absolutely certain of was how terribly much she missed him.

Joe sat in the bar nursing a beer, trying not to listen to the endless parade of country songs about heartbreak playing on the jukebox.

"At ease, at ease. Stay in your seats, boys."

Joe looked into the mirror behind the bar and saw Admiral Forrest making his way across the crowded room. The admiral sat down at the bar, next to Joe, who took another sip of his beer, not even looking up, certainly not even smiling.

"Rumor has it you survived your mission," Mac said to Joe, ordering a diet cola from the bartender. "But it looks to me like you extracted without a pulse or a sense of humor. Am I right or are you still alive over there, son?"

"Well, gee whiz, Admiral," Joe said, staring morosely into his beer. "We can't all be a barrel of laughs all the time."

Mac nodded seriously. "No, no, you're right. We can't." He nodded to the bartender as the man put a tall glass of soda on the bar. "Thanks." He glanced down the bar and nodded to Blue McCoy, who was sitting on Joe's right. "Lieutenant."

Blue nodded back. "Good to see you, Admiral."

Forrest turned back to Joe. "Hear you and some of your boys had a run-in with Salustiano Vargas two days ago."

Joe nodded, glancing up at the older man. "Yes, sir."

"Also hear from the Intel grapevine that the rumor is, Vargas was disassociated from Diosdado and the Cloud of Death some time ago."

Joe shrugged, drawing wet lines with the condensation from his mug on the surface of the bar. He exchanged a look with Blue. "Vargas wasn't able to verify FInCOM's information after we had it out with him. He was too dead to talk."

Admiral Forrest nodded. "I heard that, too," he said. He took a long sip of his soda, then set it carefully back down on the bar. "What *I* can't figure out is, if Salustiano Vargas was *not* working with Diosdado, why did earlier FInCOM reports state that members of the Cloud of Death were un-usually interested in Prince Tedric's tour schedule?"

"FInCOM isn't known for their flawless operations," Joe said, one eyebrow raised. "Someone made a mistake."

"I don't know, Joe." Mac scratched his head through his thick white hair. "I've got this gut feeling that the mistake is in assuming the reports are true about this rift between Vargas and Diosdado. I think there's still some connection between them. Those two were too close for too long." He shook his head again. "What I can't figure out is *why* Sal-ustiano Vargas—Diosdado's number-one sharpshooter—would set himself up as a suicide assassin. He didn't stand a chance at getting out of there. *And* he didn't even hit his target."

Joe took another slug of his beer. "He had the opportu-nity," he said. "I was on that stage, with my back to the bas-tard when he fired his first shot. It wasn't until the second shot went into the stage next to me that I realized he was shooting from behind me and—"

Joe froze, his glass a quarter of an inch from his lips. "Jesus, Mary and Joseph." He put his beer back on the counter and looked from Blue to the admiral. "Why would a sharpshooter of Vargas's caliber miss an easy target in broad daylight?"

"Luck," Blue suggested. "You moved out of the way of the bullet at the right split second."

"I didn't," Joe said. "I didn't move at all. He *deliberately* missed me." He stood, knocking his barstool over. "I need the telephone," he said to the bartender. "Now."

The bartender moved fast and placed the phone in front of Joe. Joe pushed it in front of the admiral.

"Who am I calling?" Forrest asked dryly. "*Why* am I calling?"

"Why would Salustiano Vargas deliberately miss his assassination target?" Joe asked. He answered his own question. "Because the assassination attempt was only a diversion, set up to make FInCOM's security force relax. Which they immediately did, right? I'm out of the picture. The rest of Alpha Squad is out of the picture. Mac, how many FInCOM agents are with Prince Tedric's tour now that the alleged danger has passed?"

Mac shrugged. "Two. I think." He leaned forward. "Joe, what are you saying?"

"That the *real* terrorist attack hasn't happened yet. Damn, at least I hope it hasn't happened yet."

Mac Forrest's mouth dropped open. "Jumping Jesse," he said. "The cruise ship?"

Joe nodded. "With only two FInCOM agents onboard, that cruise ship is a terrorist's dream come true." He picked up the telephone receiver and handed it to the admiral. "Contact them, sir. Warn them."

Forrest dialed a number and waited, his blue eyes steely in his weathered face.

Joe waited, too. Waited, and prayed. Veronica was on that ship.

Blue stood. "I'm gonna page the squad," he said quietly to Joe.

Joe nodded. "Better make it all of Team Ten," he told Blue in a low voice. "If this is going down, it's going to be big. We're going to need all the manpower we've got. While you're at it, get on the horn with the commander of Team Six. Let's put in a request to put them on standby, too."

Blue nodded and vanished in the direction of the door and the outside pay phone.

Please, God, keep Veronica safe, Joe prayed. *Please, God, let him be really, really wrong about the situation. Please God...*

Forrest put his hand over the receiver. "I got through to the naval base in Washington State," he said to Joe. "They're hailing the cruise ship now." He lifted his hand from the mouthpiece. "Yes?" he said into the telephone. "They're not?" He looked up at Joe, his eyes dark with concern. "The ship's not responding. Apparently, their radio's down. The base has them on radar, and they've gone seriously off course." He shook his head, his mouth tight with anger and frustration. "I believe we've got ourselves a crisis situation."

Veronica watched a second helicopter land on the sundeck.

This couldn't be happening. Five hours ago, she'd been having lunch with Ambassador Freder and his staff. Five hours ago, everything had been perfectly normal aboard the cruise ship *Majestic*. Tedric had been sleeping in, as was his habit. She'd been forcing down a salad even though she wasn't hungry, even though her stomach hurt from missing Joe. Lord, she didn't think it was possible to miss another person that badly. She felt hollow, empty, and hopelessly devoid of life.

And then a dozen men, dressed in black and carrying automatic rifles and submachine guns, jumped out of one helicopter and swarmed across the deck of the cruise ship, declaring that the *Majestic* was now in their control, and all her passengers were their hostages.

It seemed unreal, like some sort of strange movie that she was somehow involved in making.

There were fewer than sixty people aboard the small cruise ship, including the crew. They were all on deck, watching and waiting as the second helicopter's blades slowed and then stopped.

No one made a sound as the doors opened and several men stepped out.

One of them, a man with a pronounced limp who was wearing a baseball cap and sunglasses, smiled a greeting to the silent crowd. He had a wide, friendly, white-toothed smile set off by a thick salt-and-pepper beard. Without saying a word, he gestured to one of the other terrorists, who pulled the two FInCOM agents out in front of them all.

The terrorists had cuffed the two security agents' hands behind them, and now, as they were pushed to their knees in front of the bearded man, they fought to keep their balance.

"Who are you?" one of the agents, a woman named Maggie Forte demanded. "What is this—"

"Silence," the bearded man said. And then he pulled a revolver from his belt and shot both agents in the head.

Senator McKinley's wife screamed and started to cry.

"Just so you know our guns are quite real," the bearded man said to the rest of them in his softly accented voice, "and that we mean business. My name is Diosdado." He gestured to the other terrorists around him. "These men and women all work for me. Do as they say, and you will all be fine." He smiled again. "Of course, there are no guarantees."

Veronica stared at the bright red blood pooling beneath the FInCOM agents' bodies. They were dead. Just like that, a man and a woman were dead. The man—Charlie Griswold, he'd said his name was—had just had a new baby. He'd shown Veronica pictures. He'd been so proud, so in love with his pretty young wife. And now…

God forgive her, but all she could think was *Thank God it wasn't Joe*. Thank God Joe wasn't here. Thank God that wasn't Joe's blood spreading across the deck.

Diosdado limped toward Prince Tedric, who was standing slightly apart from the rest of them.

"So we finally meet again," the terrorist said. He used his

submachine gun to knock the Stetson cowboy hat Tedric was wearing off his head.

Tedric looked as if he might be ill.

"Did you really think I'd forget about the agreement we made?" Diosdado asked.

Tedric glanced toward the two dead agents lying on the deck. "No," he whispered.

"Then where are my long-range missiles?" Diosdado demanded. "I've been waiting and waiting for you to come through on your part of the deal."

Veronica couldn't believe what she was hearing. Prince Tedric, involved in arms smuggling? She wouldn't have believed he had the nerve.

"I said I'd *try*," Tedric hissed. "I made no promises."

Diosdado made tsking sounds. "Then it was very bad form for you to keep the money," he said.

Tedric straightened in shock. "I sent the money back," he retorted. "I wouldn't have kept it. *Mon Dieu*, I wouldn't have...dared."

Diosdado stared at him. Then he laughed. "You know, I actually believe you. It seems my good friend Salustiano intervened more than once. No wonder he wanted you dead. He'd intercepted two million of my dollars that you were returning to me." He laughed again. "Isn't this an interesting twist?" He turned to his men. "Take the other hostages below, and His Highness to the bridge. Let's see what a crown prince is worth these days. I may get my long-range missiles yet."

Navy SEAL Team Ten was airborne less than thirty minutes after Admiral Forrest contacted the naval base in Washington State. Joe sat in the air-force jet with his men, receiving nearly continuous reports from a Blackbird SR-71 spy plane that was circling at eighty-five thousand feet above the hijacked cruise ship, over the northern Pacific Ocean. The Blackbird was flying so high the terrorists and hostages on board the *Majestic* couldn't have seen it even with high-powered binoculars.

But with the Blackbird's high-tech equipment, Joe could see the cruise ship. The pictures that were coming in were very sharp and clear.

There were two bodies on the deck near two high-speed attack helicopters.

Two bodies, two pools of blood.

More detailed reports showed that one of the bodies was wearing a skirt, her legs angled awkwardly on the deck.

One man, one woman. Both dead.

Joe studied the picture, unable to see the woman's features for all the blood. Please, God, don't let it be Veronica! He glanced up to find Blue looking over his shoulder.

Blue shook his head. "I don't think it's her," he said. "I don't think it's Veronica."

Joe didn't say anything at first. "It could be," he finally said, his voice low.

"Yeah." Blue nodded. "Could be. And if it's not, it's someone that somebody else loves. It's already a no-win situation, Cat. Don't let it interfere with what we've got to do."

"I won't," he said. He smiled, but it didn't reach his eyes. "That bastard Diosdado isn't gonna know what hit him."

Veronica sat in the dining room with the other hostages, wondering what was going to come next.

Tedric sat apart from the others, staring at the walls, his jaw clenched tightly, his arms crossed in front of him.

It was funny, so many people had seen Joe and thought that he was Tedric. But to Veronica, their physical differences were so clearly obvious. Joe's eyes were bigger and darker, his lashes longer. Joe's chin was stronger, more square. Tedric's nose was narrower, and slightly pinched looking at the end.

Sure, they both had dark hair and dark eyes, but Tedric's eyes shifted as he spoke, never settling on any one thing. Veronica had worked for hours and *hours*, trying to teach the prince to look steadily into the TV cameras. Joe, on the other hand, always looked everyone straight in the eye. Tedric was in constant motion—fingers tapping, a foot jiggling, crossing and uncrossing his legs. Joe's energy was carefully contained. He could sit absolutely still, but one could feel his leashed power. He nearly throbbed with it, but it didn't distract—at least, not all the time.

Veronica closed her eyes.

Was she ever going to see Joe again? What she would give to put her arms around him, to feel his arms holding her.

But he was in Virginia. It was very likely that he hadn't even heard about the hijacking yet. And what would he think when he found out? Would he even care? He'd been so cold, so formal, so distant during their last conversation.

Diosdado had opened communications with both the U.S. and the Ustanzian governments. Ustanzia was ready to ship out the missiles the terrorists wanted, but the U.S. was against that. Now the two governments were in disagreement, with the U.S. threatening to drop all future aid if Ustanzia gave in to the terrorists' demands. But Senator McKinley was on board the *Majestic*, too. So between the senator and Crown Prince Tedric, Diosdado had hit a jackpot.

But jackpot or not, Diosdado was losing patience.

He limped into the room now, and all of the hostages tensed.

"Men on one side, and women on the other," said the leader of the Cloud of Death, drawing an imaginary line down the center of the room with his arm.

Everybody stared. No one moved.

"Now!" he commanded quite softly, lifting his gun for emphasis.

They all moved. Veronica stood on the right side of the imaginary line with the rest of the women. There were only fourteen women on board, compared to the forty men on the other side of the dining room.

Mrs. McKinley was shivering, and Veronica reached down and took the older woman's icy fingers.

"Here's how it's going to work," Diosdado said pleasantly. "We're going to start with the women. You're going to go up to the bridge, to the radio room, and talk to your government. You're going to convince them to give us what we want, *and* to keep their distance. And you're going to tell them that starting in one hour, we're going to begin eliminating our hostages, one each hour, on the hour."

There was a murmur in the crowd, and Mrs. McKinley clung more tightly to Veronica's hand.

"And," Diosdado said, "you may tell them that once again we're going to start with the women."

"No!" one of the men cried.

Diosdado turned and fired his gun, shooting the man in the head. Several people screamed, many dove for cover.

Veronica turned away, sickened. Just like that, another man was dead.

"Anyone else have any objections?" Diosdado asked pleasantly.

Except for the sound of quiet sobbing, the hostages were silent.

"You and you," the terrorist said, and it was several moments before Veronica realized he was talking to her and Mrs. McKinley. "To the radio room."

Veronica looked up into the glittering chill of Diosdado's dark eyes, and she knew. She was going to be the first. She had only one more hour to live.

One very short hour.

Even if Joe knew, even if Joe cared, there was nothing he could do to save her. He was on the other side of the country. There was no way he could reach her within an hour.

She was going to die.

Chapter Twenty-One

Joe stood in the briefing room of the USS *Watkins*, and tried to work out a plan to get SEAL Team Ten onto the *Majestic*, and the hostages off.

"Infrared surveillance shows the majority of the hostages are in the ship's dining hall," Blue reported. He pointed to the location on a cutaway schematic of the cruise ship that was spread out on the table among all the other maps and charts and photographs. "We can approach at dusk, going under their radar with inflatable boats, climb up the sides of the *Majestic*, and bring the hostages out without the terrorists even knowing."

"Once everyone's clear of the cruise ship," Harvard said with a hard smile, "we kick their butts all the way to hell."

"We'll need air support," Joe said. "At the first sign of trouble, Diosdado is going to split in one of those choppers he's got on the deck. I want to make sure we've got some fighters standing by, ready to shoot him down if necessary."

"What you *need*," Admiral Forrest said, coming into the

room, "is a go-ahead from the president. And right now, he wants to sit tight, wait and see what the terrorists do next."

The intercom from the bridge crackled on. "We have a report from the *Majestic*," a voice said over the loudspeaker. "Another hostage is dead. The terrorists say they'll kill one hostage every hour until they get either twenty million dollars or a shipment of long-range missiles."

Another hostage was dead. Joe couldn't breathe. God help Diosdado if he so much as *touched* Veronica. He looked around the room at the grim faces of his men. God help that bastard, anyway. SEAL Team Ten was after him now.

The telephone rang, and Cowboy picked it up. "Jones," he said. He held the receiver out to the admiral. "Sir, it's for you." He swallowed. "It's the president."

Forrest took the phone. "Yes, sir?" He nodded, listening hard, then looked up at Joe. He spoke only one word, but it was the word Joe had been waiting for.

"Go."

As the sun began to set, Mrs. McKinley was taken back to the dining room, leaving Veronica alone with Diosdado and one of his followers.

"Right about now, you're wondering how you ever got into this mess," Diosdado said to Veronica, offering her one of the cigarettes from his pack.

She shook her head.

"It's okay," he said. "You can smoke if you want." He laughed. "After all, you don't have to worry about dying from lung cancer, right?"

"Right about now," Veronica said with forced calm, "I'm wondering what your head would look like—on a pike."

Diosdado laughed, and touched her on the cheek. "You Brits are so bloodthirsty."

She pulled her head away, repulsed. He just laughed again.

"They're all going to die," he said. "All of the hostages. You should be thankful *your* death is going to be painless."

Joe met Blue's eyes in the dimness of the corridor outside the dining hall. They both wore headsets and mikes, but at this proximity to the terrorists, they were silent. Joe nodded once and Blue nodded back.

They were going in.

The door was open a crack, and they knew from looking in that both guards had their backs to them. Both guards were holding Uzis, but their stances were relaxed, unsuspecting of trouble.

Joe smiled grimly. Well, here came trouble with a capital *T*. He pointed to Blue and then to the guard on the left. Blue nodded. Joe held up three fingers, two fingers, one…

He pushed the door open, and he and Blue erupted into the room as if they were one body with a single controlling brain. The guard on the left spun around, bringing his Uzi up. Joe fired once, the sound of the shot muffled by his hushpuppy. He caught the Uzi as the man fell, turning to see Blue lower the other guard, his head at an unnatural angle, to the ground.

The hostages didn't make a sound. They stared, though. The entire room reeked of fear.

"Dining room secure," Blue said into his microphone. "Let's get some backup down here, boys." He turned to the hostages. "We're U.S. Navy SEALs," he told them in his gentle Southern accent as Joe searched the crowd for Veronica. "With your continued cooperation, we're here to take y'all home."

There was a babble of voices, questions, demands. Blue held up both hands. "We're not out of danger yet, folks," he said. "I'd like to ask you all to remain silent and to move quickly and quietly when we tell you to."

Veronica wasn't here. If she wasn't here, that meant…

"Veronica St. John," Joe said, his voice cracking with his effort to stay calm. Just because she wasn't here didn't necessarily mean she was dead, right? "Does anyone know where Veronica St. John is?"

An older woman with graying hair raised her hand. "On the bridge," she said in a shaky voice. "That man, that murderer, is going to kill her at six o'clock. They took the prince somewhere else, too."

The clock on the wall said five fifty-five.

Joe's watch said the same.

He turned to look at Blue, who was already speaking into his headset. "Harvard and Cowboy, get your fannies down here on the double. We've got to get these people off this ship, pronto, and you're the ones who're gonna do it."

With Blue only a few steps behind, Joe slipped the strap of the Uzi over his shoulder. Holding his HK machine gun he headed back down the corridor at a run.

"I'm sorry," Diosdado said into the radio, sounding not one bit sorry. "Your promise to deliver twenty million to my Swiss bank account isn't enough. I gave you plenty of time to get the job done. Maybe you'll do it before the *next* hostage is killed, hmm? Think about it. This communication has ended."

With a flick of his wrist, he turned the radio off. He took a sip of coffee before he faced Veronica.

"I'm so sorry," he said. "Your government has let you down. They don't think you're worth twenty million dollars."

"I thought you wanted missiles," Veronica said. "Not money."

It was 6:01 p.m. Maybe if she could keep him talking, maybe if she could stall him, something, some miracle would happen. At the very least, she'd live a few minutes longer. She'd already lived one minute more than she'd thought she would.

"Either one would be fine," Diosdado said with a shrug. He turned to his guard. "Where is our little prince? I need him in here."

The man nodded and left the room.

Veronica felt incredibly calm, remarkably poised, considering that, miracles aside, she was going to get a bullet in her head in a matter of minutes.

She wasn't going to see another sunrise. She wasn't going to see Joe's beautiful smile, hear his contagious laughter again. She wasn't going to get a chance to tell him that she'd been wrong, that she wanted him for however long he was willing to give her.

Facing her own death made her see it all so clearly. She loved Joe Catalanotto. So what if he was a Navy SEAL. It was who he was, what he did. It was quite probably the reason she'd fallen in love with him. He was the best of the best in so many different ways. If by being a SEAL, he had to live on the edge and cheat death, so be it. She would learn to cope.

But she wasn't going to have a chance to do that. Because of her own fears and weaknesses, she'd pushed Joe away. She'd given up the few moments of happiness she could have had with him. She'd given up a lingering kiss goodbye. She'd given up a phone call that could have been filled with whispered "I love you's" instead of stilted apologies and chilly regrets.

How ironic that *she* was the one who was going to die a violent and horrible death.

Four minutes past six.

"What could be taking them so long?" Diosdado mused. He smiled at Veronica. "I'm so sorry, dear. I know you must be anxious to get this over with. I'd do it myself, but when

Prince Tedric comes in, we're going to play a little game. Do you want to know the rules?"

Veronica looked into the eyes of the man who was going to kill her. "Why do you do this?" she asked.

"Because I can." The eyes narrowed slightly. "You're not afraid, are you?" he asked.

She was terrified. But she was damned if she was going to let *him* know that. She replied, "I'm saddened. There's a man that I love, and he's never going to know just how much I really do love him."

Diosdado laughed. "Isn't that tragic," he said. "You're just as pathetic as the rest of them. And to think, for a moment I was actually considering sparing you."

Five minutes past six.

He'd never had any intention of sparing her. It was just another of his head games. Veronica didn't allow any expression to cross her face.

"You didn't let me tell you about this game we're going to play," the terrorist continued. "It's called 'Who's the Killer?' When Prince Tedric comes in, I'll put a gun on the table over here." He patted the tabletop. "And then, with *my* gun on him, I'll order him to pick up that gun and fire a bullet into your head." He laughed. "Do you think he'll do it?"

"You aren't afraid he'll turn and use the gun on you?"

"Prince Tedric?" Diosdado blew out a burst of disparaging air. "No. The man has no…backbone." He shook his head. "No, it will be *your* brains on these nice windows, not mine."

The door was pushed tentatively open, and Prince Tedric came onto the bridge. He was still wearing his cowboy hat, pulled low over his face. But his jacket was unbuttoned. That was odd—surely a sign of his despondency. Veronica had never seen him look anything but fastidious.

"Your Royalness," Diosdado said. He swooped low in a mocking bow. "I believe you are familiar with Miss Veronica St. John, yes?"

Tedric nodded. "Yes," he said. "I know Ronnie."

Ronnie?

Veronica looked up at Tedric in surprise—and met Joe's warm brown gaze.

Joe! Here?

The rush of emotions was intense. Veronica had never been so glad to see anyone in her entire life. Or so frightened. *Lord, please, don't let Joe be killed, too....*

"Get down," Joe mouthed silently.

"We're going to play a little game," Diosdado was saying.

"I've got a game for you," Joe said in Tedric's Ustanzian accent. "It's called 'Show-and-Tell.'"

He pulled the biggest machine gun Veronica had ever seen in her life out from under his open jacket and aimed it at Diosdado.

"I show you my gun," Joe finished in his regular voice, "and you freeze. Then tell your army to surrender."

Diosdado didn't freeze. He lifted his gun.

Veronica dove for the floor as they opened fire. The noise was incredible, and the smell of gunpowder filled the air. But just as quickly as it started, it stopped. And then Joe was next to her on the floor, pulling her into his arms.

"Ronnie! God, tell me you're all right!"

She clung to his neck. "Oh, Joe!" She pulled back. "Are *you* all right?" He seemed to be in one piece, despite all of the bullets that had been flying just moments earlier.

"He didn't hurt you, did he?"

Veronica shook her head.

He kissed her, hard, on the mouth and she closed her eyes, pulling him closer, kissing him back with as much strength and passion. She welcomed his familiar taste, giddy

with relief and a sense of homecoming she'd never experienced before. He'd come to save her. Somehow he'd known,
and he'd come.

"Well," Joe said, his voice husky as he drew back. "I guess
this is probably the one situation where you'd be indispu-
tably glad to see me, huh?" He smiled, but there was a flash
of remorse in his eyes as he took off Tedric's jacket, revealing some kind of dark uniform and vest underneath.

He was serious. He honestly thought the only reason she
was so happy to see him was because he had come to save
her life. "No, Joe—" she said, but he stopped her, standing
and pulling her to her feet.

"Come on, baby, we've got to get moving," Joe said. "In
about thirty seconds, this place is going to be crawling
with tangos who heard that gunfire. We've got to get out
of here."

"Joe—"

"Tell me while we're moving," he said, not unkindly, as
he pulled her toward the door. She hesitated only a second,
glancing back over her shoulder at where Diosdado had
stood only moments before.

"Is he...?"

Joe nodded. "Yeah." Holding her hand, he led her gently
down the corridor. She was shaking slightly, but otherwise
seemed okay. Of course, it was entirely possible that the
shock of what she'd just been through hadn't set in. Still,
they had to move while they could. "Can you run?" he asked.

"Yes," she said.

They set off down the corridor at an easy trot.

She was still holding his hand, and she squeezed it
slightly. "I love you," she said.

Joe glanced at her. Her eyes were bright with unshed
tears, but she managed to smile as she met his gaze. "I didn't
think I'd get the chance to tell you that ever again," she ex-

plained. "And I know we're not out of danger, so I wanted to make sure you knew, in case—"

Veronica was right—they *weren't* out of danger. They were at the opposite end of the ship from the extraction point, and the tangos had surely been alerted to the fact that there were intruders on board. They had surely noticed that their hostages were missing and their leader was dead. SEAL Team Ten had stirred up one hell of a hornet's nest—and Joe and Veronica were still in the middle of it.

But Joe wasn't about to tell Veronica that. They *could* pull this off. Damn it, they *would* pull this off. He was a SEAL and he was armed to the teeth. Several dozen terrorists didn't stand a chance against him. Hell, with stakes this high, with the life of the woman he loved at risk, he could take on several hundred and win.

Joe slowed, peering around a corner, making sure they weren't about to run head-on into a pack of terrorists. Veronica loved him, and even though she didn't love him enough to want to marry him, he didn't care anymore. He honestly didn't care. If he'd been five minutes later, if that evil bastard Diosdado hadn't wanted to play games with his victims, if any number of things had been different, he would have lost Veronica permanently. The thought made him crazy. She could have been killed, and he would be alone, without her forever and ever.

But she hadn't been killed. They'd both been given a second chance, and Joe wasn't going to waste it. And he wanted to make his feelings clear to her—now—before she walked away from him again.

"When this is all over," he said almost conversationally, "after you're off this ship and safely back onshore, you're going to have to get used to me coming around to visit you. You don't have to marry me, Ronnie. It doesn't have to be anything permanent. But I've got to tell you right now—I have no intention of letting this thing between us drop, do you follow?"

Silently, she nodded.

"Good," Joe said. "You don't have to go out with me in public. You don't have to acknowledge our relationship at all—not to your friends, not to your family. I'll keep sneaking in your back door, baby, if that's the way you want it. You can just go on slumming, indefinitely. I don't give a damn, because I love you." To hell with his pride. To hell with it all. He'd take her any way he could get her.

"Slumming?" Veronica echoed, surprise in her voice. "What—"

"Beg your pardon, Romeo," came Blue's voice over Joe's headset, and Joe held up his hand, cutting Veronica off, "but I thought you might want to know that I've extracted with my royal luggage. Ronnie's the last civilian on board. The tangos know something's up, so move it, Cat—fast. The USS *Watkins* is moving into position, picking up the IBS's with the hostages. I'm coming back to the *Majestic* to assist you—"

"No," Joe interrupted. Veronica was watching him, with that look on her face that meant she was dying to speak. He shook his head, touching his headset as he spoke to his XO. "No, Blue, I need you to stay with the prince," he ordered. "But make sure there's a boat waiting for me and Ronnie at the bottom of that rope at the bow of this ship."

"You got it," Blue said. "See you on the *Watkins*."

"Check," Joe replied.

Veronica watched Joe. *Slumming?* What had he meant? Then her words came back to her. *Different worlds*. She'd talked about their different worlds when she'd turned down his marriage proposal. She'd been referring to the differences between his matter-of-fact response to danger, his thrill for adventure, and her fears of letting him go. Had he somehow misunderstood her? Had he actually thought she'd been talking about their supposed class differences—assuming something as absurd as class differences even existed? Could he actually have thought she was put off by something as ridiculous as where he came from or where he grew up?

Veronica opened her mouth, about to speak, when suddenly, from somewhere on the ship, there was an enormous, swooshing noise, like a rocket being launched.

"What was *that?*" Veronica breathed.

But Joe was listening again, listening to the voices over his headset.

"Check," he said into his microphone. He turned toward Veronica. "The T's are firing artillery at the hostages. Return fire," he ordered. He listened again. "You're gonna have to," he said tersely. "We're down below, outside the game room, but that's gonna change real soon. I'll keep you informed of my position. You just use that high-tech equipment and make sure you aim when you shoot. Fire now. Do you copy? Fire *now.*"

"My Lord!" Veronica said. Joe had just given an order for the men on the USS *Watkins* to return fire at the cruise ship—while she and Joe were still on board!

A deafening explosion the likes of which Veronica had never heard before thundered around them. The missile from the USS *Watkins* rocked the entire ship, seeming to lift it out of the water and throw it back down.

Joe grabbed Veronica's hand and pulled her with him down the hallway.

"Okay, *Watkins,*" he said over his headset. "We're heading away from the game room, toward the bow of the ship." There was a flight of stairs leading up toward the deck. Joe motioned for Veronica to hang back as he crawled up and peeked over the edge. He motioned with his hand for her to follow him. "Heading toward the recreation deck," he said into his microphone as he climbed up the steps and got his bearings, hanging back in the shadows and looking around. Veronica wasn't sure what he saw, but it didn't make him happy. "We're not going to make it to the extraction point," he said. "We've got to find another way off—"

Then Joe saw it—the perfect escape vehicle—and smiled. Diosdado's helicopters were sitting there, waiting to be hijacked. But this time by the good guys.

They were twenty yards from the helicopter. Twenty yards from freedom.

"Heading for the choppers up on the deck," he said into his mike. "Keep those missiles coming in, but keep 'em clear of us."

Fifteen yards. Ten. God, they were going to make it. They were—

All hell broke loose.

It was a small squad of T's—only about five of them— but they came out of nowhere.

Joe had his gun up and firing as he stepped in front of Veronica. He felt the slap of a bullet hit him low in his gut, beneath the edge of his flak jacket, but he felt no pain, only anger.

Damn it, he wasn't going to let Ronnie die. No way in *hell* was he going to let her die. Not now. Not when he was so close to getting her to safety...

His bullets plowed through the terrorists, taking them down, or driving them away from him to cover. But the sound of gunfire drew more of them toward him.

His mind registered the first sensations of pain. *Pain?* The word didn't come close to describing the white-hot, searing agony he felt with every step, every movement. He was gut-shot, and every pounding beat of his heart was pumping his blood out of his body. It wouldn't be long before he bled to death. Still firing his gun, he tried to stanch the flow. He'd been trained as a hospital corpsman—all SEALs were. He'd been trained to provide first aid to his men, and even to himself. He needed to apply pressure, but it was tough with a wound this size. The bullet had penetrated him, leaving an exit wound in his back, through which he also bled.

God, the pain.

Through it all, he kept going. If they could reach the chopper, he could still fly Ronnie out of here. If they could reach the chopper, bleeding or not, dying or not, he could get her to the *Watkins*.

The door to the bird was open—God was on his side—but Joe didn't seem to have the strength to push Veronica in. "Dear Lord, you're bleeding," he heard her say. He felt her push him up and into the cockpit. And then, damned if she didn't grab the Uzi, and turn and fire out the open door, keeping the T's at bay while, through a fog, Joe started the engine. He could fly anything, he told himself over and over, hoping that the litany would somehow make his brain respond. They didn't make a chopper he couldn't handle. But his arms felt like lead and his legs weren't working right. Still, he had to do it. He had to, or Veronica was going to die alongside him.

And then, miracle of miracles, they were up. They were in the air and moving away from the ship.

"We're clear of the *Majestic*," Joe rasped into his microphone. "Launch a full-scale attack."

The world blurred for a second, and then snapped sharply into focus.

That was smoke he saw coming from the engine. Sweet Jesus, the chopper must have sustained a direct hit. Somehow, Joe had gotten the damned thing up, but it wasn't going to stay in the air too much longer.

"Tell them you need a medic standing by," Veronica said.

"We've got bigger problems," Joe told her.

She saw the smoke, and her eyes widened, but her voice didn't falter as she told him again, "You've been shot. Make sure someone on the *Watkins* knows that, Joe."

"We're not going to make it to the *Watkins*," Joe said. He spoke into his microphone. "Blue, I need you, man."

"I'm here, and I see you," Blue's familiar Southern drawl sounded in his ears. "You're leaving a trail of smoke like a cheap cigar, Cat. I'm coming out to meet you."

"Good," Joe said. "Because I'm going to bring this bird low, and Ronnie's gonna jump out into the water, you copy?"

"I'm not going anywhere without you," Veronica said, adding loudly, loud enough for Blue to hear, "Joe's been hit, and he's bleeding badly."

"I have a medic standing by," Blue said to Joe. "Is it bad, Cat?"

Joe ignored Blue's question. "I'm right behind you, Ronnie," he said to Veronica, knowing damn well that he was telling her a lie. "But I'm not going to ditch this bird until you're clear."

He could see her indecision in her eyes. She didn't want to leave him.

God, he was getting light-headed, and this chopper was getting harder and harder to handle as he hovered ten feet above the water's surface. The combination was *not* good.

"Go," he said.

"Joe—"

"Baby, *please*..." He couldn't hold on much longer.

"Promise you'll be right behind me?"

He nodded, praying to God for forgiveness for his lie. "I promise."

She slid open the door. "I want us to get married right away," she said, and then she was gone.

* * *

The water was cold as ice.

It surrounded Veronica, squeezing her chest as she surfaced and tried to take in a breath of air.

But then a boat was there, and hands reached for her, pulling her up.

Veronica ignored the cold as she turned to watch the chopper, hovering above the waves, its whirling blades turning the ocean into choppy whitecaps. Someone wrapped a blanket around her— Blue, it was Blue McCoy, Joe's executive officer.

The plume of smoke from the helicopter was darker, thicker. And the chopper seemed to lurch instead of holding still.

"Why won't he jump?" she wondered aloud.

Before she finished speaking, the helicopter jerked forward and down—into the water.

She could hear shouting—it was Blue's voice—and she couldn't believe that the noise—some noise, *any* noise, wasn't coming from her own throat.

The helicopter was sinking beneath the waves, taking Joe with it, taking all her hopes and dreams for the future away from her.

"No!" she cried, the word torn from her raggedly.

"I'm going in after him." It was Blue. "Pull this boat closer."

"Sir, I can't let you do that," said a young man in a naval uniform. His face was pale. "If the chopper doesn't pull you under, the water's so cold, it'll kill you. You won't last more than five minutes before hypothermia sets in."

"Pull the damned boat closer, Ensign," Blue said, his voice as cold as the Alaskan water. "I'm a SEAL, and that's my commander down there. I'm going after him."

The water was cold as ice.

It roused Joe from his fog as it splashed him in the face.

Damn, he'd gone down. He didn't remember going down. All he remembered was Ronnie—

Ronnie telling him that she wanted to…marry him?

The last pocket of air bubbled out of the helicopter cockpit.

No way was he going to die. Ronnie wanted to *marry* him. No way was he going to *drown. Or bleed to death,* damn it.

The water was cold as hell, but it would slow his bleeding.

All he had to do was get his arms and legs to work.

But he hurt.

Every single cell in his body hurt, and it took so much goddammed effort to lift even a finger.

This was worse than anything he'd ever experienced, worse even than Hell Week, that torturous final week of SEAL training that he'd lived through so many years ago.

He'd never wanted anything as badly as he'd wanted to be a SEAL. It had kept him going through the nonstop exertion, through the pain, through the torturous physical demands. *"You got to want it badly enough,"* one of his instructors had shouted at them, day after day, hour after hour. And Joe had. He'd wanted to be a SEAL. He'd wanted it badly enough.

He'd wanted to be a SEAL almost as much as he wanted Veronica St. John.

And she was there, up there, above the surface of that freezing water, waiting for him. All he had to do was kick his legs, push himself free and he would have her. Forever. All he had to do was want it badly enough….

Veronica stared at the water, at the place where first the helicopter and then Blue had disappeared.

Please, God, if you give me this, I'll never ask for anything ever again….

Seconds ticked into one minute. Two. Three…

Was it possible for a man to hold his breath for this long, let alone search for a wounded, drowning man…?

Please, God.

And then, all at once, a body erupted from beneath the surface of the water. Veronica peered into the area lit by the searchlights. Was that one head or…

Two! Two heads! Blue had found Joe!

A cheer went up from the sailors on board the boat, and they quickly maneuvered closer to the two men, and pulled them out.

Dear God, it *was* Joe, and he was breathing. Veronica stood aside as the medics sliced his wet clothes from his body. Oh, Lord, he'd been shot in the abdomen, just above his hip. She watched, clutching her own blanket more tightly around her as he was wrapped in a blanket and an IV was attached to his arm.

"Cat was coming up as I was going down after him," Blue said, respect heavy in his voice. "I think he would have made it, even without me. He didn't want to die. Not today."

Joe was floating in and out of consciousness, yet he turned his head, searching for something, searching for…

"Ronnie." His voice was just a whisper, but he reached for her, and she took his hand.

"I'm here," she said, pressing his fingers to her lips.

"Did you mean it?" He was fighting hard to remain conscious. He was fighting, and winning. "When you said you'd marry me?"

"Yes," she said, fighting her own battle against the tears that threatened to escape.

Joe nodded. "You know, I'm not going to change," he said. "I can't pretend to be something I'm not. I'm not a prince or a duke or—"

Veronica cut him off with a kiss. "You're my prince," she said.

"Your parents are going to hate me."

"My parents are going to *love* you," she countered. "Nearly as much as I do."

He smiled then, ignoring his pain, reaching up to touch the side of her face. "You really think this could work?"

"Do you love me?" Veronica asked.

"Absolutely."

"Then it will work." The boat was pulling up alongside of the USS *Watkins*, where a doctor was waiting. From what Veronica had gathered from the medics, they believed the bullet had passed through Joe's body, narrowly missing his vital organs. He'd lost a lot of blood, and had to be stitched up and treated for infection, but it could have been worse. It could have been *far* worse.

Joe felt himself placed onto a stretcher. He had to release Ronnie's hand as he was lifted up and onto the deck of the *Watkins*.

"I love you," she called.

He was smiling as the doctor approached him, smiling as the nurse added painkiller to his intravenous tube, smiling as he gave in to the drug and let the darkness finally close in around him.

Joe stared up at the white ceiling in sick bay for a good long time before he figured out where he was and why he couldn't move. He was still strapped down to a bed. He hurt like hell. He'd been shot. He'd been stitched up.

He'd been promised a lifetime filled with happiness and Veronica St. John's beautiful smile.

Veronica Catalanotto. He smiled at the idea of her taking his name.

And then Blue was leaning over him, releasing the restraints. "Damn, Cat," he said in his familiar drawl. "The doc said you were grinning like a fool when he brought you in here, and here you are again, smiling like a fox in a henhouse."

"Where's Ronnie?" Joe whispered. His throat was so dry, and his mouth felt gummy. He tried to moisten his dry lips with his tongue.

Blue turned away, murmuring something to the nurse before he turned back to Joe, lifting a cup of water to his friend's lips. "She's getting checked by the doctor," he told Joe.

Joe's smile disappeared, the soothing drink of water forgotten. "She okay?"

Blue nodded. "She's just getting a blood test," he said. "Apparently she needs one."

"Why?"

"Because I'm hoping to get married," Ronnie said, leaning forward to kiss him gently on the mouth. "That is, if you still have that ring. If you still want me."

Joe gazed up at her. Her hair was down, loose and curling around her shoulders. She was wearing a sailor suit that was several sizes too large, white flared pants and a white shirt, sleeves rolled up several times. She was wearing no makeup, and her freshly scrubbed face looked impossibly young—and anxious—as she waited for his answer. "Hell, yes," he somehow managed to say.

She smiled, and Joe felt his mouth curve up into an answering smile as he lost himself in the ocean color of her eyes. "Do you still want *me?*"

Blue moved quietly toward the door. "I guess I'll leave you two a—"

Ronnie turned then, looking up at Joe's XO and best friend. "Wait," she said. "Please?" She looked back at Joe. "I'll marry you, but there's one condition."

Blue shifted his weight uncomfortably.

"Anything," Joe said to Veronica. "I'd promise you anything. Just name it."

"It's not something *you* can promise me," she said. She looked up at Blue again, directly into his turquoise eyes. "I need Blue's promise—to keep Joe safe and alive."

Blue nodded slowly, taking her words seriously. "I'd die for him," he said, matter-of-factly.

Veronica had seen them in action. She'd seen Blue dive into the icy Alaskan waters after Joe, and she knew he spoke the truth. It wasn't going to make her fear for Joe's safety disappear, but it *was* going to make it easier.

"I didn't want to marry you because I was—I am—afraid that you're going to get yourself killed," she said, turning back to Joe. "I knew I couldn't ask you to leave the SEALs and…"

She saw his eyes narrow slightly as he understood her words. "Then…"

Veronica felt more than saw Blue slip from the room as she leaned forward to kiss Joe's lips. "I wasn't 'slumming.'" She mock shuddered. "Nasty expression, that."

He laced his fingers through her hair, wariness and concern in his eyes. "I can't leave the SEALs, baby—"

She silenced him with another kiss. "I know. I'm not asking you to. I'm not going to quit my job and become a career navy wife, either," Veronica told Joe. "I'll travel and work—the same as you. But whenever you can get leave time, I'll be there."

As she gazed into Joe's midnight-dark eyes, the last of his reservations drained away, leaving only love—pure and powerful. But then he frowned slightly. "Your ring's back in Little Creek," he said.

"I don't need a ring to know how much you love me," Veronica whispered.

Joe touched his chest, realized he was wearing a hospital gown, then pressed the call button for the nurse.

A young man appeared almost instantly. "Problem, sir?"

"What happened to my uniform?" Joe demanded.

"There wasn't much left of it after the medics cut it off you, sir." The nurse gestured toward a small table just out of reach of the bed. "Your personal gear is in that drawer."

"Thanks, pal," Joe said.

"Can I get you anything, sir?"

"Just some privacy," Joe told him, and the nurse left as quickly as he had come.

Joe turned to Veronica. "Check in that drawer for me, will you, baby?"

Veronica stood up and crossed to the table. She pulled open the drawer. There were three guns inside, several rounds of ammunition, something that looked decidedly like a hand grenade, a deadly-looking knife, several bills of large denominations, a handful of change…

"There should be a gold pin," Joe said. "It's called a 'Budweiser.'"

A gold pin in the shape of an eagle with both an ocean trident and a gun, it was Joe's SEAL pin, one of his most precious possessions. He'd gotten it on the day he graduated, the day he became a Navy SEAL. Veronica took it from the drawer. It felt solid and heavy in her hand as she carried it to Joe.

But he didn't take it from her. He wrapped her fingers around it. "I want you to have it."

Veronica stared at him.

"There are two things I've never given anyone," he said quietly. "One is this pin. The other is my heart." He smiled at her. "Now you got 'em both. Forever."

He pulled her head down to him and kissed her so gently, so sweetly, so perfectly.

And Veronica realized again what she'd known for quite some time.

She had found her prince.

FOREVER BLUE

ACKNOWLEDGMENTS

Special thanks to the Forever Blue Project volunteers from the Team Ten list (http://groups.yahoo.com/group/teamten/) for their proofreading skills: Cocaptains Rebecca Chappell and Agnes Brach, and Jeanette Bishop, Erin Brown, Jaxine Bubis, Nicole Geary, April Gieseking, Cindy Olp, Patricia Rovensky, Mary Beth Schroeder and Neal Wyatt. Hooyah, gang! Thanks so much for helping out.

Thanks to the real teams of SEALs, and to all of the courageous men and women in the U.S. military who sacrifice so much to keep America the land of the free and the home of the brave. And last but not least, a heartfelt thank-you to the wives, husbands, children and families of these real-life military heroes and heroines. Your sacrifice is deeply appreciated!

Any mistakes I've made or liberties I've taken in writing this book are completely my own.

For Jodie Kuhlman and Patricia McMahon,
for their amazing brainstorming power
and naming skill, and for Sarah Telford,
for lending Lucy her little black dress.

Prologue

Lieutenant Blue McCoy was the point man, leading the six other men of SEAL Team Ten's Alpha Squad across the marshlike ground. He moved painstakingly slowly, inch by inch through the darkness, touching, feeling the soft, loamy earth; searching for booby traps and land mines before actually putting his weight down on any one spot.

He watched the shadows, scanning the brush in front of him, memorizing the placement of each faintly silhouetted leaf and branch, alert to even the most minute movement.

The sounds of the night surrounded him. Insects buzzed and clicked; a dog barked maybe a mile away. An owl called through the darkness, its eerie cry proclaiming itself lord of this nocturnal domain, king of this night world.

It was a world in which Blue McCoy belonged, a world where he could lead a group of men so silently and invisibly through the darkness that the crickets at their feet didn't sense their presence.

It had taken them more than an hour to cross the open

field. Five more yards and they'd be in the cover of the brush. They'd be able to move faster then. Faster, but no less cautiously.

Blue listened, so in tune with the land around him that he *was* the night. His heart beat slowly in time with the silent, age-old rhythm of the earth and he thought of nothing—nothing but survival. All the noises and sounds of the air force base where Alpha Squad had been just ten hours earlier had long since evaporated, leaving only the night. There were six other men behind him, but Blue heard not a sound from any of them. He knew they were there only from faith, but it was a faith in which he had no doubts. The other SEALs were guarding his back as he led them forward. He knew they would die to protect him, as certainly as he would give his life for them.

Blue sniffed the air and froze, catching a faint, musky odor. But a second sniff convinced him that it was only an animal, some kind of rodent that moved as silently through the night as he did. It wasn't a human smell, and human animals were the prey he was hunting tonight.

Directly through the woods, dead ahead at twelve o'clock, forty yards distant, was a cabin. According to the spooks from FInCOM—the agents from the Federal Intelligence Commission—inside the cabin was United States Senator Mike Branford's fifteen-year-old daughter, Karen. The latest infrared satellite photos of the cabin revealed that at least four members of the terrorist group that had kidnapped her were inside the cabin with her. Another ten people were sleeping in a second structure, twenty yards to the northeast. And two five-man units of terrorists patrolled the surrounding woods. Only minutes ago, one of the units had come within four feet of Blue and the Alpha Squad. The unit commander had lit a cigarette, tossing the smoking match inches from Blue's hand before ordering his men to move on.

With their faces painted green and black, and with their intensive SEAL training, experience and discipline, Alpha Squad *was* invisible, embraced by the darkness, enshrouded by the cloak of night.

As the SEALs positioned themselves in the brush that surrounded the cabin, Blue turned to look at his commanding officer and good friend, Lieutenant Joe Catalanotto. Blue could barely see Joe Cat's face in the darkness, but he saw the man's nod.

Time to go.

Out of the corner of his eye, Blue caught the stealthy movement of Cowboy, Lucky, Bobby and Wes as they faded toward the northeast and the second structure. They were going to secure that building and neutralize the terrorists inside.

That left Joe Cat and Harvard cooling their heels outside the main cabin while Blue crept inside to snatch back the girl.

H. stood guard while Joe and Blue scanned the exterior of the cabin, in particular the window that was to be Blue's insertion point, his way in.

There were no booby traps, no alarms, no extra security. That was because the quarter mile surrounding the cabin was loaded with booby traps, alarms and armed security patrols. It was also because Aldo Fricker, the terrorists' leader, had forgotten the number-one rule: Never assume. The terrorists had left their vulnerable underbelly unprotected because they'd assumed that no one would be able to penetrate the fiercely guarded outer perimeters of their compound.

They were wrong.

Al Fricker, meet SEAL Team Ten's Alpha Squad.

As Blue watched, Joe Cat quickly and quietly cut the pane of glass from the cabin's window. Harvard gave Blue a boost up, and he was inside.

Blue did a quick scan of the interior with his night-vision glasses, quickly locating the senator's young daughter. She was curled up in an old brass bed in the southeast corner of the room. From what he could see she was still alive. The four guards were in sleeping bags or stretched out on the bare floor near the door. Blue took off his NVs and waited several seconds for his eyes to grow accustomed to the dark again, listening to the quiet breathing of the sleeping guards. It wouldn't do any good to wake the girl up while wearing the NVs, looking like some kind of alien from outer space. She was going to be frightened enough as it was.

He took four syringes from his battle vest and moved silently through the room, giving each of the guards a carefully dosed guaranteed good night's sleep. He sealed the needles back up and packaged the now-empty syringes in a bag marked Biohazardous Waste. A quick search of the cabin convinced him that no other guards were lurking, so he moved toward the senator's daughter.

He flicked on his penlight, shielding the light in the palm of one hand as he looked down at the sleeping girl. She was curled in a fetal position, knees tucked into her chest, one arm up, wrist attached by handcuffs to the brass headboard of the bed. Her hair was tangled and knotted, and dirt and blood from abrasions streaked her face and bare arms and legs. She was wearing a pair of blue shorts and a sleeveless top. Both were badly torn.

The bastards had hurt her. Karen. Her name was Karen Branford. They'd beaten her. Probably raped her. Christ, she was *fifteen* years old.

Rage filled him. Hot, molten and deadly, Blue felt it seep through his body, under his skin, spreading out all the way to his fingers and toes. It was a familiar sensation in his line of business. Normally he welcomed it. But tonight his job wasn't to fight back. Tonight his job was to take this battered little girl out of here and get her to safety.

When he adjusted his headset, pulling the lip microphone closer to his mouth, his voice was steady. "Cat," he said almost silently to his commanding officer. "They hurt her."

Joe Catalanotto cursed. "Bad?"

"Yeah."

"Can she walk?"

"I don't know," Blue said.

He turned toward the girl again, sensing from the change in the sound of her breathing that she was awake. Awake and terrified.

Quickly he knelt down next to her, holding the penlight so that it lit his camouflaged face.

"I'm Lieutenant Blue McCoy, miss," he said in a low voice. "I'm a U.S. Navy SEAL, and I'm here to bring you home."

She stared at him, eyes wide, taking in his uniform, his gun, and he knew she didn't understand.

"I'm an American sailor, Karen," he said. "I'm a friend of your daddy's, and I'm gonna get you outta here."

At the mention of her father, understanding and hope flared simultaneously in her brown eyes. She had been clutching at her torn shirt in a futile attempt at modesty, but now she removed her hand to cover his light.

"Shh," she whispered. "You'll wake the guards."

"No, I won't," Blue said. "They're not going to wake up for a while. And when they do, they're going to be in jail." He extracted his lock pick from the waterproof case in his vest and set to work on her cuffs. Three seconds was all it took, and the lock snapped open.

As she rubbed her wrist, Blue slipped off his pack and battle vest and quickly unbuttoned the camouflage shirt he wore underneath it. It was damp with perspiration and probably didn't smell too good, but it was the best he could offer her under the circumstances.

She accepted it silently, slipping it on and buttoning it clear up to her neck.

Blue had to give her credit. After her initial surprise and fear, she now gazed back at him unflinchingly. Her eyes were clear and brave. He'd seen brown eyes like hers somewhere before, a lifetime ago. The owner of those eyes had been fifteen years old, too....

Lucy. Little Lucy Tait. Hell, he hadn't thought about *her* in years.

Blue glanced at his watch, double-checking to make sure his pack was secure. According to the plan, diversionary tactics should be just about ready to start. Blue took a deep breath, looked down at Karen and quietly asked, "Can you walk?"

The young girl stood up. The tail of Blue's shirt came all the way down to her knees. "Better than that," she said stoutly, "I can run."

Blue smiled for the first time in what seemed like hours. "Well, all right. Let's go."

They were halfway through the brush, when Blue heard the first shots ring out. Joe Cat and H. were right behind him, and he sensed them both turning toward the sounds of the skirmish, wondering which men of Alpha Squad were involved, wishing they could go toward the fighting and provide backup.

"This is the wrong way," Blue heard Karen gasp. She pulled free from his grasp, looking wildly around.

He took her arm again. "No, it's not—"

"Yes, it is," she insisted. "I tried running this way before. There are nothing but cliffs. There's no path down to the ocean. We'll be trapped!"

The kid had tried to escape. Blue marveled at her guts. She *was* tough. Again he couldn't help but think about Lucy Tait. He'd been a senior and Lucy had been a little freshman, and the first time they met, she had been getting the stuff kicked out of her by a gang of kids. She was bloody and clearly the odds were against her, but she had a defiant lift to her chin and a "you can't beat me" glint in her brown eyes.

Cowboy's voice came in over Blue's headset. "Cat! About four tangos broke free. They're heading in your direction!"

"Copy that," Cat replied. He turned to Blue. "Go."

"We're going to parasail down to the water," Blue told Karen. "There's a boat waiting for us."

She didn't understand. "Parasail? *How?*"

"Trust me," he said.

Karen hesitated only a fraction of a second, then nodded.

Then they were running again, this time without Cat and Harvard on their heels.

The forest opened up into a field, and Blue felt vulnerable and exposed. If one of the terrorists broke through Cat and Harvard's ambush... But they wouldn't.

"Knock the hell out of them for me," he said into his lip microphone, and he heard Joe Catalanotto chuckle.

"You bet, buddy."

Blue stopped at the edge of the cliff and made adjustments to his pack so that Karen could be latched against him and they could parasail down to the water together.

She didn't complain, didn't say a word, although he knew that the proximity of his body to hers had to remind her of the brutalities she'd endured over the past four days.

But he couldn't think about that; couldn't wonder, couldn't focus on her pain. He had to think about that ship bobbing in the darkness, made invisible by the night.

He flipped on the homing device in his vest, reassured by the series of blips and beeps that told him the ship was indeed out there.

"Hold on," he said to the girl, and then he jumped.

Blue was on the deck of the USS *Franklin* when the chopper carrying the rest of Alpha Squad touched down.

He looked closer, trying for a quick head count. It was a

reflex from the time all those years ago when Frisco had gone down. He hadn't been KIA—killed in action—but he may as well have been. He still hadn't recovered from his injuries. His leg had damn near been blown off and he was still in a wheelchair—and still mad as hell about it.

Frisco had been Alpha Squad's unofficial goodwill ambassador. He had been friendly and lighthearted, quick to talk to and make friends with everyone around him. He had a sharp sense of humor and a fast wit—he soon had strangers laughing and smiling wherever he went. And his friendliness was sincere. He was a walking party. He always had a good time, whatever the situation.

In fact, Alan "Frisco" Francisco was the only SEAL Blue knew who actually enjoyed basic training's endurance test called Hell Week.

But when Frisco was told that he would never walk again, he'd stopped smiling. To Frisco, losing the use of his leg was the worst thing that ever could have happened to him. Even worse, maybe, than dying.

Blue watched the men jump down from the big bay doors of the helicopter. Joe Cat—his dark hair worn longer and tied back in a ponytail, his stern face relaxed in a smile nearly all the time now that he was married. Harvard—his shaved head gleaming like a coffee-colored bowling ball, looking big and mean and scary as hell. Bobby and Wes—unidentical twins, one big and tall, the other wiry and short, yet they moved in unison, finished each other's sentences. Lucky O'Donlon—Frisco's swim buddy. And the new guy—Cowboy. Harlan "Cowboy" Jones—temporary replacement first for Lucky on the same rescue mission that had injured Frisco, then temporary replacement for Frisco. Except it had been years and years, and it sure as hell looked as though temporary had turned pretty damned permanent.

They were all there, and they were all walking and breathing.

Joe Cat spotted Blue and moved in his direction.

"Everything okay?" he asked.

Blue nodded, heading with Joe toward the stairs leading below deck. "The doctor checked out the girl," he drawled. "She's with the shrink and the support staff right now." He shook his head. "Four *days*, Cat. Why the hell did it take them so long to let us go in after her?"

"Because the average politician and top-brass pencil pusher doesn't have a clue what a SEAL team can do." Joe Cat unfastened his battle vest, heading directly toward the mess hall.

"So a fifteen-year-old girl is *brutalized* for four *days* while we sit around with our thumbs up our—"

Cat stopped walking, turning to face Blue. "Yeah, it bugs me too," he said. "But it's over now. Let it go."

"You think Karen Branford is gonna just let it go?"

Blue could see from Cat's dark eyes that the CO didn't like the answer to that question. "She's alive," he said quietly. "That's much better than the alternative."

Blue took a deep breath. He was right. Cat was right. He exhaled loudly. "Sorry." They started walking again. "It's just... The girl reminded me of someone I used to know back in Hatboro Creek. A girl named Lucy. Lucy Tait."

Joe Cat eyed him with feigned astonishment as they turned the corner into the mess hall. "Yo," he said. "Am I hearing you correctly? You actually knew other girls besides Jenny Lee Beaumont in Hatboro Creek? I thought the sun rose and set with Jenny Lee, and all other girls were rendered invisible by her magnificent shine."

Blue staunchly ignored Cat's teasing tone. "Lucy wasn't a girl," he said, pouring black, steaming coffee into a paper cup. "She was just...a kid."

"Maybe you should look her up while you're back in South Carolina for the wedding."

Blue shook his head. "I don't think so."

Cat took a mug from the rack, regarding Blue speculatively. "You sure you want to *go* to this wedding?" he asked. "You know, I can arrange for Alpha Squad to be part of some vital training mission if you need an excuse not to be there."

"It's my brother's wedding."

"Gerry's your *step*brother," Cat noted, "and he happens to be marrying Jenny Lee, your high-school sweetheart and the only woman I've ever heard you talk about—with the exception now of this Lucy Tait."

Blue took a swallow of the coffee. It was strong and hot and it burned all the way down. "I told him I'd be his best man."

Joe Cat's teeth were clenched as he gazed at Blue. The muscle worked in his jaw. "He shouldn't have asked you for that," he said. "He wants you there, giving him your stamp of approval, so he can stop feeling guilty about stealing Jenny Lee from you."

Blue crumpled up his empty paper cup, then tossed it into the garbage. "He didn't steal her," he said. "She was in love with him right from the start."

Chapter One

It was going to be the wedding of the year—shoot, it was going to be the wedding of the decade. And Lucy Tait was going to be there.

Oh, not that she'd be invited. No, Lucy wasn't going to get one of those fancy, gold-lettered invitations printed on heavy, cream-colored stock, no way. She was going to this wedding as a hired hand—first to keep the traffic moving outside Hatboro Creek's posh country club and then to stand inside the ballroom, guarding the pile of expensive wedding gifts.

Lucy adjusted the collar of her police uniform as she cruised Main Street in her patrol car, searching for a parking spot near Bobby Joe's Grill.

Not that she'd expected to be invited to Jenny Lee Beaumont's nuptials. She'd never run with that crowd, not even back in high school. But man, back then, back when Lucy was a scrawny freshman and blond, beautiful homecoming queen Jenny Lee had been a senior, Lucy had desperately wanted to join Jenny's exclusive club.

She would never have admitted it. The same way she would never have admitted the reason she wanted so desperately to be close to Jenny Lee—namely, Blue McCoy.

Blue McCoy.

Rumor had it he was coming back to town for his stepbrother's wedding.

Blue McCoy.

With dark blond hair and dark blue eyes that burned with an intensity that made her heart stand still, Blue McCoy had haunted all of Lucy's adolescent dreams. He was the hero of her teenaged years—a loner, quiet, dark and dangerous, capable of just about anything.

Including winning beautiful Jenny Lee Beaumont's heart.

Except Jenny Lee wasn't going to marry Blue McCoy on Saturday afternoon. She was marrying his stepbrother, Gerry. He was two years older than Blue, with a quicksilver smile, movie-star good looks and a happy-go-lucky attitude. Some people might have found Gerry the more attractive of the McCoy boys.

Apparently Jenny Lee had.

Lucy found a parking place a block down from the Grill and turned off the patrol car's powerful engine. On second thought, she turned the key again and pushed the buttons to raise the power windows. The summer sky looked threatening. Lucy was willing to bet it was going to pour before she finished her lunch.

She checked to make sure her sidearm was secured in her belt holster as she hurried down the sidewalk. She was already ten minutes late, and her friend Sarah's self-imposed work schedule didn't allow her to take more than a hour for lunch.

The Grill was crowded, as usual, but Sarah was saving a table. Lucy slid into the booth, across from her friend.

"I'm sorry I'm late."

Sarah just smiled. "I would have ordered lunch," she

said. "But Iris hasn't worked her way around to this part of the room."

Lucy leaned back against the plastic cushion of the bench seat. She let out a burst of air that lifted her bangs up off her forehead. "I haven't stopped running since 7 a.m." She eyed her friend. Sarah looked tired and hot, her dark hair pulled back from her face in a ponytail, dark circles under her hazel eyes. "How are *you?*"

"I'm nine months pregnant with a child that has obviously decided not to be born until he's old enough to vote," Sarah said dryly. "It's ninety-seven degrees in the shade, my back hurts when I lie down, my sciatic nerve acts up when I sit, I have a review deadline that I can't possibly make because I've spent the past three days cooking instead of writing, my husband has been home from his shift at the hospital four hours in the past forty-eight, my mother-in-law calls every five minutes to see if my water has broken, I miss living in Boston and this is the first chance I've had in nearly a week to complain."

Lucy grinned. "Then don't stop now."

"No, no, I'm done," Sarah said, fanning herself with her napkin.

"Afternoon, ladies." Iris took her pen from behind her ear and held it poised over her ordering pad. "What can I get you today?"

"I'd like some marzipan," Sarah said.

Iris sighed good-naturedly, pushing a stray red curl back up into her bun. "Honey, I told you before, if it's not on the menu…"

"I *need* some marzipan," Sarah said almost desperately. "Almond paste. Or maybe a piece of my mother's fruitcake. I haven't been able to think about anything else for days…."

"We'll both take a turkey club," Lucy said smoothly, "on whole wheat, mustard, no mayo, extra pickles."

"Sorry, hon," Iris murmured to Sarah as she moved on to the next table.

"My life," Sarah intoned dramatically, "is an endless string of disappointments."

Lucy had to laugh. "You're married to the nicest guy in town, you're about to have a baby, you just won a prize for your music and you're *disappointed?*"

Sarah leaned forward. "I'm insanely jealous of you," she said. "You still have a waistline. You can see your feet without craning your neck. You—" She broke off, staring across the room toward the door. "Don't look now, but I think we're being invaded."

Lucy turned around as the glass door to the grill swung open and a man in green army fatigues, carrying a heavy-looking green duffel bag casually over one shoulder, came inside.

He was clearly a soldier, except on second glance his uniform wasn't quite inspection ready. The first thing Lucy noticed was his arms. The sleeves had been torn from his green shirt at the shoulders and his arms were muscular and strong. He looked as if he could easily bench-press three times his body weight. He wore his shirt open at the collar and unbuttoned halfway down his broad chest. His fatigue pants fit him comfortably, but instead of clunky black army boots, he wore only sandals on his feet.

He had sunglasses on, but his gaze swept quickly around the room and Lucy imagined that he didn't miss much.

His hair was thick and a dark, sandy blond.

And his face was one she recognized.

Lucy would have known Blue McCoy anywhere. That strong chin, his firm, unsmiling mouth, those rugged cheekbones and straight nose. Twelve years of living had added power and strength to his already strong face. The lines around his eyes and mouth had deepened, adding a sense of compassion or wisdom to his unforgivingly stern features.

He had been good-looking as a teenaged boy. As a man, he was impossibly handsome.

Lucy was staring. She couldn't help herself. Blue McCoy was back in town, larger than life.

He finished his quick inspection of the room and his eyes returned to her. As Lucy watched, Blue took off his sunglasses. His eyes were still the brightest shade of blue she'd ever seen in her life, and as he met her gaze she felt frozen in place, hypnotized.

He nodded at her, just once, still unsmiling, and then Iris breezed past him.

"Sit anywhere, hon!" she called out to him.

The spell was broken. Blue looked away from Lucy and she turned back to the table and Sarah.

"Do you know him?" Sarah asked, her sharp eyes missing nothing—particularly not the blush that was heating Lucy's cheeks. "You do, don't you?"

"Not really, no," Lucy said, then admitted, "I mean, I know who he is, but…" She shook her head.

"Who is he?"

Lucy glanced up again, but Blue was busy stashing his duffel bag underneath a table on the far side of the room. "Blue McCoy." Lucy spoke softly, as if he might overhear even from across the noisy restaurant.

"*That's* Gerry McCoy's brother? He looks nothing like him."

"They're stepbrothers," Lucy explained. "Blue's mother married Gerry's father, only she died about five months after the wedding. Mr. McCoy adopted Blue shortly after that. The way I hear it, neither Mr. McCoy nor Blue was happy with that arrangement. Apparently they didn't get along too well, but Blue had nowhere else to go."

"I guess not, since he didn't make it back into town when Mr. McCoy died a few years ago," Sarah commented.

"Gerry told me Blue was part of Desert Storm," Lucy

said. "He couldn't get leave, not then, and Gerry didn't want to hold up the funeral, not indefinitely like that."

"Gerry's brother is in the army?"

"Navy," Lucy corrected her. "He's Special Operations—a Navy SEAL."

"A *what?*"

"SEAL," Lucy said. "It stands for Sea, Air and Land. SEALs are like supercommandos. They're experts in everything from...I don't know...underwater demolition to parachute assaults to...piloting state-of-the-art jets. They have these insane training sessions where they learn to work as a team under incredible stress. There's this one week—Hell Week—where they're allowed only four hours of sleep *all week*. They have to sleep in fifteen-minute segments, while air-raid sirens are wailing. If they quit, they're out of the program. It's pretty scary stuff. Only the toughest and most determined men make the grade and become SEALs. It's a real status symbol—for obvious reasons."

Sarah was gazing across the room, a speculative light in her eyes. "You seem to have acquired an awful lot of information about a man you claim you don't know."

"I've read about SEALs and the training they go through. That's all."

"Hmm." Sarah lifted one delicate eyebrow. "Before or after Gerry's brother joined the Navy?"

Lucy shrugged, trying hard to look casual. "So I had a crush on the guy in high school. Big deal."

Sarah rested her chin in her hand. "Out of all the people in this place, he nods at *you*," she remarked. "Did you date him?"

Lucy couldn't help laughing. "Not a chance. I was three years younger, and he was..."

"What?"

Iris approached the table, carrying two enormous sandwiches and a basket of French fries. Lucy smiled her thanks at the waitress, but waited for her to leave before answering Sarah's question.

"He was going out with Jenny Lee."

"Beaumont…?" Sarah's eyes lit up. "You mean the same Jenny Lee who's marrying his brother on Saturday?" At Lucy's nod, she chuckled. "This is getting too good."

"You didn't know?" Lucy asked. "I thought everyone in town knew. It seems it's all anyone's talking about—whether or not Blue McCoy will show up to the wedding of his stepbrother and his high-school sweetheart."

"Apparently the answer to *that* question is yes," Sarah said, glancing across the room at the man in uniform.

Lucy took a bite of her turkey sandwich, carefully *not* turning around to look at this man she found so fascinating. Sarah was right. The question about whether or not Blue would attend Gerry's wedding had been answered. Now the town would be abuzz with speculation, wondering if Blue was going to create a disturbance or rise to his feet when the preacher said "speak now or forever hold your peace."

The temptation proved too intense, and Lucy glanced over her shoulder. Blue was eating his lunch and reading the past week's edition of the *Hatboro Creek Gazette*. His blond hair fell across his forehead, almost into his eyes, and he pushed it back with a smooth motion that caused the muscles in his right arm to ripple. As if he could feel her watching him, he looked up and directly into her eyes.

Lucy's stomach did circus tricks as she quickly, guiltily, looked away. God, you would think she was fifteen again and sneaking around the marina where Blue worked, hoping for a peek at him. But he hadn't noticed her then and he certainly wouldn't notice her now. She was still decidedly not the Jenny Lee Beaumont type.

"What was his mother thinking when she named him Blue?" Sarah wondered aloud.

"His real name is Carter," Lucy said. "Blue is a nickname—it's short for 'Blue Streak.'"

"Don't tell me," Sarah said. "He talks all the time."

Lucy had to laugh at that. Blue McCoy was not known for running on at the mouth. "I don't know when he first got the nickname," she said, "but he's a runner. He broke all kinds of speed records for sprinting and long-distance races back in junior high and high school."

Sarah nodded, peering around Lucy to get another peek at Blue.

Lucy's police walkie-talkie went off at nearly the exact instant the skies opened up with a crash of thunder.

"Report of a 415 in progress at the corner of Main and Willow," Annabella's voice squawked over the radio's tinny speaker. "Possible 10-91A. Lucy, what's your location?"

Main and Willow was less than a block and a half from the Grill, in the opposite direction of her patrol car. It would take her less time to jog over there than it would to get to her car and drive. Lucy quickly swallowed a half-chewed bite of her sandwich and thumbed the talk switch to her radio. "The Grill," she said, already halfway out of the booth. "I'm on it. But unless you want me to stop at my car to check my code book, you better tell me what a 10-91A is."

The police dispatcher, Annabella Sawyer, was overly fond of the California police ten code. Never mind that they were in South Carolina. Never mind the fact that Hatboro Creek was so small that they didn't need half the codes most of the time. Never mind that the police officers weren't required to memorize any kind of code. Annabella liked using them. She clearly had watched too many episodes of "Top Cops."

Lucy knew what a 415 was, though. A disturbance. She'd heard that number enough times. Even a town as tiny as Hatboro Creek had plenty of those.

"A 10-91A is a report of a vicious animal," Annabella's voice squawked back.

Lucy swore under her breath. Leroy Hurley's brute of a dog had no doubt gotten loose again.

"Be careful," Sarah said.

"I'll wrap your sandwich," Iris called as Lucy pushed open the door and stepped out onto the sidewalk.

The rain soaked her instantly, as if someone had turned a fire hose on her from above. Her hat was back in her car, and Lucy wished for both of them—hat and car—as she headed toward Willow Street at a quick trot.

With any luck, this sudden skyburst had sent that 10-91A scurrying for shelter. With any luck, the 415 had ceased to exist. With any luck...

No such luck. Leroy Hurley's snarling Doberman had treed Merle Groggin on Andy Hayes's front lawn. Andy was shouting for Merle to get the hell out of his expensive Japanese maple. Merle was brandishing his hunting knife and shouting for Leroy to get his damned dog locked up or put down, and Leroy was laughing his size forty-six-inch waist pants off.

It was decidedly a bonafide 415.

As Lucy approached Leroy Hurley, his huge dog caught sight of her and turned. Her stomach tightened at the animal's threatening growl. She liked dogs. Most dogs. But this one had one mean streak. Just like his master.

"Leroy," Lucy said, nodding a greeting to the big man, as if they weren't both standing in a torrential downpour. "What did I tell you last week about keeping your dog chained in your yard?"

The Doberman shifted its weight, glancing from Lucy to Merle Groggin, as if deciding who would make a tastier lunch.

Leroy shrugged and grinned. "Can't help it if he breaks free."

She could smell the unmistakable scent of whiskey on his

breath. Damn, he got meaner than ever when he'd been drinking.

"Yes, you can," Lucy said, taking her ticket pad from her pocket. It was instantly soaked. "He's your dog. You're responsible for him. And in fact, to help you remember that, I'm going to slap you with a fifty-dollar fine."

The big man's smile faded. "I'm the only thing standing between you walking away from here in one piece and you getting chewed," he said, "and you're gonna *fine* me?"

Lucy stared at Leroy. "Are you threatening me, Hurley?" she asked, her voice low and tight but carrying clearly over the sound of the rain. "Because if you're threatening me, I'll run both you *and* your dog in so fast your head will spin."

Something in Leroy's eyes shifted, and Lucy felt a surge of triumph. He believed her. She'd called his bluff, he believed her and was going to back down, despite the whiskey that was screwing up the very small amount of good judgment he had to begin with.

"Call your dog off," Lucy said calmly.

But before Leroy could comply, all hell broke loose.

Andy Hayes fired a booming shot from his double-barrel shotgun, sending Merle plunging down from the tree. The Doberman leaped toward the fallen man, who struck at the dog with his big knife, drawing blood. With a howl, the animal dashed away down the street.

"Stay the *hell* away from my tree!" Andy shouted.

"You stabbed my dog!" Leroy Hurley roared at Merle.

"You coulda killed me," Merle shouted at Andy as he hurried out of the man's yard. "Why the hell didn't you just shoot the damned dog?"

Leroy moved threateningly toward Merle. "If that dog dies, I'm gonna string you up by your—"

"Hold it right there!" Lucy planted herself firmly between Merle and Leroy. She raised her voice so it would carry to the house. "Andy, you know I'm going to have to bring you in—reckless endangerment and unlawful discharge of a firearm. And as for you two—"

"I hope that stupid animal does kick." Merle spoke to Leroy Hurley right through Lucy, as if she wasn't even there. "Because if it doesn't, I'm gonna come after it one of these nights and finish it off."

"I ain't going nowhere," Andy proclaimed. "I got rights! I was protecting my property!"

"Maybe I'll just finish *you* off first!" Leroy's fleshy face was florid with anger as he shouted at Merle.

Lucy keyed the thumb switch on her radio. "Dispatch, this is Officer Tait. I need backup, corner of Willow and—"

Leroy Hurley pushed her aside with the sweep of one beefy arm, and Lucy went down, hard, on her rear in the street, dropping the radio and her ticket pad in the mud. Leroy moved up the walkway to Andy's house with a speed surprising for such a large man, and as Lucy scrambled to her feet, he grabbed Andy's shotgun and pointed it at Merle.

Merle ducked for cover behind Lucy, and Leroy swung the gun toward her.

"Leroy, put that down," Lucy ordered, pushing her rain-soaked hair back from her face with her left hand as she unsnapped the safety buttons that held her sidearm in her belt holster with her right hand.

"Freeze! Keep your hands where I can see 'em," Leroy ordered her.

Lucy lifted her hands. *Shoot.* How could this have gotten so utterly out of control? And where the hell was that backup?

Leroy was edging toward them; Merle was cowering behind her, using her as a shield; and for once Andy Hayes was silent.

"Step away from Merle," Leroy growled at her.

"Leroy, put the gun down before this goes too far," Lucy said again, trying to sound calm, to not let the desperation she was feeling show in her voice.

"If you don't step away from him," Leroy vowed, his eyes wild, "I'll just blast a hole right through you."

Dear God, he was serious. He raised the shotgun higher, closing one eye as he took aim directly at Lucy's chest. Her life flashed briefly and oh, so meaninglessly through her eyes as she stared into the barrel of that gun. She could very well die at this man's hands. Right here in the rain. And what would she have to show for her life? A six-month-old police badge. A liberal-arts degree from the state university. A computer business she no longer had any interest in. An empty house at the edge of town. No family, only a few friends...

"Don't do this, Leroy," Lucy said, inching her hand back down toward her own gun. She didn't want to die. She hadn't even begun to live. Dammit, if Leroy Hurley was going to shoot her, she was going to die trying for her gun.

"Freeze!" Leroy told her. "I said to freeze!"

"Leroy, I'm holding an Uzi nine-millimeter submachine gun," a soft voice drawled from over Lucy's shoulder. "It looks small and unassuming, but if I move my trigger finger a fraction of an inch, with a firing rate of sixteen bullets per second, I can cut even a man as big as you in two."

It was Blue McCoy. Lucy would have recognized his velvet Southern drawl anywhere.

"You have exactly two seconds to drop that shotgun," Blue continued, "or I start firing."

Leroy dropped the gun.

Lucy sprang forward before the barrel had finished clattering on the cement walkway and scooped up the gun. She cradled it in her arms as she turned to look at Blue.

His blond hair was drenched and plastered to his head. His clothes were as soaked as her own, and they clung to his body, outlining and emphasizing his muscular build. He squinted slightly through the downpour, but otherwise stood there holding a very deadly looking little submachine gun as if the sky were clear and the sun were shining.

He was still watching Leroy, but his brilliant blue eyes flickered briefly in Lucy's direction. "You okay?"

She nodded, unable to find her voice.

There was a crowd of people down the block, she realized suddenly. No doubt they had all been drawn out into the wet by the sound of Andy's first gunshot. Great. She looked like a fool, unable to handle a few troublemakers, requiring a Navy SEAL to come to her rescue. Terrific.

"Leroy, Andy, Merle," Lucy said. "You're *all* gonna take a ride to the station."

"Aw, I didn't do a damned thing," Merle complained as the long-awaited backup arrived, along with the police van for transporting the three men. "You got nothing on *me*."

"Carrying a concealed weapon ought to do the trick," Lucy said, deftly taking his hunting knife from him and handing it and the shotgun to Frank Redfield, one of the police officers who had finally made the scene.

"Talk about carrying a concealed weapon," Merle snorted, gesturing with his head toward Blue McCoy as Frank led him toward the van. "What are you going to charge *him* with?"

Lucy pushed her wet hair back from her face again, stopping to pick up her sodden ticket pad and the fallen walkie-talkie from the mud before she approached Blue.

"Merle is right, you know, Lieutenant McCoy," she said to him, hoping he would mistake the shakiness in her voice as a reaction to the excitement rather than as a result of his proximity. "I'm not sure I can let you walk around town with one of those things."

He handed the gun to her, butt first. "You let Tommy Parker walk around town with it," he said.

Tommy Parker? Tommy Parker was nine years old.... Lucy looked down at the gun she was holding. It was lightweight and… "My God," she said. "It's plastic. It's a *toy*." She looked back up into Blue's eyes. "You were bluffing."

"Of course I was bluffing," he said. "I wouldn't be caught dead with an Uzi. If I wanted an assault weapon, I'd only use a Heckler and Koch MP5-K."

Lucy stared at him and he gazed back at her. And then he smiled. His teeth were white and even and contrasted nicely with his tanned face.

"I'm kidding," he explained gently. "If I had to, I'd use an Uzi. It's not my weapon of choice, though."

Great, he must think she was some kind of imbecile, the way she was staring at him. Lucy closed her eyes briefly, but when she opened them he was still watching her.

"I'm sorry," she said, "I really owe you one. You saved my neck back there, and…well, thanks."

He nodded, gracefully acknowledging her clumsy thanks. "You're welcome," he said. "But haven't we already had this conversation? I'm getting a real sense of déjà vu here." His smile flashed again—pure sunshine in the pouring rain. "It seems every time I'm in Hatboro Creek, I end up saving little Lucy Tait's…neck."

Lucy was shocked. "You remember me?" As soon as the words were out of her mouth she was embarrassed. Of course he remembered her. Standing here soaking wet, resembling a drowned rat, she no doubt looked not too different from the skinny fifteen-year-old girl Blue had saved from a serious thrashing out on the far side of the town baseball field all those years ago.

"I'm a little surprised to see you," Blue drawled. "I'd have thought you would've packed up and left South Carolina years ago, Yankee."

Yankee. It had been her nickname all through high school. Lucy Tait, the Yankee girl. Moved to town with her widowed mom from someplace way up north. She was still referred to all the time as "Yankee girl." It had been twelve years. Twelve *years*. Her mother was no longer alive. And Lucy wasn't a girl anymore. But some things never changed.

"No," Lucy said evenly. "I'm still here in Hatboro Creek."

"I can see that."

Blue gazed at Lucy, taking in her long, brown—wet— hair, tied back in a utilitarian ponytail; her unforgettable dark brown eyes; the lovely, almost delicate shape of her face; and her tall, slender body. Little Lucy Tait wasn't so little anymore. The rain had softened the stiff fabric of her police uniform, molding it against her female curves. Yes, Lucy Tait had definitely grown up. Blue felt an unmistakable surge of physical attraction and he had to smile. At age eighteen, he *never* would have believed that the sight of scrawny little Lucy Tait standing in the rain could possibly turn him on.

But if there was one thing he learned in his stint as a Navy SEAL, it was that times—and people—were always changing. Nothing ever stayed the same.

"How long have you been an officer of the law?" he asked. The crowd was gone and the police van was pulling away. The rain was relentless but warm. Blue liked the way it felt on his face, and Lucy didn't seem to be in any hurry to get to shelter.

Lucy crossed her arms. "Six months."

Blue nodded.

She lifted her chin. "I'm the first woman on the Hatboro Creek police force."

Blue tried to hide his smile, but it slipped through. "First *Yankee* on the force, too, no doubt."

Lucy must have realized how defensive she looked, because she slowly smiled, too—at first almost sheepishly, then wider. "Yeah," she said. "I suppose I've been setting all kinds of new Hatboro Creek records lately."

Her face wasn't exactly what you'd call pretty. At least, not at first glance. Her mouth was too wide, too generous, too big for her face—except when she smiled. Her smile transformed her totally, making her eyes dance and sparkle and charming dimples appear in the perfect, smooth, slightly olive-tinted complexion of her cheeks. Her nose was straight and large, but not too big for her face, revealing a faintly Mediterranean ancestry. Her eyes were warm and the deepest shade of brown, framed by thick, dark eyelashes. Her ears were small and amazingly delicate looking. Blue found himself watching, fascinated, as a drop of rain clung to her unpierced earlobe before dripping onto her shoulder.

"I'm surprised Chief Bradley lets you patrol alone," Blue said.

Lucy's smile vanished. "Why? Because I'm a woman or because I'm a Yankee?"

"Because you're a rookie."

"I had Leroy Hurley handled," Lucy remarked, her dark eyes flashing. "Until Andy got his gun."

Blue nodded, forcing his gaze out and into the distance, down Main Street, toward the marina. How long had it been since he'd been with a woman? Two months? Three? Longer? He honestly couldn't remember. He usually didn't pay his sexual appetite much mind—until it sat up and demanded priority attention.

Like right now.

In a flash he could picture Lucy standing in the warm rain, sans uniform, water washing down her lean, shapely female body—full, soft breasts; flat stomach; slim hips; dangerously long, well-muscled thighs…. The image sent an intense rush of heat through him, heat he knew she'd be able to see in his eyes.

It was strange. In the past, Blue had always been attracted to the overly feminine type—the helpless type of woman who wore lots of frills and lace and needed to be rescued. It was true that he had in fact come to Lucy's rescue more than once, but both times she'd certainly been doing her best to save herself. She was independent and strong. Even though she was soaking wet and only a rookie, she wore her police uniform and the gun at her side with an air of authority and competence. That should have pushed him back a step or two. Instead, he found himself inching forward, trying to get closer.

"I assumed Andy was harmless," Lucy was saying with a frown. "I focused on Leroy and didn't pay Andy any attention. That was my big mistake."

"Never assume anything," Blue said. He could tell from the way she met his gaze, then suddenly looked away, that she had gotten a glimpse of the fire in his eyes. She blushed, a tinge of pink darkening her cheeks as she looked down at the mud-encrusted radio and ticket pad she still held in her hands. She slipped the pad into her belt and tried to wipe the radio clean. She appeared to be intent on fixing her equipment, but she couldn't keep from glancing at him out of the corners of her eyes.

Suddenly, Blue remembered the rumor he'd heard his senior year in high school that the little Yankee freshman girl had a crush on him. He'd been flattered and amused, and as kind to the girl as he could be without leading her on.

Was it possible that Lucy's high-school crush had survived all these years?

Blue had noticed right from the first moment he'd spotted her sitting in the Grill that she wasn't wearing a wedding band. Was it possible that Lucy was still single, still unattached?

Blue had come to Hatboro Creek today out of obligation. He'd come with every intention of enduring his visit—he hadn't planned to enjoy any of it. But he was on leave, and his leave time was infrequent and irregular. Why not take hold of an opportunity and have a little pleasure, especially since that pleasure seemed to be handing itself to him on a silver platter? Why not? Especially since the attraction he was feeling right now was stronger than anything he'd felt in a long, *long* time.

"I, um, I better go," Lucy said. "I'll need to fill out a report and…" She turned toward him, using the back of one hand to push her wet hair from her face, but succeeding in leaving a streak of mud on her cheek. "Can I give you a ride somewhere? Are you staying at your brother's?"

As Lucy watched, Blue glanced up at the cloudy sky as if noticing the rain for the first time. It was finally starting to let up. He pushed his hair back from his face but didn't meet Lucy's eyes again. "No," he said. "Jenny Lee has already moved into Gerry's place. I thought it would be better if I stayed at the motel. And it's not far. I can walk there probably faster than you could drive."

Lucy nodded, wishing almost inanely that he would smile at her again, or that he would look at her and let her get a second glance at that slow-burning heat she'd imagined she'd seen in his eyes. But it had to be just that—imagined. Blue McCoy would never be interested in her.

Would he?

"I wish I could think of a way to thank you properly for what you did," she said, backing away.

He stepped toward her, following. "*I* can think of a way," he said in his soft drawl. "There's a party tonight at the country club, a sort of rehearsal dinner for Saturday's wedding. Come as my date."

Lucy stopped short. Her first reaction was to laugh. This had to be some sort of joke. Go to Hatboro Creek's exclusive country club—on a *date* with Blue McCoy, her childhood hero? But Blue wasn't laughing. He was…serious?

Why? Lucy searched his eyes, looking for the reason he'd asked her out. Why? There had to be a reason.

She found the answer in the heat in his eyes, as clear as day.

Sex.

He was a man and she was a woman, and although his invitation had been to attend a fancy, high-society party, what he *really* wanted to do with her wouldn't require any kind of party dress at all. She could see all that in his eyes—and more.

Lucy was floored.

Blue McCoy wanted her. He wanted *her*. He was actually physically attracted to and interested in the tall, skinny, gawky, awkward Yankee tomboy, Lucy Tait.

Oh, she had no misconceptions about the extent of his desire. It was purely sexual. There were no emotions involved. At least not from his end. But it was clear from the look in his eyes that if she went on this date with him, he was going to do his damnedest to see that she didn't get home tonight until well after dawn.

A clear and extremely erotic image of Blue pulling her down with him onto his bed at the Lighthouse Motel flashed through Lucy's mind. Tangled arms and legs, seeking mouths, straining bodies, skin slick with sweat and desire... Strobelike pictures bombarded Lucy's senses, along with a thousand other thoughts.

She had been plenty reckless and wild before—but never in her personal life. As crazy as she'd been with her career, Lucy had always been extremely careful when it came to relationships. But ever since she'd first laid eyes on Blue McCoy at age fifteen, she'd desperately wanted to run her fingers through his thick, dark blond hair.

Lucy knew she meant nothing to Blue and would no doubt continue to mean nothing to him, even if he slept with her. She'd never made love to a man before without knowing that their relationship was going to grow, without *hoping* for some kind of permanence. Yet Blue was in town for only a few days—a week at the most. Chances were that he wouldn't be back. Maybe not for another twelve years.

As she gazed up at Blue, he reached out and touched the side of her face, gently wiping what was no doubt a smudge of dirt from her cheek with his thumb. His hand was warm, warmer even than the rain, and his touch sent a wave of fire spiraling through her, down to the depths of her very soul.

She couldn't help herself. She reached up and touched his hair. It was wet, but still soft and thick. It was remarkable. One small movement and she was living one of her wildest dreams.

Blue's eyelids grew heavy at her touch, heavy with pleasure—and satisfaction. He'd won, and he knew it.

"I'll pick you up at 1900…seven o'clock," Blue said, his voice barely louder than a whisper. "Or would you rather meet me over there, at the club?"

Lucy found herself nodding. Yes. "I'll meet you there," she breathed. Dear God, yes, she was going to do this. She was going to go to this party with Blue McCoy, and later… Later, she was going to live out one of her most powerful, most decadent fantasies.

It wasn't until after he walked her back to her patrol car, until after he went inside the Grill for the rest of his lunch and his duffel bag and with a nod headed toward the motel, and until after Sarah drove by in her little black Honda Accord, giving Lucy a toot of her horn and a big thumbs-up, that reality crashed in.

What the hell did Lucy think she was doing? Was a one-night stand with Blue McCoy—no matter that he was the man of her hottest dreams—worth the talk and gossip and speculative looks she'd have to endure weeks and even months after he'd gone? Was one night—or even two or three nights—worth the silence that was sure to follow? Because Lucy had no false expectations. Blue would not write.

He would not call. He could be killed on a training mission, and she'd be the very last to know.

Could she really love a man she knew would be loving someone else, some other woman, this time next month— or hell, maybe even next *week*?

She wished she could call Edgar, wished she could tell him about Blue's invitation, wished they could talk it over, hash it out. But even though Edgar wasn't around, Lucy knew exactly what he would have said.

Go for it.

Edgar was the only person Lucy had ever told about her high-school crush on Blue. He was the only one who had known that she still carried a torch for a guy she never even really knew.

Yeah, go for it was what Edgar would have said.

And then he would have reminded her to have safe sex. Safe sex. Now there was an oxymoron if Lucy had ever heard one. A condom would help with some of the physical dangers. But what about her emotional safety? What kind of protection could she use to ensure herself that?

Down at the police station, Lucy went through the motions, taking a shower; putting on a clean, dry uniform; filling out the forms and reports. But all afternoon, she asked herself the same questions over and over again. Could she really go out with Blue tonight, knowing damn well where it was going to lead?

The answer wavered between Edgar's possible *go for it* and *no*. No, it wasn't worth it. No, she couldn't do this. Could she? How could she pass up her wildest, hottest sexual fantasy?

But every time she told herself no and started to pick up the phone to dial the Lighthouse Motel, where Blue was staying, Lucy remembered the liquid desire in his eyes and the hot touch of his hand on her face.

She remembered the answering pull of her own longing

and need, the promise of a wild, reckless passion the likes of which she'd never known.

And she knew exactly why she'd said yes.

Chapter Two

Lucy pulled her truck into the Hatboro Country Club's elegant driveway, feeling out of place. She parked in the back lot, unwilling to leave the keys to her trusty but beat-up old Ford four-by-four with the valets. She couldn't stand the thought of them snickering as they pulled it alongside the Town Cars and Cadillacs. She also wasn't sure she could handle walking in the front entrance of the posh country club wearing this little black dress she'd borrowed from Sarah. *Little* was the key word. It was sleeveless, with a sweetheart neckline and a keyhole back, and it hugged Lucy's body, ending many, *many* inches above her knees. On Sarah, the tight skirt had been short, but Lucy was at least four inches taller than her friend. Aided further by high heels, the dress made Lucy's long legs appear as if they went on forever—an effect, Sarah had pointed out, that would *not* be lost on Blue McCoy.

Lucy glanced in one of the mirrors that lined the hall as she went in the country club's back door.

Sarah had fixed her hair, too, piling it on top of her head. It seemed as if Lucy had casually swept it up off her neck, but in reality the carefree look had taken the solid part of a half hour to achieve.

She was also wearing more than her usual dab of lip gloss. Mascara, liner and shadow adorned her brown eyes, and blush accentuated her wide cheekbones.

Lucy looked like…somebody else. Instead of skinny, she looked slender, her legs long and graceful. Instead of girl-next-door average, she looked exotic, glamorous and mysteriously sexy.

Blue probably wasn't going to recognize her. She could barely recognize herself.

Which made sense, because Lucy certainly didn't recognize this odd sensation she felt, knowing that she was here to meet a man who was practically a stranger—a stranger who could very well be her lover before the night was through.

Blue McCoy.

But he *wasn't* a stranger. Not really. After all, he'd been her hero for years. He was pure masculine perfection—if you went for the big, brooding, enigmatic type. And Lucy definitely did.

Music was playing in the country club's big ballroom, and it filtered down toward Lucy. She started up the stairs, heart pounding; she knew that Blue was somewhere up there near that pulsating music.

The country club had undergone changes in its interior decor since the last time she had been there. She couldn't remember what color the thick wall-to-wall carpeting had been, but she was positive that it hadn't been this deep, almost smoky shade of pink. The wallpaper was different, too, a muted collection of flowers and squiggles, in tasteful off-whites and beiges and various shades of that same dark pink.

Her high heels made no noise at all on the plush carpeting as she moved down the corridor toward the ballroom.

The lights in the ballroom had been dimmed, and hundreds of candles had been placed around the room—on the dining tables, on the serving tables, even in candlesticks mounted on the walls. The effect was lovely, giving the entire room a flickering, golden, fairy-tale like glow.

The dining tables covered half the room, leaving the other half of the hardwood floor open for dancing. A small band—drums, keyboard and guitar—was set up in the corner opposite the bar.

Lucy recognized many of the people scattered about the big room. It was a who's who of the county's wealthiest and most powerful citizens. The police chief and his wife were there, as was the president of the bank. The mayor and his wife were chatting with the owner of Carolina Island, the seaside resort located several miles north of the Hatboro Creek town line.

The women wore glittering gowns and the men were dressed in black tuxedos—all except for one. One man—Blue McCoy—was dressed in the resplendent, almost shimmering white of a naval dress uniform. As he turned, the candlelight gleamed on the rows and rows and *rows* of ribbons and medals he wore on his chest.

His shoulders appeared impossibly broad, with his well-tailored uniform jacket tapering down to his lean hips. He wore officer's insignia, and Lucy was reminded that Blue was a full lieutenant—unless he'd been even further promoted since the last time she'd asked Gerry about his stepbrother's naval career.

He was carrying a white hat in his hands. His hair, a dark, shining golden blond, reflected the dim light. He was talking to Mitch Casey, the chairman of Hatboro Creek's chamber of commerce. Blue's tanned face looked so serious, so stern, as he nodded at something Casey was saying. He was listening intently, but his blue eyes kept straying toward the front entrance, as if he were waiting for someone. Her? Lucy felt a flash of pleasure. He was. Blue McCoy was watching and waiting for *her*.

He held himself slightly stiffly, as if he wasn't quite comfortable in his surroundings. But why should he be? Gerry and his father were the ones who had had the memberships to the country club. Throughout high school, Blue had chosen to hang out and work down by the docks where he kept his little powerboat.

Even when Blue was dating Jenny Lee Beaumont he had stayed away from the country-club set. He'd been a loner back in high school, with only one or two friends who were also outcasts or misfits. He wore a leather jacket and rode a motorcycle that he'd rebuilt from parts, yet unlike the other tough kids, his grades were exceptionally above average. Still, he had a reputation for being a troublemaker simply because he looked the part.

Even back in high school Blue had been slow to smile. He'd been serious and quietly watchful, missing nothing but rarely stepping in. Unless, of course, the cruel teenaged teasing and rudeness went beyond the limits—like the time five members of the boys' junior-varsity baseball team decided to demonstrate just how unhappy they were that a girl, a Yankee girl, had made the cut and gotten onto the team.

Lucy could hold her own in a fair fight, but five to one were tough odds.

Until Blue fearlessly stepped in, ending the violence with his mere presence. The other kids had learned to keep their distance from him, wary of his quietly seething temper and his ability—and willingness—to fight. And to fight dirty, if he had to.

Apparently he'd had to more than a few times.

According to the story Lucy had heard, Blue had been five when Gerry's father had adopted the little boy out of obligation. Apparently neither Blue nor Mr. McCoy had been overly happy about that, but Blue had had nowhere else to go. Blue had grown up in his elder stepbrother's shadow, clearly a burden to his stepfather. Was it any wonder that the little boy should have quickly become self-sufficient and self-reliant? And quietly grim?

Was it any wonder that both the boy and the man he'd become were watchful, intensely serious and slow to smile?

Lucy remembered the way Blue had smiled at her that afternoon. Had Blue smiled at Jenny Lee that way back in high school? It was hard to believe that he had. If he had, with a smile like that, surely Jenny would be marrying Blue this coming Saturday rather than his elder stepbrother.

As Lucy watched, Blue's attention was pulled away from both the main entrance and Mitch Casey when Gerry McCoy and Jenny Lee Beaumont swept onto the dance floor.

Jenny was wearing a long, pink dress that set off her soft, blond curls and her peaches-and-cream complexion. It had been fifteen years since she'd been in high school, but her skin was still smooth and clear. She still looked like the captain of the cheerleading squad, with her sweet smile and perfect, beautiful features—a fact that no doubt had helped her land her job as entertainment news reporter for the local TV station.

Gerry, however, looked tense, his smile forced as he led his bride-to-be in a slow dance. Was he feeling threatened, perhaps, by his stepbrother's larger-than-life presence?

Physically, the two men couldn't have been less alike. Gerry was taller than Blue but slighter, almost willowy, if that word could be used to describe a man. Although they both had blond hair, Gerry's was a lighter, paler shade, and his hair was fine and slightly thinning on top, not thick and wavy like Blue's. And though Blue's smiles were scarce, Gerry's were almost constant. In fact, Gerry's carefree, fun-time, no-worries attitude contrasted so sharply with Blue's serious intensity that Lucy found it hard to believe the two men had lived under the same roof as young boys. It seemed almost impossible that they'd shared a home and not driven each other crazy with their different approaches to life.

But the talk around town was that despite their differences, Gerry and Blue had been closer than many blood brothers, that their strengths and weaknesses had complemented one another. Lucy didn't know for sure that that was true. By the time she and her mother had moved to Hatboro Creek, Gerry was off at college, and by the time Gerry returned after college, Blue had already left to join the Navy.

Lucy gazed across the ballroom, studying Blue's face, watching him as he watched Gerry dance with Jenny Lee.

His gaze swept around the room, passing directly over Lucy with no glint of recognition, as if she weren't even there—or as if he'd forgotten that she even existed, as if she paled so absolutely compared with Jenny Lee.

Lucy's stomach clenched in disappointment. But really now, she scolded herself. What did she expect? Did she honestly think she'd be anything to Blue but a poor substitute for the woman he truly wanted? She had to keep her imagination in line here. If she wasn't careful, she'd start believing that Blue had unconsciously reached out to her because deep down he was searching desperately for a good woman to love. Or she might start believing that she could make Blue fall in love with her, that just one glorious night of lovemaking with Lucy would soften his damaged heart.

No, the sad truth was, Lucy had come here tonight with her eyes wide open. She knew exactly what Blue wanted from her. He wanted sex. No strings, no desperate search, no falling in love, no softening hearts.

She knew that, and she'd come anyway.

Except now the way Blue's eyes seemed to look right through her signified a decided lack of interest on his part.

Lucy was a fool for thinking she could ever compete with

Jenny Lee. Even though Jenny was engaged to marry another man, she was so pretty and sweet it was crazy to think
that Blue wouldn't be carrying a torch for her. No doubt
he'd asked Lucy here tonight hoping for a distraction—a
distraction that she'd failed to provide.

Lucy knew she should turn away, walk out of the room
and down the long corridor to the stairs that led out to the
back parking lot. But she couldn't move. She could only
gaze at Blue and wish that things were different.

His rugged features were impassive, his eyes revealing
nothing—no emotion, nothing. And that, of course, convinced Lucy that there *was* something Blue was working so
hard to hide.

On the other hand, she had to admit it was a no-win situation for Blue. She knew that she was not the only person in the room watching him for his reaction to his
stepbrother and his former sweetheart's dance. If he smiled,
it would be with "bittersweet longing." If he frowned, it
would be with "barely concealed jealousy."

No, Blue's were not easy shoes to be in right now, and Lucy
had to give the man credit for showing up in the first place.

Shoes. Blue wasn't wearing shoes, Lucy realized suddenly.
He was wearing sandals. He was wearing his gleaming white
navy dress uniform with rows and rows of ribbons and medals on his chest, and a pair of leather sandals on his feet.

As more and more people moved out onto the dance
floor, Blue turned away and headed for the French doors
that led out onto the patio. The doors were closed tonight.
It was too hot to keep them open. The air-conditioning
would escape and the muggy night air would be let in.

With his hand on the doorknob, Blue turned back and
looked across the room—directly at Lucy. This time he
didn't look through her. This time he met her eyes. He
moved his head almost imperceptibly, but his message was
clear. Follow him outside.

Lucy's heart was pounding as she moved along the ballroom wall toward the patio doors. Perhaps she'd been wrong. Blue did recognize her. He did know she was here. It took her several minutes to work her way around the room, but finally she reached the French doors and slipped out onto the patio.

The sounds of the music and laughter from the party became muffled and distant as she shut the door behind her. The heat brushed against her face and arms like something solid. The moon was nearly full and it glowed through a haze of high clouds.

The patio was wide and made of carefully evened-off flagstones, with a decorative cast-iron railing surrounding it. Several chairs and tables with flickering citronella candles were set up around the edges. Japanese lanterns were strung overhead, but the pale light they cast couldn't compete with the moonlight.

As Lucy stood and let her eyes grow accustomed to the dimness, she saw Blue in the shadows, leaning against the railing, just watching her.

Blue couldn't believe his eyes. That was strange, because he'd been a lot of places, seen both the best and the worst that humanity could offer, and he'd begun to think that nothing could ever surprise him.

But Lucy Tait, dressed to kill in a sexy black dress, with her legs looking at least seven miles long, with her hair piled sophisticatedly atop her head and her brown eyes made up and smoldering, had proven him wrong.

He'd expected her to arrive at the country club wearing something demure and functional. He'd expected he would have to use his imagination to see beyond her clothing to the woman he suspected was underneath.

She started toward him, and he felt his pulse kick into the double time of anticipation, which he immediately tried to squelch. He hadn't been thinking straight when he'd asked her to come to this party with him. It wasn't until he arrived and realized that he was the focus of covert— and some not so covert—attention that it occurred to him that, as his date, Lucy would be subjected to the same curious stares and speculation.

She didn't deserve that. He had to send her home before anyone saw them together.

That was why, when he first noticed her standing on the other side of the room, he didn't allow himself to react. He didn't even let himself do the double take he so desperately wanted to do.

But here in the darkness, away from all the prying eyes, Blue could do all the double takes he wanted.

Mercy.

She could have been the poster model for carnal desire. But as he gazed into her eyes, he realized that it was entirely possible that Lucy didn't know how incredibly sexy she looked. He could see hesitation in her eyes, and a kind of vulnerability that, combined with her incredible outfit, made her seem a curious mix of experience and innocence.

Blue couldn't remember the last time he'd seen a woman and wanted her more than the way he wanted Lucy right now.

He pushed himself up off the railing as she drew closer. The sexy black spike heels of her shoes made her nearly his own height and she gazed directly into his eyes.

"Seems I've been away from town longer than I thought," Blue said softly. He felt his body tighten as he dropped his gaze to her mouth to watch her nervously moisten her lips with the pink tip of her tongue.

"Twelve years," she murmured.

He nodded. "So…why aren't you married…settled down with a couple of kids and all?"

She crossed her arms, one dark eyebrow lifting slightly. "Why aren't *you?*"

"I never met someone I couldn't live without," he said bluntly. "I guess I'm picky that way."

Lucy lifted her chin challengingly. "And what makes you think I'm not?"

Blue had to smile. "Touché." With that defiant gleam in her eyes, she looked so like the girl he'd first met all those years ago—and so unlike her, all at the same time.

He could still remember the way fifteen-year-old Lucy had tried to hide her pain, even after the boys who had been beating on her had run off. Her nose had been bleeding slightly, and she was holding her side. Though Blue had seen one of the boys kick her savagely in the ribs when she was down on the ground, she never cried, and tried not to let on that she was badly hurt. But there was a sheen of perspiration on her face that had told Blue otherwise.

She'd sat on the grass, knees pulled in tightly to her chest, and he'd sat down next to her. "You all right, Yankee?"

"Yeah," she said, wiping the blood from her nose with the back of one hand. "Yeah, I'm…fine."

"You don't look so fine."

"I just…need to sit here for a minute."

"Okay," Blue said quietly. "Mind if I sit here for a minute, too?"

She shook her head. No, she didn't mind.

"Those boys give you a reason for kicking the bejesus out of you?" Blue asked.

"They don't think a girl belongs on the baseball team," Lucy said.

"Well, it *is* called the *boys'* baseball team," Blue commented.

Lucy's eyes flashed. "So where's the girls' team?"

Blue shrugged. "'Round these parts, girls try out for the cheerleading squad."

"The coach said I'm the best shortstop this hick town has

ever seen," Lucy said flatly. "And from what I've seen, he might be right. He put me in the starting lineup and has me batting lead-off. And you want me to be a *cheer*leader?"

Blue hid a smile. "You're pretty sure of yourself, aren't you?"

"There are some things boys can do better than girls— like pee standing up," Lucy told him, her eyes narrowed dangerously, "but playing baseball is *not* one of them. I'm going to stick it in those creeps' faces by winning MVP this year—and accepting the award in a *dress*."

Blue might have even laughed out loud at that, except a spasm of pain made Lucy wince. She closed her eyes and clenched her teeth. Her face looked so pale.

"How about I give your mama a call?" Blue asked.

Lucy shook her head. "She's working."

"You're hurt—"

"I'm fine."

Blue stood up. "She works in the office at the mill, doesn't she?"

"I said, I'm fine!" Lucy scrambled to her feet, and the effort made her sway.

Blue reached for her, holding her up. "You got a broken rib, Yankee. I'm taking you over to Doc Gray's."

"No, please!" Lucy's dark-brown eyes were wide, her voice beseeching as she gazed up at him. "It's only a crack. The doctor will tape me up and tell me I can't play ball for three weeks. By then I'll have been off the starting lineup for so long I'll have lost my place. I'll spend the rest of the season on the bench."

"Sometimes you gotta sit out."

"Not this time," Lucy said desperately. "If I sit out, those creeps will win. I can't let that happen."

Blue was silent.

"I'll tape myself up," Lucy had told him, chin held high. "It'll hurt, but I'm damned if I'm not going to play."

She *had* played, and sure enough, that year she'd won the coveted Most Valuable Player award for the junior-varsity team. She'd had one hell of a stubborn streak back then, and from the way she was holding her head at that same challenging angle, it seemed that she still had those same guts and grit now. Inside, she wasn't that different. It was the outer packaging that had changed some. A whole lot of some.

Blue let his gaze travel over Lucy's formfitting black dress and down her long, nylon-clad legs. "I guess what I really meant," he said, gazing back into her eyes, "was that I can't believe you're unattached. I can't believe you could walk into this place alone, looking the way you do."

"But I'm not alone," she said softly. "I'm with you."

Desire knifed sharply through Blue, and despite all his best intentions, he knew there was no way he could send Lucy home. Not unless he went, too.

But maybe he could go. In half an hour or so he could make his excuses to Gerry and Jenny Lee and bow out before dinner was served. Until then, he and Lucy could stay out here on the patio. No one would see them. No one would have to know.

Lucy held Blue's gaze, wondering almost desperately what he was thinking. And he *was* thinking. He was planning, deciding. There was more than desire in his eyes—although there was plenty of that, too. She'd have to tell Sarah, she thought almost inanely, that her little black dress was a raging success.

"May I have this dance?" Blue finally said, his smooth Southern drawl like black velvet in the darkness.

Oh, yes. But… "Right here?" Lucy asked, breaking free from the magnetic hold of his eyes to glance around the deserted patio.

Blue smiled crookedly, just a slight lifting of one side of his mouth. "Yeah," he said. He hooked the rim of his hat over one of the posts of the cast-iron railing. And then he reached for her.

Inside the country club, the band was playing an old, slow, familiar tune. The music seemed to drift in the stillness of the night, distant and haunting and pure.

Lucy slipped her right hand into Blue's, resting her other hand on the solidness of his shoulder. She felt his arm encircle her waist, felt the warmth of his hand on her back.

Dear God, she was slow-dancing with Blue McCoy.

He was graceful and surefooted, and when his thigh brushed hers, she knew it was not by accident. Slowly and so surely he pulled her in, closer to him, until her breasts touched his broad chest, until their legs touched continuously. His hand moved upward, exploring the back of her dress, finding the round keyhole of exposed skin.

Lucy felt herself sigh, felt herself tighten her hold on Blue as his slightly work-roughened fingers caressed her back. Gently she pulled her fingers free from his and ran her hand up his arm and shoulders to meet her other hand at the back of his neck.

She could see satisfaction in the ocean-colored depths of Blue's eyes. He knew as well as she did that she was probably going to end up in his bed tonight. It was clear that pleased him. It was also clear that he desired her, too—she couldn't help but be aware of that from the way their bodies were molded together.

Any moment now, he was going to kiss her. Any moment now, he was going to lean forward and touch his lips to hers and they were both going to explode with passion. She could imagine them making a beeline for Blue's motel room, undressing each other as they climbed into the cab of her truck, barely making it inside before...

Lucy felt dizzy. This was moving much too quickly. Yes, she wanted to make love to this man. She'd come here tonight knowing that the clothes she was wearing sent a message, knowing that her mere *presence* was a loud and clear affirmative to Blue's unspoken sexual question. But she'd imagined them having dinner first—shoot, at least having a drink and a certain amount of conversation—before giving in to the animal attraction that flashed between them.

But polite conversation and small talk had no place in this relationship. Her body understood that, heat flooding her, readying her for what she really wanted—the most basic and intimate of acts.

Lucy didn't wait for Blue to kiss her. Pulling his mouth down to hers, *she* kissed *him*.

She felt more than heard his surprised laughter—laughter that lasted only a fraction of a second before he angled his head and returned her kiss with an urgency that took her breath away.

He pulled her with him deeper into the darkness of the shadows. His hands explored her body, covering her breasts, slipping down to cup her derriere, reaching for the edge of her dress and sliding up underneath the hem, pushing her miniskirt up along her nylon-smooth thigh. He discovered the edge of her thigh-high stockings and groaned, kissing her harder, deeper, as his fingers caressed the soft smoothness of her skin, as he found the silky lace of her panties.

They weren't even going to make it back to his hotel room. The thought flashed crazily through Lucy's head. But they had to. There were laws against making love in public. For God's sake, she was a police officer. She couldn't do this. Not here.

Lucy pulled back slightly. "Blue..."

"Come back to my room with me." His velvet voice was rough, hoarse, and out of breath.

She nodded. "Yes."

Blue kissed her again and she clung to him, shutting her eyes tightly against the regrets that were sure to come in the morning and all the rest of her tomorrows. But for the first time in her life, Lucy refused to think beyond the here and now. She lost herself again in his kiss.

He tasted the way she'd always imagined he would— sweet and clean and wonderful.

He broke away from her, taking her hand and pulling her toward the gate. "Come on."

"We're just going to leave?"

His eyes were blazing hot in the dim glow from the Japanese lanterns. "You bet."

"But…"

"Come on, Yankee. Let's go make all my dreams come true." His voice was low, vibrating with his desire as he tugged on her hand.

"Your brother will look for you." His brother and a hundred or so odd guests. "He'll wonder where you went."

"If Gerry caught sight of you walking into that country club, he'll know *exactly* where I went."

Lucy blushed. "I'm serious," she said, pulling her hand free from his grasp. "You know how small-town gossip can be. Everyone is going to think that you left because you couldn't stand watching Gerry with Jenny Lee."

"Me and Jenny Lee," Blue said, shaking his head. "That's ancient history."

Lucy could almost believe him. Almost. "That's not the way it's going to look," she said quietly. "No one is going to know that you left with me—no one has even seen us together."

"And I don't want 'em to," Blue said. "I don't want 'em talking about you, too."

Lucy smiled ruefully. "Whatever they'd be saying, it would probably be true, wouldn't it?"

He smiled, a tight, sexy, dangerous smile. "Well, yeah," he said, "if they say I took one look at you and lost control."

His soft words made Lucy's heart leap into her throat. But

they were just words, she reminded herself. "I'd be willing to bet," she said, "that you don't ever lose control."

His eyes were unreadable, mysterious. "There's always a first time." His voice dropped to a nearly inaudible level. "All I know is, I'd do damn near anything to make love to you right now, Lucy."

"Well, shoot," Lucy said, crossing her arms and smiling to hide the way his words made her pulse race. "Maybe if I play my cards right, we can make that wedding on Saturday a double ceremony."

She was baiting him, watching to see if her words made him back off. "I said *damn near* anything," Blue said, smiling at her expression—she thought she had him retreating. So he called her bluff. "I guess getting married falls into that description. Sure. But why wait till Saturday? We can fly out to Las Vegas and get hitched tonight. Right now."

Lucy surrendered. "We both know you don't have to marry me to get what you want—what *I* want, too."

He stepped toward her. "Then what are we waiting for?"

She lifted her chin. "*We're* waiting for *you* to go inside and make your excuses to Gerry and Jenny Lee."

Blue smiled again—damn, he couldn't remember the last time he'd smiled and laughed so much. But this was fun. Lucy Tait was able to hold her own against him. She was a worthy sparring opponent, and he liked that. He liked it a lot.

He'd moved close enough to her to put his arms around her waist, close enough to lean forward for another long, sensuous kiss. But Lucy reached out for him first, sweeping her hands along the lapels of his jacket, lightly tracing the ribbons and medals he wore on his chest with one finger.

"Look at all these," she mused. "What are you, some kind of hero?"

"Just a SEAL," Blue murmured, mesmerized by the elegant curve of her lips, by the spattering of freckles that ran across her cheekbones and the bridge of her nose, by the delicate shell-like curve of her ears.

She leaned forward so that her lips were only a whisper away from his. "Go find your brother," she breathed.

He kissed her again—he couldn't resist—drowning in her softness, marveling how one woman could be such a complete montage of sweetness and spice. When he finally pulled away, his voice didn't sound like his own. "Don't go anywhere."

Lucy smiled. "I won't."

Chapter Three

Blue searched the country-club dining room for any sign of Gerry. The band was still playing in the corner, and couples were still out on the dance floor, but most of the crowd were starting to get seated at the round banquet tables that dotted half the room.

His sharp eyes finally picked Gerry out of the crowd. He was in the corner, having what looked like a serious discussion with R. W. Fisher, the Tobacco King.

Fisher had sold his tobacco farms and cigarette factories in Virginia and moved his massive fortune to Hatboro Creek about the same time Blue had moved to town with his mother. It had been more than twenty-five years since Fisher had earned his wages from growing and selling tobacco, but he would no doubt be known as the Tobacco King until the day he died.

Gerry was forever trying to work his way into R. W. Fisher's exclusive circle of friends and business acquaintances. Blue knew better than to disturb his stepbrother now.

On the other hand, Lucy was waiting for him out on the patio....

He could just as easily make his excuses for leaving to Jenny Lee, tell her that he'd talk to Gerry in the morning. Blue turned back to the table where he'd last seen his stepbrother's bride-to-be talking with several of her friends.

He worked his way across the room, and Jenny Lee glanced up. She rose to her feet, smiling a welcome, her cheeks dimpling prettily. Her friends were noticeably quiet, watching them both.

"Carter," Jenny said in her soft Southern accent. "We haven't properly said hello yet, have we?"

She held out her hand to him, and he reached for it automatically. Jenny Lee Beaumont. There had once been a time when he'd wanted this girl more than life itself. Her blond hair and blue eyes, her diminutive yet well-rounded figure, her lacy, frilly clothes had all seemed the definition of femaleness. It was funny, but now she seemed overdone— a caricature of the Southern belle, all peaches and sugar and girlish charm.

Funny, but somewhere during the past twelve years he'd developed a definite preference for spice. And for full-grown women.

Jenny Lee's fragrant scent enveloped him, cloyingly sweet and chokingly strong. Hell, he used to love the way she smelled. Now he had to fight a nearly overpowering urge to step back, away from her, to find some fresh air.

As she smiled up into his eyes, Blue felt nothing.

He *had* been afraid to see her again, he realized suddenly. He'd been scared that all the old wants and needs and hurts would come flooding back.

But he felt nothing.

Except an urge to get back out to that patio, where Lucy Tait was waiting for him.

"Jenny, I'm sorry," he said, gently disengaging his hand from hers, "but I can't stay for dinner. I've got to head out."

"Oh, dear. I was hoping to get a chance to talk to you."

As her smile faded, Blue could see lines of worry on Jenny's usually smooth face. And when she smiled again, he could see that it was forced and unnatural.

Blue glanced at the tableful of women, all still listening, as if they were watching an episode of "As the World Turns." Whatever Jenny had to say, she didn't want to say it in front of an audience.

"Of course, I really can't leave without at least one dance," Blue said, knowing that whatever was bothering her, she could tell him on the privacy of the dance floor.

Relief flashed through Jenny's eyes. "Of course," she said, letting him lead her out into the middle of the room. The women at the table were still watching, but at least they wouldn't be able to hear them.

"Is everything all right?" Blue asked. Dancing with Jenny was odd after he'd held Lucy in his arms. Lucy was nearly his own height, a perfect fit; Jenny was so much shorter. He felt awkward, as if he had to bend clear over to talk to her.

"I don't know what's going on," Jenny said. "Gerry has been acting so strangely the past few days…so worried and upset. I can't figure out why. Business has been better than ever. He just bought a new car, and the honeymoon plans he's made are *extravagant*…. It's not financial worries that have him down, that's for sure."

Her eyes were bright with tears, but Blue still felt nothing. Nothing more than brotherly concern for Gerry's future wife. She looked as if she was going to say more, so he waited.

"I just wonder…"

If she were Lucy, she would have spit out whatever was bugging her the moment they'd begun to dance. Lucy was straightforward and to the point. She said what was on her mind. It was refreshing, Blue realized. He liked it much better than Jenny Lee's approach, where every tiny piece of information had to be wheedled out of her.

"What is it, Jenny Lee?" he asked. "Just tell me."

She couldn't look him in the eye, embarrassment making her blush. "I just can't help but wonder if I haven't made a colossal mistake by inviting you here," she whispered.

Ten minutes stretched into fifteen, and all Lucy's doubts and reservations grew bigger and bigger.

What was she doing? Now that she was taking the time to think about it, the incredible power of the passion she felt from Blue's kisses scared her to death.

What if she did something really stupid? What if she fell in love with this guy?

Fell in love? Lord help her, she was already halfway over the edge. Could she really have sex with Blue, keeping the physical and emotional totally separate? Or would the physical intimacy send her into a tailspin from which she could never pull free?

Where *was* he? What was taking him so long?

Lucy had no questions, no doubts, when she gazed into Blue's eyes. She could move in no other direction but ahead. It was only when he wasn't around that she started to back away.

She opened the French doors and went back into the country club. Blue had probably gotten into some deep discussion with Gerry and couldn't get free. And she—she needed a drink, something with a kick to give her the courage to keep from running away.

Halfway to the bar, she saw him.

Blue was out on the dance floor, with Jenny Lee Beaumont in his arms.

Didn't it figure.

Lucy turned away, too disgusted with her own self to

feel angry at Blue. Blue and Jenny Lee, ancient history? Lucy had almost believed it. That made her as big a fool as Blue.

She had to get away from here, fast, so she headed for the doors to the corridor. She was nearly there when the shouting started.

Lucy turned back, her police officer's training not allowing her to run from sounds of trouble. What she saw made her heart sink.

Gerry, his face livid, was standing in the middle of the dance floor, between Blue and Jenny. And even though he'd lowered his voice, he pushed at Blue repeatedly, clearly upset and angry.

Lucy could see from Blue's stance and from the way he held both hands in the air, palms out and facing his stepbrother, that he had no intention of letting this argument become violent. But Jenny was in tears, and Gerry pushed Blue harder and harder with every sentence he spoke. Lucy moved closer, wondering whether she should step in even though she wasn't on duty. Not that she'd had much luck settling this afternoon's disturbance….

The room was silent. Even the band had stopped playing. Sheldon Bradley, the chief of police, moved quickly to Gerry's side, and Lucy was glad. He had far more experience than she did, in addition to being one of Gerry's friends.

"I want him *out* of here." Gerry's voice started to get louder again. "Who the hell gave him permission to dance with Jenny Lee anyway?"

Was his speech slurred? He sounded funny, as if he were…

"Gerry, you're drunk," Jenny Lee said.

"It was *your* idea to invite him," Gerry shot back harshly, turning to berate his fiancée. "Stepbrother or not, I didn't think it was right to invite one of your ex-lovers to my wedding. But maybe you had some other kind of reason to want him here…?"

"When you sober up, brother," Blue drawled softly, "you're going to feel like a real idiot."

"Stay the *hell* out of my life," Gerry said, his eyes wild. "You're not my brother. I don't want you hanging around. I didn't when we were kids, and I sure as hell don't *now*."

The flash of pain that appeared in Blue's eyes left so quickly that Lucy was sure she was the only one who'd seen it. But she *had* seen it. Gerry's bitter words had hurt Blue deeply.

"Come on now, boys." Chief Bradley tried to step between the two men.

"Besides, Jenny Lee is mine now." Gerry glared past Bradley at Blue. "You had your chance. You can't have her."

"She's not going to be yours too much longer if you keep this up," Blue said evenly, quietly.

"Is that some kind of threat? Because if that was some kind of a threat, I'm gonna…" Gerry swung at Blue.

Blue caught his hand effortlessly, stopping his stepbrother's punch midswing.

"Now, come on," the police chief said, "is this any way for brothers to treat each other?"

"He's not my brother." Gerry pulled his hand free from Blue's. "If my old man hadn't felt guilty for picking up and bedding Blue's white-trash mama—"

Blue reacted so quickly that Lucy didn't even see his movement. One moment he was standing several feet away from Gerry, and the next he had backed his stepbrother up against a support pillar and was holding on to the taller man by the lapels of his expensive tuxedo.

Chief Bradley looked as if he were thinking twice about getting on the wrong side of Blue. Still, he stepped forward. "Here now, boys. Let's not—"

Blue ignored Bradley, glaring into Gerry's eyes. "That time you went too far," he said softly. "I don't give a damn what you say about me, but you keep my mother out of this."

"Blue," the police chief said. "Son, I'm going to have to ask you to leave."

"You so much as breathe her name again," Blue continued, "and there'll be hell to pay, you understand me?"

Gerry nodded, finally silenced.

Chief Bradley wasn't used to being ignored. "Blue McCoy, I'm going to have to ask you to unhand your brother."

But Blue didn't move. "You apologize to Jenny Lee, and then you go on home and sober up," he said to Gerry, still in that same low, dangerous voice.

Gerry seemed to wilt, to sag, his arms going around Blue in an odd kind of embrace. He may have said something, whispered something in Blue's ear, but he spoke so softly Lucy couldn't hear it.

"As far as *I* can see, son, *you're* the one who needs to be making apologies and clearing on out of here." Chief Bradley looked around the room, searching for any kind of support. He spotted Lucy. "You on duty tonight, Tait?"

"No, sir. I'm here as—"

"Consider yourself on duty as of right now," Bradley said grimly. "I'm ordering you to escort Lieutenant McCoy back to his motel. See that he gets there without any more trouble."

"But…" Lucy glanced at Blue, who had let go of Gerry.

Blue turned to Jenny Lee. "I'm sorry," he said.

"I am, too," she said. She held her head high despite the tears that were in her eyes, and with a withering look at Gerry, she swept out of the room.

Blue turned and headed for the other door. Chief Bradley had pulled Gerry aside and was talking to him in a low voice. Lucy briefly considered waiting and voicing her arguments about being suddenly placed on duty during her night off, but she knew it wouldn't make any difference. Sheldon Bradley ran the Hatboro Creek Police Department according to his own set of rules. With a sigh, Lucy turned and followed Blue. She had to run to catch up with him.

"McCoy—wait!"

He turned and waited, his face impassive, his eyes expressionless. Together, they walked in silence out to Lucy's truck.

It wasn't until Lucy was pulling out of the country-club driveway that Blue spoke.

"I'm sorry about that," he murmured.

She glanced at him. He was watching her in the dim light from the dashboard. "You can't help the way you feel," she said quietly.

He shifted in his seat, turning so that he was facing her. "You don't think I was…" He stopped and started over. "Do you really think I would make a move on Jenny Lee at the rehearsal dinner for her wedding to my stepbrother?"

Lucy pulled carefully up to the stop sign at the corner of Main Street and Seaside Road. "Everyone at that party was waiting for something to happen between you and Jenny Lee," she said, taking a left onto Main Street. "Everyone at that party saw you dancing with her and came to the same conclusion—that you're here to stir up trouble, that you want to win Jenny Lee back."

Blue's face was in the shadows, but she knew that he was watching her.

"Everyone at the party. Including you?"

She had to be honest. "Yes."

"And if I told you everyone at the party was wrong? That I feel nothing for Jenny Lee…?"

"I'd have to assume you were only saying that in a last-ditch effort to get me to spend the night with you," Lucy said bluntly, pulling her truck into the motel parking lot and rolling to a stop.

"That's not true," Blue said quietly. "Yes, I want you in my bed, but I wouldn't lie to get you there. Come on, Yankee, let's just leave the past in the past." He reached out across the cab of the truck, gently touching her hair.

Lucy shifted away from him. "Don't."

"Lucy—"

She closed her eyes, trying to shut him out. "I can't do this," she said. "I thought I could, but I can't." She opened her eyes and looked at Blue. "I can't be a substitute for Jenny Lee."

Blue laughed, a flare of impatience in his eyes. "You're *not*—"

"Look, McCoy, I've got to go—"

"Why don't we go get a beer and talk about this?" he suggested. "Is that roadhouse—what's it called? The Rebel Yell. Is it still around? Why don't we go there?"

"No. Believe it or not, I'm actually on duty now. I've got to go back to the station and file a report."

"You know damn well you could do that in the morning."

"Yeah," Lucy said. "But I *want* to do it now."

Silence. Lucy stared out the front windshield, hoping and wishing that Blue would just open the door and climb out of the truck's cab. She heard him sigh.

"Damn Gerry to hell," he said tiredly. "I should have wrung his neck while I had the chance."

He opened the door and climbed out of the truck. "It was a genuine pleasure seeing you again, Lucy Tait," he said in his soft drawl. "I've got to tell you—I wish it could have been an even bigger pleasure. If you're ever in California, give me a call."

She turned to look at him—she couldn't help it. "Are you leaving town?"

His blond hair glistened in the cab's overhead light as he nodded. "I'm heading out on the next bus. I don't care where it goes, as long as it's a city big enough to have an airport."

He was leaving as soon as he could. Lucy looked away

from him, afraid that he'd see the disappointment that surely crossed her face.

"Bye, Lucy," Blue whispered. He closed the cab door and was gone.

Lucy's phone rang well before dawn, waking her from a restless sleep.

It was Annabella Sawyer, the police dispatcher. "You better get down to the station," she said in her raspy voice, without any words of greeting. "All hell has broken loose. The chief is calling in all available manpower."

Lucy rolled over and looked at her clock. It was a few minutes after 4 a.m. "What's going on?"

"It started as a 10-65," Annabella said. "Jenny Beaumont called in at 2:11 a.m., reporting Gerry McCoy missing. He hadn't come home. Fifteen minutes ago, Tom Harper came across Gerry's motor vehicle by the side of Gate's Hill Road. Shortly after that, the 10-65 became a 10-54. At 3:56, Doc Harrington verified it. We've got ourselves a 187."

Lucy tiredly closed her eyes. "You mind translating that for me, Annabella?"

"The missing person became a report of a dead body," Annabella said. "We've got a homicide on our hands."

Lucy sat up. "*What?*"

"Gerry McCoy is dead," Annabella intoned. "He's been murdered."

Chapter Four

Lucy rushed into the police station, pulling her hair back into a ponytail and trying to rein in her growing sense of dread. Gerry McCoy was dead, and Lucy was almost positive that the tragedy wasn't over yet.

Officer Frank Redfield was behind the front desk, on the phone, but he nodded to her, holding up one finger, signaling her to wait.

"All right," he said into the telephone. His thinning brown hair was standing up straight, as if he'd rolled directly out of bed. "I understand, Chief. I'll get right on it." He hung up the receiver and turned to Lucy. "Hell of a situation," he said to her, taking a long swig of black coffee. "You been filled in on the specifics?"

"I've heard that Gerry McCoy's body was found up off Gate's Hill Road," Lucy said, pouring her own mug of coffee from the urn in the lobby. "I don't know any of the details. How did he die? Gunshot?" Nearly all the deaths in the county were gun related.

"Come on," Frank said, gesturing for her to follow him. "I've got to put out an all-points bulletin, but I'll try to bring you up to speed while I'm entering the info into the computer."

Lucy hurried down the hall after him. Frank was about four inches shorter than she was, and thin as a rail. But what he lacked in weight, he made up for in speed and good nature. It certainly wasn't his fault that, standing next to him, Lucy felt like some kind of Amazon. He was always friendly and respectful. In fact, Frank and his best friend, Tom Harper—tall and black and built like a defensive lineman—were the only men on the Hatboro Creek police force who hadn't muttered and complained about Lucy joining their previously exclusively male organization.

"First of all," Frank said in his thick South Carolina accent, "cause of death wasn't gun related. Gerry McCoy died from a broken neck."

"We're certain it wasn't accidental?" Lucy asked. "Sustained in a fall?"

"Gerry's body was found in the middle of a clearing," he said. "Unless he fell out of the sky, there was no way his injuries were accidental." He sat down at the computer desk, glancing up at her and grimacing. "Doc Harrington reported that his neck was broke clean through. Snapped like a twig." He shuddered. "Doc estimated time of death to be a little bit after eleven. We'll get a more accurate time when the forensics guy gets out here in the morning."

"Who's the APB for?"

"The stepbrother," Frank said, typing the information into the computer, fingers moving at his usual breathtaking speed.

Lucy's dread deepened. "Blue McCoy." Of course they were going to want to talk to Gerry's stepbrother—particularly since Blue was seen publicly arguing with the deceased hours before the estimated time of death. Family members were always high on the suspect list early on in a murder investigation. Statistically, most murders were committed by someone near and dear to the victim. Yet Blue wasn't a cold-blooded killer. He was a soldier, a warrior, but not a murderer.

Still, *damn Gerry to hell*, Blue had said. *I should have wrung his neck while I had the chance.*

Wrung his neck, he'd said. And now here Gerry was, dead—that very same neck snapped in two.

My God, was it possible...?

No, Lucy couldn't believe it. She *wouldn't* believe it.

"We want to bring him in for questioning," Frank said.

"You don't need an APB for that," Lucy said. Questioning. Being brought in for questioning was marginally better than being brought in with charges already filed. "Blue McCoy is staying over at the Lighthouse Motel."

"Not any more," Frank said. "Chief just called in and reported that Gerry's brother checked out of the motel at around 1 a.m. Jedd Southeby over at the Lighthouse said Blue paid his bill and just walked out of there with some kind of heavy duffel bag over his shoulder." He looked up at Lucy. "In fact, now that you know as much as we know, you better get on the ball and join the search. A man on foot carrying a heavy load couldn't have gotten far."

What was it Blue had said as they were saying goodbye? *I'm heading out on the next bus. I don't care where it goes...*

Lucy picked up the phone and dialed information. "Yeah, I need the number of the bus station in Georgetown." She scribbled it on a piece of paper as Frank glanced over at her in barely concealed disbelief.

"There's no way in hell the stepbrother could've gone to Georgetown," he said. "It's nearly fifteen miles away. Use your head, Luce. This time of night the roads are quiet. He couldn't even get there by hitching. Nobody is around to pick him up."

"Georgetown has the nearest all-night bus station," Lucy said, dialing the number she was given. "And fifteen miles is an after-dinner stroll to a Navy SEAL."

"You're wasting your time," Frank said in a singsong voice.

After nearly seventeen rings, the phone at the Georgetown bus station was picked up. Lucy identified herself and was forwarded to the manager. "I need the schedule of all buses that have left or are leaving your terminal, starting at 3:00 a.m.," she said. It was unlikely that Blue had arrived in Georgetown that early, but she wanted to be safe.

"No buses left between 2:00 a.m. and 3:55," the bus station manager told her. "At 3:55, we had a departure for Columbia and Greenville. At 4:20, just a few minutes ago, a bus left for Charleston, and the next bus… Let's see—"

"Isn't there a naval base in Charleston?" Lucy asked Frank. He nodded. "Yeah."

"That's the bus," Lucy said. It had to be the one Blue would take. He'd ride the bus to Charleston, and at the naval base he'd catch the next flight out of state, probably back to California. "Is there any way to contact the bus driver?"

"Not short of chasing him and flagging him down. The local buses aren't equipped with radios," the manager told her. "We can contact the bus depot in Charleston, but that's about it."

"What time does that bus get in?"

"It's not an express," the manager said, "so it stops in nearly every town along Route 17 from here to Charleston. It won't arrive at the final destination until 6:45 p.m. That's if they're running on time."

"Thank you," Lucy said, hanging up the phone. "I'm going to Charleston," she said to Frank.

"What you're going on is a wild-goose chase," he told her.

"Aren't my orders to join in the search to find Blue McCoy?" Lucy asked.

"Well, yeah, but—"

"I'm joining in," Lucy said, heading for the door.

"Chief is gonna get riled—"

"Tell the chief," Lucy said, "that I'll be back before eight o'clock—with Blue McCoy."

Blue was drifting in and out of sleep. It seemed incredible that he had spent most of last night hiking to the bus station in Georgetown. It seemed amazing that he had worked so hard just to get on this crummy old bus.

It seemed particularly incredible that he had worked so hard to leave Hatboro Creek, because for the first time in his life, Hatboro Creek was precisely where he wanted to be.

Because a woman named Lucy Tait was there, and try as he might, he couldn't get her off his mind.

She still lived in the same big, old house that she'd shared with her mother back when Blue had been in high school. Unable to sleep, he'd gone for a walk last night and found himself standing and staring at her darkened windows, wanting to go up to her door and knowing that he shouldn't.

He could have rung her doorbell, finagled an invitation inside. Once in Lucy's living room, it wouldn't have taken much to seduce her. He already knew that she found the attraction between them nearly impossible to resist.

He'd forced himself to turn around, to turn his back on the paradise that making love to Lucy Tait would bring. Why? He didn't know for sure, but he suspected his motivation was due to wariness. There was something inside that warned him that maybe, just maybe, this Lucy Tait was someone special. And Blue knew, plain as day, that he had no room in his life for anyone, particularly not someone who was special.

He knew from watching Joe Catalanotto, the commander of SEAL Team Ten's Alpha Squad and Blue's closest friend, that finding someone special wasn't all hearts and flowers. Yeah, Joe seemed happy most of the time. Yeah, in general he smiled more and got irritated and frustrated less. But during the times when Alpha Squad was on a mission, when it had been weeks since Joe had seen his wife, Veronica, and weeks, possibly even months, until he'd get a chance to see her again, Joe would grow quieter and quieter. Joe never complained, never spoke about it, but Blue knew his friend. He knew that Joe missed the woman he loved, and that he worried about her when he was gone for so long.

Blue didn't want that, didn't need that. No, sir—no, thanks.

So why was he sitting here on this bus, dozing and fantasizing about Lucy Tait, as if he could conjure her up just by wishing and wanting? When he pulled into Charleston, he'd look up one of the women he knew from back when he'd been stationed at the naval base, and...

"What the hell...?" he heard someone say. "Why are we pulling over here?"

"This stop ain't on the route," another voice said.

Blue opened his eyes. Sure enough, the bus was moving to the side of the road. Two men in work clothes, sitting across the aisle and several seats toward the front, were the only ones on the sparsely filled bus who were talking.

"Aw, hell," the first man said. "Driver must've been speeding. We're getting pulled over by a cop."

"If I don't get to Charleston by 7:00, I'm going to lose my job," the second voice complained. "I've been late too many times before."

Blue tried to see out of his window, but couldn't see a police cruiser, couldn't see anything, so he closed his eyes again. It didn't matter to him if this took five minutes or an hour. He'd get to Charleston when he got there.

He heard the hiss as the driver opened the door, heard the murmur of voices from the front of the bus.

"Oh, sugar," the first man said. "Come and arrest *me*."

"Where do I sign up to get frisked?" the other man asked with a giggle.

"I've heard that one before," a third voice said, "so unless you can come up with something original, why don't you just keep your mouths shut?"

Lucy?

Blue opened his eyes, and sure enough, there she was, standing in the aisle, looking down at him.

"McCoy, you've got to grab your stuff and come off the bus with me," she said.

She looked tired, and her face had been wiped clean of last night's makeup. Her hair was up in a utilitarian ponytail, and her uniform shirt hid the soft curves of her body. Still, she looked *damn* good and Blue felt his mouth curve up into a smile of pleasure.

"Hey," he said, his voice rusty from sleep. He cleared his throat. "Yankee. Didn't think I'd see *you* again."

"Come on, we're holding these people up," Lucy said.

She wouldn't look him in the eye, as if she were afraid of the inferno of attraction he knew was burning there.

"Am I under arrest?" he teased, tilting his head so that she was forced to meet his gaze.

But she didn't smile. "No," she said. "Not yet."

Blue felt his own smile fade as he searched her eyes. She wasn't kidding when she'd said "not yet." Whatever Lucy was doing here, it wasn't gonna be good. "What happened?" he asked, suddenly concerned. Clearly she hadn't followed him halfway to Charleston because of their unconsummated, sizzling attraction to each other. "Something happened, didn't it?"

She gestured with her head toward the front of the bus. "Get off the bus and I'll fill you in."

Blue stood up and swung his duffel bag down from the overhead rack. He followed Lucy down the aisle and out the narrow stairs onto the dusty road. Something was going on here. Something *bad*.

As the bus pulled back onto Route 17, he dropped his duffel bag onto the street. "Spill it."

"Why don't you get into the car?" she suggested.

Blue didn't move. "Don't play games, Lucy. It's not your style. Just tell me what's going on."

"I've got bad news," she said tightly. "I'd like you to sit down."

Bad news.

Bad news meant death or the equivalent.

Last time Blue got "bad news," he'd been in the hospital, waiting with the rest of Alpha Squad for word about Frisco. For hours, they didn't know if he was going to live or die. And *I've got bad news* was what the doctor had said when he'd come out of surgery. Frisco was going to live, but he wasn't going to walk ever again.

That doctor knew about Navy SEALs. He knew that losing mobility, losing the ability to run and jump and even walk, was bad news akin to death.

And in a way, Frisco *had* died in Baghdad. The unsmiling man lying in that hospital bed with lines of pain around his eyes and mouth was nothing like the laughing, upbeat SEAL Blue had once known.

Bad news.

Someone had died. He could see it in Lucy's eyes. But who? Blue didn't want to guess. He just wanted her to tell him.

Lucy felt a rush of relief as she looked at Blue. He was gazing into her eyes as if he were trying to read her mind. He honestly didn't know what she was about to tell him. He didn't know—he honestly didn't know that Gerry was dead. He couldn't possibly be the killer. No one was that good a liar.

"I don't need to sit down to get bad news," Blue said in his soft drawl.

Lucy knew that she was just supposed to tell him that his

stepbrother was dead. That way she could gauge his reaction, further verify that he didn't know anything about the killing. But it seemed so cruel, so heartless. Although recently Blue and Gerry hadn't been on the best of terms, they *had* been friends in their youth.

"Come on, Yankee," Blue said softly. "If it's gonna hurt, do it fast, get it over with."

Lucy nodded, moistening her lips. "Gerry is dead."

Blue squinted slightly, as if the sun were suddenly too bright for him. "Gerry," he said, looking out over the farmland that stretched into the distance as the muscle in his jaw clenched again and again. "Dear God. How?"

"He was killed sometime last night," Lucy said.

Blue turned to look sharply at her, his blue eyes neon and intense in the morning light. "Killed," he repeated. "As in...murdered?"

Lucy nodded. "His neck was broken."

Blue swore under his breath. "Who would've done that to him—three days before his wedding?"

"We don't know yet. The homicide investigation has just started."

Something changed in his eyes and his entire body became stiffer, more tense. "Am I a suspect?"

"Right now everyone in town is a suspect," Lucy told him. "As a family member, you just happen to be up a little higher on the list."

"I can't believe he's dead." Blue shook his head. "Gerry. When I was a kid, I thought he was immortal. One of the gods." He laughed, but it held no humor. "The last thing I said to him I said in anger, and now he's dead." He fixed Lucy with his brilliant blue gaze, and she caught her breath at the depth of the pain she saw in his eyes.

"I loved him," Blue said simply. "He was my brother. I wouldn't kill my brother."

Chapter Five

"I believe him," Lucy said.

Sarah gazed back at her silently for several long moments from her prone position on the couch. "Richard told me that Gerry's neck was broken cleanly," Sarah said. "He said that in order to do that, a man either had to be a martial-arts expert or have extreme upper-body strength." She paused for a moment, pushing herself up on one elbow to take a cooling sip from a tall glass of orange juice. "Speaking of upper-body strength, didn't you tell me something about Navy SEALs being able to bench-press three or four hundred pounds or something like that?"

Lucy shook her head. "I know what you're getting at," she said. "Yes, you're right. Blue McCoy probably has the strength and ability to break a man's neck the way Gerry's was broken. But I don't think he did it."

"Have they arrested him?" Sarah asked, her hazel eyes sympathetic.

"No," Lucy said. "They don't have enough to hold him.

The fact that he was—quote, unquote—'fleeing the scene of the crime' is only circumstantial evidence."

The phone rang jarringly loudly, disrupting the calm of Sarah's living room. Lucy jumped and Sarah winced, making a face in apology. "Richard got a ring amplifier for the phone," she explained. "He was afraid he'd sleep straight through some medical emergency because he wouldn't hear the phone ringing in the middle of the night. I tell you, it's tough being married to a small-town doctor." Her smile turned impish. "Or maybe it's just tough being married to Richard. Excuse me for a sec." Sarah reached out and took the cordless phone from its resting place on the coffee table in front of her. "Hello?"

Lucy gazed around Sarah's living room. It wasn't until the baby was well on its way that Sarah and Richard had gotten around to furnishing their new house. For nearly a year, there had been almost nothing in the living room. But now everything was finally out of boxes. The house was filled with furniture that was toddler friendly. There were no sharp edges or breakable surfaces; everything was softly rounded, designed for being bumped by small heads and grabbed by tiny fingers. Yet despite its functional furnishings, the living room was tastefully decorated. Sarah wouldn't have had it any other way.

"No," she was saying into the phone. "I'm still waiting for this baby to decide that it's time to be born." She laughed. "Don't worry, you'll get a call." She paused, glancing up at Lucy. "Yes, she's here. Do you want to talk to her?"

"Who is it?" Lucy mouthed.

"Tom Harper," Sarah mouthed back. "Oh, okay. I'll give her that message. Consider her on her way." She laughed. "Sure, Tom. Thanks. Bye." Sarah pressed the off button, looking up at Lucy. "Tom was calling with a message from the chief. You're wanted down at the station. Immediately."

Lucy drained the last of her orange juice. "Did he happen to say why?"

Sarah smiled. "He mentioned something about Chief Bradley putting you in charge of the entire investigation since you did such a good job tracking Blue McCoy down."

Lucy nearly dropped her glass. "*Me?*"

"I don't understand," Lucy said vehemently, climbing into her truck. "Every other person on this police force is better qualified to handle this investigation. Why *me?*"

Blue stowed his duffel bag under his feet and calmly closed the passenger door, locking it with his elbow. "Because every other person on this police force thinks that I killed Gerry."

"And since when does Chief Bradley let the prime suspect select the officer in charge of the investigation?" she sputtered.

"Drive this thing, will you?" Blue said, squinting as he gazed out the front windshield. "I want to get out of here."

It was clear that he wasn't going to answer any of her questions until she put her truck in gear and pulled out of the parking lot.

It wasn't until she was on Bluff Drive, heading down toward the beach, that Blue started to talk. "Bradley doesn't know that *I* chose you," he said in his soft drawl. "He thinks *he* did. He was trying to get me to sign a confession and he claimed that the case against me was gonna be open and shut. Even though they don't have enough evidence to hold me today, the chief said this one was so easy that even the dumbest, greenest rookie on the force would be able to collect the necessary evidence to send me to jail within forty-eight hours. I took the opportunity to maneuver him into standing by his claim."

"And I'm that dumbest, greenest rookie," Lucy said dryly.

"You're green, Yankee," Blue said, "but you're not dumb.

And you're not going to overlook any evidence that supports my innocence in your zeal to hang me."

Lucy was silent for a moment. "What if I only find evidence that will help convict you?" she finally asked.

Blue pointed toward the beach parking lot. "Pull in," he said. "Please."

Lucy did. At this time of the late afternoon, the parking lot was almost empty, the last of the beachgoers heading home. She pulled up to the big boulders that lined the lot and turned off the engine. When she was in high school, this was where kids had come at night to park and make out. She'd never gone, but she was willing to bet that Blue had brought Jenny Lee here plenty of times.

Blue turned in his seat to face her. "I have a gut feeling," he said slowly, "that you're only going to find evidence that points to my guilt." He held up one hand, stopping her before she could speak. "Something about this whole thing reeks of setup. Whoever killed Gerry wants it to look like I'm the murderer. I don't know who's involved, or how far they're willing to take this. Until I do know, there's only one person I'm going to trust in this town, and that's you."

Lucy stared at him in disbelief. He was serious. Out of all the people he could have turned to for help, he'd turned to *her*.

But as the officer in charge of the investigation, her job wasn't to play favorites with a suspect. Her job was to find the killer—no matter who that killer turned out to be.

Lucy rested her head on her folded arms atop the steering wheel. "What if I decide you're guilty?"

"I believe you already decided that I'm not."

Lucy lifted her head. "I need to question you," she said. "you need to tell me where you were at the time of Gerry's death."

"I don't have an alibi," Blue told her. "I was by myself."

Lucy took her notebook out of her pocket and opened the truck door. "Let's walk on the beach," she suggested.

Blue nodded. "I'd like that," he said, following her out of the truck.

The sand crunched beneath Lucy's shoes. Blue had kicked off his sandals, she noticed, and his feet were now bare. He had nice feet. They were strong looking, with high arches and long, straight toes.

Lucy held her questions until they reached the edge of the water. They headed south along the coast in silence, watching the play of the early evening sun on the ocean.

"We're in an interesting position here," Lucy finally said. It wasn't easy, but she had to be honest with him because she *needed* him to be honest with her. "Last night we were on the verge of a...certain kind of relationship, but today that relationship has to be something entirely different."

Blue was quiet, just listening, so she pushed on. "I'm going to ask you a whole bunch of questions, and you've got to answer them honestly, do you understand?"

Lucy moved away slightly so that a wave rushing up to shore wouldn't get her shoes wet. Blue let the water wash over his bare feet. It soaked the hem of his pants, but he didn't seem to notice or care. He glanced up as if he felt Lucy watching him, and nodded. Yes, he understood.

"Okay." Lucy exhaled a burst of air. She hadn't realized it, but she had been holding her breath. "I dropped you off at your motel room around 8:30 p.m.," she said. "Tell me everything you did from then till the time you checked out."

Blue narrowed his eyes, thinking. "I went inside the room, took a shower and changed out of my dress uniform. I got some fried fish and a salad to go from the Grill, went back to my room and watched part of a movie on cable while I ate dinner," he said. "It wasn't very good—the movie, not the food—so I turned it off before the end. It was probably around ten at that point. The air conditioner wasn't working real well, and I was...restless, so I went outside, for a walk."

Restless. Lucy had been restless last night, too. She knew he was watching her, so she kept her eyes carefully on her notebook. "Where did you go? It's possible someone saw you while you were out."

"I went down Main and cut over some back lots to the marina," Blue said. "I sat down there for a while—I don't even know how long." He paused. "And then I walked up toward Fox Run Road."

Lucy couldn't keep from turning and looking at him. Her house was on Fox Run Road.

"That's right," he said. "I went to see if maybe you were still awake, like me."

She had been. She'd been awake last night until well into the early hours of the morning. She'd stared at the shadows on her ceiling, wishing that she had been reckless and bold, wishing that Blue were there with her. But even as she'd wished for his presence, she knew that what she *really* wished for was some kind of fairy-tale ending, for him to kiss her and confess that he couldn't live without her, that his only hope of finding true happiness was there in her arms.

She'd told herself all along that she was walking into a short, hot, love affair, a one-night stand. She'd tried to convince herself that that would be enough. But all along, she'd hoped—secretly, even from herself—that something magical would happen and Blue would stay in town.

Lucy stared down at the neat lines of notes in her pad, but her eyes were unfocused, and the notes looked more like the tracks of seabirds in the sand than words. Blue *was* going to stay in town, but the something that had happened was far from magical. It was evil and deadly.

If Blue hadn't killed Gerry—and he was right; she didn't believe that he had—then the real killer had long since disappeared or, worse, was somewhere out there, watching and waiting, biding his time.

Lucy glanced up to find Blue still gazing at her. "There wasn't a light on in your house," he said, "but even if there had been, I wouldn't have knocked. You made it clear when you dropped me off at the motel that you didn't want me around."

That wasn't true. She *had* wanted him around. But it just got way too complicated when she'd seen him holding Jenny Lee in his arms out on the country-club dance floor.

"I don't know why I even walked over to your place," Blue continued, glancing away from her, out at the ocean. "I guess maybe I hoped I'd find you out dancing naked on your back lawn or something."

Lucy had to laugh. "I don't spend much time dancing naked these days," she said.

"Too bad," he said, looking back at her with a slow smile.

Too bad. It *was* too bad that Blue hadn't knocked on her door last night. And it was too bad that Lucy had turned down his invitation to come into his hotel room earlier. "If I'd spent the night with you, you would have had an alibi," she noted.

Blue met her eyes, the heat in his gaze suddenly dangerously high. "That's right," he said softly.

Lucy looked away, scanning her notes again, knowing without a doubt that it was time to get into the sticky questions, the ones she'd been avoiding asking. She needed to know about Blue's conversation with Jenny Lee and the ensuing argument with Gerry. That would keep them from drifting into these dangerous waters.

"Let's backtrack a bit," Lucy said. "Last night, at the country club…"

"I arrived at the club a little before six-thirty," Blue said. "See, I'd called Gerry's office in the afternoon, after I'd checked into my room at the motel. His secretary said he would be in meetings all day and that he'd said he would see me at the party, that I should come early to talk to him."

Lucy stopped walking. "What did you talk about?"

"He never showed." Blue drew a line in the wet sand with his toe and watched as a gentle wave erased all but part of it. "I watched for him until after seven, but the first I saw of him was when he and Jenny Lee made their grand entrance."

Blue had been looking for his stepbrother at the country club last night, Lucy realized. He hadn't been watching and waiting for her as she'd thought. Disappointment washed over her, and she forced herself to ignore it. There was no room for such emotions in their current relationship as investigator and suspect.

"Any idea what he wanted to talk to you about?"

Blue raked his fingers through his thick, blond hair, pushing it back from his face. The breeze immediately made a wavy lock fall forward again. It danced lightly about on his forehead. "I thought it was just a casual meeting," he said. "You know 'Hey, how are you? How's it goin'? Whatcha been up to in the past two years since I last saw you?' Catching up. That stuff."

"But…?"

Again Lucy saw that glimmer of hurt on his otherwise expressionless face. If she hadn't seen it before, she might not have noticed it. He started forward down the beach and she walked backward, in order to watch his face as he spoke.

"After that little show on the dance floor," Blue said. "I'm thinking Gerry was originally intending to give me his 'get lost' speech in private, before the party started."

"You can't blame him for being jealous," Lucy remarked. "You *were* dancing with his fiancée." She caught herself, turning away, facing forward now, as if she were intent on reading her notes. She wasn't here to give her opinions on the situation. She was supposed to be gathering facts.

"Okay, I know where you were from seven-fifteen until a few minutes before eight."

"I remember that part pretty damn clearly, too," Blue said.

Lucy knew that if she glanced up, she'd find him gazing at her, so she kept her eyes carefully locked on her notebook. "You went inside to talk to Gerry," she said. "Apparently you didn't find him."

"He was in the middle of a business conversation with Mr. Fisher," Blue told her. "So I gave my regrets to Jenny Lee."

"By asking her to dance?" Lucy couldn't keep the incredulousness from her voice. God, she sounded like a jealous girlfriend. She immediately backpedaled. "I'm sorry. Please continue. What happened then?"

But Blue didn't continue. He stopped walking and looked at her, studying her face and her eyes, his gaze probing, searching. The sensation was not unlike being underneath a microscope.

"You didn't believe me when I told you that the only thing between Jenny Lee and me was ancient history," Blue finally said. "When you saw me dancing with her—that's what changed your mind about spending the night with me, wasn't it?"

"That has nothing to do with this investigation—"

"Come on, Yankee," Blue drawled. "I'm answering all *your* questions honestly. The least you can do is answer one of mine."

Lucy lifted her head and looked him squarely in the eye. "Yes," she said. But it was only half the truth. The real answer was yes *and* no. Seeing Blue with Jenny Lee had somehow broken the spell he'd cast over her. Seeing him with her made Lucy remember that she didn't do things like sleep with sailors who were in town for only a few days.

Blue was watching her. He moved a step toward her and then another step. Lucy found herself immobilized, unable to back away. He reached out and gently tucked a loose strand of her hair behind her ear.

"Let's get back to Jenny Lee," Lucy said desperately. The mention of Blue's former girlfriend was successful, as usual, in dissolving the odd power he had over her.

"When I told her I was leaving the party," Blue said, "she told me that she wanted to talk to me." He crouched and picked up a smooth rock from the beach, wiping the sand off it, weighing it in the palm of his hand. "She seemed really worried, really upset about something. It was clear that she wanted the conversation to be private, and since pulling her off into some secluded corner of the room seemed inappropriate, I asked her to dance."

Blue straightened up and flung the rock out into the ocean, past the breaking waves. It skipped several times before it vanished. "You probably won't believe me," he said, his voice still matter-of-fact. "But what I'm gonna tell you is God's own truth, Lucy."

Lucy nodded, her pen poised to take notes.

Blue wiped the remaining sand from his hands, glancing at her notebook. "You don't need that," he said. "This doesn't have anything to do with the case." His gaze was steady. "I just wanted you to know that the entire time I was dancing with Jenny Lee, I was wishing it was you in my arms."

Lucy closed her eyes. My God! Was it possible Blue still thought he had a chance with her? Was it possible that he didn't realize that their current roles didn't allow for any type of romantic interaction whatsoever? And, really, did he honestly think she was so naive she would believe he'd prefer her over Jenny Lee Beaumont?

"Let's stay focused on the case," she said. "I'd rather hear God's own truth about what Jenny Lee said to you while you were dancing."

Lucy didn't believe him. Blue hadn't really expected her

to. But now, perhaps, was not the best time to convince her otherwise.

"Jenny Lee told me that she was worried about Gerry," Blue said. "He was acting strangely, as if he was under a lot of stress. She told me that she believed she'd made a mistake in inviting me to the wedding. Apparently it was her idea to ask me to be best man. She thought Gerry liked the idea—if he didn't, he didn't tell her otherwise. But over the past few days, Jenny Lee was starting to wonder if Gerry's upset was caused by my coming back to town, considering my and Jenny's history." He paused. "In short, Jenny asked me to leave."

Lucy nodded, scribbling in her notebook, lower lip clasped gently between her teeth in concentration.

Blue couldn't help but remember how soft those lips had felt, how delicious Lucy's mouth had tasted, how willing she'd been to take that kiss to a more intimate level. Before he left town again, he was going to find a way back to that moment they'd shared. And when he did, the attraction that ignited between them like rocket fuel was going to launch them past the point of no return. It was going to be good. It was going to be very, *very* good.

It was also going to be good to track down the son of a bitch who'd killed Gerry, to see him brought to justice. Although Blue and Gerry had had their disagreements in the recent past, and despite Gerry's harsh words to Blue last night, Blue couldn't forget the friendship he'd shared with his stepbrother during his childhood and adolescence. And he still couldn't believe that Gerry was really dead. The thought that he'd never see Gerry's upbeat smile again made him feel empty.

"I'd like to take a look at the body," Blue said. "See if there's anything that the police might've missed."

Lucy shook her head. "The state medical examiner's office is performing an autopsy. It's required on all suspicious deaths. If everything goes smoothly, the body will be returned to town on Friday for Saturday funeral services."

"Who's taking care of the funeral arrangements?" Blue asked.

Lucy looked up from her notebook. "Jenny Lee is."

Jenny Lee. Hell, whatever pain Blue was feeling at Gerry's death, it surely was amplified hundreds of times over for poor Jenny Lee. Instead of marrying Gerry on Saturday, she was going to be burying him.

"How's Jenny holding up?"

"As well as can be expected, I guess," Lucy told him. As always, when Jenny Lee's name came up, her dark eyes were guarded. The shadows were getting very long, and she turned, looking back down the beach in the direction they had come. "We'd better head back."

"This whole thing stinks," Blue said in a low voice.

Lucy glanced at him again, compassion in her eyes. "This must be hard for you," she said. "Everyone has been so busy making accusations. No one has offered you condolences on your stepbrother's death."

"It doesn't matter."

"Yes, it does," Lucy said. "At times like this, you need to know that people care."

Blue smiled. "I know *you* care, Yankee," he said. "And that's all I need."

Chapter Six

Lucy dropped Blue off at the Lighthouse Motel, then swung back onto Main Street, heading for the Grill. It was well past suppertime, and she was far too exhausted to cook. She pulled into a parking spot on the street in front of the tiny restaurant, dreaming about a cheeseburger and french fries and knowing that she'd end up ordering vegetable soup and a salad.

She hadn't been inside and sitting at a booth by the window of the crowded Grill for more than five minutes, when the door opened and Blue McCoy came in.

All conversation stopped.

Blue headed for the only empty table—the one next to Lucy's. Giving Lucy a nod hello, he dropped his duffel bag on the floor and sat down. He glanced around the still-silent room, as if noticing for the first time that he was the center of attention. Some people were downright rude as they stared at him, hostility in their eyes.

Iris came out to Blue's table. The normally friendly waitress wasn't smiling. In fact, she looked worried. "I'm sorry," she said to Blue, and it was clear that she was. "But that table is reserved for someone else."

Lucy knew it damn well wasn't. Tables at the Grill had always been, and would always be, first come, first served.

Blue knew that, too, but he reached down under the table and picked up his duffel bag.

"Why don't you come sit with me, McCoy?" Lucy called out. "I've got this big booth all to myself." She looked up at Iris challengingly. "Unless *it's* suddenly reserved for someone else, too."

Iris flushed, but she faced Lucy and then Blue. "I feel real bad about this, but I'm going to have to ask you to leave," she said to Blue. "I can't risk trouble getting stirred up inside my establishment, and you, sir, are trouble."

The crowd murmured its agreement. "Get him out of here," said a voice, as Iris disappeared into the back.

"Yeah." Travis Southeby stood up, light glinting off his police badge. "Eating dinner with Gerry McCoy's killer in the room is gonna give me gas."

Lucy raised her voice to be heard over the sudden din. "Whatever happened to innocent until proven guilty?" she asked, looking directly at Travis. "Blue McCoy hasn't been convicted of any crimes—he hasn't even been *charged*."

From the other side of the room, a chair scraped across the floor as it was pushed back from a table. Leroy Hurley stood up and Lucy's heart sank.

"Whatever happened to the good old days," Leroy asked the crowd, "when a town didn't have to pay millions of dollars to convict a cold-blooded killer? Anyone remember back then? My granddaddy used to tell me about those times. They didn't need no judge or jury. No, sir. They just needed the townfolk, the guilty man and a sturdy length of rope."

Travis Southeby grinned. "It sure saved the taxpayers a heap of money."

As Blue watched, Lucy pushed herself to her feet. She was spitting mad. Her cheeks were flushed and her brown eyes were alight with an unholy flame. Her teeth were clenched and she had one hand on the handle of her sidearm. He was glad as hell that she was on *his* side.

"Are you talking about a *lynching?*" Her voice was low and dangerous. She turned to glare at the stocky police officer. "Shame on you, Travis, for making light of this. You should know better than that." She turned back to Leroy. "How about it, Hurley? Shall I run you in for attempting to incite a riot, or shall I charge you with attempted murder? Because times have changed since your dear old granddaddy was allowed to run amok in this town. These days we've got another name for a lynching, pal. It's called first-degree murder." She looked around the room. "Are you all clear on that? Does anyone have any questions? I wouldn't want to leave anyone confused about this matter."

Leroy Hurley stomped out of the Grill, and the rest of the customers turned back to their food. Travis Southeby still stood, a pink tinge of anger on his puffy face.

He gestured toward Blue. "If I was in charge of this investigation, *he'd* be locked up by now."

"Well, you're not in charge," Lucy said tartly. "So just sit down and finish your dinner, Travis. If you have any complaints, take them to Chief Bradley."

Travis threw down several dollar bills and left the Grill, his dinner barely touched.

Before Lucy could sit down, Iris appeared from the kitchen, carrying a big paper bag. "It's enough for both of you," she said, looking from Lucy to Blue and back. "And it's on the house." She moved to the front door and opened it wide. "As long as you take it outside."

Lucy shook her head. "I'm disappointed in you," she said to Iris.

Blue silently slipped his duffel bag over his shoulder as

Iris said, "Last time there was a fight in here, that big plate-glass window broke. Insurance company wouldn't cover it, and we were paying off the debt for three months straight. Billy Joe and me, we've got a kid in college now, Lucy. We can't afford that again. You know that."

Blue went out the door first and Lucy followed. "I'm sorry," Iris said again as she shut the door tightly behind them both.

"I'm sorry about that, too," Lucy said to Blue.

"People get passionate," he said quietly. "They don't always stop to think."

She looked at the heavy bag he was still carrying over his shoulder. "Why didn't you leave your stuff in the motel?"

He shook his head. "I'm not staying over there."

"There's nowhere else in town to stay," Lucy said. "What are you going to do? Sleep outside?"

Blue shrugged. "Yeah," he said. "I guess."

She looked closely at him, her eyes narrowing. "What's going on?"

He gazed at her several long moments before answering. "Jedd Southeby informed me that there are no vacancies at the motel at this time," Blue finally said.

Lucy's mouth got tight, and she flung open the driver's-side door to her truck with more force than necessary. "Get in," she said.

Blue climbed into the truck and watched with interest as she jammed the key into the ignition, revved the motor much higher than necessary and threw the truck into reverse.

"There are *never* no vacancies at the Lighthouse Motel," she said grimly. "That's total bull. I know for a fact that there are at least fifteen rooms unoccupied right this very moment."

It took less than a minute to drive to the motel. Lucy came to a halt with a squeal of tires.

"Jedd Southeby, what is wrong with you?" she fumed, marching into the motel office lobby. "No vacancy, my foot!"

Jedd didn't even get out of his chair. "He's not welcome here," he said coldly, motioning to Blue with his chin. He was small and angular, in contrast to his brother Travis, who was small and beefy.

"That's illegal," Lucy said, crossing her arms. "You can't discriminate against—"

"I most certainly can," Jedd told her smugly. "I reserve the right to turn down any paying guest if I have justifiable reason to believe he will cause injury to my property, himself or my other paying guests. Considering Blue is suspected of killing his stepbrother, I'd have to say that I have a damned good justifiable reason, wouldn't you?"

Lucy was aghast. "So where is Blue supposed to stay?" She shook her head. "Chief Bradley told him not to leave town. If you won't rent him a room…"

"There's room in the town jail," Jedd said. He looked at Blue and smiled nastily. "You might as well get used to sleeping in a room with bars on the windows, McCoy."

Lucy took a deep breath and forced a smile. "Jedd." She carefully kept her voice steady, reasonable. "Your own brother is on the police force. I'm sure he's told you that no one gets any sleep at the station at night. The lights are always up, it's noisy, the TV is on and—"

"Blue shoulda thought of that before he killed Gerry, huh?"

"What if it rains tonight?" Lucy asked, slapping her hand down on the counter as she lost her cool. "Are you going to sit there and tell me that you're going to make this man—who, I might point out, has not been accused of *any* crime—sleep out in the rain?"

"I don't give a flying fig where he sleeps." Jedd turned back to his television set.

"Dammit!" Lucy turned away, pushing open the glass door and stepping out into the muggy heat of the night.

Giving in to her urge to slap Jedd Southeby's smug smile off his face wouldn't do Blue or her career any good. *"Dammit!"*

"I'm a SEAL. I've slept in the rain before," Blue said calmly. He looked up at the sky. "Besides, it's not gonna rain."

"Get in the truck," Lucy fumed, climbing back into the driver's seat of her Ford.

Blue looked at her through the open passenger-side window. "Where are we going?" he asked. "Because I'd honestly rather sleep out in the rain than spend the night in the Hatboro Creek jail house."

"Don't worry, I'm not taking you to the jail," she said. She took in a deep breath, then let it slowly out in an attempt to calm herself down. This was not the best solution, but it was the only one she could think of at the moment. "You can spend the night at my house."

Blue opened the door and climbed into the truck. "That sounds like the best idea anyone has had all day."

Lucy shot him a dangerous look. "In one of the spare bedrooms."

He smiled back at her. "Whatever you say."

Lucy's house was a great big, rambling old thing on top of the hill off Fox Run Road. It had been built sometime around the turn of the century, Blue guessed. He knew that it had stood empty for a few years before the Taits had moved into town. No one had wanted to buy it—it would have cost way too much to keep up—and Lucy's mother had gotten it for a song. Of course, the Taits had spent every weekend and most weekday evenings scraping paint and sanding and painting and repairing the old monster. When they finished with the inside, they started in on the outside.

Even in the eerie glow of twilight, Blue could see that all their hard work had paid off. The big, old house was gorgeous. They'd painted it white, with dark green shutters and trim. It looked clean and fresh and as if it might even glow in the dark.

"Place looks great," Blue said.

"Thanks."

"Still as big as ever."

"Yep. Too big since my mom died." She snorted. "Too big before that, too."

"Maybe you should sell it," Blue said.

Lucy looked up at the house as she climbed out of the truck. "I could. Betty Stedman over at the real-estate agency makes me an offer on the place every few months or so. It's just… It's the reason I'm still here in town," she admitted. "If I sold it, I'd have to find someplace else to go."

"There are about a million choices out there," Blue said dryly, pushing himself up so that he was sitting on the hood of her truck, "and in my opinion just about every one of 'em is better than Hatboro Creek."

"You *were* in a big hurry to get out of this town, weren't you?" Lucy asked, gazing up at him.

"I made a promise I'd get my high-school diploma. I knew I needed it to get where I wanted to go in the navy," Blue said, "or I would've left town the day I turned sixteen."

"If you had, I never would've met you," Lucy mused. "I would've had the devil kicked out of me, or worse—remember that day the boys from the baseball team tried to beat me up?"

Blue nodded. "Yes, ma'am." He leaned forward slightly to see her face in the darkening twilight. "What do you mean, 'or worse'?"

"Nothing really." Lucy hefted the paper bag that Iris had handed her. "What do you say we sit on the porch and eat some of this food?"

Blue slid down off the hood of the truck, following her up the path to the house. "You wouldn't have said 'or worse' if you meant nothing." He caught her arm before she went up the stairs. "Lucy, what did those boys do to you? Did they ever come near you again?"

Her eyes were wide as she looked down at where he was holding on to her arm, but he wouldn't let go.

"They just…" She sighed. "They were jerks. They told me that if I stayed on the baseball team they'd take me out in the woods and show me the only thing a girl was good for—and I don't think they had cooking and cleaning in mind. I was too embarrassed to tell you—or anyone—about their threats."

She gently pulled free from his grasp and went up the stairs and onto the porch.

"Did they…?" He could hardly get even that much of the question out as she sat down on a porch swing.

"They never touched me again," Lucy said. "Not after you did your superhero imitation. They thought I was high up on your list of friends." She glanced up at him, a smile playing about the corners of her mouth. "Of course, I helped perpetuate that myth by telling them how Blue McCoy was going to take me fishing, or how I was helping Blue McCoy fix up his boat…. I had quite the little fantasy world going, and they bought into every word of it."

When Lucy smiled at him like that, Blue forgot about everything—about Gerry's untimely and tragic death, about the murder charges looming over him, about how the people in this town had turned their backs on him yet again. He could only think about Lucy—about the way she'd had that same sparkling smile back when she was a high-school freshman, back when she'd had a crush on him.

If he had known then what he knew now, things would have been mighty different for him. He probably wouldn't have left town with his heart stomped into a thousand pieces. No, he would have left Lucy with *her* young heart trashed and broken, instead. But that really wasn't more appealing than the way things *had* worked out. Of course…

maybe...if Lucy Tait had been his girlfriend back in high school, Blue wouldn't have left town at all.

Now, where the hell had *that* thought come from? Blue had wanted to leave Hatboro Creek from the first moment he'd pulled into town at the tender age of five. Even if things had turned out differently between Blue and Jenny Lee, even if she had truly loved him rather than tried to use him to reach Gerry, he *still* wouldn't have stayed in town. And if Jenny Lee Beaumont, with her considerable charms, couldn't keep Blue from leaving town, what made him think Lucy Tait could have done otherwise?

"It looks like Iris packed a couple of burgers, a vegetable soup, some of her fish chowder, two turkeys on whole wheat, an order of fries and some onion rings," Lucy said, spreading the feast out on the porch railing. "There are even plastic spoons. I've got dibs on the veggie soup, but everything else is up for grabs."

Blue picked up the waxed cardboard soup bowl that held the fish chowder and pried off the lid. He gave the fragrant soup a stir with one of Iris's plastic spoons, then sat down next to Lucy on the porch swing. He sensed her stiffen, and knew the words were coming before she even spoke.

"I'd appreciate it if you didn't sit quite so close."

"Come on, Yankee. You know you've got to have two on one of these swings to get the proper balance."

Lucy didn't look up at him. She wouldn't meet his eyes. She just stared down into her vegetable soup as if it held the answers to all the questions in the universe.

And when she finally did speak, she surprised him again with her frankness. "I know you're probably thinking about me as a sure thing," Lucy said. When he started to protest, she held up one hand, stopping him, her dark eyes serious. "I mean, here we are at my house. I brought you home to spend the night, right? Sure, I said you'd have to sleep in the spare bedroom, but you're figuring I probably didn't mean it. How could I mean it after last night? We nearly went all the way on the patio outside the country club. And if we had gone straight to your motel room from that patio, things would have turned out really different than they did."

She set her soup down on the railing and turned to face him. "Yes," she continued. "In some ways you're right. Yes, we came very close to having sex last night. You wanted to. I wanted to. And if we'd been anywhere but out in public, we most likely would have. Even though it's not something I'm comfortable admitting, and even though I've never done anything so reckless in my life before last night, I can't deny that.

"It puts a very odd spin on our relationship today—because today if there is one thing that I absolutely, positively *cannot* do, it's engage in sexual activity with you. I'm the investigator. You're the suspect. If I were to allow us to have sex, I'd be breaking every rule in the book and then some."

She took a deep breath. "So there, I've said it."

Blue nodded, trying to hide his smile. Damn, but he liked this girl. She didn't play games. She just laid the facts out straight, just lined 'em all up on the table in full view. "No chance of changing your mind?" he asked.

She didn't realize he was kidding. She shook her head. "No way. I'd lose my job. *And* my self-respect."

"Well, all right," Blue said. "I guess there's only one thing we can do."

Lucy was watching him, her eyes nearly luminous in the porch light.

He *wanted* to kiss her. Instead, he stood. "We start with me easing back a bit. We don't want any spontaneous combustion," he added. "Then we wake up tomorrow morning, bright and early, and work our butts off to find a way to eliminate me from the list of suspects. And tomorrow night…we can take it from the porch swing."

Lucy sighed, closing her eyes briefly. "I wish it were that simple."

Blue tossed his empty chowder bowl into the brown paper bag. "It *is* simple."

But Lucy didn't look convinced. She looked tired and wistful and very weighed down by responsibility.

Blue wanted to put his arms around her and ease her burden. But right now he knew that would only make it harder to bear.

Chapter Seven

Lucy's alarm clock rang at 5:45, pulling her up and out of a deep, dreamless sleep. She'd finally fallen asleep sometime after midnight. Before that she'd lain awake in her bedroom, listening to the familiar quiet noises of her house, straining to hear any hint of Blue moving around upstairs in the guest bedroom.

She'd heard the thump of the pipes as he turned on the shower, and the hum of the pump and the hissing of the water as it was pushed up from the deep well. Several minutes later, she'd heard another thump as the water was turned off, but then...nothing. Silence. No footsteps. No noise.

Not that she'd expected to hear anything. Blue was Alpha Squad's point man. She'd asked, and he'd told her that last night, after she'd shown him to the guest room and gotten several clean towels down from the linen closet.

"I lead the squad in combat or clandestine situations," he said.

Blue didn't know it, but Lucy already knew what a point

man was. A point man could lead his team of SEALs silently right up to an enemy encampment without being discovered. A point man could lead his squad single file through a mine field without a single injury. A point man moved silently, carefully, always alert and watchful, responsible for the safety of his men.

Lucy already knew all this because she'd read every book about SEALs that she could get her hands on. She'd read the first book in high school because she'd been thinking about Blue, and had heard through the local grapevine that he'd been accepted into the SEAL training program.

She'd read the rest of the books not because of Blue, but because the first book had fascinated her so thoroughly. The concept of a Special Operations team like the SEALs intrigued her. They were unconventional in every sense of the word. They were trained as counterterrorists, taught to think and look and act, even *smell*, like the enemy. Due to the special skills of individual team members in areas such as language and cultural knowledge, they were able to lose themselves in any country and infiltrate any organization.

They were tough, smart, mean and dedicated. They were a different kind of American hero.

And Blue McCoy was one of them.

Every man in a SEAL unit was an expert in half a dozen different fields, including computers, technical warfare, engine repair, piloting state-of-the-art helicopters and aircraft. Each SEAL in the elite Team Ten was an expert marksman, intimately familiar with all types of firearms. Each was an expert scuba diver and extensively trained in demolition techniques—both on land and underwater. Each could parachute out of nearly any type of aircraft at nearly any altitude.

They seemed superhuman, strong and rugged and very, very dangerous.

And Blue McCoy, already her hero, was one of them.

She was attracted to him. There was no point in denying that. And Blue had made it quite clear that the feeling was mutual. He'd told her that he'd thought about her as he'd danced with Jenny Lee at the country club.

That was a hard one to swallow—Blue McCoy thinking about Lucy Tait while he was dancing with Jenny Lee Beaumont.

Still, he'd told the truth about his conversation with Jenny. Lucy had read Jenny Lee's statement about the events leading up to the time of Gerry's death. The statement had included a description of Jenny's conversation with Blue at the country club. Jenny's version was identical to Blue's.

But there was no way to verify exactly what Blue had been feeling when he'd danced with Jenny, holding her in his arms.

Lucy knew that Blue wanted to make love to her. She saw that truth in his eyes every time he looked in her direction. The power of his desire was dizzying. But she was brought down to earth quickly enough by the thought that Blue probably only wanted her because Jenny Lee was not available.

Lucy moved quietly into her bathroom and took a quick shower before pulling on a clean uniform. She brushed out her hair, leaving it down as it dried, grabbed an apple from the kitchen and left the house. She'd be back before Blue even woke up.

Blue saw Lucy's truck pull away from the house as he finished his morning run.

He'd slept only two hours last night. He'd gotten up well before sunrise, wide awake and alert, filled with a restless kind of energy and anticipation he'd felt in the past before going into combat situations. This time, however, it was laced with an undercurrent of sexual tension that sharpened the feeling of anticipation, giving it a knifelike edge.

He had run five miles before dawn, another five as the sun rose, and still the edginess wouldn't go away.

He watched the dust rise as Lucy's truck pulled out of the driveway. She looked as if she had on her uniform, and he was willing to bet she was heading down to the police station. She was probably going to fill the chief in on all that Blue had told her yesterday and find out if anything new had come in from the autopsy report.

Blue climbed the stairs to the porch and tried the kitchen door. It was locked. He'd left his bedroom window open all the way up on the third floor. He knew he could get in that way; still, there was bound to be another window open a bit closer to the ground.

The ground-floor window over the kitchen sink was open, but the sill was lined with plants being rooted in jars of water. He spotted an open window on the second floor, recognizing it instantly as Lucy's room by its location.

He climbed easily up the side of the porch and was outside the window in a matter of moments. There was nothing to knock over inside, just a filmy white curtain blowing gently in the morning breeze.

He unfastened the screen and slipped into the house.

Lucy's room was big—at one time it had no doubt been a front parlor or a sitting room. She'd put her bed in an offset area, surrounded on almost three sides by big bay windows. Her bed was unmade, her sheets a bold pattern of dark blues and reds and greens. A white bedspread had been pushed off the bed onto the highly polished hardwood floor. A white throw rug was spread on the floor. It was unnecessary in the summer heat, but it would be nice in the winter when the bare floors would be cold.

The walls were white, with a collection of framed watercolors breaking up the monotony. The pictures were mostly seascapes with bright-colored sailboats out on the water or beach scenes. There were only two framed photographs, and they sat on a dresser. Blue recognized Lucy's mother in one, smiling through a hole in the half-finished wall of the kitchen. The other was a photo of Lucy, her arms around a tall, thin man he didn't recognize. The man had his arms around Lucy's shoulders, and the two of them were laughing into the camera.

Who the hell was he? What did he mean to Lucy that she should keep this picture in her bedroom? Was he a former lover? A *current* lover? If so, where was he? Did he live across the street, or across the country?

Lucy hadn't mentioned having a boyfriend. She hadn't acted as if she had one, either. But on the other hand, Blue had no right to feel these pangs of jealousy. He wasn't looking for commitment, just a night or two of great sex. If Lucy had some kind of steady thing going on the side, that was her problem, not his.

So why did the thought of Lucy laughing like this as she leaned forward to kiss this other man leave such a bad taste in Blue's mouth? Why did he have this compelling urge to tear this photograph in two?

Blue headed for the door, suddenly very aware that he was invading Lucy's privacy. But he turned and looked back over his shoulder before he headed for the stairs up to his bedroom and the third-floor shower.

It was a nice room, a pleasant room, spacious and as uncluttered as the rest of the house. Lucy wasn't the sort of person who had to fill every available space with doodads and souvenirs. She wasn't afraid of a clean surface or an empty wall. Yeah, he liked this room. He hoped he had a chance to see it again—from the perspective of Lucy's bed.

"Lucy!"

Lucy turned to see Chief Bradley jogging down the corridor toward her.

"Hey, glad I caught you, darlin'," he said, out of breath.

"I see you picked up a copy of the autopsy report. Good. Good. Did you also get the message from Travis Southeby? He just happened to be talking to Andy Hayes over at the Rebel Yell last night and found out that Andy saw Blue McCoy leave his motel room at about ten o'clock on the night of Gerry's murder."

Lucy nodded. "Yes, sir," she said. "That fits with what Blue told me as to his whereabouts that evening."

Sheldon Bradley nodded, running his fingers through his thinning gray hair. "Did he also mention that Matt Parker was just in, not more than a few minutes ago, saying how he thought he saw someone who looked just like Blue McCoy arguing with Gerry at around 11 p.m., up in the woods near where the body was found? He saw them there just twenty minutes before the established time of death."

"Matt *thought* he saw someone who looked like Blue?" Lucy allowed her skepticism to show. "No, I didn't get that message. I'll make a point to go over and talk to both Matt and Andy this afternoon."

"Let me know what else you come up with," the chief said.

"I'll have another report typed up and on your desk by the end of the day," Lucy told him. She opened the door, but again Bradley stopped her.

"Oh, and one more thing," he said. "Leroy Hurley mentioned that he saw Blue McCoy here in town with an automatic weapon."

"Chief, it wasn't a real—"

He held up his hand. "As a result, it came to my attention that as of yet no one has confiscated whatever weapons McCoy might have—and I've heard some of those Special Forces types walk around carrying an arsenal."

"It's Special Operations. And without a warrant, I'm not sure we have the right to—"

"Actually, we do," Bradley told her. "It's an old town law, dates back from Reconstruction, from when folks ran a little wild. The Hatboro Creek peacekeeping officers have the right to gain possession of any individual's personal weapons until that individual crosses back over the town line. We never did get around to amending that law. It was brought up at a meeting a few years back, but then Hurricane Rosie came through, knocked it off the town agenda."

"I'll ask him if he has any weapons—"

"You'll search the son of a bitch," the chief told her. "Or you'll bring him down here so that we can search him, if you're not up to it."

Lucy lifted her chin. "I'm up to it. But you should know that the gun Hurley saw him with was just a plastic toy."

"Either way, I won't have him running around my town with an Uzi or the likes," Bradley said. "Whatever he's got, I want it locked up in my safe by noon, is that clear?"

Lucy nodded. "Yes, sir."

"And get a move on with this investigation," Bradley added, heading back down the hallway. "I want Blue McCoy locked up, too, before sundown tomorrow."

Lucy pulled her truck into her driveway, unable to shake the feeling of dread in her stomach, dread that had started with the chief's news that someone had allegedly seen Blue arguing with Gerry near the murder site. Matt Parker. He was an upstanding citizen. He'd recently had his share of bad luck, though. He'd even been the cause of one of Annabella's 415 dispatches earlier in the summer when he and his wife got to fighting about his recent unemployment just a little too loudly. But other than that, he wasn't one of the town troublemakers or one of Leroy Hurley's wild friends. Parker stayed mostly to himself, kept up his house and yard and showed up at church every Sunday without fail.

Why would Parker lie about what he'd seen the night of Gerry's murder?"

And if he wasn't lying, did that mean Blue was?

No. Blue had looked her in the eye and told her that he wasn't the one who had killed his stepbrother. Lucy believed him. He wasn't lying. The air of calm that seemed to surround him, his definite tone of voice, his steady eye contact all reinforced her belief.

Lucy got out of the truck and walked up the path to the house. It was only 9:30 in the morning, and already she felt as if she couldn't wait for the day to end.

She had to search Blue McCoy for concealed weapons. That was going to be fun. Lucy rolled her eyes. She couldn't get within three feet of the man without risking third-degree burns. How on earth was she supposed to *search* him? She was going to have to make him assume the classic body-search position, arms stretched out in front of him, legs spread, hands against the wall. Because God help her, if he simply held out his arms while she patted him down and she happened to glance up and into his eyes... What was it that Blue had said last night? Spontaneous combustion. It was an accurate description of the way she'd felt at the country club when he'd held her in his arms and she'd kissed him. What a kiss that had been.

God, maybe she *should* take Blue down to the station, let Frank Redfield or Tom Harper search him. But that would be admitting that she wasn't "up to it," as Chief Bradley had said.

Lucy unlocked the kitchen door. She'd picked up a bag of doughnuts and two cups of coffee at the bakery in town, and she put them on the table. The house was quiet. Was it possible Blue was still asleep?

Then she saw it. There was a note on the kitchen table. Blue had written a message to her on a paper napkin. He'd taken care to write neatly, printing in clear block letters: "Seven a.m. Went to scout out woods off Gate's Hill Road. C.M."

C.M.?

It took Lucy a moment to realize that C.M. were Blue's initials. His real, given name was Carter McCoy. Why hadn't he signed the note Blue? Did he think of himself as Carter? Or was he just so used to initialing Navy paperwork that the C.M. had come out automatically?

Either way, he was already up and out, doing *her* job. Lucy grabbed the doughnuts and coffee, locked the kitchen door behind her and went back to her truck.

Chapter Eight

Lucy didn't find Blue up in the woods by Gate's Hill Road. Blue found Lucy.

He just sort of appeared next to her. One minute she was alone at the edge of the clearing where Gerry's body had been discovered, and the next Blue was standing right beside her.

She'd been expecting him to do something like that, so she didn't jump. At least not too high. She handed him a paper cup of coffee, instead.

"Hope you like it black," she said.

He nodded, sunlight glinting off his golden hair. "Thanks."

The day was promising to be another hot, muggy one. Blue was still wearing his army fatigue shirt with the sleeves cut off, but he had it unbuttoned most of the way, allowing Lucy tantalizing glimpses of his rock-solid, tanned chest.

She handed him the doughnut bag. "I also hope you like jelly doughnuts," she said, wishing that it were winter and thirty degrees so he'd have to wear a parka zipped up to his chin. "I ate all the honey glazed. That's what you get for coming out here without me."

Blue smiled. "Serves me right. What's the latest news down at the station?"

"The autopsy report is in." Lucy took a sip of her own coffee, leaning back against a tree as she gazed at him. His blue eyes were clear, his face unmarked by fatigue. He'd probably gotten eight hours of dreamless, perfect sleep, damn him. He didn't look as if he'd tossed and turned for one moment last night, distracted not a whit by the thought of her sleeping several rooms away.

Lucy had tossed and turned enough for both of them.

"The cause of Gerry's death was definitely a broken neck," she continued, "but we already knew that. It *was* a clean break, though, and the medical examiner found some slight bruising on his head and neck, indicating some kind of stranglehold. Whoever killed him knew what he was doing. It wasn't accidental, and apparently the bruising wasn't severe enough to indicate a long, passionate struggle. The killer knew exactly what he intended to do before he even got his hands on Gerry."

Blue looked away, swearing softly.

"The good news is that Gerry didn't feel it," Lucy said quietly. "He probably didn't even know."

"Yeah, I know that." His mouth was tight as he looked up at Lucy again. "What else was in the report?"

She shook her head. "I just skimmed the first few paragraphs. I'll read it more thoroughly later. You can look at it, too, if you want." She sighed, knowing that she had to tell him about what Matt Parker allegedly saw.

"You've got more bad news," Blue said, reading her face. "What is it?"

"A couple of witnesses have surfaced," Lucy said. "One of them places you up here, arguing with Gerry, about twenty minutes before his established time of death."

Blue didn't say a word. His lips just got tighter.

"Either this witness is lying," Lucy continued, "or he saw someone or something up here that could give us a lead to finding out what really happened."

"Someone was up here, all right," Blue said. He set his coffee cup and the bag of doughnuts down on a rock and headed out into the center of the clearing, motioning for Lucy to follow.

"Gerry's body was found right about here," he told her, pointing at an area where the weeds were trampled flat. "I didn't expect to find anything new. Too many people, both police and paramedics, added their footprints before a proper investigation could be made." He straightened up. "What I did this morning was search the clearing and the woods, moving out in circles away from the place where Gerry was found."

He headed into the woods, and Lucy followed him through the thick underbrush.

"I don't think the police searched out this far from the murder site," Blue said over his shoulder as they walked for what seemed like half a mile. "But I didn't have anything better to do this morning, so I just kept going."

He stopped at a trail that was cut through the dense growth. It was little more than two tire paths, ruts worn into the side of the hill for a truck or Jeep to get through.

Blue crouched, pointing at the damp earth. "Tire tracks," he said. "*Big* tires. Wider than your average truck tires by a good four inches. And whatever it was those great big tires were attached to, it was big and heavy, too."

Sure enough, the tracks sank deeply into the dark soil. The mud was starting to dry. Whatever had left this track had been here directly after the last rain—probably around the time of Gerry's death.

"Was it some kind of monster truck?" Lucy mused, crouching next to him.

"That or an all-terrain vehicle," Blue said.

"The tires look new," Lucy remarked. "The tread is barely worn. God, we can take a print of this and make an easy match, find out who else was up here that night—if they're still in town."

"And look over here," Blue said, standing up and pointing farther down the trail. "Whoever drove this thing left in one hell of a big hurry."

Lucy straightened too, wiping her hands on her pants. "This is great! Let's go back to my truck and radio for assistance. I'll have the crime team take some photos and make a mold of these tire tracks." She grinned. "McCoy, I think you may have just saved your own neck."

Blue smiled at her enthusiasm as he followed her toward the main road, where she'd parked her truck. "Careful, or folks are going to say that this isn't an unbiased investigation."

"Yeah, well, it's not," Lucy admitted.

When she glanced over her shoulder at him, he could see a healthy dose of that simmering heat that could turn his blood boiling hot in less than a blink. But he could also see admiration shining in her eyes. He could see admiration and respect and something akin to hero worship.

And in that instant, Blue realized that Lucy still had that old schoolgirl crush on him—no, not on him, but on some larger-than-life heroic image of him. He was a superhero who'd saved the day, chasing away her attackers twelve years ago. He was a member of the elite Navy SEALs—and he knew from the shelf of books about the Navy and the SEALs that he'd found in Lucy's living room that she'd read all about the legendary heroism and patriotism and loyalty of the SEAL units. To Lucy, he was a living legend.

And that made him attractive to her—probably more attractive than any normal, mortal man she'd ever known.

The truth was, Lucy didn't really know Blue at all. Because he *was* mortal. But all her powerful attraction, all her respect and admiration, was based on some idea of how he *should* be. It was based on an image of the way she *thought* he was.

Still, what did he expect? Since he'd arrived, he'd done nothing to straighten her out. He'd told her none of his secrets, shared none of his feelings. As a matter of fact, Blue could count the people he'd shared his feelings and secrets with on the fingers of one hand.

Frisco was one. But it had been years since Blue had really talked to the injured SEAL. He'd gone to see him in the Veterans' Hospital and the rehab center a few times right after he'd been wounded. But Frisco didn't want to talk. And Blue finally stopped going to see him.

It was hard to visit. It was hard to handle the guilt of knowing that he, Blue, could stand up and walk out of the hospital, while Frisco never would. It was hard to smile and offer hope in the face of Frisco's pain. And now it had been so long since Blue had visited Frisco, he wouldn't know what to say to the man.

But Blue could still talk to Joe Catalanotto, the commander of Alpha Squad. And Daryl "Harvard" Becker, Alpha Squad's chief. But that was it. Hell, forget his fingers. These days, Blue could count the people he let in to his life on his thumbs.

He watched the sunlight play in Lucy's long, brown hair as she opened the door to her truck and took out the microphone attached to her radio. She smiled at him—a flash of white teeth and sparkling brown eyes.

What did he care that she wanted to sleep with him because of some overblown heroic image she'd been carrying around in her head for a dozen years? The key part of that sentence was that she wanted to sleep with him. Everyone had motives. Jenny Lee's motive back in high school had been to hang around Gerry's house to catch the attention of Blue's elder brother. The women he'd had relationships with since then had had their motives, too. They'd wanted to break away from the boredom of their lives, live on the edge for a while, go the distance with a good-looking stranger who was going to slip out of their lives in a day or two. So what if Lucy's motive was that she wanted to sleep with Superman?

Of course, she wasn't entirely convinced that she should sleep with anybody. She had a solid streak of good girl running through her that had been overpowered by emotions and lust and the pull of the full moon the other night at the country club.

Blue watched Lucy radio in the information about the tire tracks he'd found. She was so alive, so animated. Even though she was speaking to the dispatcher over the radio, she talked with her hands, gesturing, shrugging, moving, smiling. He was struck again by just how beautiful she was.

It wasn't the kind of beauty that would draw stares or whistles when she walked down the street. In fact, dressed as she was right now in her police uniform, most men wouldn't give her a second glance.

But Blue knew better. He knew the encompassing warmth of her smile; the powerful draw of her fresh, funny, upbeat personality; the dazzling sparkle of her eyes. And he knew the seductive taste of her kisses and the unforgettable feel of her incredible body against his.

As he watched, her body language changed, subtly, slightly. He tuned himself in to her words.

She glanced at her watch. "I realize the time," she said. "I know it's almost eleven, but this is more important than—"

"The chief says he'll send someone out right away," a woman's scratchy voice said over the radio, "but you better get your rear end back here to the station before noon with whatever weapons McCoy is hiding, or there'll be hell to pay."

Whatever weapons McCoy is hiding?

It wasn't really that much of a surprise. Blue had figured it was going to come sooner or later. They'd search him, hoping to find and take away whatever he had on him, hoping to make him less dangerous.

Lucy was doing her best to postpone the inevitable. "Annabella—"

"The chief is yelling for me, Lucy. I can't stay on and argue with you right now," the dispatcher said. "Do your job. This transmission is over."

"No, Annabella..." Lucy swore sharply, leaning into the truck to adjust the radio. "She turned it off." She hooked the microphone back into its slot and looked at Blue. "She actually *turned off* the police station's radio."

"You know, Yankee, if there's something you have to do back at the station, I can hang here and wait for the crime team to show up," Blue volunteered.

Lucy shook her head. "That won't work," she said. "Because *you're* what I have to do."

Blue smiled. "While I truly like the way that sounds," he drawled, "I've got a feeling that's not exactly what you meant."

Lucy felt her face flush. Still, she forced herself to look into his eyes. "I have to confiscate your weapons, McCoy," she told him. "I need to search you. And then we have to go down to the station so you can fill out the paperwork to get your property back when this is over."

Blue nodded slowly. "This is easy," he said. "You're not going to find any weapons on me. We don't have to go anywhere. You can just radio that information in."

He hadn't said he didn't have any weapons. He'd said she wouldn't *find* them. Lucy held his gaze. "Look me in the eye and tell me you're not carrying," she said softly.

"I'm not carrying," he said, his eyes steady.

The rush of disappointment that went through her almost knocked her down. "Well, damn," she said. "I guess now we've established that you *will* lie to me."

Blue didn't say anything. He just watched her.

Her eyes blazed fire as she looked up at him again. "You want to try that one more time?" she asked.

He didn't bat an eyelash. "I'm not carrying."

Blue thought for a moment that Lucy was going to haul back and punch him in the stomach. Instead, she crossed her arms. "Hands against the truck, and spread 'em, mister."

"Lucy, it's not going to do any good—"

"Because I won't find anything?" she finished for him. "You want to make a bet on that?" She gestured to the truck. "Come on, move it, McCoy. Assume the position."

"This isn't necessary."

Lucy exploded. "You're a SEAL, dammit," she said, slapping the side of her truck with one opened hand. The sound echoed in the stillness. "*I* know you didn't come into town unarmed, and Chief Bradley knows you didn't come into town unarmed, either. He's not stupid and I'm not stupid, and—"

"And *I'm* not stupid, either." Blue caught her chin in one hand, pulling her head around so that she was forced to look into his eyes. In one swift movement he was standing close to her, penning her in against the side of her truck. His thigh was pressed against hers, the sensation nearly making him forget everything but his enormous need to feel her lips against his again. Nearly. Somehow he centered his focus and returned to the task at hand.

"You're right," he whispered. "I'm a SEAL. And I can't forget that somebody out there killed Gerry. I'm not walking around unarmed—virtually *naked*—with a killer on the loose. And if that means I have to lie to you, Yankee, then I'm gonna have to lie to you. It's not personal. Don't think that it is. There's not a SEAL alive who wouldn't lie to

Mother Teresa herself to stay armed in a potentially dangerous situation like this one."

Lucy tried to pull away from him, but he held her tightly.

"You look me in the eye," Blue continued, "and you tell me that if I admitted to you that I was armed you wouldn't insist on confiscating those weapons." His eyes were like blue steel, hard and unrelenting. "You tell me that you'd simply say, 'Well, thank you very much, Blue. Thank you for telling me the truth. I know how much having that sidearm and that knife on your person means to you, so I won't include that information in my report to Chief Bradley.'"

Lucy was silent.

"Can't tell me that, huh?" Blue nodded. "In that case, I'll say it again. I'm not carrying."

Lucy lifted her chin even higher. "And *I* said, hands against the truck and spread your legs, mister."

Blue had to laugh. She was so clearly overpowered, so obviously in a position of being dominated, yet she wouldn't give in. She refused to back down. As annoying as that was, he had to like her for it. And he did. Mercy, he did like her.

"Are you going to let go of me and do as I say, or do I have to haul you to jail first?" Her brown eyes were flashing again, her mouth trembling slightly in anger. It was all that Blue could do not to kiss her. Dear, sweet Lord, he wanted to kiss her something fierce. He wanted to, and dammit, he was going to.

"Come on, Yankee," he said softly. "Let's not fight. We're on the same side here, aren't we?"

She glared at him. "I'm not so sure of that anymore."

"Yes," he said definitely. "We *are* on the same side. So let's just kiss and make up."

Lucy's eyes widened as he leaned forward, lowering his mouth to hers. His lips grazed the softness of her sweet lips and he was milliseconds from sheer, total paradise when she spoke.

"Don't," she breathed. "Please, Blue—don't."

He didn't. He didn't kiss her. He pulled back. Out of all the tough things he'd done in his life, it was quite possibly the toughest.

"I can't do this," Lucy whispered. "Remember? Until I'm through investigating Gerry's murder, you're a suspect, and I cannot do this."

"It's just a kiss." His voice sounded raspy and strained in his own ears.

Lucy shook her head. "No," she said. "It most definitely is not just a kiss." Somehow he'd lost his ability to hold her, and she broke free from his arms, pushing herself away from the truck and moving a safe distance away from him. She turned to face him. "It's not *just* a kiss, and you know that as well as I do."

Her hand shook slightly as she pushed her hair back behind her ear, and she folded her arms tightly across her chest as if she had to hold herself steady. Her eyes looked big and almost bruised, and she clasped her lower lip between her front teeth. But still she gazed directly at him, her chin held high.

"Either way, it's totally inappropriate," she added. She took a deep breath, exhaling it quickly in a loud burst of air. "So let's just get on with it, then, okay?"

Was she talking about...?

Son of a bitch, she still intended to frisk him. Blue swore under his breath.

Lucy tried to slow her hammering heart, waiting and watching as Blue slowly turned back to the truck. The muscles in his powerful arms flexed as he used them to support most of his weight, his feet planted and his long legs spread.

He turned his head and looked at her over his shoulder. The heat in his eyes was unmistakable.

Not quite a minute ago, he'd been about to kiss her, and now she was supposed to frisk him, patting him down all over his body to make sure he had no weapons concealed underneath his clothing. Or concealed *in* his clothing, she realized, looking at the big, metal buckle of his belt. Still, this was weird. Too weird.

"Well, come on," he said. "Don't keep a man waiting."

Lucy stepped forward, uncertain exactly where to begin. Blue was watching her with one of those slow, lazy half smiles on his handsome face, though, so she started with his back. It seemed a whole hell of a lot less dangerous than the long, sturdy lengths of his legs or, Lord help her, his perfect, athletic rear end.

Or *was* it less dangerous? As she ran her hands down the soft, worn cotton of his shirt, she could feel the ridges and bulges of his muscles. It was only his back. How could he have so many muscles in his *back?* But she wasn't supposed to be looking for muscles. She was looking for any kind of concealable weapon. A handgun. A knife. Who knows, maybe even some kind of grenade. He was carrying something, and despite what he said, she was going to find it.

Lucy could feel a bead of sweat dripping down her own back as she slid her hands around to his sides.

Jackpot. He was wearing a shoulder holster under his left arm. Triumphantly, she slipped her hands up underneath his shirt, only to find the holster was…empty?

"Where's the gun, McCoy?" she asked.

"I told you," he said. "I'm not carrying."

"Yeah, right," she said. She was standing there with her hands inside his shirt, the back of her fingers resting against the smooth warmth of his skin. She moved her hands quickly away. "I'm supposed to believe you wear the holster empty because you're so used to wearing it you'd feel off balance if you didn't have it on, gun or no gun. Right?"

"Exactly," Blue said with a smile. "I couldn't have said it better myself."

Lucy humphed, searching through the contents of his

shirt pockets, trying hard not to touch his satiny-smooth skin again. In his right-hand shirt pocket she came up with a Swiss Army knife.

It was Blue's turn to humph. "That's no weapon," he scoffed. "I use the knife on that thing to spread peanut butter on my sandwiches."

"From what I've read about Navy SEALs," Lucy said, "a *shoe* could be a weapon."

"I'm not wearing shoes," Blue drawled. "Although if I were, you'd want to be sure to check for the secret SEAL submachine gun that's hidden in the soles."

"Just be quiet and let me get this over with," Lucy muttered, bending to pat his right ankle, her hands moving slowly up his leg. He had disgustingly nice legs.

"Get this over with?" Blue murmured. "Shoot, I thought you were enjoying this. *I* sure as hell am. I figure if you want to touch me all over, and I mean *all* over, well, that's more than fine with me. I'd sure prefer it if we'd do it back in the privacy of your bedroom, though, instead of out in the open like this. But…whatever turns you on."

Lucy tried to move her hands over the hard muscles of his legs quickly and impersonally, until she realized what he was doing. He was purposely trying to fluster her, to keep her from taking her time. There was something here that he was trying to hide.

Her hands moved up one strong thigh, all the way to the juncture of his legs. But then she hesitated. Dear Lord, how exactly did a woman search a man thoroughly without embarrassing them both? And then there was the question of his belt….

"Don't stop there, honey," Blue drawled.

And Lucy suddenly knew that he only said that because he *wanted* her to stop there. He was trying to freak her out, make her back away.

Well, fine. She'd play it his way—but only for a while.

She went back to his left ankle, working her way up, again, to the top of his thigh. Again she stopped short.

She patted his rear end and hips rather gingerly—to make him think he was winning the game.

"Nice belt," she said, continuing with the ineffective patting around his waist. Then she dropped her bomb. "A big, metal buckle like that must set off all the bells and whistles at the airport, huh? I bet airport security makes you take that belt off and walk back through the metal detector without it on all the time."

Blue shrugged "It's happened once or twice," he said.

"You don't mind if I take this off and have a look at it," Lucy said, unfastening the buckle. "A much *closer* look?"

She had to hand it to him. He didn't react as she pulled his belt free from the belt loops on his pants. He didn't show his surprise. He didn't sigh, didn't groan, didn't even clear his throat in acceptance of his defeat. And he *had* to know it was coming.

He just said, very matter-of-factly, "That belt holds up my pants."

"Looks like it does more than that," Lucy said, examining the inside of the buckle. Sure enough, hidden inside the buckle, and extending down through part of the thick leather of the belt, was a short but very deadly looking switchblade knife.

Blue glanced at both her and the knife over his shoulder, but still said nothing.

"What you use this one for?" Lucy asked, putting the knife back into the belt buckle. "And don't tell me it's the grape-jelly knife."

He met her eyes steadily. She could see no remorse on his face. "I guess I underestimated you," he said, starting to straighten.

Lucy stopped him. "We're not done," she said, smiling

sweetly. "As long as you've got your belt off, maybe you want to unfasten your pants and give me that gun I know you're hiding in your shorts."

He smiled. Then he laughed. And then he called her bluff. "You *think* I'm hiding something there," he said. "But you're wrong. 'Course, feel free to check and see for yourself."

He knew she wouldn't do it. No, he *thought* he knew— but he was wrong again.

The worst that would happen was that Lucy was mistaken and she'd end up briefly handling a man she'd daydreamed about since she was fifteen. Of course, if she *was* mistaken, he'd probably never let her live it down.

But she *wasn't* mistaken. She couldn't be. God only knows where the gun from his shoulder holster had gone. Still, Blue had surely had a second gun tucked into the small of his back. It wouldn't have taken too much to push it down into his shorts and then wriggle it to a place where most women wouldn't search very carefully—if at all.

Praying that she was right, she reached for him and her fingers found…

Metal.

"Ouch," Blue said. "Careful. Please."

"Sorry," Lucy said sweetly. "You want to get that thing out of there, or should I? Of course, God forbid that it's loaded and I accidentally knock the safety off and—"

Blue scowled at her, reaching into his pants. He pulled the tiny handgun out.

And aimed it at her, dropping into a firing stance. "Hands up," he shouted, and she raised her hands in alarm.

Stepping away from him, Lucy tripped over a tree root and went down in the dirt right on her rear end.

Blue popped the safety back on and helped her up with one hand while handing her the gun with the other. "Dammit, Lucy," he said. "You ID'd a weapon on my person, and you had me get it out myself? That's damned stupid. If I were the bad guy, I would've come out shooting and you'd be dead right now. Next time you're in a similar situation, you aim your own firearm at the guy's head and order him to drop his pants *and* his shorts, and let his weapon fall on the ground. Whereupon *you* pick it up. Do you understand?"

Lucy nodded. Her heart was still pounding, adrenaline surging through her veins. This was one lesson she was never going to forget. But she had one to give him, too.

"If you ever," she said coolly, "*ever* aim a gun at me again in the course of this investigation, I will arrest you and hold you on charges of threatening a police officer. Do *you* understand?"

Down the road she could spot a police cruiser heading in their direction. It was Frank Redfield and Tom Harper. They'd come out to take photos and a plaster casting of the tire tracks.

Blue looked from the cruiser to Lucy and nodded. "Sounds fair to me," he said. Then he smiled. "Provided you can catch me and contain me after I do it."

Lucy didn't smile. She just stared coldly at him. She'd triumphed by finding two weapons he hadn't thought her capable of finding, but he'd kept the upper hand by making her look a fool.

"Stick my gun and my belt in your lockbox," Blue told her. "We just have time to take these guys out to see the tire prints before we have to head into the station and surrender my gear."

Lucy picked Blue's belt with the knife hidden inside it up off the ground, praying that she wasn't about to become an even bigger fool. Instead of holding on to the belt, she handed it back to him.

"You said you needed this to hold up your pants," she told him. She pulled her keys out of her pocket and unlocked the heavy steel box that was attached to the bed of her truck. She stashed Blue's gun and the Swiss Army knife inside and locked it back up. "I know you said never to assume," she added, turning to look at him, "but in this case, I'm assuming that the occupant of your shoulder holster isn't too far away. Otherwise I'd give you the gun back, too. Too bad I can't complete the scenario by thanking you for telling me the truth."

Blue hadn't moved. He stood staring at her, just holding his belt. There was an odd mixture of surprise on his face—surprise and something else that she couldn't quite pinpoint. Whatever it was, it was clear he hadn't expected her to break any rules on his account.

Lucy walked past him, heading toward where Frank had parked the patrol car. She glanced over her shoulder at Blue. "I guess you did underestimate me," she said.

Blue didn't say a word, but the expression in his eyes spoke volumes.

Lucy helped Tom and Frank lug the heavy equipment and supplies they needed to make a plaster casting of the tire tracks up through the woods. The three of them huffed and puffed and sounded like an entire army crashing through the thick growth. Only Blue managed to move silently despite the fact that he carried at least as much—and maybe even more—gear.

They were halfway up the hill, when Blue held up a hand, stopping them.

There was a sound in the distance. It was little more than an odd buzzing, a midrange-pitched whine.

It wasn't until Blue turned and began to run toward the tire tracks that Lucy realized what that sound was.

Dirt bikes.

It was the sound of a group of dirt bikes. With very little effort, the dirt bikes could obscure the tire tracks on the trail, bringing the investigation back to square one.

Lucy dropped the bucket of dried plaster she was carrying and ran after Blue. She shouted over her shoulder for Frank and Tom to follow.

Blue was moving so quickly through the trees it was nearly impossible to keep up with him. Still Lucy tried, leaping over rocks and roots as leaf-filled branches slapped her in the face and arms.

The sound of the dirt bikes grew louder and then more distant, and when Lucy saw Blue just standing up ahead, she feared that the worst had happened. She slowed, and he surely heard her approaching, but he didn't turn around. He just stood, looking down at the trail.

The imprint of the big tires had been totally flattened and erased. There was nothing worth saving, nothing they could use to get a match on the vehicle that had been here the night of Gerry's murder.

Blue's face was tight, expressionless, and when he glanced at her, his eyes were cold.

"I should have stayed up here," he said softly. "I should have guarded the tracks until the casting was done. This was my mistake."

"Mine, too," Lucy whispered. "Oh, Blue, I'm sorry."

Blue was silent as they drove back to her house. He was silent as she did a cursory search of his duffel bag, silent as they drove down to the police station and turned in one of his guns to Chief Bradley.

It wasn't until they'd left the station that he spoke.

"Sheldon Bradley is involved," Blue said.

Lucy turned to look at him in surprise. "Involved in what?"

"This setup," he said. "This frame. And probably in Gerry's murder."

"You think the chief of police," Lucy repeated skeptically, "murdered Gerry and is trying to pin it on you?"

"I didn't say that," Blue said. "I said I think Bradley is

somehow involved. Bradley or someone else on the police force."

"Look, I know you're upset about this," Lucy said. "It was bad timing that those dirt bikes were up on that trail—"

"I thought the timing was pretty damn perfect myself," Blue interrupted. "You radio in to the station, tell Bradley about the tire tracks, and not forty minutes later dirt bikers ride on that very same trail, erasing the evidence?"

Lucy sighed. "You're right," she admitted. "It does seem a little too coincidental. But it doesn't mean that the chief is involved. Anyone listening in on the scanner could have heard that we found those tracks." She pulled her truck up in front of the Grill. "What do you say we get some lunch?"

Blue took a five-dollar bill from his wallet. "Better get mine to go," he said, handing it to her.

Lucy nodded. "I'll be right out."

The Grill was crowded, as usual, but Lucy caught Iris's eye and quickly gave her an order for a couple of sandwiches. Sarah waved at her from a table in the corner, and Lucy walked over.

"Hey," she said, sitting down across from Sarah.

Sarah made an obvious point of looking out the window, out at Lucy's truck, where Blue was sitting. "Can't he come in and order his own lunch?" she asked. "Or does he have too many Y chromosomes to do that?"

Lucy sighed. "Last time he was in here, we almost had a riot," she said. "Most of the town has already found Blue guilty of murder."

"Not you, though," Sarah said, watching her friend.

"No, not me," Lucy agreed.

"Are you sure you're not getting in too deep with this guy?"

Lucy forced a smile. "Can we talk about something else?" she asked.

Sarah hesitated. She clearly had more to say on the subject.

"Please?"

"Okay," Sarah said evenly. "Here's something new—some good news. Remember that demo tape I sent to the Charleston Music Society? They want me to be part of their winter concert series as a featured artist. They've asked me to do a program of French art songs."

Lucy smiled at her friend. "That's great! Did they give you a date?"

"Sometime in December," Sarah said. She made a face. "That's assuming I've had the baby by then."

Lucy had to laugh. "That's six months away. No one has ever been pregnant for fifteen months."

"Not yet, anyway."

"Lucy," Iris called out. "Your order is up."

Lucy stood. "Congratulations," she said.

"Thanks," Sarah said. "Call me later, okay?" She leaned forward and lowered her voice. "Lucy, I've got to ask you if it's true what I've heard—that the superhunk is staying at your place? With you?"

Lucy closed her eyes, swearing silently. She sat back down at Sarah's table. "You heard that?" she asked.

Sarah nodded. "People are talking," she said, "and what they're saying isn't very nice."

"Jedd Southeby wouldn't give Blue a room at the motel," Lucy said. "What was I supposed to do, make him sleep in the jail?"

Sarah nodded. "Yes," she said. "It's a shame, but…yes."

Lucy shook her head, standing up again. "I can't do that," she said. "Thanks for telling me, but…" She shrugged. "I guess people are just going to have to talk."

"Lucy, he *could* have done it, you know." Worry showed in Sarah's hazel eyes. "You're opening your house to a man who could very well be a killer. I know you probably don't see it that way—he's a man you've always respected and admired. Don't let that cloud your good judgment."

"I appreciate your concern," Lucy said. "I really do."

"But…"

"I'll talk to you later."

Lucy could feel Sarah's eyes on her as she paid Iris for the lunch and carried the paper bag of food with her out to the sidewalk. She started for her truck and stopped.

Blue was gone.

This time she didn't swear silently. She turned around, did a complete three-sixty, searching for any sign of where he might have gone.

Tom Harper's police cruiser went past, moving faster than usual, and on a hunch, Lucy climbed into her truck, tossed the bag with the sandwiches onto the passenger seat and followed.

Tom's patrol car pulled up in front of the vacant lot next to the gas station, several blocks down Main Street.

Sure enough, there was Blue. He was facing off with three men, looking as if he was intending to fight them all simultaneously. One of the men had a chain and another had a length of two-by-four, but Blue was the one advancing. A small crowd had gathered to watch.

As she jumped out of her truck and ran toward them, Lucy could see that one of the men was Merle Groggin. Another was Matt Parker. And the third was Leroy Hurley. Matt's nose was bleeding, Merle had what appeared to be the start of a black eye and Leroy was hot and sweaty. Blue didn't even look ruffled. Just mad as hell.

"All right, break it up," Lucy called out, Tom Harper just a step behind her.

"You call *him* off," Merle said, gesturing to Blue. "He's the one threatened to tear us limb from limb."

"You jumped me," Blue drawled. "Remember?"

"McCoy, back off," Lucy said sharply.

He glanced at her, and she could see anger in his eyes. Real, hot, molten, deadly anger.

"These boys just came back from a joy ride on some dirt bikes," he told her. "Shiny, brand-new dirt bikes. Who do you suppose gave them those bikes? They tell me they found 'em, that they fell off a truck that went past on the state highway. I figured they needed a little encouragement to tell me the real story—like who called them and told them to take that ride on that trail over by Gate's Hill Road—so I asked them to think a little harder. That's when they jumped me."

"He's crazy," Leroy said. "It's the truth that we found those bikes. The packing crates are still up there on Route 17. We'll show you where, if you want. We didn't think it would do 'em any harm to take 'em for a test drive."

Blue's voice was low, dangerous. "You are so full of garbage. You and your 'buddy' Merle just happened to be out for a stroll along the state highway? Or maybe you were the one who found 'em and you thought, 'Gee, maybe I should give Merle a call, see if he wants to take a ride.' Never mind the fact that two days ago you were threatening to *kill* him."

Leroy brandished the two-by-four he was holding. "Are you calling me a liar?"

"Hell, yes." Blue's eyes were shooting fire. "You're a liar and a drunk and a son of a bitch, and I aim to get the truth out of you if it's the last thing you do."

Leroy bristled. "Call me a liar again, and I'll—"

"You want to hit me with that stick, go on and do it, you lying sack of—"

Leroy sprang, the two-by-four slicing down through the air. But Blue had moved. He was no longer where he had been standing. He spun, kicking as he turned, his foot connecting solidly with Leroy's arm. The piece of wood went flying, and there was a loud crack that had to be the sound of breaking bone.

Leroy screamed.

Lucy threw herself in front of Blue, grabbing his arms, trying to hold him back. "Stop it," she hissed. "Right now!"

Leroy was curled up on the ground, moaning and holding his arm.

"Tell me who gave you those bikes," Blue demanded.

Leroy spit on the dirt.

Blue looked at Lucy. His eyes were wild and he was still breathing hard. "I can make him tell me," he said.

She shook her head. "No, you can't," she said.

"Radio for medical assistance," Tom told her. "We better bring 'em all in."

Lucy was angry at Blue.

Her anger was a palpable thing that filled the inside of her truck, surrounding them both. She was angry as she pulled out of the police-station parking lot, angry as she drove down Main Street. She was still angry as she took the right-hand turn onto Fox Run Road and skidded to a stop in her gravel driveway.

She climbed angrily down from the truck cab and stalked up the front walk and onto the porch. She unlocked the kitchen door and pushed it open.

"I want you to go inside," she said tightly, "and I want you to stay there until I get back."

Blue's own temper sparked. "Since when did you start telling me what to do?"

"Since you started acting like an idiot," Lucy said. "God Almighty, McCoy, what were you thinking? Did you honestly figure you could beat up Leroy Hurley, make him tell you what you wanted to know and not risk imprisonment? I had to talk rings around Chief Bradley to keep him from locking you up." She pushed her hair off her face in frustration as she stalked into the kitchen and paced back and forth across the floor. "I don't know how it works in the SEALs, but in this part of America, you just can't go around terrorizing people because you're mad. Lord, I expected more from you."

I expected more from you. Her words pushed Blue over the edge, sending him down into a spiral of emotion and anger that he couldn't pull out of. He tried, but it enveloped him completely, and he lost his temper.

"If you expected more from me," Blue exploded, "that's *your* problem, Yankee, not mine. Because guess what? I'm not perfect. I never have been."

The force of his words pushed Lucy back against the kitchen counter. He could see shock in her eyes, alarm on her face, but once he'd started, he couldn't stop.

"You see me as some kind of damned hero, but I'm not. I'm flesh and blood, and just as capable of screwing up as the next guy.

"Guess what else?" he continued. "I yell sometimes. I *like* to yell. I *like* to fight. But I don't always win, because I'm *not* a hero. I'm *not* always right. I'm *not* always in control. I make mistakes, sometimes *stupid* mistakes. I get angry. I get hurt. I get scared. And right now I'm all *three* of those things." His voice got softer, and he looked away from her, out the kitchen window. "Only I can't tell you that, can I? Because…you expect more from me."

The silence that surrounded them seemed almost unnatural, artificial. Blue could hear the hum of the refrigerator, the almost inaudible ticking of the clock. Outside, a breeze blew and a tree branch bumped the house.

He heard Lucy take a step toward him and then another step, and then he felt her hand on his back. It was a touch meant to give comfort. Blue didn't know what he wanted from her, but he was almost certain it wasn't comfort. Still, when he turned and saw the sheen of tears in her eyes, he knew without a doubt that he was going to take whatever she had to offer. And maybe even then some.

She went into his arms, holding him as tightly as he held her, and the longing that welled up inside him was sharp and painful as hell. This wasn't comfort; it was torture.

"I'm so sorry," she murmured.

He felt her hands on his back, in his hair, meant to soothe and calm. It wasn't working.

"Lucy, I want you," he whispered, "and I don't think I can stand it anymore."

He felt her stiffen at his words. She lifted her head and he gazed directly into her eyes.

"Blue—"

He touched her lips with one finger, silencing her.

"I'm not what you think I am," he said. "You think I'm some kind of gentleman. You think all you have to do is tell me 'no,' and 'don't,' even though you damn well want it as much as I do. You think that because I'm some kind of hero I'll keep both of us from going too far. You think you can look at me with these big, brown eyes, not bothering to hide how much you want me, too. You think you can put me upstairs in some guest room, while you sleep one flight away, with your bedroom door unlocked and open, as if I'm strong enough to keep us apart. But guess what? You leave that door open and unlocked tonight, and I'm going to take it as the invitation that it is—because I'm *not* strong enough. I don't want to be strong enough anymore. I'm not a hero, Lucy, and I'm tired as hell of playing one."

She was trembling, actually trembling, in his arms. "Blue, I can't. You're right. Part of me wants to be with you that way, but I can't—"

"Maybe you can't, but I sure as hell can."

Blue kissed her. He covered Lucy's mouth with his and drank her in. She tasted sweet and hot and she so absolutely set him on fire. If she resisted his kiss, she resisted for all of a half a second. And then her tongue welcomed him fiercely, pulling him into her mouth, harder, deeper.

The power of her answering passion took his breath away. He kissed her again and again, trying desperately to get even closer, to fill his senses with her, to have more, *more*.

He reached for her shirt, yanking the tails up and out of the waist of her pants. He found the softness of her skin and moaned at the smooth sensation beneath his fingertips.

And still he kissed her and she kissed him. It was wild, incredible, amazing. He couldn't get enough, would never get enough. Her hands were in his hair, on his back, on the curve of his rear end, pulling him closer to her.

She could surely feel him pressed against her, fully aroused. He was so hard he hurt.

Blue picked her up and her legs locked around his waist. He was dizzy, delirious with the knowledge that he was going to have her. Right here and right now, he could take her and she wouldn't refuse.

He pulled his shirt off over his head and quickly unbuckled his shoulder holster, then tossed it onto the kitchen table. Lucy's hands were everywhere, skimming across the muscles in his shoulders and chest and back, touching him, caressing his skin, just lightly enough to drive him totally insane.

I can't.

Blue's eyes opened. Lucy hadn't spoken. She was still kissing him. She hadn't given voice to her protest again. But still, it echoed in his head, over and over and over.

I can't.

If they didn't stop, she'd lose her job and her self-respect, just as she'd told him.

And if they did stop, he'd lose his mind. After all, he was no hero.

But even so, how could he willingly do something that would destroy her?

As if she felt his hesitation, Lucy lifted her head, staring with sudden shock into Blue's eyes.

"Oh, my God," she said. "What are we doing? What am *I* doing? Blue, I can't do this...."

Blue gently set her down, away from him, on the kitchen

counter. He had to look away from her—she looked too damn good with her hair messed and her clothing askew. He picked up his holster from the table and his shirt from the floor, keeping his eyes averted.

"I'll be outside," he said, barely getting the words out through his clenched teeth, "getting some air."

Chapter Nine

When Lucy came home from the police station, the sun had already set. Her house was dark. There were no lights on, and she climbed out of her truck filled with trepidation. Where had Blue gone this time?

She'd told him to stay here, but that didn't mean he'd be here.

Hoping she'd find another note on the kitchen table, Lucy wearily climbed the stairs to the porch, searching for her key in the darkness.

"It's unlocked."

Lucy jumped. My God. Blue was sitting out on the porch in the dark.

"You're here," she said inanely.

"You asked me to stick around."

As her eyes adjusted to the darkness, she could see that he was on the porch swing, rocking slightly, just watching her.

"And you told me you were going to do what you wanted."

"Not entirely," he said softly, his meaning clear. He was referring to this afternoon—to when they had almost made love.

Lucy sat down on the steps. It was as far as she could get from him and still be on the porch.

"I'm sorry about before," he murmured.

She turned to look at him. From this distance, she couldn't quite make out his features in the darkness. "Which part of before?" she asked bluntly. "The part where you yelled at me, or the part where we almost had sex?"

"I'm sorry for yelling."

"But not for the other."

He chuckled. "I'm sorry about that, too—but only that we didn't get to finish what we started."

Lucy was silent for several long minutes, just looking up at the stars. Another man probably wouldn't have admitted that. Another man would have pretended to apologize.

Of course, another man wouldn't have blithely lied about the fact that he was carrying three different concealed weapons. Another man wouldn't have egged on an angry man holding a two-by-four.

Blue McCoy wasn't a hero. He was a man, with a man's strengths and weaknesses. Until his outburst, Lucy hadn't allowed herself to see past the comic book-perfect facade she'd constructed for him. She hadn't allowed him to have any real human emotions or fears. But he did.

The moon came out from behind the clouds. It was still quite full, and it lit the yard and made the white paint of the porch seem to glow.

"Are you really afraid?" Lucy asked.

She heard him sigh. "Normally, I wouldn't admit something like that more than once a decade," he said. "But, yeah, Yankee. I'm scared."

She turned to face him, leaning back against the banister, tucking her knees in to her chest and holding them with her arms. "You don't act like you're afraid of anything."

"I'm not afraid of fighting," he said. "I know what to do when it comes down to violence. I know how to respond to that. I know I'm good at it. The thought of getting hurt doesn't frighten me, either—I've been hurt before. Pain ends. Bodies heal. I'm not afraid of dying, either." He looked up at the moon, squinting slightly as he studied it. "I've got my faith," he added quietly.

He turned to gaze at her, and his eyes reflected the moon's silvery light, making him appear otherworldly.

"But I'm terrified of getting caught in a legal system that's corrupt—and possibly controlled by the people who are trying to frame me. I feel like I'm in the middle of a war that I don't know how to fight."

He closed his eyes briefly, and Lucy knew that this wasn't easy for him.

"I'm afraid of going to jail, Lucy. It damn near scares me to death. I won't let them lock me up. I swear, I'll run before that happens."

Lucy sat forward. "But don't you see? That'll make you look guilty."

"I already look guilty as hell," Blue said flatly. "Everyone in town thinks I did it."

"Well, *I* know you didn't kill Gerry," Lucy said fiercely, "and I'm going to make damn sure that you don't go to jail for something you didn't do."

She could see an odd play of emotions cross his face in the moonlight.

"You still believe in me," he said. He sounded faintly surprised.

"Of course."

"Even though I'm not…some kind of superhero?"

The truth was, Lucy liked him better this way. The human Blue seemed so much warmer, so much more real.

Realizing he had imperfections and weaknesses added a depth and dimension to her image of him. He was still outrageously attractive—maybe even more so, because she knew now that he was human, with a full array of human emotions. His vulnerabilities contrasted with his strengths, giving him a sensitivity she hadn't realized he'd possessed.

"What does that have to do with whether I think you killed your stepbrother?" she asked evenly.

"I don't know," he admitted. He paused. "I guess maybe I misunderstood your reasons for wanting to help me."

Lucy laughed softly. "I assure you my reasons are only pure," she said. "The pursuit of justice. The defeat of evil. Things like that. Whether you can leap tall buildings has nothing to do with it."

Blue was silent. She knew he was thinking about Gerry. In Gerry's case, evil had won. And Lucy knew that if she didn't come up with some new evidence exonerating Blue, Chief Bradley was going to bring charges against him. With Matt Parker's damning testimony and without the hard proof of the tire tracks they'd seen, it was only a matter of time. She'd talked to Matt Parker today. He insisted that Leroy's story about finding the dirt bikes on the side of Route 17 was true. And he swore it was Blue he saw up in the woods on the night Gerry had died.

"Maybe you should call someone," Lucy said. "Get a lawyer."

Blue shifted his weight, making the swing rock slowly.

"I tried calling Joe Cat this afternoon—Joe Catalanotto. He's my commanding officer in the Alpha Squad. And he's my friend," Blue told her. "I figured he'd know how to proceed, maybe even get me a good Navy lawyer, get this mess cleared up. But I found out that Alpha Squad is out on a training mission until further notice. And SEAL Team Ten's normal liaison, Admiral Forrest, is suddenly unavailable." His normally relaxed voice sounded tense, tight. "I spoke to some pencil-pushing commander from Internal Affairs, who says he's handling all of Alpha Squad's paperwork and messages until further notice. IA does this every few years when it's time for budget cuts. This commander is looking for dirt—for reasons to get rid of Alpha Squad. I didn't dare tell him I wanted to talk to a lawyer. If he found out that one of the members of Alpha Squad was going to be up on murder charges…" Blue shook his head. "I've got to get through this on my own."

"But you're not on your own," Lucy said softly. "You've got me."

Across the porch, Blue tried to smile. "Thanks, Yankee, but…"

"I'm not part of Alpha Squad," she finished for him.

He nodded. "We've been trained to work as a team," he tried to explain.

"I know," Lucy said. "I know how the SEAL teams operate. And from what I've read about Alpha Squad, some of you guys have been together since basic training."

Blue nodded. "Joe Cat and I went through BUD/S together more than ten years ago. We were swim buddies. Still are."

Swim buddies. That meant that all throughout BUD/S—Basic Underwater Demolition/SEAL training—Blue and his friend Joe Cat had stuck together like glue. Where one went, the other had to follow. They had no doubt formed a bond that went way beyond friendship, based on respect and determination and an unswerving responsibility toward each other and Alpha Squad.

"I've read about Hell Week," Lucy said, resting her chin in the palm of her hand as she gazed up at him. "It sounds awful. Was it true that you had only four hours of sleep all week?"

"Yeah," Blue said with a smile. "Both Cat and I were hallucinating before it was over. Fortunately, when I was seeing sea monsters he took charge. And when *he* was the one foaming at the mouth I was able to grab him and set him back on track. That was one hell of a week. I guess that's why they call it that."

"Will you tell me about it?" Lucy asked.

Blue gave the porch swing another push with his foot and it creaked rhythmically as it swung back and forth. He gazed at her, his expression unreadable for many long moments.

"Please?" she added.

"'You gotta want it badly enough,'" Blue said.

For a second, Lucy was confused. But then he explained.

"That's what one of the SEAL instructors used to shout at us, and it's the single most lucid thing I remember about Hell Week."

The moon slipped back behind a cloud, taking its silvery light with it. Blue became a dark outline on the other side of the porch, but his voice surrounded her, as warm and smooth and completely enveloping as the darkness.

"The instructors would shout at us over these bullhorns," he said. "It was relentless. They would ridicule and torment us all the time as they hit us with surf torture or made us run endless laps on the beach or do sugar-cookie drills. But there was this one bastard—his nickname was Captain Blood—and he was the meanest, toughest instructor of them all. He was out for blood, literally. But one of the first things he ever said to us through his megaphone was 'You gotta want it badly enough.'"

Blue laughed softly. "It must've been on the first day. We were in the water. It was *cold* water, less than sixty degrees. We had to lock arms and just sit in the surf and try not to freeze our asses off. They called it surf torture and it was designed to see how much we could endure, the thought being that someday we'd find ourselves swimming for hours in the ice water off Alaska.

"Anyway, we were in the freezing mother of an ocean for

about an hour, when the first man quit. It was so damn cold. I'd never been that cold before in my life. All around me I could hear other guys complaining. What were we doing this for? Why did we need to do this? What were the instructors trying to prove?"

The clouds covering the moon thinned and then broke apart and Blue paused. Lucy gazed up at him. She could picture him sitting in the freezing water, silently enduring the cold, his handsome face tight, his teeth clenched.

"As I sat there," Blue continued, "these other guys started to give up. Just like that. It got too uncomfortable, too tough, too painful, so they just up and quit. But I wasn't going anywhere. And I looked at Joe Cat, and I knew he wasn't going anywhere, either. I could tell from the expression on his face that he was thinking the same thing I was thinking—'You gotta want it badly enough.' And we did. We wanted to make it through, get our SEAL pin."

Blue smiled down at her, and Lucy found herself smiling almost foolishly back at him. His eyes seemed to caress her face and he shook his head slightly, as if he were bemused. "You *are* pretty, aren't you?" he asked softly.

Lucy had to look away. Everyone was pretty in the moonlight.

"You sure you don't want to sit up here on the swing, next to me?" Blue added.

She met his eyes evenly. "You know I can't."

"I know you *won't*," he countered.

"Either way," she said. "I better stay where I am."

"We could just hold hands," Blue said. "Like sweethearts. Nothing more. It'd be real innocent."

Lucy had to laugh. "You don't have a single innocent cell in your body, McCoy. You know as well as I do that holding hands would lead to a kiss, and we both know where *that* would go."

Blue's eyes turned hot. "Yeah, I sure do," he said softly. "I spent most of the evening fantasizing about it."

Lucy stood up. "I think it's time for this conversation to end."

Blue sat up. He didn't want her to go. More, even more than he wanted to make love to Lucy, he wanted her company. Her smile and her beautiful midnight eyes kept all his demon fears at bay. "You sure you don't want to hear more about Hell Week?" he asked.

He'd never talked so much in his entire life. He'd never told his stories, recounted his past the way some of the other guys in the squad did over and over again. It wasn't that he didn't have good tales to tell—he just always preferred to listen.

And he and Joe Cat didn't talk that much. They knew each other so well that they shared each other's thoughts, communicating with a look or a nod.

His friendship with Daryl Becker—nicknamed Harvard because of his Ivy League college education—was filled with talk of books and philosophy, of science and art and technology and anything—you name it and they'd touched on it. But Harvard did most of the talking, thinking aloud, rattling off ideas before they'd even become fully formed. Blue kept his thinking to himself, carefully forming his opinions before he spoke. As a result, his comments were always short and sweet.

But tonight, even though he was nearly hoarse from doing so much talking, he was willing to keep going if it meant Lucy would stay with him just a bit longer.

Lucy was still standing by the steps, her arms crossed in front of her. "Are you going to let me sit over here?" she asked warily.

He nodded. "Yeah."

She sat down, just gazing at him expectantly in the moonlight.

It took Blue a minute to remember he'd promised to tell her more about Hell Week. Except he was damned if he could think of a single thing to say.

"I'm not sure what you want to hear about," he said lamely.

Lucy shifted, getting more comfortable on the hard wood of the steps. "I've read about something called 'rock portage,'" she said. "Did you have to do that in basic training?"

"Yeah. Halfway through Hell Week we had to do a night-time coastal landing in our IBS—our rubber life raft." Blue nodded again, glad she had given him something to talk about. Or had she? The night his BUD/S team had done rock portage was a nightmare blur. He hesitated. "I don't remember much about it," he admitted. "I remember wondering how the hell we were going to get safely ashore with our boat intact. The surf was rough and the coast was nothing but a jagged line of rocks. It wouldn't take much to crush a man between the rocks and our boat." He looked down at his hands, wondering what else he could tell her. "We were exhausted and freezing and some of our boat crew had injuries. I can't really tell you exactly how we got ashore, just that we did."

Blue glanced up to find Lucy still watching him. She was listening, her dark eyes luminous and warm in the moon-light. And he knew then what he could tell her. He could tell her the truth.

"I remember being scared to death while we were doing it," he added quietly. "I felt like such a coward."

His words hung in the air. He'd never admitted that to anyone before. Not Joe Cat, not Frisco or Harvard. He'd barely even admitted it to himself. The sounds of the night surrounded him as he gazed into Lucy's eyes, wondering what she would do with this intimate truth that he'd shared with her.

She smiled. "You weren't a coward," she said. "A coward

doesn't keep on doing something that scares him to death. A coward quits. Only a very strong, very brave person perseveres in the face of fear."

Blue nodded, smiling back at her. "I know that now," he said. "But I was younger then."

"I bet a lot of guys quit during rock portage," Lucy said.

"Our boat crew's senior officer did," Blue told her. "He took one look at those rocks and checked out of the program. We made our landing that night without a senior officer—just us grunts, getting the job done."

Lucy was fascinated, hanging on his every word. Blue knew that as long as he could keep talking, she'd stay there with him. And he wanted her to stay.

"By the end of the week, only half the class was left," he continued, the words flowing more easily now. "We were running down the beach and my entire boat crew was limping—we were a mess. Like I said, our senior officer had quit on us, and Joe Cat and me, even though we were grunts—just enlisted men—we took command. Someone had to. But by this time, Cat was really hurting. Turned out he had a stress fracture in his leg, but we didn't know it at the time."

"He was running on a *broken* leg?"

"Yeah." Blue nodded, watching all of Lucy's emotions play across her face. She gazed up into his eyes, waiting for his response, one hundred percent of her attention focused on him. He had to smile. He quite possibly had never had a woman's total, undivided attention before—at least not while they both had all their clothes on. Maybe there was something to this storytelling thing after all.

"Anyway, Cat was damned if he was going to get pulled because of his injury," Blue said, "so we hid him from the instructors. We carried him when we could, surrounded him, held him up, dragged him when no one was looking. But Captain Blood finally spotted him and started in on how Cat was slowing us up, taking us down with him. He shouted into his damned bullhorn how we should ditch him, just leave him behind, toss him into the surf."

Blue grinned. "Well, Joe Cat and me, we'd both about had enough. This was day seven. We were sleep deprived. We were psychologically abused. We were hurting. Cat was in excruciating physical pain, and I don't think there was a single part of me that didn't ache or sting. We were cold and wet and hungry. And Cat, he gets really annoyed when he's cold and wet and hungry. But I get mean. So I tell Captain Blood to go to hell, going into detail about just exactly what he should do with himself when he gets there. Then I order the rest of the boat crew to put Cat up on top of our IBS. We'd carry him on the life raft.

"But as we're doing that, Captain Blood realizes that Cat is hurt worse than he thought, and he orders him out of the line. He's gonna pull him because of his injury, and he starts calling in for an ambulance. I look up at Cat, sitting on top of that raft, and he's got this expression on his face, like his entire world has come to an end. There are five hours left in Hell Week. Five lousy hours, and he's gonna get pulled.

"So I get in Captain Blood's face and I interrupt that phone call. I tell him that Joe Cat's leg is fine—and to prove it to him, Cat will do a mile lap down the beach. The captain knows I'm full of it, but he's into playing games, so he tells me, fine. If Cat can run a mile, he can stay in till the end."

The moon went behind the clouds again, plunging the porch into darkness. But Blue could hear Lucy's quiet breathing. He heard her shift her weight, saw her shadowy form. He could feel the power of her attention as if it were a tangible thing, as if she were next to him, touching him.

"Cat is ready to jump down off that IBS to try to do a five-minute mile right then and there," Blue continued. "But I know he'll never make it. Just putting his weight on his damned leg is enough to make him start to black out. So I put Joe Cat's arm around my shoulder. I'd figured we could run down the beach together, kind of like a three-legged race, with Cat staying off his bad leg. But he was hurt worse than I thought, so I ended up picking him up and carrying him on my back."

Blue heard Lucy's soft inhale. "You *carried* him for a *mile?*" she whispered.

"We were swim buddies," Blue said simply. "Cat is no lightweight—he's about five inches taller than me and he's built like a tank—so about a quarter mile in, I'm starting to move really slowly. But I'm still running, 'cause I want it badly enough, and I know Cat does, too, and I'm not gonna let him get pulled. But I start to wonder how the hell I'm going to find the strength to do this. And then I look up, and the rest of our boat crew is running right next to me. Me and Cat, we're not alone. Our crew is with us. Crow and Harvard and all the rest of the guys. They're all hurting, too, but they're with us. We all took turns carrying Cat that entire mile down the beach. It was no five-minute mile—it took more like a half an hour.

"But when we were done, Captain Blood looks at Cat and he looks at me, and then he nods and says to our boat crew, 'You boys are secure.' Just like that, four and a half hours early, Hell Week was over for our entire crew. We'd made it—all of us. And I swear to God, Captain Blood turned and gave us a salute. An officer, saluting a bunch of enlisted men. That was a sight to see."

Lucy had tears in her eyes and goose bumps on her arms. She sat hugging her knees to her chest, glad for the darkness that hid her emotional response to his soft words. It was an amazing story. And Blue had told it so matter-of-factly, as if he didn't realize how rare and moving his loyalty to his friend truly was.

She knew that Blue's loyalty had to be a two-sided thing, and she knew that if this Joe Cat hadn't been on a training mission, he would be on his way here to Hatboro Creek. Lord knows Blue could use some help. Lucy was doing the best that she could, but she knew without a doubt that her best wasn't enough. She didn't have the experience to pull this investigation off.

And the one thing she did know how to do, she couldn't. She couldn't let herself love Blue—not on the physical level that he so desperately wanted, and not even on an emotional, spiritual level. She couldn't fall in love with him; she couldn't allow herself to feel more than dispassionate compassion for him.

But she did. She felt far more than that. She ached at his pain, suffered his worries, felt the cold of his fears.

She couldn't fall in love with him…but that was exactly what she was beginning to do. Right here, in the darkness, with the echo of his velvet voice in her ears, she was sliding deeper in love with Blue McCoy.

It was ironic. Until this afternoon, until Blue's outburst had jolted her, she would have labeled her feelings for Blue as a crush. It had been a very surface-level mixture of awe and admiration and lust—mere hero worship.

But then, with his actions and his words, Blue had stripped off his superhero costume, revealing the imperfections of the flesh-and-blood man underneath.

The hero could only be worshipped.

But the man could be loved.

It was crazy. Even if she succeeded in clearing his name, Blue would be gone in a matter of days, probably hours. How could she let herself fall in love with a man who would never love her in return?

But the point was moot. She couldn't let herself love him. She had to stop herself from falling. Because right now her hands were securely tied by her responsibility to the murder investigation.

"Try calling Joe Cat again in the morning," she said. Her

voice was husky with emotion, and she cleared her throat. "If he's not there, try again in the afternoon."

"I will," he said. "Sooner or later he'll be back."

She stood up, and she felt, more than heard, him tense. "Lucy," he said softly. "Don't go inside yet. Please?"

She could hear loneliness in his voice and knew how much he wanted her to stay, how much it had taken him to ask her not to go.

But she couldn't stay. Every word he spoke brought him a little deeper into her heart. She wasn't strong enough to resist him. Even here in the darkness, six feet apart, she found the sexual pull, the animal attraction between them, alarmingly strong. And the emotional pull that she felt was overpowering.

But she couldn't tell him that.

"I'm sorry, I'm exhausted," she said. She crossed the porch and opened the kitchen door. "I'm going up to take a shower and then go to bed."

She could feel his disappointment, but he didn't try to change her mind.

"All right," he said quietly. "Good night."

The screen door closed after her, and she was halfway through the kitchen before she heard Blue's soft voice.

"Lucy?"

She stopped, but she didn't turn around. She heard him move so that he was standing on the other side of the screen.

"Lock your door tonight," he said quietly.

Lucy nodded. "I will."

The clouds that covered last night's moon brought a dismal, gloomy rain to the day. It was an appropriate backdrop for Gerry's funeral.

Most of the town had been there, many of the people slanting dark looks in Blue's direction.

He had sat alone in a pew toward the front of the church, wearing his gleaming white dress uniform. Only Jenny Lee Beaumont spoke to him, and just briefly, as she was led from the church, following Gerry's gleaming white coffin out to the waiting hearse.

This was supposed to be Lucy's day off, but she'd gone into the police station intending to carry on with the investigation into Gerry's murder. Except, when he saw her there, Chief Bradley had taken the liberty of temporarily assigning Lucy to the task of directing the funeral traffic. She now stood in the rain, halting traffic and giving the right-of-way to the funeral procession heading out to the cemetery.

Blue had borrowed Lucy's truck and he met her eyes briefly through the windshield as he pulled out of the church parking lot. Lucy had gone into the church for the ceremony and had seen that he clearly wasn't welcome at his stepbrother's funeral. He hadn't been asked to carry the casket. He'd been virtually ignored. The minister of the church hadn't even mentioned Blue in his short eulogy to Gerry's life.

Lucy's heart ached for Blue. As she stood getting wetter with each drop of rain that fell, she prayed for a break in the case.

Today wouldn't be a good day to talk to Jenny Lee Beaumont, but maybe tomorrow Lucy could go over to the house that Jenny and Gerry had shared. If she wanted to find Gerry's killer, maybe she should start by looking for a motive. Why would someone want Gerry dead? Did he have any enemies? Was he in the middle of any fights, any business disputes? Maybe Jenny would know.

And if Jenny didn't, someone in town had to know. Lucy was going to start out on Gate's Hill Road, near where the murder had taken place, and work her way through town, knocking on doors and asking questions. Somebody saw or heard something that night. Somebody knew who really killed Gerry McCoy.

And then there were Leroy Hurley and Matt Parker. Blue was right about them. Their story about finding the dirt bikes by the side of the road was ludicrous. Someone had paid them off to obscure those tire tracks. And it was possibly the same someone who was paying Matt Parker to say he'd seen Blue up in the woods with Gerry.

The last of the cars pulled out of the church lot and Lucy watched their taillights vanish as they made a left at the corner of Main and Willow.

Turning, she pushed her wet hair out of her face, adjusted her soggy hat and headed for home. It was nearly three o'clock, and she wanted to change out of her soaked uniform and have something to eat. She'd make herself a salad and actually sit down at her kitchen table to eat it. And in order not to feel as if she were wasting time, she'd take the opportunity to really read over Gerry's autopsy reports.

It was three-fifteen before she got home, three-thirty before she got out of the shower and nearly four o'clock before she sat down with her salad at the kitchen table. She'd pulled on a short pair of cutoff jeans and a tank top, and brushed out her wet hair.

She skimmed through the autopsy report, then went back to read it more carefully. It wasn't until the third time through that she saw it.

There was almost no alcohol present in Gerry's blood.

No alcohol?

She checked the numbers again, and sure enough, according to these figures, Gerry couldn't have had more than one beer all evening long on the night he died.

That had to be wrong.

She'd seen Gerry's drunken behavior with her own eyes. He had looked and acted inebriated at the party at 8:15, yet had been dead at 11:06, not quite three hours later, with only the slightest trace of alcohol in his blood.

It didn't make sense. Either the autopsy report was wrong...

Or...

Was it possible that Gerry's drunken behavior had been an act? Had he been stone sober at the country club, only pretending to be drunk? And if so, why? What purpose could it possibly have served? He'd embarrassed himself and Blue *and* Jenny Lee. Why would he have done that intentionally?

It didn't make sense.

Lucy had to tell someone. She had to ask questions, talk to Jenny herself, find out if Gerry had seemed sober or drunk earlier at the party. And R. W. Fisher. Blue said he'd seen his stepbrother talking to the Tobacco King right before Gerry's outburst. Lucy had to talk to Fisher, see if he'd noticed anything odd about Gerry during their conversation.

Lucy stood up, stuffed her feet into her running shoes and grabbed her raincoat from its hook by the kitchen door. She was out on the porch before she realized that she didn't have her keys—or her truck.

Okay. That was okay. She'd take a few minutes, go inside, change out of her shorts and into a pair of jeans. As hot as it was with the humidity from the rain, it wouldn't do her any good to appear at the police station in shorts.

Lucy took the stairs to her room two at a time and quickly kicked off her sneakers. She wriggled out of her shorts and pulled on her jeans. She fished her cowboy boots out from under her bed and pulled them on, too.

She was reaching for the phone, about to call down to the station, looking for a ride, when she heard the kitchen door open and shut.

Blue was back.

Lucy clattered down the stairs and into the kitchen, stopping short when she realized that Blue was taking off his dripping clothes right there in the doorway.

But his clothes weren't just wet, she realized. They were also muddy and torn. And smeared with blood. *His* blood.

Blue had been in a fight.

He'd taken off his jacket and the shirt he wore underneath. His arm was bleeding, his fingers dripping with blood. Lucy got a glimpse of a nasty cut across his biceps before he pressed his shirt against it, trying to stop the flow of blood.

Fear welled up in her. He'd been out there, in town, all alone, without her. He could have been badly hurt. Or even killed. "Are you all right?"

He met her eyes briefly as he stepped out of his muddy pants. "I could use a first-aid kit," he said. "And I'll need some ice for my leg."

Lucy saw that he had the beginnings of a truly dreadful-looking bruise on his left thigh.

Silently she moved to the cabinet and took out her first-aid kit, with its vast array of bandages and gauze. As she set it on the kitchen table, she saw that Blue was still standing in the doorway, awkwardly holding his filthy clothes.

"I don't want to get your floor any dirtier," he apologized.

"Just put them down," she said, hoping he wouldn't notice how her voice was shaking. "The floor can be washed."

He nodded, setting his clothes on the floor.

"What happened?" Lucy asked, since it was clear he wasn't going to volunteer the information himself. She filled a wash basin with warm water and set it on the table next to the first-aid kit.

"Fight," Blue said, gingerly lowering himself onto one of the kitchen chairs.

Lucy took a soft washcloth from the shelf, throwing him an exasperated look over her shoulder. "You want to be a little more specific there, McCoy?"

She handed him the washcloth, then went to the freezer to get an ice pack for his leg.

"No."

His knuckles and hands were torn up, and he had a scrape across his left cheekbone. It was still bleeding, and he tried futilely to blot the blood with the back of his hand.

Lucy's cold fear turned hot with frustration. "No," she repeated. She wrapped the ice pack in a small towel and crossed toward him.

"It was nothing I care to issue a complaint about," he said. He lifted his wad of shirt from the cut on his arm, and it welled with blood. He quickly covered the wound with the soapy washcloth, applying pressure.

"Issue a complaint?" Lucy stared at him. "I asked you what happened. I didn't ask you if you wanted to file a complaint."

"I'm not trying to start another fight here," Blue said, glancing up at her. His eyes were startlingly blue. "It's just…you've been careful about remaining in your role as a police officer at other times, I figured what happened to me this afternoon was something you wouldn't want to know."

Lucy was shocked. "Is that all I am to you, a police officer?"

"I thought that was your choice," Blue said, rinsing the washcloth in the basin, then using it to reapply pressure to his slashed arm. "I thought you were the one who set those limits."

"I can't be your lover," Lucy told him. "*That's* my limit. But I thought at least I was your friend."

He looked up at her again, his eyes sweeping down the length of her body and back up before settling on her face. "My friends don't look that good in their jeans."

"I suppose you don't have a single friend who's a woman."

"No, I don't."

"You do now," she said grimly. She crouched next to him, not certain of the best way to put the ice pack on his leg. The bruise looked incredibly painful. It was turning all sorts of shades of purple, with a long, darker welt in the center, as if… "My God, were you hit with a pipe?"

He briefly met her eyes again. "Yeah. I think that's what it was." He took a bottle of antiseptic spray from the first-aid kit and sprayed it on his arm. It had to sting, but he didn't even blink.

"God, Blue, if they'd hit you with this much force on your head…" Lucy sat back on her heels, feeling sick to her stomach. He could have been killed.

"They didn't," he said. "I was careful not to let them do that."

"Please tell me what happened." Slowly, carefully, trying to be gentle, Lucy lowered the ice pack onto Blue's leg. He didn't wince; he merely clenched his teeth a little tighter at the contact.

"I stayed behind at the cemetery," Blue said, using a roll of gauze to wrap up his arm.

"Do you want me to do that?" Lucy asked, interrupting him.

He sent her a tight smile. "No," he said. "Thanks. It's tricky doing it with only one hand, and that's keeping my focus off my leg."

"It must really hurt."

"Like a bitch," he agreed.

"It could be broken," Lucy said, worried.

"It's not," Blue said. "I've felt broken before and it's not."

He was sitting in the middle of her kitchen, wearing only a pair of white briefs, Lucy realized suddenly. Even battered and bruised, he was drop-dead gorgeous. Every inch of him was trim and fit and muscular and tanned a delicious golden brown.

"I hung back to visit my mother's grave," he was saying, continuing his story.

Lucy forced herself to pay attention to his words, not his body.

"I thought everyone had gone home from Gerry's burial, but apparently I was wrong. I was walking back to your truck, and I was jumped."

He'd rinsed the washcloth clean and was now using it to wipe rather ineffectively at the cut on his cheek. Lucy pulled another chair over and took the cloth from his hand, leaning across him to wash the cut for him. She had to use her left hand to push his hair back from his face. It felt thick and soft underneath her fingers. She tried not to think about it, tried not to think about his mouth, only inches away from hers.

"Did you see who it was who jumped you?" she asked evenly.

"My old friend Leroy Hurley was there," Blue said. "And Jedd Southeby. He was the owner of the pipe, I believe. I'm not sure who else was at the party. There were an awful lot of 'em."

Lucy pulled back slightly so she could look into his eyes. "How many?"

"I don't know."

She searched his eyes. Did he really not know, or was he keeping the truth from her? "Make a guess."

"More than fifteen, fewer than twenty."

Lucy's mouth dropped open. "*That* many?"

"Most of 'em weren't a real threat," Blue said. "When it was clear that I wasn't going to curl up into a little ball and die, most of 'em ran away."

Lucy's gaze dropped to the bandage on his arm. "Who exactly was the owner of the knife?" she asked.

"We weren't introduced," Blue said, "but he'll be the gentleman checking in to the county hospital with a broken hand."

Lucy laughed. She had to laugh, or she would start to cry. Still, her eyes welled with tears.

"Hey," Blue said softly. He gently touched the side of her

face with the tips of his fingers. "I'm okay, Yankee. It's the other fifteen guys who don't look so good right now."

"More than fifteen guys attack you, and *they're* the ones who don't look so good?" Lucy laughed again, and this time the tears escaped, flowing down her cheeks. "What if one of them had had a gun?"

"Someone probably would've been shot," Blue said, gently running his fingers back through her hair. "But there wasn't a gun. No one was badly hurt."

Lucy almost couldn't help herself. She almost put her arms around Blue's neck and held him close.

He could see it in her eyes, she knew, because his own eyes grew hotter, more liquid. Other than that, he didn't move a muscle.

Lucy made herself back away, wiping her face free of tears with her hands.

"I have to go down to the station," she said, taking a tissue from a box on the kitchen counter and blowing her nose, trying desperately to break the highly charged mood that lingered in the room. She emptied the basin of water and rinsed out the washcloth. "I read the autopsy report and found something odd. Gerry had almost no alcohol in his bloodstream when he died."

Blue frowned. "It must be a lab error," he said. "Gerry was corked that night."

"Was he?" Lucy asked, turning to face him. "Or was he only trying to make you *think* he was? Did you actually smell alcohol on his breath?"

Blue was silent, trying to remember. "I don't know," he finally admitted.

"I was thinking about that whole incident," Lucy said, leaning back against the sink, "and it occurred to me—I've never asked what Gerry whispered to you before you left the country club. Do you remember?"

Blue nodded, the muscle working in his jaw. "He said,

'I'm sorry, but you have to leave town.' You know, I thought he was referring to Jenny Lee—that he didn't want me around stirring up the past during his wedding. But now…'"

"What if he knew something bad was going to happen?" Lucy asked. "What if he staged that whole drunk scene because it was the only way he could communicate with you?"

Blue stared down at the ice pack on his leg. "That was one hell of a way to communicate," he said. "Why wouldn't he just pull me aside and talk to me?"

"Maybe he couldn't," Lucy said, excitement tingeing her voice. "Maybe he knew he was in danger. Maybe he knew someone was going to kill him."

"Why wouldn't he tell me about it?" Blue asked, looking back up at her, his frustration vibrating in his own voice. "I could've helped him. I could've kept him safe."

Lucy shook her head. "I don't know," she admitted. "But the first thing I've got to do is talk to some of the people who were at that party—people who interacted with Gerry. And I'll have the lab double-check the results of the autopsy blood test. I want to find out for sure if Gerry *was* sober that night."

She picked up her raincoat from where she'd thrown it over the back of a chair. "I'm going down to the station right now," she said. "Will you be all right alone?"

He smiled. "I'll be fine."

Lucy started for the door, but then turned back. "My bathroom has a Jacuzzi in it," she said. "Maybe it would help your leg to sit in it for a while."

Blue shook his head. "That's all right. I don't want to invade your personal space—"

"Please," she said. "Use it. I'll be back as soon as I can."

Chapter Ten

Sheldon Bradley sat behind his big, oak desk and stared at Lucy. "That's ridiculous," the police chief said. "Whether or not Gerry McCoy was drunk at a party has nothing to do with the events that transpired nearly three hours later—events that led to his death."

"I think it does," she said, stubbornly holding her ground. "I intend to talk to the people who were there—people who spoke to Gerry before his outburst. R. W. Fisher had a long conversation with Gerry—"

"No," Bradley said, rising to his feet. "Absolutely not. This has gone too far. I'm taking you off this case. In fact, I'm temporarily suspending you from the force."

Shocked, Lucy stood up, too. "What?"

"I've had word of your inappropriate behavior concerning Blue McCoy," the chief said. "Clearly, your judgment is skewed."

He sat down again, opening a file—her personnel file, Lucy realized. "Sir, I have done *nothing* that could be considered inappropriate."

Bradley looked up at her, eyebrows raised. "Do you deny then that the chief suspect in this case is sharing your house with you? And before you perjure yourself, darlin', be warned that neighbors *have* seen McCoy come home with you at night and leave with you in the morning."

"He needed a place to stay!"

"So naturally, you offer him your bed?"

"I did no such thing—"

"Officially, the charge would be sexual misconduct," Bradley told her, "and the punishment would be dismissal, not mere suspension. But you're young and you're new, and I give everyone here one mistake. This one is certainly yours."

"But, sir—"

"I suggest you keep your mouth closed, Ms. Tait," Bradley said, "because I am going to say this only once, *and* this matter is *not* negotiable. I'm suspending you for at least one week, your return subject to my approval. You'll turn in your badge and your sidearm." He held up his hand. "However, I'll record the suspension in your permanent file as an unpaid vacation. There'll be no further questions asked, no more talk about this matter and no ugly blot on your record. Unless, of course, you raise a racket about it."

Lucy shook her head. She felt numb. "But I did nothing wrong."

"I'm not asking you for a signed confession," he said. "Like I said, as of this moment, there will be no more questions asked—"

"Yet I'm suspended."

"Yes, you are."

"Because you think I had sex with Blue McCoy."

Bradley winced at her lack of delicacy. "I don't wish to discuss the details—"

"But I'm telling you that I *didn't*."

"Other individuals have expressed their concerns and

suspicions, fearing that you have allowed yourself to…shall we say, fall under the suspect's…influence." Bradley closed her file. "I have no desire to attempt to judge exactly who is right or wrong in this matter—"

"But you are," Lucy said. "By suspending me, you're finding me guilty of something that I did *not* do."

"Are you telling me that your opinions about this case are one hundred percent impartial?"

Lucy couldn't answer that, and she knew her silence damned her.

Bradley leaned forward. "Do yourself a favor, Lucy," he said. "Take a vacation. Leave town for a few days—at least until this mess is over."

"I can't do that," Lucy said. She was so angry her voice shook.

"Don't make this worse than it has to be," Bradley said. "Don't make me have to fire you."

"If you're charging me with sexual misconduct, I want to be officially charged."

"If I charge you," Bradley said tightly, "the penalty will *not* be suspension. As I said, you will be removed from the force."

"*If* I'm found guilty," Lucy said.

Bradley had had enough. "Fine," he said. "I find you guilty. Hearing closed. You're fired, darlin'." He tossed her personnel file into the garbage can. "Leave your badge and your gun on my desk and get the hell out of my office."

"If that's your idea of a fair hearing, then I don't want to work for you. You can't fire me—I quit!"

She nearly threw her badge and her gun down onto Bradley's desk.

"I'll pass along your reports on the investigation to Travis Southeby," the chief said.

Travis Southeby? "You're letting Travis take over the investigation?" Lucy was aghast.

Travis Southeby, whose brother Jedd had been among the group of men who'd attacked Blue just this afternoon. Travis Southeby, who'd stood up in the Grill because he didn't want to eat dinner in the same room as Gerry's "killer."

Travis Southeby? Impartial investigator?

Not even close.

Frustration and anger bubbled inside Lucy, and she left Chief Bradley's office, slamming the door behind her.

Blue closed his eyes, leaning back in the tub and letting the water gently massage his aching leg.

When Lucy had first told him about the Jacuzzi in her tub, he'd imagined it was one of those little tiny ones. Instead, it was a great big hot tub with room enough to throw a party.

He tried to imagine Lucy serving champagne and wine as she and a bunch of her friends sat laughing and talking in this tub. But he couldn't picture it. It seemed too out of character. He tried to imagine her sitting in this tub with the man in that photo on her dresser, having a very, very private party. That picture came far too easily, and he shook his head, trying to clear his mind of that image. He didn't want to picture that.

He tried to imagine her, instead, coming back from the police station. He could picture her clearly, dressed in those sinfully snug-fitting blue jeans and those black cowboy boots, black tank top clinging to her curves, her shining hair loose around her shoulders. She'd lean in the doorway for a moment, watching him with the temperature in her dark-brown eyes soaring way past that of the hot tub. Then she'd straighten up and pull her shirt up and over her head and—

Blue opened his eyes at the sound of the kitchen door opening. Lucy was back. He heard her toss her keys down onto the kitchen table. The refrigerator door opened.

"Blue, you want a beer?" he heard her call out.

He didn't have to think about it. "Yeah. Thanks." Damn, he would have accepted an offer of hemlock if it meant she'd bring it up here to him.

He heard the thump of the refrigerator door as she closed it. A drawer opened in the kitchen and she fished around, looking for something. Then he heard the sound of bottle caps being removed, a thud as she put what had to be a bottle opener down on the table and two smaller thuds as she tossed the caps into the trash.

Then he heard her climbing up the stairs. Mercy, just the thought of Lucy walking in here had made him hard as rock. He forced himself to keep breathing, to relax. She was bringing him a beer. Nothing more. But maybe if he wasn't shooting pheromones into the air, if he could look as if he didn't want to gobble her up, maybe then she'd sit down and talk to him awhile.

That was really what he wanted. True, he'd give damn near anything to have sex with this woman, but he wouldn't risk scaring her away. Because he needed her company tonight—her smile, the sound of her husky laughter, the warmth of her eyes and maybe most important her patient and unswerving belief in him. He needed all that more than he needed sexual relief.

And then she was standing in the doorway.

Blue could sense her tension. He picked up her undercurrent of anger and frustration before she even spoke.

"I hope American beer is okay," she said, handing him the dark-brown bottle. She turned to pull the shade down on the window. "It was on sale and—"

"It's fine," he said. Her hands were shaking and her voice was unnaturally tight. But she was working so hard to hide it from him, he wasn't sure if he should ask her what was wrong. "How'd it go in town?" he asked instead, keeping the question neutral, his voice light.

"Well, it went," she said, taking a long pull of her beer. "It went straight to hell in a handbasket." She turned and gazed directly into his eyes. "Mind if I climb in there with you?"

Blue's heart stopped. And then it jump-started in double time. "No," he somehow managed to say.

Lucy leaned against the sink to pull off her boots and socks. She tossed them into the bedroom, then unzipped her pants.

As Blue watched, she wriggled out of her blue jeans. Her legs were longer and even more shapely than he remembered. Her panties were bright white against her tanned skin. Mercy. He was going to die.

She didn't look at him as she peeled her shirt up and over her head and threw it down on top of her jeans. Her bra was also white, and she unfastened the front clasp as if she casually stripped naked in front of a man every day of her life. Her breasts were beautiful, so full and firm, with dark-brown tips that tightened under his gaze. Her body was exactly as he'd imagined it. She was slender, yet she had some real muscle in her arms and legs and torso, giving her body shape and definition. Her stomach was flat, her hips curving softly out.

He was going to explode, Blue realized. Out of all the ways he'd imagined that this evening would end, he hadn't considered the possibility that Lucy would throw all her cautions and reserves to the wind and make love to him. He'd fantasized about it, but he never believed it could possibly happen. Just last night she'd locked her door tightly against him. He knew she'd locked it—he'd tried the knob.

So what had happened between now and then? What had happened between now and just a few hours ago, when Lucy had maintained that they stay friends instead of lovers?

Lucy slid her panties down her legs and moved up the steps to the top edge of the hot tub. She paused for a moment, looking down at him, boldly meeting his eyes. "You seem to have run out of things to say," she said.

She slid down, letting the water slowly cover her body. She sat, a full half circle away from him. Closing her eyes, she let her head fall back against the side of the tub.

"I'm just trying to figure out when I died and went to heaven," Blue said.

Lucy opened her eyes. "You're not in heaven, McCoy— at least not yet."

Blue had to laugh. This was just too much. He couldn't have written a better script for a sexual fantasy himself. "Lucy, I'm confused as hell," he admitted. "What's going on here?"

"I decided I'd come home and seduce you." Her eyes suddenly looked uncertain, vulnerable. Her voice got very soft. "Am I doing it wrong?"

"Oh, no," Blue said quickly. "No, you're doing it perfectly. I just don't understand *why* you're doing it."

"I was suspended from the police force," she said in that same low voice. "For sexual misconduct."

"But—"

"I had no real hearing and no chance to challenge the charges," she said, her voice growing stronger. There was a spark of anger in her eyes. "Bradley removed me from the investigation and gave me a one-week suspension, disguised as a vacation. I argued—he fired me—I quit."

Blue swore. "This is my fault."

"You didn't do anything wrong," Lucy said. "And I didn't, either. But I figured as long as I've been tried, convicted and I'm serving sentence for breaking a rule I didn't break, well, hell, I might as well break that rule, right?"

Blue didn't know what to do, what to say. She wasn't here because she honestly wanted to be. She was here in some kind of knee-jerk reaction to her altercation with Chief Bradley.

With any other woman, Blue wouldn't have hesitated. With any other woman, he would have already been on the other side of the hot tub, performing a seduction of his own. She'd taken it this far; he could easily see it through to its climax, so to speak.

But...Lucy was his friend. She had been right earlier today. Something had developed between them that could only be called friendship. And as much as Blue wanted her, he didn't want her this way.

So he kept his distance and waited for her to answer her own question.

"But this really isn't me," she finally said. "I mean, I don't...do things like this. I've never tried to seduce someone before...."

"Yankee, I do believe you're a natural," Blue said with a slow smile.

Lucy laughed, covering her face with her hands. "I'm feeling pretty stupid."

"Don't be," he said. "I'm in serious pain."

"Then why are you sitting way over there?"

Her soft question made the bathroom seem suddenly very, *very* quiet. Blue could hear his watch ticking from underneath the pile of clean clothes he'd brought into the room. He moistened his dry lips. Damn, he couldn't remember ever being this nervous with a woman before. "Do you want me to sit next to you?" he asked.

Her eyes were wide and a bottomless shade of brown as she gazed at him. "I don't know what I want," she admitted.

Blue took a deep breath, trying to slow his raging pulse, trying to lower his soaring blood pressure. "When *you* know," he said, "then you let *me* know."

She was silent, just staring at him. "I can't believe you're turning me down," she said at last.

"I'm not turning you down, because you haven't made me a real offer," Blue said quietly. "You make me an offer, Lucy, and I assure you, I will not turn you down."

There was wonder in her eyes, wonder and the sheen of tears. "You told me you weren't a gentleman," she said.

"I'm not."

Which was why he had to get out of there. Right now. Blue stood, water sheeting off him. He climbed up the stairs and out of the tub, trying not to limp. He could feel Lucy's eyes on him, skimming over his nakedness, and he wrapped his towel around his waist. She couldn't have missed his state of arousal. Even though he'd tried his best to calm his raging libido, he could have sat in the tub forever and still it wouldn't have completely gone away.

"What do you say we go downstairs and I cook us both some dinner?" Blue said. He didn't wait for her to say no. "Throw some clothes on and meet me in the kitchen."

It was nearly ten o'clock before dinner was over.

Lucy had gone into the kitchen with some trepidation, but Blue did or said nothing to remind her how foolishly she'd behaved up in the bathroom.

He made her set the table and then sit and do nothing but watch as he cooked up a fragrant pot of spaghetti sauce and pasta.

As he cooked, and then as they ate, he told her the story of how his friend and swim buddy, Joe Cat, had met his wife, Veronica. She was a seemingly prim-and-proper media consultant who worked for European royalty. He was a rough, tough Navy SEAL from a bad part of New Jersey. According to Blue, it was love at first sight—only, both Joe Cat and Veronica stubbornly refused to acknowledge it.

"Do you really believe in love at first sight?" Lucy asked Blue as he began washing up the dishes.

"Yeah," he admitted. "I know it sounds corny, but, yeah, I do. I saw it happen with Cat. Something just grabbed him and wouldn't let go. It scared the hell out of me. One day everything was normal, and the next Cat was totally out of control."

Lucy was silent. She understood. She was falling in love with Blue, and it was way, way beyond her control.

"Cat and Veronica both tried to run away from what they felt," Blue said in his slow Southern drawl. "But you can't run away from something that's inside you. I saw that first-hand. Cat was miserable without Veronica."

And Lucy would be miserable without Blue. But why force herself to be miserable *with* him, too? She *could* have him— even if only for a few days, even if only on a physical level.

She knew Blue wanted their relationship to be a sexual one. Even though he'd gallantly turned her down up in the hot tub, he'd made that more than clear. She could have his body. All she had to do was ask. It was more than nothing, and it would have to be enough.

Why should she refuse herself even just an hour or two of happiness and pleasure? Yes, Blue was going to leave. No, Blue wasn't in love with her. Yes, she'd probably be just a substitute for Jenny Lee Beaumont. But Lucy didn't have to think about that. She didn't have to make herself miserable. She had the entire rest of her life to do that. She deserved at least a day or two of happiness now, even if it was only false happiness.

But how was Lucy supposed to tell him that she finally knew what she wanted—that she wanted to make love to him?

Another seduction attempt? The thought made her squirm.

Make me an offer, he'd said. That kind of offer seemed so unromantic, so calculated and cold.

Maybe instead of an offer, she could issue an invitation.

Lucy stood. "I'm going to head upstairs," she said. "Unless you want me to help clean up?"

Blue glanced at her over his shoulder and then at his

watch. It was still early, and he was clearly disappointed that she was leaving. "No, that's all right," he said. "I'm almost done down here."

"Good night, then," she said, and started out of the room. "Lucy."

Lock your door. He didn't have to say it aloud. "I know," she said. Heading up the stairs, she smiled.

Blue tried calling California from the telephone in the kitchen as he finished up the dishes. Yes, Lieutenant Joe Catalanotto was still out on a training mission. Yes, Admiral Mac Forrest was still not available.

He hung up the phone, fighting a feeling of dread.

Lucy was no longer in charge of Gerry's murder investigation. Travis Southeby was. Blue figured it was only a matter of days, maybe even hours, before Southeby found what he felt was enough evidence to lock Blue up. Tomorrow Blue very well might be in jail.

And today Blue had had heaven in his hands, and like a damn fool, he'd let it slip away.

It was still early—before midnight, anyway—and he was feeling way too restless to sleep. His leg hurt too badly to go for a run, but a walk might do him good.

He headed upstairs to get his handgun and…

The door to Lucy's room was unlocked and open a crack.

Her room was dark inside, but the door had definitely been left open.

Dammit, he wasn't strong enough for this. He'd turned her down once tonight, but there was no way he could handle twice. He knocked loudly on her door. "Hey," he said crossly. "Yankee. You forgot to lock up."

"No, I didn't." Her voice was soft, but very certain.

The meaning of her words crashed down around him, and Blue had to hold on to the door frame for a moment to keep his balance. She'd left the door open. Intentionally.

"May I…come in?" he asked.

He heard her husky laugh. "How many invitations do you want, McCoy?"

Blue pushed open the door. The dim light from the hallway spilled all the way across Lucy's room, falling onto her bed. She was sitting there, wearing an old extra large T-shirt and a pair of panties and quite probably nothing else.

Her hair was down around her shoulders and she had no makeup on her face. She looked clean and fresh, and as she smiled hesitantly at him, he couldn't believe how utterly beautiful she was.

She held out her arms, shrugging slightly, her smile turning almost apologetic. "This is me," she said, laughing self-consciously. "What you see right now is really me. No negligee. No borrowed little black dress or spike heels. No fancy hairdo. No hot-tub seduction. Just an old University of South Carolina T-shirt and a pair of cotton underpants. White. No frills. Just like me. If you decide to…accept my…invitation, this is what you get."

Blue knew instantly that this was what he'd been waiting for. She had no police badge to hide behind, no hesitation, no more doubts. She'd worked their relationship down to the simplest equation: she wanted him and he wanted her.

And oh, how he wanted her. He'd had his share of women wearing fancy negligees and seductive clothing, but none of them looked even half as sexy as Lucy Tait did in an old university T-shirt with her hair tumbling down her back, her face clean of makeup. No frills, she'd said. Maybe not. Maybe just one hundred percent pure woman.

Blue sat down on the bed next to Lucy and gave her his answer in a kiss. Despite all the fire surging through his veins it was a sweet kiss—the sweetest he'd ever known. He felt her fingers on his chest, unfastening the buttons of his shirt and he put his hand over hers, stopping her, slowing her down.

"We've got all night," he whispered, pulling back to look at her.

He closed his eyes as she ran her fingers through his hair. It felt sinfully, deliciously, good.

"Then you won't mind if I just sit here and do this for about an hour," Lucy said.

"Not as long as I can kiss you, Yankee," Blue murmured, pressing his lips to hers.

He pulled her back with him onto the bed, and their legs intertwined, and still he kissed her. He gave her long, slow, deep kiss after long, slow, deep kiss, until her breath grew short, her hands gripped him tighter and her body strained against his.

Deftly, he removed her T-shirt, pulling it up and over her head in one quick motion. And then all of her smooth, sleek skin was his to touch, to caress, to kiss.

Lucy was delirious. She'd known that making love with Blue was going to be an extraordinary experience, but she'd never imagined that his hands could be so gentle. She'd never dreamed that he could kiss her so slowly, so completely.

She'd imagined a frantic, urgent joining, not this languorous, sensuous worship of her body. She clung to him as he brought his lips down first to one breast and then the other, laving her tender nipples with his tongue, drawing them slowly into his mouth.

She tugged at his shirt and he slipped it off, tossing it onto the floor along with his shoulder holster. As she ran her fingers across the satiny skin of his back, careful of the bandage on his arm, his mouth journeyed downward, to her stomach, stopping to explore the softness of her belly button.

Heat pooled through her, sending liquid fire through her veins. Her love for this man seemed such a tangible thing that Lucy was almost certain he could see it.

"You're so beautiful," he whispered, meeting her gaze and

smiling as he slid her panties down her legs. The heat in his eyes was more than lust. It was more powerful, more pure—almost transcendental, making the blue of his eyes seem luminous and soft.

For the first time in her life, Lucy felt cherished.

She knew it couldn't possibly be so. In reality, Blue didn't love her. He would never love her. But she fought that reality, allowing herself the complete illusion tonight. Tonight, she would be cherished.

He kissed the inside of her knee, parting her legs as he slowly moved his mouth down toward the sensitive skin of her thigh. And farther. Lucy gripped the bed as he touched her, kissed her, first gently, then harder, deeper.

The sensation was beyond pleasure, beyond ecstasy, beyond anything she had ever felt or known before. And that, in tandem with her love for this man, catapulted her up and over the edge.

She heard herself cry out as he held her tighter, as a sudden and unexpected release cannonballed through her, seeming to rip her apart with wave upon wave upon unending wave of sheer, excruciatingly wild pleasure.

Finally, *finally*, it came to an end. She reached for Blue, pulling him up and across her. He was laughing, real delight in his eyes.

"Hoo-yah," he said.

"Oh, man," Lucy gasped.

"Do you do that all the time, Yankee?" he asked, smoothing her hair back from her face.

"No," she breathed. "Never. Not like that."

His smile grew broader, satisfied. "Good."

He kissed her, slowly, tenderly, but that wasn't what she wanted. She deepened their kiss and reached for his belt, unbuckling it.

"Mercy." Blue pulled back, laughing again. "You want *more?*"

"Yes." Lucy unzipped his pants, tracing his length with her fingers. There was so much of him. She ached to feel him inside her. "Please." She reached down into his shorts, touching him, encircling him with her hand as she kissed him fiercely.

She heard him groan, felt him pull away as he pushed and kicked his pants from his legs. She tried to help, but she suspected she only made the process more difficult. Still, she wanted to touch him, to run her hands along the lengths of his long, muscular legs—

Oh, shoot, she'd forgotten all about his injured leg. She pulled back. "Oh, Blue, have I hurt you?"

He just laughed at that, catching her mouth with his and kissing her, hard. She felt herself melt against him, opening herself to him in every possible way. She reached down to touch him again and found he'd already ensheathed himself with a condom he must have taken from his pocket.

He kissed her again, a kiss of fire and passion, and she felt something shift, as if the powerful kick of their rocket fuel-powered attraction was ready now to ignite. She knew instantly that this phase of their lovemaking would be neither slow nor languorous.

Blue felt Lucy arch her hips up toward him, seeking him, and he felt the first tier of his ragged control start to crack. He needed to feel her surrounding him. Now.

He plunged into her, hard and fast…and mercy! He had to slow down, take care. He didn't want to hurt her.

Yet she was anything but hurt. "Yes," she was murmuring into his ear, "yes," pulling him closer, meeting each of his thrusts with a dizzying passion.

This was too good. No one should ever be allowed to feel this good. The thought made him laugh aloud and he kissed Lucy again, spinning with the joy and exhilaration of knowing he was exactly, precisely, where he wanted to be.

He rolled over onto his back, pulling her with him so she

sat straddling him. She flicked her hair back out of her eyes, moving hard and fast, the way he liked it. She grinned down at him, her eyes sparkling and dancing with sheer pleasure, and more of his precious control crumbled.

He reached for her, his hands covering her breasts, and she arched her body, pressing herself more fully into his palms. She threw her head back, her smile fading, and Blue felt her body tense and tighten. She cried out his name, her voiced ecstasy music to his ears. Her release was as powerful as before, only this time she took him with her.

Never before had his pleasure been so perfect. Never before had the rush of his passionate explosion sent him soaring quite so high, quite so far. Never before had he wanted to take a moment in time and freeze it for all eternity.

But it wasn't the moment of mind-blowing, raw sexual pleasure that he'd freeze. It was this moment afterward, as he held Lucy tightly against him, his face buried in her hair, their two hearts still beating wildly as they drifted slowly back to earth. This was the moment he wanted to save and keep forever. Because never before had he felt such peace, such completeness.

His chest ached and his eyes burned, and he wanted to speak, wanted to tell her something, but he didn't know what to say. He didn't know what words he could use that could possibly describe this feeling. So he kissed her, instead, sweetly, gently, hoping she'd understand.

Chapter Eleven

Blue woke up several hours after dawn. He stretched and yawned, feeling oddly rested. He hadn't slept this well in a long time and...

He opened his eyes.

He was in Lucy's bed. She was lying next to him, still sleeping peacefully, the sheets tangled around her.

Memories of last night came roaring back to him in a rush, and for a moment he could barely breathe, barely think. The things they'd done, the things he'd felt...

Mercy.

But the sun had crept up above the tree line, and it was shining in Lucy's windows. The night had ended and it was morning.

Morning. The time of regrets and recriminations. The time of awkward silences and uncomfortable conversations. Like some broken spell, the magic of the night before always shriveled and died in the morning light.

A night of sex was understood by all to be nothing more than a good time. But when breakfast was added to the equation, that night of sex became something else entirely. It became a relationship. It became a possibility, an expectation, a future commitment. Blue had long since learned to clear out of a lady's bedroom well before dawn.

This time he hadn't. This time the spell he'd been under had held him in its power and he'd slept the dreamless sleep of the enchanted. But now he eased himself up and off the bed. There was still time to make his escape.

Lucy remained asleep. But as he looked at her lying there, his eyes followed the exposed curve of her derriere, the gentle swell of her breast as she lay on her stomach, her arms tucked up underneath the pillow. He felt an unexpected surge of desire.

The few times he'd stayed with a woman until the morning, he'd awoken with his lust abated, his sexual attraction fading fast. Aided by the harsh morning light, his lover's slept-in and smudged makeup, disheveled hair and usually bloodshot eyes left him wanting nothing more than to leave, and leave quickly.

But Lucy looked like some kind of angel in the early-morning light. Her skin seemed to glow, it was so smooth and perfect. He wanted to reach out and touch her. He wanted to feel her softness beneath his fingers again. Her hair was messed, but on her it looked sexy. And her face...

She was impossibly beautiful. Her lashes were long and dark and they lay against cheeks that had been kissed by the sun. Her mouth was open very slightly, and her lips looked so moist....

Lucy stirred slightly and Blue ran, noiselessly leaving her room before her eyes opened. He ran because he'd always run away before.

"'Morning," Blue said, clearly ill at ease, not quite meeting Lucy's eyes as he opened the refrigerator and took out the pitcher of orange juice.

Lucy had been down in the kitchen for nearly an hour before he'd appeared. As she watched, he helped himself to a glass from the cabinet and poured the juice, still not looking at her.

The last of Lucy's hopes shattered into a million tiny pieces.

She was a fool. She knew when she'd awakened to see Blue making his clandestine escape from her room that he was most likely regretting their lovemaking. Of course, he might have been leaving to replenish his supply of condoms. But when he didn't return even after she'd stepped out of the shower, even after she'd taken her time getting dressed, even after she'd opened her door and stood staring at the quite obviously closed door to his room, she knew.

Still, she'd hoped that he wasn't having true regrets. Maybe he was having only mild doubts, second thoughts. But looking at him standing there in her kitchen, poised as if ready to turn and run, she knew for sure.

For him, last night had been nothing but a big, fat, giant mistake. She was a fool for hoping he'd feel otherwise. She was a fool for hoping that somehow, someway, he'd fall in love with her. A very small, *very* foolish part of her had actually dreamed that Blue McCoy would make love to her— to no-frills, white-cotton Lucy Tait—and the earth would shake and the skies would open and he would realize that she was his life, his future, his reason for living.

Oh, yeah, she was a fool.

But at least she was a sensible fool. Her fantasies crushed and useless, she swept them away, out of sight, at least for now. She'd have plenty of time to feel badly later.

"Do you want breakfast?" she asked, her voice remarkably even as she busied herself with washing up her own breakfast dishes.

"I'll just fix myself some toast."

"That's good," she said. "You can bring it with you."

She could feel his surprise, even though her back was to him.

"We going someplace?"

Lucy wrung out the dish sponge and set it on the edge of the sink before she turned to face him. "I called Jenny Lee and asked if she would mind if we stopped by. She said yes, we should come around nine-thirty, and that that would also be a convenient time for us to take a look at Gerry's home office and—"

"Wait a minute, you lost me somewhere back around bringing my toast along to Jenny Lee's. I don't understand. Why are we going to her place?"

Lucy turned and stared at him. He truly didn't understand. For the first time since he'd come downstairs, he was looking at her, really looking at her, instead of through her or over her or under her or around her.

"I thought you were taken off the investigation," Blue said. "You said you quit. You're not even on the police force anymore."

Lucy nodded. "That's right."

"You don't need to do this," he said.

She nodded again. "Yeah, I know. But I *want* to do this. We're the only ones who want to find out who really killed Gerry. Travis Southeby is going to mess around until he finds enough circumstantial evidence to haul you in. If we don't try to discover who might've had a motive for wanting Gerry dead, the real killer is going to run free while you go directly to jail." She shrugged. "I currently seem to be between jobs and I have some free time on my hands, so..."

Blue was silent. He'd looked away from her again, and was studying the wide antique boards of the kitchen floor.

"You don't intend to just roll over and die, do you?" Lucy asked.

He glanced up. "No, but—"

"Neither do I," she said, well aware that her words had a deeper, hidden meaning.

"Why do you want to help me?" His question was point-blank, and it came with no warning. He was watching her again, his eyes almost piercing in intensity.

Because I love you. But she couldn't tell him that. Not so long as a small portion of her pride was still intact. "Because I know you didn't kill Gerry," she said, instead. "Because right now you've got no one else. And because I'm your friend."

He was silent again, still watching her, and she knew exactly what he was thinking. He was thinking about last night, about how their lovemaking had permanently altered their so-called friendship. What they were to each other wasn't as simple as being friends anymore. But it was clear that Blue didn't want them to continue on as lovers, so where, exactly, did that leave them?

He so obviously wanted to pack his bag and walk away from her. But where would he go? What would he do?

Blue needed her right now, whether he knew it or not. Lucy believed that. She *had* to believe that. It was all she had left.

"I *am* your friend," she told him quietly. "Last night we were lovers, but today I'm your friend again, McCoy. I expect nothing from you. I didn't last night, and I certainly don't this morning—nothing, that is, but friendship. So you can stop tiptoeing around me as if I'm going to act all hurt and upset because last night wasn't the start of happily ever after. I know nothing has changed, except that now I know exactly where to touch you to really turn you on."

He laughed, his voice tinged with a mixture of disbelief and respect. "Hell, you're not afraid to get right to the heart of the matter, are you?"

Lucy raised her eyebrows, crossing her arms in front of

her. "Was I supposed to pretend I didn't notice you having some kind of morning-after anxiety attack?"

"Well, I don't know. Yeah. Most women would...."

"I was just supposed to let you walk away because suddenly *you're* uncomfortable with the fact that last night we got naked and had sex—*great* sex, I might add." Lucy glared at him. "You honestly expected me to just throw away your friendship? Forget it, McCoy. I can deal with your thinking that I might overreact. It's probably been your poor, pathetic experience that 'most women' do. But thinking I would just ditch your friendship...*that* hurts."

"I'm sorry," he said, and he actually looked as if he was. "It's just... I've never slept with a...a friend before. This is a new one for me. I'm not sure what to say to you...or what to do."

"You could say, 'Good morning, Lucy. Gee, you really rocked my world last night,'" she told him. She took the loaf of bread from the bread box on the counter and tossed it to him with a touch more force than necessary. "And then you could make your damned toast so we could get to work finding out who killed Gerry."

Blue sat in Lucy's truck and watched her drive. Going to Jenny Lee's hadn't given them any more answers.

No, Gerry didn't seem to have any enemies. Yes, his behavior had been odd over the past several days, but Jenny had believed it was due to Blue's impending arrival. Business had been picking up for his construction company over the past year. Gerry had had a number of projects in development and several in progress. Money was coming in and going out on a regular basis. His staff were all steadily employed; in fact, he'd had to hire carpenters and construction workers from an employment agency for a recent job.

A search of Gerry's office had provided no additional information. Nothing was unusual about any of his current projects. His files were all in order, his desk free from any mention or warning of any threats. His date book had no appointments circled in red saying "lunch with killers."

Gerry had had a normal amount of business meetings listed in his date book. Lucy had gone painstakingly through all the different names, matching them to his current projects. Some of them were clients he was wooing. And some of them were social appointments. He'd had lunch with Jenny Lee frequently, and he'd also apparently recently joined the Hatboro Creek Men's Club, R. W. Fisher's invitation-only elite organization that took on community projects. According to Gerry's notes, they were currently raising money to repair the roof of the county hospital.

No, this trip to the house that Gerry had shared with Jenny Lee hadn't provided any answers. However, it had raised some new questions for Blue.

Such as, why exactly was Lucy Tait going to all this trouble for him? Why had she slept with him last night? What did she really want? If there was one thing Blue had learned in life, it was that most people had motives for every little thing they did. What was Lucy's motive here?

She'd said she was helping him out of friendship, that she'd slept with him because she'd wanted to, no strings attached. But Blue found that hard to believe. Of course, he was suspicious by nature. Since he was small he'd had only himself to rely on. Trusting other people meant risking pain, so he'd learned to trust no one.

But then he'd become a SEAL, and he'd literally had to put his life in his teammates' hands. He'd learned to trust the men in his squad and unit, and that trust had grown deep and strong, bonded by friendship and loyalty.

SEALs had no ulterior motives, at least not beyond unit integrity. Sure, they had career drives and personal goals, but in the heat of battle, in the midst of an operation, getting the job done and getting everyone out alive and in one piece became the single motivating force.

Lucy Tait wasn't a SEAL, but she said she was his friend.

He had to smile when he remembered her direct confrontation in the kitchen this morning. He had to hand it to her; she was tough. He himself would jump into a fistfight without a moment's hesitation, but if the battle was an emotional one, he'd do all that he could to beat a retreat. Lucy, instead, had attacked.

Blue was glad that she had. Even though they'd gotten nowhere with their investigation by talking to Jenny Lee, he was glad Lucy hadn't let him walk away, glad he was sitting here next to her in her truck.

He liked having Lucy for a friend. It was odd—she was a woman, yet she *was* his friend. Even odder was the fact that they'd had incredibly intense sex last night, and this morning Lucy, somehow, was *still* his friend.

Blue couldn't remember ever having had a sexual experience as powerful. She *had* rocked his world last night. So why the hell had he backed away this morning? Why had he allowed the night to end? Why hadn't he stayed in her bed? They could have been there still, up in her bedroom, making love all day long. He could have been holding her, kissing her, gazing into her beautiful eyes, commanding her complete and total attention as he told her stories of the operations he'd been on, the high-risk missions he'd completed.

Why had he backed away?

Because he always backed away. He hadn't even considered the possibility of sticking around, of turning their one-night stand into a longer affair. He hadn't known that Lucy could still be his friend after becoming his lover. He simply hadn't known.

But could they honestly be friends during the day and lovers at night? Could that really work?

Something about it didn't sit right with him. Now that he'd had time to think about it, he felt as if he were taking advantage of her. It seemed as if he were using her. And he wouldn't—couldn't—do that to a friend.

It would probably be best if they kept sex out of their friendship. It wouldn't be easy, not with the memories of last night crashing into him every time he looked in Lucy's direction. No, it wouldn't be easy, but it would be the right thing to do.

Maybe Lucy was telling the truth and she was helping him find Gerry's killer purely out of friendship. If that was so, the least he could do was treat her with an equal respect.

Blue watched Lucy as she drove. She handled her big truck with the same air of calm confidence that she handled damn near everything. She wasn't wearing her uniform—she couldn't now that she'd resigned from the police force. Instead, she had on her worn-out blue jeans and cowboy boots and a plain T-shirt—white, cotton, no frills. Damn, but she looked good.

She glanced over, as if she felt him watching her. "What do you say we go over and talk to Matt Parker before lunch?"

Matt Parker. The "witness" who had "seen" Blue arguing with Gerry in the woods off Gate's Hill Road moments before Gerry's death. He had also been one of the joyriding dirt bikers who had obscured the tire tracks Blue had found. Blue nodded and smiled tightly. He definitely wanted to have a little talk with Parker. "Yeah."

Lucy looked at him again, concern darkening her eyes. "Just a talk, McCoy," she said. "Do you understand what I'm saying?"

He met her gaze evenly. "He's not going to tell us anything new unless we use a new approach. Like scaring the devil out of him."

"And if he turns around and calls Chief Bradley with an assault complaint, there's nothing I could do to keep you out of jail," Lucy countered. "And you know as well as I do that Travis Southeby is itching for a reason to lock you up."

Lucy could see real frustration in Blue's eyes.

"Why bother talking to Parker at all?" he asked.

"Because somebody is paying him to say what he's saying," she said, "and I'm betting no matter how much money he's making, he's feeling lousy about having to lie. I'm betting he won't be able to look you in the eye, because deep down he's probably a decent man, and he knows his story is a solid part of the case they're building against you."

"And you think he's going to take one look at me and confess?" Blue's voice dripped with skepticism.

"No," Lucy said calmly. "I think we're going to go over there, and he's going to stick to his story, and we're going to leave. And then he's not going to be able to sleep tonight, because he's going to be thinking about his words sending an innocent man to prison."

Blue laughed. "Get real, Pollyanna," he said. "He's gonna spend the evening counting his blood money and drinking himself into a stupor. The fate of my sorry ass won't even drift across his soggy mind."

"He may not even let us in the door," Lucy admitted. "But we have to try." She pulled her truck to a stop outside the Parkers' little bungalow. "After lunch, I want to go up to Gate's Hill Road and start canvassing the neighborhood. Somebody had to see or hear something unusual that night."

"And if nobody did?"

She met his gaze evenly. "Then we're going to check motor-vehicle registration records, find a list of all the owners of trucks with oversize tires. We'll go check 'em all out, find out whose tires still have new treads. And if that doesn't give us a lead, we'll get a copy of the guest list for that country-club party and go and talk to every single person on it. I still want to find out if Gerry was only pretending to be drunk at the party. Someone somewhere knows something."

Blue's face softened as he smiled at her. "You're not going to give up on this, are you, Yankee?"

Lucy shook her head. "No." He should know that she wasn't going to give up on this case—or on him. If she could endure that visit with Jenny Lee Beaumont, she could handle just about anything. Shoot, watching Blue put his arms around Jenny in a comforting embrace had been deadly. And sitting there like that in Jenny Lee's picture-perfect living room had been awkward—Blue together with both his high-school sweetheart and his lover from last night. Of course, Jenny probably hadn't known that Lucy and Blue were lovers. But Lucy had, and it was weird.

Lucy had expended a great deal of energy trying *not* to watch for signs of Blue's old chemistry with Jenny. Still, she couldn't help but wonder if Blue had closed his eyes and pictured himself making love to Jenny Lee last night. Lucy had had temporary possession of Blue's body, but Jenny probably still owned Blue's heart.

Lucy would have given just about anything to have even a short-term lease on Blue's heart. But that wasn't going to happen. He'd made *that* more than clear this morning.

The silence in the truck dragged on much longer than it should have as Lucy lost herself in the hot depths of Blue's eyes. He still wanted her. She could see desire swirling in among the blue. She could see it in the set of his jaw, in the tension in his lips. What had transpired between them last night hadn't been enough. He wanted more.

But he turned away, clearly intent on denying himself even the warm pleasure of the memory of their lovemaking. Was it seeing Jenny Lee again? Lucy wondered. Could Blue's former girlfriend still have that much power over him? Lucy's stomach hurt. She'd told Blue just this morning that she was his friend. But she was his lover now, too. She knew that if he came to her room again tonight, she wouldn't be able to refuse him anything he wanted or needed. She loved him that much.

But what about what Lucy needed?

Blue looked out the windshield at Matt Parker's house and took a deep breath. "Let's get this over with."

Chapter Twelve

They were in luck. Little Tommy Parker answered the door and let them in the house.

Lucy knew from the look in Matt Parker's eyes that he wouldn't even have opened the screen door to talk to them. But now they were here, in his tiny living room.

She looked around. The furniture was shabby, but clean. In fact, the entire house looked well kept. The ancient orange shag carpeting had been recently vacuumed and the surfaces of the end tables were clear and free from dust and clutter.

She could hear the sounds of Sunday dinner being cooked down the short hallway that led to the kitchen. Utensils banged against pots, and dishes clattered as a table was set. The fragrant smell of onions frying drifted out into the living room.

Blue went farther into the room and turned off the TV that was on.

"Travis told me *he* was handling this case now." Parker's

eyes shifted from Lucy to Blue and then back. He was clearly remembering the fight outside the gas station. His nose was still swollen, and he touched it gingerly. "McCoy is not welcome in my house."

"We just want to ask you some questions," Lucy said soothingly. "You don't have a reason to want to hide the truth from us, do you, Matt?"

His eyes flicked back to Blue. "Of course not." He shifted slightly in his seat in a well-worn reclining chair. "But I answered all these questions already. My statement is down at the police station. Why don't you just get a copy of that, instead of bugging me again?"

"Well, we do have a copy of your statement," Lucy said, carefully keeping her voice reasonable and calm. "However, it raised an additional question or two, because Blue wasn't anywhere near Gate's Hill Road at the time you allegedly saw him there with Gerry."

Parker stood up. "Are you saying I'm a liar?"

"No, sir." Lucy gazed steadily at him. "You're too smart to get yourself into a situation where you'd have to perjure yourself in a court of law. You know the punishment for that can be a hefty fine along with jail time." She shook her head. "No, you're just mistaken about exactly what you saw. You must've seen someone else—not Blue. I'd like you to spend some time tonight thinking about it, because it would sure be a shame if your testimony sent an innocent man to prison, wouldn't it?"

She turned, heading back toward the door, and from the corner of her eyes she saw a shadow in the hallway, near the kitchen. It was Matt's wife, Darlene, but she disappeared before Lucy could even say hello.

"Let me know if you think of anything new," Lucy told Parker. She opened the front door and Blue followed her outside.

She could feel Parker—or maybe it was Darlene—watching them as they walked down the path to the street and her truck.

"You did okay," Blue told her as they got into her truck. "You said just enough to make the guilt stick—provided Parker has a conscience."

"Thanks." Lucy put the truck in gear and headed back toward the main road. "You did okay, too."

"I just stood there."

"Exactly." She glanced at him, unable to hide a smile. "You *didn't* slam him against the wall and threaten to tear his throat out. I know that's what you wanted to do."

His lips twitched upward into an answering smile. "I'm hurt and offended you could think such a thing, Yankee."

"Am I wrong?"

His smile became a grin. It transformed his face, making him look younger—and nearly paralyzingly handsome. "No, ma'am."

Lucy had to laugh. But when their eyes met, something sparked, something molten, something hot and liquid and filled with the trembling echoes of last night. As he'd done before, Blue was the first to look away.

Lucy turned her attention back to the road, trying not to care. Yet she couldn't help but feel disappointed. And she knew with a dreadful certainty exactly what she wanted, precisely what she needed.

She needed Blue McCoy by her side for the rest of her life.

Fat chance of *that* happening. But maybe if she played it right, she'd have Blue by her side again tonight. It was a pathetic substitute for what she really wanted, but it was all she could hope for.

Except Blue was still clearly uncomfortable with the hazy definition of their relationship. Were they friends, or were they lovers? He didn't seem to understand that they could be both. He didn't seem to realize that the best of lovers always were the best of friends, too.

If only she had enough time, she could set him straight. But time was not on her side.

Lucy glanced back at Blue, forcing a smile. "Come on, McCoy. Let's go knock on some doors up near Gate's Hill Road before lunch. Let's shake this town up. Maybe something of interest will fall out."

Dinner was over. The dishes had been cleaned up.

Lucy had gone out onto the porch to look up at the night sky and get a breath of fresh air.

Blue knew he shouldn't follow her out there. He'd told himself at least a hundred times during dinner and probably a thousand times during the course of the day that sex could not be a regular part of his relationship with Lucy. He respected her too much to use her that way. Unfortunately, that didn't stop him from wanting her. And he did. He wanted her so badly it hurt. But he'd lived through pain before. He could do it again.

They'd talked about the investigation over dinner, going over and over the same facts again and again, trying to find whatever it was that they were missing, searching for some kind of lead.

They'd learned nothing from their endless knocking on doors and questioning the folks who lived near the spot where Gerry had died. They'd learned nothing from Jenny Lee, nothing from Matt Parker.

It was frustrating as hell.

Blue picked up the phone and tried calling the naval base in California again. But Alpha Squad was still off base and the officer from Internal Affairs was still taking all calls. Blue tried to squash the frustration that rose inside him. He needed some serious help, yet here he was, on his own.

Not entirely on his own—he had Lucy Tait on his side.

Wanting desperately to see her warm, familiar smile, Blue pushed open the door and stepped outside onto the porch. He was coming out here to say good-night to her. Only to say good-night.

She was sitting on the steps, looking at the stars. She glanced up when she heard the door and smiled. Blue felt simultaneously better and worse. Mercy, he wanted to make love to her again tonight.

But he couldn't let himself. It wouldn't be right.

He sat down dangerously close to her—on the steps instead of across the porch on the swing—even though he knew sparks were going to fly. But he was a demolitions expert. He was used to handling volatile substances. He could sit here, close enough to breathe in Lucy's clean, fresh scent, and he could still find the strength to stand up and walk away from her. He knew he could.

"Pleiades," she said, pointing up to the stars. "It's my favorite constellation. It's the—"

"That little tiny cluster of stars," Blue said. "I know the constellations."

Lucy looked at him. "Don't tell me SEALs are trained in astronomy."

"Intergalactic space navigation," he corrected her. "In case we need to run a rescue mission on some planet in the Andromeda galaxy."

She looked at him and laughed. He loved the sound of her laughter. He had to fight to keep from reaching out and pushing a strand of her hair back behind her ear.

"You know you say things like that so seriously I almost believe you," she told him.

"Alpha Squad *has* trained to fly the space shuttle," he said. "We haven't had the opportunity yet, but if the need arose, we'd be ready."

"You sound so casual about it," Lucy said, turning slightly on the stairs so that she was facing him. "As if hundreds, probably *thousands*, of hours of training are insignificant."

She'd changed from her jeans to a pair of cutoff shorts

when they'd arrived home and Blue couldn't keep his eyes from traveling the long, smooth lengths of her legs. Just last night he'd run his hands and his mouth over every inch of those beautiful, sexy legs....

He forced himself to shrug, bringing his gaze back up to her face. "That particular training op was fun. Some of them aren't."

"Like what?"

He shrugged again. "Some of the guys really hate the submarine work. It's pretty claustrophobic stuff. Others turn green at the high-altitude parachute jumps. And most SEALs didn't have fun during the Arctic survival training."

"But those things didn't bother you."

"No." He smiled. "I could handle the physical training. My personal hell was trying to learn a different language. I busted my ass for that one."

Blue could see amusement shining in Lucy's eyes. "Are you serious?"

"I am now fluent in German," he continued. "And I can *parlez-vous* enough to get by in French and Arabic, but let me tell you it was a real uphill battle. I would've gladly taken a repeat session on Arctic survival, instead."

"Why did you have to learn a language, too?" Lucy asked. "I thought you said Joe Cat was the language specialist in your unit."

Blue shifted down several steps, leaning back on the porch with his elbows and stretching his legs out in front of him. He'd hoped his movement would get him away from the magnetic pull of Lucy's eyes, but now he was inches from the satiny skin of her thighs. He felt sweat trickle down the middle of his back.

"He is," he answered her. "But we all need to have at least one language besides English that we can speak fluently. It's important on an overseas mission *not* to look and sound like an American. That can be a real kiss of death. Part of SEAL

Team Ten's counterterrorist training is learning how to insert into a country and blend in. Hide in plain sight." He sighed, shaking his head. "But I tell you, it was frustrating as hell watching Cat plow through language after language, sounding like a native after only a day or two of listening to the tapes. He was learning two different dialects of Russian while I was still stumbling over '*Guten Tag, wie geht es dir? Meine Nahme ist Fritz.*'"

"Your name is Fritz?" Lucy repeated, covering her mouth with her hand as she tried not to laugh.

"Fritz or Hans or Johann," Blue said, smiling back at her. "When I go on an overseas mission to someplace like Cairo or Kathmandu, I play a German because of my hair. I've even learned to speak English with a heavy Deutsch accent."

Lucy looked away from him and up at the stars again, trying to imagine the extent of the effort Blue had put in to become a SEAL. Clearly it wasn't all physical training. He had worked hard to get where he was. He'd truly wanted it badly enough.

The sound of insects scratching and buzzing and humming and rattling filled the night air. "You never fail to amaze me," Lucy finally said, so softly he had to lean forward to hear her.

"You're pretty amazing yourself, Yankee." Their gazes locked, and Blue felt himself drop into a wild free-fall of sexual energy that rivaled his most intense skydiving jumps. Except right now he wasn't wearing any kind of parachute. God only knows how he was going to land without hurting himself. Or Lucy.

"I'm not amazing. I'm a coward," she said, looking away from him. "You've gone so many different places and had so many adventures." She sighed. "You were right about Hatboro Creek. There are places that I'd rather be, but look at me. I ended up back here." She stood and gazed up at her big Victorian house, looming above them in the darkness. "Living here was my mother's dream, not mine."

"What's keeping you from selling and moving on?" Blue asked quietly.

Lucy held out her hand for him, and he hesitated only a moment before taking it and letting her pull him to his feet. But she let go of him almost immediately. He followed her in the soft moonlight around to the side of the house.

"I know exactly what I'm getting in Hatboro Creek," she said as they walked slowly into the backyard. "It's safe and secure—no risk. Like I told you, I'm a coward."

"Just because it's hard for you to throw away your mother's dreams," Blue said softly, "doesn't make you a coward."

Lucy turned and looked at him, the moonlight reflecting the surprise in her eyes. "Don't tell me. SEALs are trained in basic psychology."

"The psychology we learn isn't basic," he said with a smile. But then his smile faded and he gazed at her steadily, his eyes serious. "No, I'm talking from experience, Lucy. I stayed in Hatboro Creek as long as I did because it was my mother's dream."

Lucy's pace had slowed. She was watching him as they walked, waiting for him to tell her more. But now that he'd started this conversation, he wasn't sure that he could. He'd never talked to anyone about his mother, not even Joe Cat. But he wanted to make Lucy understand that she wasn't alone. It was the least he could do for a friend.

"My mother married Arthur McCoy because he was an honest and decent man. He wasn't necessarily a kind man, but she did the best she could in the time she had," Blue said. "See, she knew she had cancer—she knew she was dying. She married Arthur for me—so that I wouldn't be all alone in the world after she was gone."

Lucy was silent, just listening.

Blue took a deep breath and went on. "It was her dream

that there would be someone in Hatboro Creek who would take care of me, someone who would love me and keep me safe. She wanted to know that I'd grow up here, in this little town, in a good home. She made me promise I'd stay until I finished school."

They'd walked all the way back to the end of the yard and up the trail through the woods to the back field where there was a small pond. The moon reflected almost perfectly on the glass-calm surface of the water. It was beautiful, but Lucy couldn't look away from Blue's face as he continued to talk.

"I made a promise, so I stayed." Blue's voice was softer now. "Even when it was clear that her dream wasn't going to come true—that Arthur McCoy had nothing to spare for me outside of a bed to sleep in and food to eat."

Lucy gazed at Blue in the moonlight. He was a man for whom talk did not come easily, and this was particularly difficult for him to talk about. As she looked in his eyes, she could see a distant reflection of the little boy he'd been, lost and alone. His basic needs had been taken care of, but he'd truly needed so much more. He still did.

Lucy knew at that moment that she loved Blue McCoy without any doubts, without any reservations. It had seemed so complicated last night and this morning, but it really wasn't. It was as simple as it could possibly be.

Her heart ached, and she had to wonder if anyone, *anyone*, had ever told this man that he or she loved him. She knew if she spoke the words that he would back away. She knew that he no longer wanted love, that he saw it as a burden, an unlucky twist of fate, a weight to be carried. And she knew that even if he were to change his mind, he wouldn't want her to be the one who loved him. He'd want someone perfect and feminine. Someone special and sweet…like Jenny Lee.

But he wasn't alone, and he wasn't unloved. Not as long as Lucy's heart was still beating.

"I always felt like there was something wrong with me," Blue told Lucy, "because here I was, living this dream of my mother's and hating every damn minute of it. It wasn't until I was older that I realized it was *her* dream, Yankee. Not mine. Sure, it would have been nice if it had all worked out, but it didn't, and that wasn't my fault."

Maybe that dream of Blue's mother had just taken a whole lot longer to work out than she'd anticipated. Because right now there *was* someone in Hatboro Creek— someone who would do her damnedest to take care of Blue and keep him safe. Someone who loved him. Someone named Lucy Tait.

But that, too, was something Lucy couldn't tell Blue. Her words would scare him away. Instead of telling him in words that she loved him, she would show him how she felt.

She reached out and took his hand, lacing her fingers through his.

But there was regret in his eyes as he looked down at her. "Lucy, I don't think—"

"Shh," she said, lifting herself slightly onto her toes to kiss him. His mouth was soft and warm and tasted like sweetened coffee. He groaned as she ran her tongue lightly across his lips and he pulled her into his arms, deepening the kiss.

Blue was spinning. One kiss, and he couldn't stop. One kiss, and he'd finally discovered the meaning of the word *impossible*. All his life he'd refused to acknowledge that anything could be undo-able. All his life *impossible* wasn't a word that was in his working vocabulary. Before this kiss, nothing was impossible. But now he knew he'd been mistaken. Staying away from Lucy, keeping the hot-burning sex, the uncontrollable *need*, out of their relationship was proving to be just that.

Her hands were up underneath the edge of his shirt, her fingers cool against his skin despite the heat of the night.

Her touch left no doubt in his mind exactly what Lucy wanted. She wanted him. All of him. And she wanted him now.

And dear Lord, as much as he knew that he shouldn't, the truth was that he wanted her, too. He wanted her with a power that shook him to his very soul, a power that steamrolled over his resolve to keep sex out of their friendship, a power that neutralized his need to meet the impossible head-on and win.

Staying away from Lucy was going to be impossible, because as much as he wanted to do the right thing, he wanted even more to make love to her, to please her, to hear that incredible, sexy catch in her breath as he filled her. He wanted all that so much more.

He wanted to stop, but he didn't want to stop badly enough.

She was unfastening his shirt, and he helped her with the last button, then let it slide from his arms onto the grass. He unbuckled his shoulder holster as she pulled her T-shirt over her head. The moonlight glistened enticingly on her beautiful, smooth skin, on the curve of her breasts and the white lace of her bra. And then she was in his arms again and he was touching her.

Mercy! All day long he'd fought the urge to touch her. All day long he'd told himself Lucy couldn't possibly be as soft and as smooth and as delicious to touch and kiss and taste as he remembered. What they'd done last night had been damn good, but his imagination and raging libido had surely taken those memories and inflated them beyond reason.

He was wrong.

She was perfection.

And she was his.

"Let's go for a swim," she whispered, unbuckling his belt. Her eyes were shining a promise that took his breath away as she smiled at him. Blue knew without a doubt that she could have suggested that they go down into the darkest reaches of Hell and he would have gladly followed.

He kicked off his sandals and stripped off the rest of his clothes as Lucy did the same.

She was beautiful in the moonlight—so much so that his chest felt painfully tight at the sight of her. She started toward the water, but then stopped and turned to face him, as if she somehow knew that he wanted to take a moment to look at her. Her dark hair hung thick and shining around her shoulders—shoulders that were both strong and feminine at the same time. She was muscular and sleek, yet soft in all the right places. Her legs were long and well toned, leading up to slim hips and a flat stomach. The silvery light gleamed off her golden skin, casting enticing shadows, emphasizing the soft curve of her hips, the fullness of her breasts. Her nipples were taut with anticipation and need.

That need was echoed on her beautiful face. Her lips were moist and parted slightly and her usually dancing eyes were heavy-lidded and filled with a molten desire as she gazed back at him.

Lucy *hadn't* turned back to let him look at her, Blue realized suddenly, a jolt of new fire flooding through his veins. She'd turned back because *she* wanted to look at *him*.

Her gaze was almost as palpable as a caress as her eyes skimmed across his body. She boldly took her time when she reached the obvious evidence of his arousal. When she finally looked up again, she smiled into his eyes, a smile sweet and hot and filled with pleasure.

Then she turned, and a few short steps brought her to the edge of the pond. She did a surface dive out into the center, barely making a splash, then disappeared into the darkness of the water.

Blue followed more slowly, watching as she emerged on the other side of the small pond.

"Hell," he said as he stepped off the edge and found himself suddenly waist deep in icy water. "This water is *cold*."

"There's some kind of underground cold spring feeding into this pond," Lucy said, drifting toward him. "It's great—normally around here a pond this size would become stagnant and turn into a swamp within a matter of months. But this thing has been around for years. I used to come out here and skinny-dip all the time back in high school."

"If only I'd known," Blue murmured, lowering himself so that the cool water went up to his chin. The cut on his arm stung for a moment, but only for a moment.

"I invited you out here for a swim once," Lucy said, treading water as she gazed at him. "I told you all about this pond. But you never showed."

He didn't remember.

"It was a really hot day, and you stopped to talk to me," Lucy said. "It was the only other time we actually spoke—besides that time you came to my rescue."

"You mean the time those damn fools broke your rib out on the baseball field."

"It was only cracked."

"Same difference."

"It was almost exactly a month after that happened," she said. "And it's not the same difference. It takes less time for a cracked rib to heal."

"I know. I've experienced both," Blue said. "Neither is any fun." He smiled at her. "Both times I thought about you, Yankee, while the doctor was taping me up."

Lucy splashed water in his direction. "You did not."

"God's truth," he said, dodging the water. "I honestly did. I thought what a tough kid you must've been to handle that kind of pain."

"You're just saying that to make up for not remembering the only other time we ever talked back in high school," Lucy teased to cover up her embarrassment. "Shoot, it was one of the highlights of my freshman year, and you don't have even the vaguest recollection."

Blue protested. "Remind me more about it," he said. "Maybe I'll remember."

"It was about a month after that fight. You and I nearly had a head-on collision in the hall outside the locker rooms," Lucy told him. "I was coming inside after a practice."

Blue felt his memory stirring. "And I just finished some long-distance run?"

"And it was about a million degrees out," Lucy said. "We were having some kind of weird heat wave."

"Yeah, that's right. It was October, right?" Blue said. He could see her, standing in the hallway of the school. She was wearing her baseball uniform, her knees all torn up from fielding ground balls, her hair falling out of a ponytail. Somehow he hadn't noticed her five-thousand-watt smile and her beautiful, sparkling eyes. He must have been blind, or a damned fool, or both. "But it was around ninety degrees, wasn't it? I do remember, Yankee. I was dying of heat."

"You were literally dripping with sweat."

"I was disgusting."

"You were sexy as hell."

She was sexy as hell right now, with the cool water barely covering the tops of her breasts. The first shock of the water had cooled Blue's overheated body down, but now he was getting used to the chilly temperature. And the thought of Lucy wrapping her long legs around his waist was creating quite a bit of new heat. Any minute now, this cold-water pond was going to start boiling.

"You were fifteen years old," he said. "You didn't even know what that word meant."

"Sexy?" Lucy's eyebrows went up. "Wanna make a bet, McCoy? One look at you and I was practically paralyzed."

He laughed again. "I thought you were just shy."

"Me? No way." She smiled at him. "No, I was just over-dosing on a sudden release of hormones."

He could relate to that phenomenon, but it didn't make him paralyzed. She was still drifting in the water, about six feet away from Blue, but he meant to change that soon.

"I think I asked you how the baseball team was doing, right?" he inquired, moving in a big, lazy circle around her. He went briefly under the water and came back up, tossing his wet hair out of his face.

"You did." She turned in the water to keep facing him, paddling with her hands to stay afloat. "I told you we'd won our first six games, but that the team still had some personality problems to work through. I said that just that afternoon, the catcher and the center fielder got into a fistfight. You said that the unseasonable heat and humidity were making everyone more irritable."

Blue stopped swimming. "You really remember all that?"

Lucy smiled. "I wrote a word-for-word account in my journal," she confessed.

"That's when you told me about this pond of yours," Blue said. "You invited me over for a swim. I remember. It sounded really nice, and I told you maybe I'd drop by."

"But you didn't show. I was heartbroken."

Her voice was light and teasing, but Blue knew there had to be at least a touch of truth to her words.

"I was a fool, Lucy."

"I was way out of my league."

"You *were* a little young," Blue admitted. "I knew you maybe had a crush on me, but I didn't take it seriously. If I had—if I'd really looked at you…"

"You had Jenny Lee," Lucy said. "She was perfect. I was the poster model for bad-hair days."

"At least you weren't afraid to go swimming and get your hair wet," Blue said. "I swear, the entire time Jenny and I dated, she never went into the water."

"That's the problem with perfection," Lucy said wist-fully. "Once you've got it, I imagine you spend a great deal of time worrying about losing it."

Blue knew that she was talking about more than just Jenny Lee Beaumont's hair. But as if she sensed him about to question her, she dove underneath the water. When she came back up, her hair was sleek against her head. She ran her hands back across it, pushing out most of the water.

Lucy met his eyes and smiled. "I used to see you down at the beach and over at the marina," she said. "I always won-dered why Jenny wasn't with you. I didn't realize it was a hair thing." She shook her head and laughed. "God, if I had been your girlfriend, I would have followed you everywhere, including into the water."

If Lucy had been his girlfriend... Jenny Lee had given Blue an intense physical relationship, but she hadn't cared about him, not really. Lucy would have cared.

"It was more than a hair thing with Jenny Lee," Blue said. He started to swim in circles around her again. Each circle was tighter, bringing him closer to her. "If I had been smart, I would've had a cute Yankee freshman for my girlfriend."

"You had your chance," Lucy said. She started swimming in circles, too, at the same leisurely speed. At this pace, he'd never reach her. "I invited you out here for a swim. I had the perfect evening planned. You were the one who didn't show up."

"You quit too soon," Blue said. "What happened to that famous Yankee tenacity I always read about? You could've done something to get me to notice you."

Lucy snorted. "You wouldn't have noticed me even if I'd juggled chain saws. You wouldn't have been able to see me past Jenny Lee's big—"

Blue had to laugh at that. "Give me a break," he said. "I was eighteen years old, and Jenny just sort of hand-deliv-ered herself to me. Did you know she asked me out first?"

Lucy silently shook her head.

He raked his wet hair back with one hand. "The first three times we went out, Jenny called me," Blue said. "Before I knew it, we were going steady." He laughed in disbelief. "I figured she really did love me, because all she ever wanted to do was come over to my house and hang out, just the two of us. We'd watch TV and you know…get real cozy on the couch. Truth was, there were more than two of us in that TV room. There was Jenny and there was me and there was Gerry—or at least the possibility that Gerry would appear. He came home from college a lot on the weekends. See, it turned out that Jenny was using me to get close to Gerry. Even back then, he was the one she wanted."

What was he doing, dissecting his relationship with Jenny Lee in front of Lucy? She didn't want to hear about this, so why was he telling her? He should be kissing her, not talking. All he seemed to do these days was talk.

But it was so easy to talk to Lucy. Blue never got the sense that she was listening with only half an ear. When she listened to him talk, she really paid attention. And she wasn't afraid of silence, like most people. Most people felt a need to fill in a pause in a conversation. Lucy seemed to understand that—at least for him—the pauses and silence added to what he was saying.

She was quiet now, just watching him. He wanted desperately to get back to where they'd been heading before he'd brought up the sobering subject of Jenny Lee.

Purposely, he made his voice light. "So tell me. This perfect evening you had planned for me that hot October night. What would've happened if I had shown?"

"You really want to know?"

"I certainly do," Blue said, smiling at her.

Lucy pushed herself backward in the water, treading with her arms and letting her legs float. Her toes broke the surface and she stared at them pensively.

"Well, you would've walked up here and found me already in the water, just like this," she said.

"Uh-huh."

"I would've smiled and waved and said, 'Come on in—the water is nice.'"

"And I would have."

"Nope." Lucy looked up at him and smiled, mischief lighting her eyes. "You would've said…" She mimicked his Southern drawl. "'Do you think your mama would mind if I went into the house and changed into my swimsuit?' And I would've said, 'You don't need a suit to swim in this pond, Blue McCoy. Don't worry—if you're shy, I'll close my eyes until you're in the water.'"

Blue laughed. "*Then* I would've gone in."

"Nope." Lucy bit her lower lip, barely able to keep from laughing. Her eyes were sparkling with amusement. "*Then* you would've stood there on the grass, deciding whether or not to be shy, and I would've said, 'I'm not wearing a suit, either. See?' and I would've done this."

Lucy had reached a shallow spot in the pond, and she now stood up, like a goddess rising from the deep, the moonlight glistening on her wet breasts, her nipples tightly peaked from the cold. The water didn't quite reach her belly button and she looked indescribably sexy as she smiled at him.

She laughed aloud at the look on his face. Her voice was musical in the night air.

"Sure, I was a little skinnier when I was fifteen," she told him, "but I can't imagine that you would've spent more than oh, five or ten more minutes up on shore, deciding whether or not to come into the water."

"Try five seconds," Blue said, starting toward her.

"After successfully enticing you into the pond," Lucy said, backing away from him, her eyes dancing with laughter, "I would've suddenly disappeared beneath the water.

You would have stood there, wondering where I went—until suddenly I appeared."

Blue reached for her, but she deftly moved away, vanishing, just as she'd described, underneath the water. Only a small ripple or two marred the surface of the pond before it once again became still. He watched for any sign of bubbles, waited for any movement. But all he could see was the moon's silvery reflection. All he could hear was the sound of the crickets and his own breathing.

And then the water swirled around him, and Lucy was there beneath the water, swimming around his legs, touching him. She erupted, up and out of the water, sliding against him as she roped her arms around his neck and kissed him.

The sensation of her sleek, naked body suddenly pressed against his was unbearably perfect. He heard himself cry out at the pure, gut-wrenching pleasure of her kisses, and he swept his hands across her wet skin, unable to get enough of her, wanting more.

She pulled back, catching her breath and laughing.

"No way would you have done that back when we were in high school," he said. His voice sounded hoarse in the still night air.

Lucy's eyes were brimming with laughter as she pushed her wet hair from her face. "Of course not," she said. "I was fifteen years old. Just because I knew what sexy meant didn't mean I had a clue what to do with you if I got you alone." She shook her head, closing her eyes in pleasure as he swept his hands again over her slick body. "No, my perfect evening with you would have been taking a swim—*with* bathing suits on. Then we would have headed back to the house and watched the baseball game on TV while we ate popcorn. I would have been in teenage heaven."

She kissed him along the side of his jaw, pressing herself closer to him. "But I'm not fifteen anymore. And my definition of heaven has changed a little bit."

Blue's definition of heaven was right here in his arms.

He kissed Lucy hard and deep, and she locked her arms around his neck and her legs around his waist. She was ready for him—he could feel her smooth, slick heat as their bodies strained to become one.

But he pulled back at the same moment she did.

"Condom," she breathed, her eyes wide as she gazed at him.

"Yeah."

"Will it work in the water?"

"Oh, yeah."

He scrambled up to the grass, to where he'd thrown his shirt. He rummaged quickly through his pocket, and was back beside her in a matter of moments. And then she was in his arms once more and he kissed her yet again. She pulled him closer to her, opening herself to him, moving her hips and sending him thrusting deeply into her hot tightness.

The sensation was incredible. Lucy's wet body was his to touch, to mold around him. As her strong legs locked around his waist, he held her derriere, pressing her tightly against him as together they set a feverish, passionate, primitive rhythm.

She pushed her wet hair out of her face, then swept Blue's hair back, too. She ran her fingers through the wetness and pulled his mouth up to hers for a hard, fierce kiss.

Blue couldn't believe he'd spent all day trying to convince himself that this shouldn't happen again. He couldn't believe he'd actually thought he'd be able to turn Lucy down. He couldn't believe he'd climbed out of her bed this morning, thinking he should run or try to hide from her.

Without a doubt, he was going to be in her bed again tonight. And this time he was going to do his damnedest to never leave.

Never leave.

Never.

The words surrounded him, pressing down on his chest with more suffocating force than the water around him. Blue could barely breathe—he was drowning in emotion. Damn, but where had that crazy thought come from? And it *was* crazy. He was career Navy. He was a SEAL. And SEALs left. That's what they did. They left. Always. There was always someplace new to go, something else to do.

He wasn't in love with this woman. He couldn't possibly be. He'd felt no lightning bolt. He'd had no vision, seen no special sign. Fireworks hadn't exploded overhead the first time he'd gazed into her eyes. The earth hadn't moved under his feet.

But, mercy, it sure as hell was moving now.

His strange thought about never leaving had to be some kind of reaction to this intense physical pleasure. He had found his perfect sexual match in Lucy Tait; that was for damn sure. He'd always liked sex—hell, that was an understatement—but it had never been even remotely like this before.

Never.

Blue felt Lucy's lithe body tighten against his, and he knew she was close to her release. He was right there with her, and all his thoughts fled.

"Oh, Blue."

She pulled back to gaze into his eyes, letting him see the power he held over her. He saw something else, too. Something warm and loving. Something more than the raw physical lust that bound them together.

He knew in that instant that he wanted to take her with him to a place she'd probably never been before. He wanted to make this single moment she was sharing with him one that she'd never forget.

"Breathe," he told her hoarsely. "Take a deep breath."

The faintest flash of confusion appeared in her eyes, and then she understood. She breathed, filling her lungs and holding the air in. And then Blue pulled her back with him, underneath the surface of the water.

It was dark and so utterly silent. Blue loved it down there, in that other world beneath the water. He couldn't get enough of the strangely quiet blueness, of the sense of peace that being underwater gave him. He'd clocked a lot of hours with his scuba gear, and never passed up an opportunity to dive. Still, he knew that many people felt claustrophobic and closed in underwater. He loosened his hold on Lucy, ready to let her go if she panicked and suddenly sought the surface. She wasn't afraid, though. She kissed him with an urgency he matched, air bubbling up around their faces.

With his hearing muffled and his vision reduced, Blue's remaining senses heightened. The taste of Lucy's mouth turned sweeter. And his tactile sense sharpened, the sensation of their rhythmic movement making him delirious from the sheer, pure, focused pleasure.

Blue pulled Lucy up with him, up to the surface of the water, up to the air, and together they gasped for breath as still their rhythm didn't slow, didn't stop.

"More," she gasped.

It was all he had to hear. He waited only for her to draw in another long, deep breath, and then he pulled her back down under the water again, and again the magical silence surrounded them.

Lucy's hair floated around them, moving slowly, lazily, a direct counterpoint to the wild movement of their bodies. Blue found her breast with his mouth, drawing her taut nipple in, sucking, pulling. He felt her grip him even tighter, felt the turbulence as the waves of her release began. Then, there in the silence beneath the water, Blue lost control. He was totally decimated. Every cell in his body exploded in a dizzying rush of exquisite pleasure so overwhelmingly pure, so incredibly sweet.

He drew in a breath in an attempt to steady himself—and got a cold lungful of water.

Blue pulled Lucy up to the surface with him, sputtering and coughing. But his footing was unsure and he slipped, dunking himself again. The water closed over his head, and he felt a flash of panic as his lungs burned and his chest heaved. He was desperate to expel the water he'd inhaled, desperate for air.

But Lucy was there, pulling him up and out. With her help, he crawled out of the water and collapsed, facedown, on the grass, coughing and retching as his body fought to clear his lungs.

Finally, *finally* he could breathe, but still it took several minutes longer before he could speak. He could feel Lucy, sitting patiently beside him, soothingly stroking his hair.

He lifted his head and glanced up at her, chagrined.

"Are you all right?" she asked.

Blue nodded. His throat burned and his eyes watered, but he was okay. "I'm embarrassed as hell." He could do little more than whisper in a raspy voice.

Her eyes were dancing with amusement and she was trying as hard as she could not to smile. "It's not every day I have to save a Navy SEAL from drowning."

"It's not every day I try to breathe H_2O. You'd have thought I would've learned *that* day one of BUD/S training." Blue pushed himself up and slid back down into the pond. He cupped his hands and brought some of the cold, clean water up to his mouth, swishing it around before he spit it back out.

Lucy's smile slipped out as she watched him. "You were distracted."

Blue couldn't argue with that. She was still distracting as hell, sitting so casually on the grass, the moon bathing her naked body with its silvery light. But the real truth was that he'd lost control. Totally. Without question. For the first time in his life he had been out of control.

The emotional impact of that hit him square in the gut, and he had to look away from her. He'd been out of control. Hell, he was *still* out of control.

He heard her stand up and turned to see her gathering up her clothes. "Let's head inside," she said, "before I become one giant mosquito bite." She nudged his shoulder holster with one toe. "Come on, McCoy. Grab your stuff."

Come on, McCoy. She spoke to him casually, lightly— the way she'd speak to a friend, not a lover. And she didn't wait for him to come out of the water. She started walking back toward the house without him. Doubt churned inside Blue, and he wondered if maybe she hadn't had the same incredible depth of sensations—he didn't dare call them feelings—that *he'd* had when they made love. But he could have sworn he'd seen something besides friendship and desire in her eyes.

But maybe he'd been wrong.

Of course, he was the one who hadn't held her in his arms after they'd made love. He should have kissed her, stayed close to her as the calming afterglow of their lovemaking surrounded them. Instead he'd tried to breathe water, and their intimacy had ended far too abruptly.

He pulled himself out of the water, then gathered up his things and sprinted after Lucy.

She was walking through her backyard buck naked, and he had to smile at her matter-of-factness. It was clear that she'd gone skinny-dipping in her pond on more than one occasion. She was quite comfortable walking back to her house without her clothes on. And she had every right to be. The neighbors' houses were some distance away, and the trees and bushes around the edges gave the big yard additional privacy.

On a whim, he dropped his bundle of clothes as he caught

up with her. He pulled her into his arms and spun her around in an inexperienced attempt at a dance move. He'd never done more than a slow rock-and-grind the times he'd danced with women in the various bars and roadhouses that Alpha Squad had visited. But despite his clumsiness, Lucy dropped her own clothes on the lawn, spinning around him with a fluid grace.

"So you do dance naked in your backyard," he said. "I knew it."

She laughed. God, he loved the sound of her laughter.

"Only in the company of *very* good friends."

Friends. There was that word again. And again it was accompanied by that nagging sense of doubt, and an unidentifiable but decidedly unpleasant feeling in the pit of his stomach.

He spun her back toward him and into his arms, holding her close as they moved slowly back and forth in time with the silent melody of the night. Unrestricted by clothing, Lucy's body swayed against his, her soft breasts touching his chest, her stomach brushing his arousal. And he was aroused. Again. Or maybe not again, maybe *still* aroused. Maybe he was going to be aroused for the rest of his life, regardless of how many times he made love to this woman.

Lucy was looking up at him, her eyes wide, her smile fading at the sudden intensity of the moment. She felt it, too— she *had* to feel it, too. Whatever this was, this almost palpable connection between them, this sensation of breathless, out-of-control wonder as he gazed into her eyes, she felt it, too.

Blue lowered his mouth and kissed her, a slow, soft kiss that made his eyes tear from its sweetness. When he spoke his voice was husky. "You gonna invite me in?"

"I thought I already did." Her voice shook slightly.

"You didn't invite me up to your room."

"My door is still unlocked."

"I didn't want to—"

Lucy finished for him. "Assume. I know. Never assume." She threaded her fingers through the hair at his nape, smiling up into his eyes. "Although I'm going to risk assuming that you'd like to go upstairs in the very near future…"

"*That* assumption is correct." Blue smiled. "Of course it's based on fact—"

"A hard fact," Lucy agreed, her grin making her cheeks dimple. "A *very* hard fact."

Blue kissed her again. This kiss was still as sweet, but it was laced with a searing fire. She pressed herself against him and he had to release her. If he didn't, he knew they'd never make it inside the house. He grabbed their clothes from the ground and tugged her toward the back porch.

It was crazy, insane. They'd just made love. They'd just had a sexual experience so intense that Blue had lost all sense of up and down.

But already he wanted her again. Right there in the backyard. Right on the lawn. Or on the porch. Right there on the porch. He pulled her to him, kissing her feverishly as she opened the screen door and pulled him inside. Or maybe on the kitchen table. That was as good a place as any. He threw down their clothes, freeing his hands to touch her, to fill his palms with her softness as he kissed her again. But she escaped, pulling him with her up the stairs and down the hall to her bedroom.

The intensity of his desire would have been frightening if not for the fact that she clearly felt it, too.

She clung to him, kissing him fiercely as he somehow managed to cover himself, to protect them both.

And then she pulled him back with her onto the colorful sheets of her bed, crying out with pleasure as he filled her.

Oh, *yeah.*

This thing that he felt, whatever it was, Blue knew she *had* to feel it, too.

Chapter Thirteen

"Who's the man in the picture?"

Lucy was lying with her head on Blue's shoulder, tracing the hills and valleys of the well-developed muscles of his chest. His words didn't make sense—not until she lifted her head and looked into his eyes. Even then she wasn't sure what he was talking about.

"What picture?"

"The one on your dresser," he said, gesturing with his head toward the other side of the room. "There's a framed photo of you with a man."

"Edgar Winston." She realized which picture Blue was talking about and pushed herself up so that she could look at him more comfortably. She rested her head on one hand, supported by her elbow. "He was a friend of mine."

Blue looked away from her, across the dimly lit room toward the chest of drawers where the photo sat. He couldn't possibly have seen the picture's details from here. Lucy knew he must have noticed it at some other time. But the thought of him in here without her, looking at her things, didn't upset or offend her. In fact, her response was quite the opposite. It made her feel good, warm. Blue was curious about her. He wanted to know more.

"A friend," he said quietly. He turned back to her, gazing into her eyes. His were serious and very blue. "The way I'm your friend?"

Was it possible that Blue was jealous? Lucy's heart started beating a little harder. If he was jealous, then maybe he felt more for her than simple friendship.

"Are you talking about sex?" she asked. "Do you mean, like, did I sleep with him?"

He smiled, the laughter lines around his eyes crinkling. "You know, that's what I do love about you, Lucy. You just grab right hold of the point of a conversation and shake it by the neck. No tiptoeing around."

That's what I do love about you... In the context of Blue's sentence, it was only a figure of speech. Lucy ached for it to be true. If only he loved her. The way he'd made love to her tonight, both out at the pond and here in her bed, she could almost believe that he felt something for her. Something powerful and strong. Something a lot like love.

But that was just her own wishful thinking.

"Isn't that what you're trying to find out?" she asked Blue. "Whether or not sex was part of my relationship with Edgar?"

"Yeah," he said, laughing silently. "You're right. That's exactly what I'm trying to find out." He leaned forward, propping himself up on his elbows in order to kiss her. "I'm sorry, though. It's not my business. I shouldn't have asked. You don't have to tell me."

"Don't you want me to tell you?"

He knew she was teasing him and he grinned good-naturedly. "What I *want*," he said, "is for you to tell me everything there is to know about this Edgar guy, starting with the fact that there's no chance at all he's going to show up here angry as hell, wielding a double-barrel shotgun and threatening to blow me to kingdom come."

"There's no chance of that," Lucy said quietly. "He's dead."

Blue closed his eyes, silently cursing himself out. Of all the insensitive things he could have said…. "Aw, Lucy, I'm sorry."

"You didn't know. How could you have known?"

"I'm still sorry," he said again.

She reached out, touching the side of his face. Her fingers were cool against his skin and she touched him so gently. "He was my business partner," Lucy said. "And, yes, our relationship was totally platonic. No sex. Even if he was still alive, he wouldn't have shown up waving a shotgun. He would've approved of you. He had a thing for well-built blondes himself."

Her words took a moment to sink in. "You mean, he was…?"

"Gay," Lucy said. "I met Edgar in college. Two days after we first met, it was as if we'd been best friends forever. We went into business together after we graduated. Computer software design. We had an office in Charleston and we made money like crazy."

"I didn't know you had your own business," Blue said, taking her hand and lacing their fingers together. Her hands were slender but strong, with long fingers and short nails.

She made a face at him. "What did you think I did between college and six months ago when I joined the Hatboro Creek police force?"

He shook his head. "I don't know. I guess…" He shrugged. "I didn't think about it. I just always pictured you here in town all that time. But you were living in the city."

"Actually, I moved back to Hatboro Creek about a year ago," Lucy told him. "Right after Edgar died…."

He rarely saw her when she wasn't smiling, Blue realized.

Lucy was usually so upbeat, with a smile or a grin at least lurking, ready to break free. But now her eyes were filled with a quiet sadness that made him ache for her.

"I'm sorry," Blue murmured. "How did he…?"

"AIDS," she said flatly. "It was awful. He got so sick. I just watched him…disappear." Her voice broke and she had to look away from him. Blue didn't want to hear this.

But he did. He touched the side of her face, gently pushing her hair behind her ear. Lucy glanced up into eyes so warm and blue and sympathetic she felt her own eyes fill with tears.

"It's hard to watch someone you love die," he said softly. "It's hard to know what to say or do." He paused. "I have a friend—Frisco. Alan Francisco. He didn't die, but he's wheelchair-bound. I never know what to say to him anymore. I don't know how to treat him."

"You treat him exactly the same way you did before," Lucy said. With her free hand, she wiped the tears from her eyes.

"Even when he shuts me out?"

"Especially when he shuts you out," Lucy said. "When Edgar got depressed, I stayed with him. I moved into his condo. I wouldn't let him give in. Did you know that it's a scientific theory that laughter and humor increase the odds of survival among patients with terminal illnesses?"

Blue shook his head. "No, I didn't know that."

"I stayed with Edgar till the end," Lucy said quietly. "I was holding his hand when he died."

"You don't run away from anything, Yankee, do you?" Blue continued. He smiled slightly. "You should've been a SEAL."

She had to smile at that. "Yeah, right."

"What happened to your software business?" Blue asked.

"When Edgar got sick, it was at the point where it could run itself," she explained. "We hired some key people to do the work for us and booked ourselves passage on a cruise around the world, but it was already too late. By the time

Edgar found out he had AIDS, it was too far along. I think he knew he was sick for quite a while. He just put off getting tested. So we never got to Egypt and Kathmandu. Instead, I held his hand as he fought off all sorts of viral infections and three different kinds of pneumonia. The pneumonia finally won."

She took a deep breath. Blue was still listening, so she went on. "After he was…gone, I went to the office for the first time in months. I wasn't there for more than thirty seconds before I knew that I couldn't go back. I didn't want to be there without Edgar. The woman I'd hired as acting president asked me not to sell, at least not right away. She was afraid one of the larger companies would buy us out and all the employees would be excessed. I didn't want that, but I knew I couldn't stick around. So I just kept things as they were."

"That's when you came back here, huh?"

Lucy nodded. "My mother left me this house when she died. Hatboro Creek seemed like the logical place to go. And then the job opened up on the police force…."

"Law enforcement is pretty different from computer software design," Blue said.

"That was the idea. I wanted to do something entirely different. And it *was*. You should've seen me learn to shoot. At the risk of bragging, I got a high percentage of bull's-eyes the first time I was on the firing range. I was good at it. I figured the rest of being a cop would come even easier. Boy, was I wrong."

Blue watched Lucy, realizing that this was the first time she'd ever really told him about herself. He'd done a great deal of talking over the past several days and she'd mostly listened. It honestly hadn't occurred to him that she had had a life beyond Hatboro Creek. But it suddenly made incredible sense.

He knew she was a rookie—that she'd been on the police force for only six months. He *hadn't* known that before that she'd lived and worked in the city. She'd owned her own successful computer business. She'd probably gone to meetings with clients, worn business suits, high heels....

Well, probably not. Lucy probably had one of those laid-back, jeans-and-T-shirts kind of computer business. That was more her style. But either way, she'd definitely had a life beyond Hatboro Creek.

He was glad for her, and saddened for what she'd been through with her friend.

"Being a cop isn't that easy." Lucy forced herself to smile, trying to disguise the unhappiness in her eyes.

Blue pulled Lucy to him, hugging her tightly. He bet she'd smiled at her friend Edgar all those endless months as he'd died. He could picture her smiling for Edgar's sake, even though she was crying inside. She was a remarkable person.

As he held her close, as she buried her face in his neck, Blue suddenly felt his own heart beating. It was slow and steady and quite possibly stronger and louder than he'd ever felt it beating before. He felt a sense of calm, a state of peace, more powerful and complete than any he'd ever felt in his entire life.

And that was odd as hell, since he was currently the main suspect in the murder of his stepbrother. He should feel turmoil, anger, frustration and grief.

But all those chaotic feelings were pushed aside, dwarfed by a powerful sense of completeness.

He was in love with Lucy Tait.

The thought popped into his mind out of nowhere, and his first reaction was to dismiss it entirely out of hand. That was ridiculous. He couldn't be. Love didn't happen this way. Love hit fast and hard and devastatingly intensely, like a wildcat bringing down its prey.

These feelings he had for Lucy—whatever they were—

had crept up on him while he wasn't paying attention. He had become slowly and steadily surrounded by this gentle warmth, this calm happiness.

He liked her. He really, *really* liked her. Maybe that was what this was.

But he really liked Joe Cat, too, and the thought of being apart from Cat didn't shake him the way the thought of leaving Lucy did.

It was more than the sex, though Lord knows he'd miss *that* less than five minutes after he left her. It was her smile, her laugh, her bluntness, her cheerful honesty that he'd really miss.

Lucy lifted her head and still tried to smile. "I'm finding out the hard way that I'm better at designing software," she told him. "The truth is, I was a lousy cop."

"No, you weren't."

She shook her head, covering his mouth with her hand. "You know I wasn't cut out for the job, so do me a favor and don't try to pretend that I was," Lucy said. "I prefer the truth, McCoy—no matter how difficult it may be. Don't ever lie just to be nice."

He pulled her hand away, lightly kissing her fingers first. "I wouldn't," Blue said. "Honesty is real important to me, too, Lucy. All my life I've seen people use other people." He was quiet for a moment, then he added, "Do you know that you're the first woman I've…been involved with…who hasn't had some ulterior motive for being with me?"

Lucy looked away, hoping Blue wouldn't be able to see the secrets she was hiding. Because she did have an ulterior motive. She was in love with him—and she wanted him to love her, too. That was one major ulterior motive. "You're exaggerating," she said. "You've got to be."

"I'm not."

"You're telling me that you know for a *fact* that every single one of *all* the women you've ever been—"

"There haven't been that many," he interrupted quietly.

"That's hard to believe."

"It's true."

"And not one of them was with you simply because they liked you?"

"None of them ever tried to get to know me." He paused. "Except for you."

His soft words made her cheeks heat with a flush. If only she didn't want more from him—more than an easygoing friendship spiced with hot sex. But she did want more. She wanted so much more.

"Even back in high school," Blue told her. "Even Jenny Lee…." Something shifted in his eyes. It was almost imperceptible. Almost. "In some ways, she was the worst. It took me a long time to get over her using me the way she did. After that I started to expect it. Some women liked being with a man in a uniform. Others were after an officer—it didn't matter who you were as long as you had some kind of rank. I once met a girl—she seemed really nice. Turned out she and her brother were writing a book about SEAL Team Ten."

Lucy sat up, her eyes narrowed slightly. "You, of course," she said, "having higher moral standards than those women, have never used another person in any way in your entire life. Every time you went home with a woman, you were searching for a meaningful relationship—something long-lasting, something special, right?"

Blue bowed his head in mock surrender. "Your point is taken. It's just that Jenny Lee…" He interrupted himself. "Let's not talk about Jenny anymore."

Good idea.

Lucy looked up at him. "So tell me honestly," she said. "Do you know how to break a man's neck the way Gerry's was broken?"

Blue nodded. "Yeah," he said. "I do."

She digested that information, still studying his face, her dark-brown eyes serious. "Have you…" She stopped herself. "Maybe I shouldn't ask you this."

"Have I ever done it?" Blue asked the question for her. "I've been in plenty of combat or counterterrorist situations where the enemy has to be permanently neutralized, often silently. So, yeah, I have done it. It's effective and efficient."

Lucy's eyes narrowed again. "You're talking about *killing* another person."

Blue shook his head. "A terrorist who kidnaps and tortures and murders a cruise ship full of civilians isn't a person to me."

"But that's how you feel in the heat of battle, so to speak," Lucy said. "After it's over don't you wonder who they were? Don't you feel badly then?"

"No," he said bluntly. "No guilt. No remorse. What good would feeling bad do me? The way I look at it is, I didn't kill them—they killed themselves by putting themselves in a situation where they'd have to go up against me."

"But every life is sacred," Lucy argued.

"You tell that to the terrorists," Blue said mildly. "If you can convince them of that fact, I'll be more than ready to agree. Until then, my job is to protect and defend—by deadly force, if necessary. I'm not an ambassador or a diplomat, Lucy. I'm a soldier. I'd far prefer it if the ambassadors and diplomats could get the job done. I'd be the first on my feet for a standing ovation if the entire world could live in perfect harmony. Hell, I'd gladly spend the rest of my life rescuing victims of natural disasters. But that's not the way it's gonna be anytime in the near future."

"I know that," Lucy said with a sigh.

"We're doing more research into weapons that aren't deadly," Blue said. "If there was some kind of stun gun or tranquilizer gun that guaranteed neutralization for a definite, extended period of time, we'd consider using it. In certain situations, when the terrorists are asleep, for instance, we do inject tranquilizers, using syringes. But tangos who aren't sleeping don't often sit still and wait for you to stick 'em with a needle. And with a gun, it's harder to be accurate.

"And that makes it tough when you're in a life-and-death situation. Everything you do is focused on staying alive, on keeping your squad alive. If you only tranquilize Terrorist X instead of killing him, you're going to expend a certain amount of energy and brain power wondering if maybe you didn't do it right, and maybe he's going to pop back up and mow down half your squad with his HK-93. But dead is dead. You do it right, and you know it. Terrorist X doesn't pop back up and kill anyone after his neck has been broken."

Lucy was still watching him. "I see your point of view," she said. She didn't necessarily agree with him, but it was clear that he'd given this a great deal of thought. He was a soldier. He had taken others' lives—not because he wanted to, but because he *had* to. She'd read about some Spec Op operators—Navy SEALs and Green Berets and others—who'd actually enjoyed the act of killing. Blue clearly wasn't one of them.

But he also wasn't going to apologize for what he did. Protect and defend. Lucy knew he would give his life; he would *die* in order to get his job done.

How many people did she know who could say the same?

She glanced up at him. He was watching her. She could see in his eyes that he was waiting for her to make some kind of negative comment. He was bracing himself for her condemnation or disapproval.

"You know, I really like you, Blue McCoy," Lucy said with a smile.

Blue had to smile, too. Her comment was pure Lucy. She

really liked him. It made him feel warm inside. Warm, but wistful, too. Was it possible he would have rather heard her tell him that she *loved* him?

Mercy, the complications that that would bring were mind-boggling. But he wanted it, he realized. He wanted her to love him.

"We should try to sleep," Lucy said, lying back in the bed. "We've got a big day tomorrow."

"Are we planning to crack the case?"

Lucy sighed as he put his arms around her, pulling her so that her back fit snugly against his chest. "No," she said. "Tomorrow we're going to drive into Charleston and hire a private investigator—someone with more than six months' experience. He or she will crack the case."

"Excuse me, Officer Tait…?"

Lucy glanced up from filling her truck's gas tank to see a tired-looking woman on the other side of the self-serve pump, filling the tank in her own car.

It was Darlene Parker, Matt's wife. Her old station wagon was loaded full to the top, and Tommy, her young son, sat in the front seat. Matt was nowhere in sight.

"I was going to send this to you," Darlene said, handing Lucy an envelope, glancing furtively around to make sure no one was watching them, "but as long as you're right here, I figured I may as well risk hand-delivering it. Don't let anyone see."

"Are you leaving town?" Lucy asked, folding it in two and putting it in the back pocket of her jeans.

Darlene nodded. She seemed relieved that the envelope was out of sight. She lowered her voice even further, her thin face pinched and nervous. "I wrote to tell you what really happened the night Gerry McCoy died."

Lucy felt a surge of hope. "You know who killed Gerry McCoy?"

But Darlene shook her head as she finished filling the tank and replaced the gas cap. "No. But I know that Matthew was paid quite a bit of money to make up that story about seeing Blue up in the woods, arguing with his stepbrother. I know for a fact that Matt didn't see anything of the sort. He was with me that entire night. It's all in the letter. When you read it, you'll see."

Darlene hurried to the gas-station office to pay. As Lucy watched through the window, Darlene quickly threw several bills onto the counter. She headed back to her car, but Lucy intercepted her.

"If you leave town," Lucy said quietly, "you won't be able to make a statement about this to the police."

Darlene was already shaking her head. "No," she said. "I'm not going to do that. I've already done more than I should. They killed Gerry McCoy. They won't think twice about killing again."

"Who are 'they'?"

"R. W. Fisher," Darlene whispered. "And the police. You're the only police officer I was absolutely certain wasn't involved."

The police? And R. W. Fisher? Killed Gerry McCoy? Lucy's head was spinning.

Darlene pushed past her and opened the door to her car. "I'm leaving with Tommy while I still can," she said. "Matt is gonna wind up with his own neck broken, but that's his own damn fault."

She closed the door with a slam, then locked it. Lucy leaned in the open window. Tommy gazed sullenly at her from where he was sitting, surrounded by bags and unpacked things his mother had thrown, last minute, into the car.

"How do you know about this?" she asked. "Darlene, I need to know where you got this information."

Darlene started the car with a roar. "I've already told you too much."

"At least give me your forwarding address, so that I can reach you in case—"

"You're kidding, right?"

Darlene put the car into gear and pressed the gas pedal. Lucy had to jump away to keep the rear tire from rolling over her boots.

Darlene's reedy voice floated back through the open window. "If I were you, I'd get out of town before you end up like Gerry McCoy, too."

Lucy pulled the envelope Darlene had given her out of her pocket. She dug in her other pocket for a pen and jotted down the station wagon's license-plate number. Just in case. She paid for her gas and got back into her truck before opening the envelope.

It was a single-page, handwritten letter. Darlene's cursive writing was scratchy and hard to read.

A glance told Lucy that the letter wasn't signed. Without Darlene around in person to back up the contents, it would do little to discredit Matt Parker's story. Still, she read it slowly, working through the nearly illegible words.

Just as Darlene had said, she'd written that Matt had been home all evening on the night that Gerry McCoy had died. She said that after Matt had issued a statement that he'd seen Gerry and Blue near Gate's Hill Road that night, he suddenly had lots of money. When Darlene asked him about it, since he was currently unemployed, he told her to mind her own business.

But later Matt had told her that he'd gotten the money from R. W. Fisher, and that in a few months, after the uproar died down, he was going to have a guaranteed job working for the Tobacco King.

R. W. Fisher.

It seemed ludicrous. The wealthiest, most successful man in town involved in murder?

And the police were supposedly involved, too. Darlene

didn't say why she thought that was true or who had given her that information. She just stated that the police couldn't be trusted.

Lucy looked up from the letter, staring sightlessly at the morning sky. Blue had seen Fisher deep in discussion with Gerry at the country club on the night Gerry had been killed.

She'd wanted to go and talk to R. W. Fisher in connection to the autopsy report's odd findings about Gerry's blood-alcohol levels at the time of his death. She'd wanted to ask Fisher if he'd thought that Gerry was drunk prior to the dance-floor altercation with Blue and Jenny.

She'd told Chief Bradley about wanting to talk to Fisher....

And he'd responded not just by taking her off the case, but by suspending her from the police force and telling her to get out of town.

What if Darlene was right and the police—including Sheldon Bradley—were involved in some sort of conspiracy?

And what if, by wanting to talk to Fisher, she'd been getting too close to the real truth?

Whatever had come in with the morning mail was causing quite a stir in Chief Bradley's office. Despite that, Annabella stopped Lucy as she was heading past her desk.

"I thought you got axed," the older woman said with her usual sensitivity, lighting a cigarette with a snap of a match.

"I'm just getting...something from my locker," Lucy said. "Packing up some of my stuff." Curiosity got the better of her, and she motioned toward the commotion. "What's going on?"

"Blue McCoy's military records just arrived," the raspy-voiced dispatcher told her, exhaling a cloud of smoke. "Did you know that he's got some kind of expert status in martial arts-style hand-to-hand combat?"

"Well, yeah, umm…actually, I did," Lucy said.

Lucy couldn't quite believe she'd dared to come inside the police station. The normally bland beige walls seemed to be dripping with conspiracy. The familiar faces of her co-workers seemed suddenly sinister.

She was probably overreacting. She was going on the unsubstantiated statement of Darlene Parker—a woman who, for all Lucy knew, could have paranoid delusions. If R. W. Fisher and the *entire* police department had killed Gerry McCoy, there had to be some kind of reason, some sort of motive. Darlene hadn't provided her with one of those, and Lucy was having a hard time coming up with one of her own.

But she couldn't totally discount what Darlene had told her. In fact, Lucy took Darlene's warnings seriously enough to want to be armed. Of course, she'd turned in her police-issue weapon when she'd had it out with Chief Bradley two days ago. But she had a personal license for a smaller gun— which happened to be inconveniently stored in her locker in the basement of the police station.

This entire day wasn't going at all the way she'd planned. She'd awakened alone again and had a moment of frustration until she caught the fragrant smell of coffee and frying pancakes floating up from the kitchen. When she went downstairs she found Blue cooking breakfast. He'd greeted her with a smile and a maple syrup-flavored kiss. That was nice—she couldn't complain about that.

But after breakfast, Lucy had left the house alone, intending to drive into town to the library to photocopy the Yellow Pages listings of private investigators from the Charleston phone book. Today she had intended to seek professional assistance in this murder investigation.

Instead, here she was, spooked by Darlene Parker's crazy suspicions, creeping down the police-station stairs, hoping she'd get to her locker, get her gun and get the hell out of there before anyone besides Annabella noticed her.

Not a chance.

Chief Bradley stopped her in the hall on her way back to the door.

Lucy kept her face carefully expressionless, hoping the fact that she suspected him to be part of some wild, murderous townwide conspiracy didn't show in her eyes.

But he didn't ask her what she was doing there. He glared at her and said, "You knew Blue McCoy had extensive martial-arts training?"

Lucy looked down toward Annabella's desk, where the dispatcher was smoking yet another cigarette, watching with unabashed curiosity.

"All Navy SEALs do," she said evenly. "I'm surprised you didn't know that."

"No, I did not know that," Bradley fumed. "Just now Annabella told me you knew about McCoy's martial-arts training. And I happened to be talking to Doc Harrington's pretty little wife yesterday, and *she* mentioned the fact that you're some kind of walking fountain of information about the military's Special Forces divisions."

"Special Operations. And Sarah was exaggerating. I don't know *that* much—"

"What I want to know is why the hell didn't any of that information bubble over onto my desk?"

"I didn't think—"

Bradley shoved several pieces of paper into Lucy's hands. It appeared to be pages photocopied from Blue's personnel file. Much of the text was blacked out, censored no doubt for security reasons. But there was a full listing of the areas in which Blue held expert-level—or higher—status. Martial arts and hand-to-hand combat were high on the list.

Lucy flipped the page, fascinated by Blue's private file, despite the fact that she was surrounded by people who were allegedly involved in Gerry McCoy's death.

She skimmed the brief psychological evaluation that

was written at the bottom of the second page. "Carter McCoy is a perfect candidate for the SEAL program," she said. "He is a tenacious, usually steady, thoughtful individual who is not afraid to take action. Negatively, his temper can be volatile at times. He also is very much of a loner, unwilling or unable to share his thoughts and feelings with anyone other than his very closest friends, if even them. Carter McCoy is—"

"You look at that file," Chief Bradley interrupted her, "and you tell me if you think McCoy has the skill and training necessary for him to be able to snap a man's neck."

Lucy gazed up at him. She didn't want to answer that. She *couldn't* answer that, not without damning Blue. But if she refused to answer, Bradley would assume she was hiding the truth.

"Blue McCoy is a lieutenant in the Navy SEALs," she told the chief. "He's the executive officer of SEAL Team Ten's Alpha Squad." She slapped the papers against her hand. "According to this, he's won countless medals for bravery—"

"I didn't ask you for a background sketch of the man," Bradley said. "I asked if Blue McCoy has the skill and training to kill in that manner—"

"He'd never do such a thing," Lucy protested.

"It's a yes or no question, Tait. Does he or does he not have the skill and training to break a man's neck?"

Bradley was watching her. Annabella was watching her. Farther down the hall, Travis Southeby and Tom Harper were watching her. They were all waiting for her answer.

"*All* SEALs do—"

But Chief Bradley wasn't listening any longer. "That sounded like a yes to me. Run next door to the judge's chambers," he said to Travis. "Let's get a warrant and bring that son of a bitch in. We got motive and now we've got means."

"Motive?" Lucy asked, following Bradley down the hall, back toward his office. "What motive did Blue McCoy have for killing his brother?"

Bradley stopped and looked at her as if she were first cousin to the village idiot. "Jenny Lee Beaumont," he said. "She's motive enough for damn near any man."

"That's ridiculous—"

"You got a better motive?" Bradley said, turning back to glare at her. "Or maybe you've got an entirely different suspect in mind?"

They killed Gerry McCoy, Darlene Parker had said ominously. *They won't think twice about killing again.*

Lucy shook her head, backing slowly away. "No," she said. "No, I don't." She gazed into the chief's eyes, trying to see if he was capable of murder. As much as she disliked the man, she found it hard to believe. But she'd been wrong about a lot of things before.

"Got the warrant, Chief," Travis called.

"Take Tom and go pick up McCoy," Bradley said to Travis. He turned to Lucy. "He still staying out at your place?" He smiled knowingly. "In the *guest* bedroom?"

Lucy's stomach was in a knot. They were going to arrest Blue. They were going to bring him in, charge him with murdering his stepbrother. Or maybe they *weren't* going to bring him in. Maybe they were simply going to kill him instead, claiming he resisted arrest.

"Let me go along," she said to Bradley, her mind going a mile a minute as she searched for a way out. "I can talk him into coming in quietly."

"Yeah, or you can tip him off—warn him so that he gets away. You don't work for me anymore, remember?" Bradley said. He nodded to Travis, who headed for the door, Tom Harper one step behind. "No, I want you to sit down right here in my office and stay until I receive word that McCoy is behind bars."

"You can't keep me here," Lucy said tightly, her fear for Blue stronger and sharper than her concern for her personal safety.

"Yes, I can," Bradley said. "We can do it one of two ways. You can sit down nice and quiet, or I can have you arrested. Which will it be?"

Lucy walked out into the hall, toward the front door. "Arrest me."

"Have it your way," the chief said. He called down the hall, "Annabella, get Frank Redfield up here to arrest Lucy Tait."

Lucy could see Annabella flipping frantically through her code book, trying to find an appropriate ten code for the situation. The dispatcher finally gave up and just picked up the phone.

But Frank was already upstairs. He stepped out into the hallway in front of Lucy, blocking her exit out of the building."

"Come on, Lucy," he said. "Why do you want to make trouble for yourself?"

"If you're arresting me," she said, "what are the charges?"

"Attempted obstruction of justice," Chief Bradley volunteered.

"That's ridiculous," Lucy said, turning to face him, "and you know it. You *try* arresting me for that. Just try it."

She stepped around Frank, who looked down the hall at the chief, waiting for instruction. But the chief didn't say a word. He was silent as Lucy pushed open the door and went down the stairs into the hot morning sunshine.

She'd called Bradley's bluff.

Lucy ran for her truck, and started the engine with a roar even before she shut the door. She pulled out of the parking lot with a squeal of tires and headed up toward Fox Run Road, praying that she wasn't too late.

Chapter Fourteen

Blue went out onto the porch as the police car pulled into the drive.

Lucy was still downtown, and he recognized Travis Southeby behind the wheel. That wasn't good. But at least Tom Harper was with him. Tom had no doubt read all of his civil-rights handbook, while Travis had clearly skipped a few chapters.

They'd come to arrest him. He knew that even before they got out of the car. And the two police officers got out of the car with almost comedic differences in style.

Tom stood up and straightened his pants, nodding a greeting to Blue, closing the car door behind him.

Travis drew his weapon, and, flinging his car door open and using it as a shield, he aimed his gun at Blue.

"Blue McCoy, you are under arrest," he shrilly announced.

Tom glanced at Travis, then looked apologetically at

Blue. "We've got to bring you in," he said. "We're making the charges official."

"I didn't kill Gerry," Blue said evenly. "If I had, I would've been long gone."

"Keep your hands where I can see 'em," Travis said sharply.

Blue glanced back at Travis and his gun. "You're too far away to get an accurate aim with that thing," he said. "Put it away before you accidentally hurt someone." He turned back to Tom. "You're making a big mistake here. You're wasting your time on me while Gerry's real killer is running around free."

Tom actually looked sorry as he snapped a pair of handcuffs on Blue. He quickly searched him as he recited Blue's Miranda rights.

Travis approached, obviously keeping his hand close to his reholstered gun. "We've got enough evidence to put you away, McCoy," he said. "We've got a motive of jealousy—"

"That's total bull."

"Is it really? I didn't think so. Chief didn't, either," Travis said. "We've got a witness who places you with the victim at the scene of the crime—"

"You've got a liar who's probably getting paid a small fortune to make up stories," Blue countered.

"We've also got a hundred other witnesses who saw you threaten the victim earlier that evening. Are *they* all getting paid off, too?" Travis was enjoying this way too much.

Tom opened the door to the patrol car, and Blue started to climb in. It wasn't easy with his hands bound together behind his back.

"And," Travis said, playing his winning card with a flourish, "we've got military records that peg you as a martial-arts expert *and* we've got our own local military scholar—of sorts—who will be called to testify that as a Navy SEAL martial-arts expert you have the knowledge and skill nec-

526   SUZANNE BROCKMANN

essary to be able to break a man's neck the way Gerry's was broken."

Blue straightened up. Was he talking about...?

Travis smiled at the look on Blue's face. "That's right," he said. "Lucy Tait. And she'll be doubly valuable to the prosecution considering you've been shacking up with her for the past few days. Imagine how that'll look to the jury—your own lover testifying against you." He made tsking sounds.

"Lucy would never do that," Blue said. He could feel anger starting inside him, burning hot and tightly contained.

"She will if she's subpoenaed," Travis said. "And she'll be subpoenaed. All she'll have to do is repeat what she said this morning down at the station."

Blue got into the car. "Play your head games with someone else, Southeby," he said shortly. "I know for a fact that Lucy wasn't at the police station this morning."

"Well, I know for a fact that she was," Travis said, slamming the door behind Blue and climbing in behind the driver's wheel. He put his arm along the back of the front seat, twisting to look at Blue. "She came in to give you up. She provided us with that last bit of information we needed to come on out here and bring you in."

Blue just laughed and told Travis in quite specific language exactly what he could do with himself.

Travis turned to look at Tom, who'd climbed into the car and was fastening his seat belt. "McCoy thinks I'm telling tall tales," he said. "He thinks I'm making this all up. Isn't that exactly what happened this morning, Tom? Lucy Tait walked in, told the chief that McCoy had the martial-arts training needed to cleanly snap a man's neck, and five minutes later I was holding the warrant for McCoy's arrest in my hand."

Tom glanced at Blue, clearly sympathetic. "I don't know exactly how it happened," he said. "I didn't hear all of it, but Lucy *was* at the station this morning, and I did hear the chief ask her if you had the skill to break a man's neck. Right after that, we had the warrant."

Part of Blue up and died. Just like that. Sudden, instant, tragic death.

He stared out the window of the police car as Travis pulled out of Lucy's driveway. Summer had hit full stride, and the trees and meadows were bursting with life and color. Wildflowers were everywhere. A breeze ruffled the green leaves, making the trees seem like some giant, moving, living thing. There was all that life out there, yet Blue felt dead inside. Dead and brown and dried up and broken.

So tell me honestly, Lucy had said to him last night, after they'd made love for the second—or was it the third?—time. *Do you know how to break a man's neck the way Gerry's neck was broken?* Their legs were still intertwined, and he had been running his fingers down her back, from her shoulder all the way to her thighs. Her skin was so soft and smooth he couldn't stop touching her.

They'd just talked about honesty, about how Lucy was the first woman Blue had known who hadn't had some sort of ulterior motive for being with him.

But she had. She'd had one hell of an ulterior motive, hadn't she? She'd used sex and the intimacy it created between them to get the information she'd needed to send him to jail.

He'd almost let himself love her. Damn, he was such a fool.

Blue was silent as Travis Southeby and Tom Harper led him into the station, silent as they took his fingerprints and mug shots, silent as they told him his bail would be set that afternoon, silent as they put him in the holding cell and locked the door.

It wasn't until Travis came back, telling him that Lucy Tait was outside, that she wanted to see him, that Blue spoke.

"I don't want to see her," he said, amazed that someone who felt so dead inside could still speak.

Lucy stared at Travis Southeby. "But…"

"He said he doesn't want to see you," Travis repeated. He smiled. "Can't say I blame him, seeing how you were the one who provided the final piece of evidence in the case against him. He wasn't too happy when I told him about that."

"You told him *what?*"

"Nothing but the truth," Travis said smugly. "You came in here to tell the chief that Blue McCoy had the ability to break a man's neck. Not everyone knew that he had that particular skill, you know. Your little tidbit of information proved vital in our case against him."

"You *son* of a bitch!"

Could Blue really believe that she would betray him that way? She wouldn't have thought so, but apparently he had.

"Watch your mouth, missy," Travis said primly.

Lucy took a deep breath. Slamming her fist into Travis's smug face wasn't going to do her—or Blue—any good. She forced herself to calm down. "I'm sorry." She took another deep breath. She'd gotten to her house too late. Blue was gone and Travis's patrol car was nowhere in sight. She'd turned right around and come back to the station. "Please, you've got to let me see him anyway."

"Can't do that."

The front doors opened, and Lucy turned to see Jenny Lee Beaumont walk into the police-station lobby. She was wearing a rose-colored suit with a frilly white blouse. The frills made her generous bosom look even larger. Her hair was up in an elegant bun and she had high heels on her tiny feet, pushing her height up to a full five foot three.

Travis moved toward her. "Ms. Beaumont," he said. "What can I do for you, ma'am?"

Jenny took off her sunglasses. Her eyes still looked smudged and bruised from grieving. "I received a call from Blue McCoy," she said in her breathy Southern accent. "I'm here to see him."

Travis nodded. "Right this way, ma'am."

As Lucy watched, Jenny turned back to Annabella, who was sitting at the dispatcher's desk. "My lawyer should be arriving soon. Will you please bring her back to us when she comes?"

Lucy watched as Jenny Lee Beaumont was ushered down the hall, toward the holding cells. Blue had called Jenny Lee. *Jenny's* lawyer was coming to help him. He trusted Jenny, not Lucy....

But Jenny didn't know that some—if not all—of the police officers on the Hatboro Creek force were involved in the cover-up of Gerry's death. And Jenny didn't know that R. W. Fisher had allegedly paid Matt Parker large sums of money to make up his story about seeing Blue in the woods with Gerry on the night of his death.

And Jenny didn't love Blue.

Lucy did.

And somehow Lucy was going to find Gerry's killer. Somehow she was going to prove Blue's innocence. Somehow she was going to prove to him that she *didn't* betray him.

Or she was going to die trying.

"Bail is set...for five-hundred-thousand dollars."

A murmur went through the courtroom. Half a million dollars. Lucy's stomach clenched. Where was Blue going to get half a million dollars?

"Can the defendant make bail?"

As Lucy watched, Blue turned and glanced at his lawyer,

who turned and looked back at Jenny Lee. Jenny shook her head. "Not at this time, Your Honor," the lawyer said. She stood up. "Your Honor, my client is a lieutenant in the U.S. Navy. A Navy attorney will be arriving sometime next week. May I suggest my client remain in custody in Hatboro Creek until that time?"

The judge shook his head. "Those facilities aren't adequate," he said. "The defendant will be transferred immediately to the correctional institution at Northgate."

Several armed guards approached Blue. He stood up and let them lead him away. He had to know Lucy was there, in the back of the room, but he didn't look up. He didn't even glance in her direction.

Blue hated Northgate prison. He hated the feeling of being locked up. He hated being stripped of his clothes and forced to wear ill-fitting blue jeans, and a white T-shirt, and sneakers on his feet. He particularly hated the sneakers.

He stood in the courtyard alone, watching from the corners of his eyes as a large group of men gathered, then approached him. They were clearly the prison's movers and shakers—among the inmates, they were the ones in charge. They surrounded him, their body language threatening.

He ignored them. It wasn't until one of the men got right in his face that Blue even looked up.

"You Popeye the sailor man?" the inmate asked, grinning at his own clever humor.

"No," Blue said. "I'm Blue McCoy, the Navy SEAL."

At least one person in the crowd knew what that meant, and as Blue stood there, a murmur spread from man to man. He couldn't hear the words, but he knew what was being said. A Navy SEAL. A snake eater. One of the toughest sons of bitches in the military.

Like magic, the crowd disappeared. No one wanted to pick a fight with a man they couldn't possibly beat.

Blue was almost disappointed. He could have used a good brawl to get this pain out of his system, this heartache of knowing that Lucy had used and then betrayed him.

She was so damn good—he hadn't suspected a thing. Her sunny smile had been genuine. Her kisses had been so sincere. How had she done it? How had she looked at him with all that emotion in her eyes without feeling a thing?

Blue wanted to be out of this prison. He wanted to be far away from South Carolina and Lucy Tait. Damn, he never wanted to see her again.

He wanted to take a sailboat out onto the ocean, out of sight of land, and just be one with the water and sky. He wanted to erase Lucy's face from his memory.

It wasn't going to happen.

He wanted to stop thinking about her, but she followed him everywhere, filling his mind, overwhelming him with her presence.

Why had she done it? How could she have done it? It didn't make sense. Did she really think he'd killed Gerry? Or worse, could she possibly be part of some conspiracy against him?

It didn't make sense.

It didn't make any sense at all.

He closed his eyes, and she was there, in his mind, arms crossed, mouth tight, glaring at him with barely concealed impatience.

"Why?" he asked, speaking the word aloud, causing some of the inmates to look curiously at him and then to move farther away.

Blue needed to know why. Of course, Lucy couldn't answer.

Lucy sat outside the gates of R. W. Fisher's plantation-style mansion, slumped in the front seat of Sarah's car.

She'd borrowed her friend's shiny black Honda because she knew her own battered truck would stand out on this well-manicured street like a sore thumb. She had also borrowed a microcassette recorder from Sarah's husband's office, and she'd dug up a pair of binoculars from her own attic.

The night was endlessly long. It was only 3:00 a.m. and she felt as if she'd been sitting out here for half an eternity instead of eight hours. She'd followed R. W. Fisher home from his office at a little after seven. He'd gone inside and hadn't come out since.

The binoculars weren't much use. The house was dark, and through the binoculars it was simply larger and dark.

The microcassette recorder wasn't much use, either. Lucy managed to amuse herself for about five minutes by recording her voice as she sang the latest country hits, and then playing back the tape. But since most of the popular songs were about heartache and love gone wrong, she quickly stopped.

She forced herself to stay awake by chewing some caffeinated gum that she'd picked up at a truck stop. She didn't dare drink any of the coffee she'd brought, for fear she'd have to leave her stakeout to find a bathroom.

The night was sticky and hot, but she didn't turn the car on and sit in air-conditioned comfort; she was afraid a neighbor would notice the running car engine and call the police.

The very same police who were somehow involved in a murderous plot with R. W. Fisher.

So Lucy just sat. And sweated. And wished that Blue hadn't been so quick to doubt her. She wondered if Northgate was as awful as she had heard. She wondered where Blue was, if he was sleeping or still awake. She prayed that he was safe.

At 5:57 a.m., Fisher's gate swung open. Lucy sat up straight, then scrunched down even farther in her seat to hide. Fisher appeared, driving a big, off-road vehicle with oversized tires. Lucy would have bet both her house and the computer software company she owned in Charleston that the tread on those big tires was nearly brand-new. And she would have gone double or nothing on those tires being the same ones that had left those tracks Blue found in the woods near where Gerry's body was discovered.

As she watched, Fisher turned to the right out of his driveway and moved swiftly down the street.

She started Sarah's car, waiting until he was some distance away before pulling out after him.

He didn't go far. He made a right into the parking lot of the middle school and stopped.

Lucy drove past without even braking, but quickly pulled off the road several hundred yards farther down. She grabbed the microcassette recorder—just in case—and scrambled out of the car, backtracking on foot through the woods.

Fisher stood near his truck, one foot on the bumper as he tightened the laces of his sneakers. He was wearing running shorts and a T-shirt, and for someone pushing seventy, he was in outrageously good shape.

He did several more stretches, adjusted his headphones and Walkman, then started running along the edge of the middle-school playing field. Lucy followed, running a parallel course through some impossibly dense woods.

He was in *hideously* good shape, she realized when she was out of breath after only a short distance. Of course, Fisher wasn't running in long jeans and cowboy boots, leaping over roots and rocks and getting smacked in the face with tree branches and vines. She saw that she was losing him and she pushed herself harder, faster.

He reached the corner edge of the field and took a trail

that led into the woods. He slowed his pace slightly, but not much.

Lucy was glad for the headphones Fisher was wearing, glad he couldn't hear her. She was making more noise than a herd of wild elephants. She remembered the way Blue had been able to run silently through the woods. And tirelessly, too. As a particularly thick branch smacked her square in the forehead, she wished that he were there with her. But he wasn't. If she wanted to keep up with Fisher, she was going to have to do it on her own.

You gotta want it badly enough. The words of Blue's SEAL training instructor flashed in her mind. She did. She wanted it. Badly. She wanted a happy ending to this nightmare. She wanted to find the proof that would free Blue from jail. She wanted him to walk out of the county prison and into her arms. And as long as she was making up happy endings, she wanted him to kiss her and tell her that he loved her. She wanted to marry him and live happily ever after.

God, she was stupid. It wasn't going to happen that way. Even if she didn't get herself killed, even if she succeeded in getting Blue out of jail, he was going to ride off into the sunset with perfect, pink, frilly Jenny Lee Beaumont.

Lucy cursed as she tripped over a root and fell, tearing a hole in the knee of her jeans. She ignored the pain, ignored the scrape and the blood, and picked herself up and ran.

R. W. Fisher was way ahead of her along the trail.

Of course, if Fisher really was just out for a morning run, Lucy was going to feel pretty idiotic. She was praying that he was meeting someone, praying that something would happen to—

Lucy stopped suddenly, dropping down into the underbrush.

Fisher had stopped running. He stood now in the middle of the trail, catching his breath, headphones off, leaning against a huge boulder. He hadn't heard or seen her, thank God.

Slowly, carefully, trying her hardest not to make a sound, Lucy crept forward.

Please, she was praying in rhythm with her pounding heart. Please, please, please, please, let him be meeting someone, please, please, please....

Then she heard it. The sound of a dirt bike coming along the trail. She used the cover of its engine to creep even closer and to take out the microcassette recorder.

But then Lucy realized it was not one dirt bike she'd heard but two. The riders braked to a stop and cut the engines. They were both wearing helmets, and as she watched, they pulled them off.

Travis Southeby. And... Frank Redfield? Oh, my God, if kind, gentlemanly Frank was involved in this, maybe Tom Harper was, also. And Chief Bradley—why not him, too?

"What are we going to do about McCoy?" Fisher asked. His voice carried clearly to Lucy. She quickly switched on the recorder and pushed the microphone level up to high. Fisher shook his head in disbelief. "Jesus, didn't I just ask that same question a week ago? Didn't we just have this conversation?"

"This time it's a different McCoy," Travis said. "But I don't think we have a problem, Mr. Fisher. Blue McCoy is in Northgate prison, and he's gonna stay there. There's no way in hell he can make that bail."

"Seems he's got some special Navy lawyer flying in," Fisher said. "When I heard about that, I came very close to calling New York and—"

"Snake doesn't want to get involved," Travis said. "He did his bit—"

"By breaking Gerry's neck?" scoffed Fisher. "He should've

made it look like some kind of accident. But a broken neck…? That was asinine."

"Blue was easy to frame," Travis said. "He'll take the fall."

"But what about this Navy lawyer?"

"It's not a problem," Frank interjected. "McCoy is up at Northgate, right? There's going to be a fight in the cafeteria at noon. Blue McCoy is not going to survive. I can guarantee it."

Lucy stopped breathing. Blue McCoy was not going to survive? Not as long as she was alive and kicking.

Fisher nodded, his well-lined face looking suddenly tired and old. "All right."

"What *I'm* interested in knowing is how you plan to fill the gap that Gerry's death left," Travis said. "How the *hell* are we going to get that money into the system and back to New York by the syndicate's deadline?"

"Matt Parker," Fisher said. "He's been willing to help up until now. I'm sure he'll be happy to continue our relationship. I'll arrange a loan with the bank. Nothing that draws attention in our direction, of course. But it'll enable Matt to purchase a suitable business—maybe even McCoy's construction company. Construction was the perfect way to launder the money."

"Too bad Gerry chickened out," Travis said.

New York syndicate. Launder money. My God, that was what this was all about. Someone named "Snake," probably from that same New York syndicate, had broken Gerry's neck because Gerry hadn't wanted to play along.

"We'll be rich yet, gentlemen," Frank said, putting his helmet back on. "Next year at this time, we'll be rolling in money."

Lucy lay hidden in the underbrush long after the dirt bikes had pulled away, long after Fisher had run back down the trail. She wasn't sure exactly where she'd be next year at this time, but she knew one thing for certain. R. W. Fisher and Frank Redfield and Travis Southeby and anyone else involved in Gerry's murder were going to be in jail.

Even if she had to put them there herself.

Chapter Fifteen

Lucy ran back toward Sarah's car, faster even than she'd run while following R. W. Fisher.

According to her watch, it was nearly six forty-five. She had to get up to Northgate by ten-thirty for morning visiting hours to warn Blue that he was in danger. It was about an hour's drive, but that was okay. She could make it.

Of course, once she got there, there was no guarantee that Blue would see her.

She was drenched with sweat and covered with burrs and dirt as she climbed into the car. She started the engine with a roar and headed quickly for home.

She had to call someone. Say what she'd overheard—what she'd gotten on tape.

She couldn't call the local police. They were involved. She knew that for sure. How about the state troopers? Hell, there was no guarantee *they* weren't in on the deal. And the local federal agents? Shoot, she was so paranoid now she was afraid to call anyone.

Lucy pulled into her driveway with a spray of gravel. She ran up her porch steps and quickly unlocked her kitchen door, then closed it behind her.

Think. She had to think.

She picked up the phone, then hung it back up. Then, with a sudden burst of inspiration, she picked the phone back up and pushed the redial button. She closed her eyes and prayed that Blue had been the last person to use the phone and that the last call he'd made had been to SEAL Team Ten's headquarters in California.

It was ringing. Wherever she'd dialed, it was ringing. She could only hope it wasn't ringing in the local pizzeria.

"Night shift," said a deep voice on the other end of the phone.

My God, of course, it was three hours earlier in California. Out there, it was five o'clock in the morning.

"Who's this?" she asked.

There was a pause. "Who's this?" came the wary reply.

Lucy took a deep breath and a big chance. "My name is Lucy Tait, and I'm a friend of Blue McCoy's," she said. "He's in big trouble, and I need to speak to Joe Cat right away."

Another pause, then, "Where are you calling from, ma'am?" the voice asked.

"Hatboro Creek, South Carolina," she said.

"Can you be more specific about this 'trouble' you say Lieutenant McCoy is in?"

"Who is this, please? I can't say more until I know who I'm talking to."

There was another brief silence, then, "My name is Daryl Becker," the voice said. "Blue calls me 'Harvard.'"

Harvard. She'd heard that name before. "You went through BUD/S with Blue and Joe Cat," she said.

"How do you know that?" he asked suspiciously.

"Blue told me."

"We talking about the same Blue McCoy?" Harvard

asked. "The Blue McCoy who hasn't said more than three full sentences in his entire life?"

"He talks to me," Lucy said. "Please, you've got to help. I need to speak with Joe Cat."

"It's 0500 here on the West Coast," Harvard said. "We just got back last night after several weeks away. Joe is with his lady tonight."

"Veronica," Lucy said.

Harvard laughed. "If you know about her, Blue *has* been yapping his mouth off. You must be special, Lucy Tait."

"No, just a friend."

"I'm his friend, too," Harvard said. "So tell me what's going on."

Lucy did, telling him everything from the money-laundering scheme to Gerry's murder, the charges against Blue and the impending murder attempt at Northgate prison. Afterward, Harvard was silent.

"Damn," he said. "When that redneck white boy gets in trouble, he gets in *big* trouble, doesn't he?"

"I need help," Lucy said. "I can't do this on my own, but I don't know who to call. I need to know who I can trust."

"Okay, Lucy Tait," Harvard said. "This one is too big for me, too. Lay your telephone number on me. I'll risk certain death by calling Cat and waking him from his blissful slumber. He'll know what to do. I'll have him call you right back."

"Thank you," Lucy said, giving him her number.

She hung up the phone and opened the refrigerator, pouring herself a glass of orange juice as she tried not to watch the clock. God, she was a mess. She was soaked with sweat and dirt, her hair straggly and stringy, her knee still bleeding through the hole in her torn jeans.

Three minutes and forty seconds after she hung up from Harvard, the telephone rang.

Lucy scooped it up. "Yes?"

"Lucy? This is Joe Catalanotto from Alpha Squad."

Lucy closed her eyes. "Thank God."

"Look, Lucy, Harvard filled me in on what's happening out there. I've already called the admiral and arranged for emergency leave. I'm on my way, but it's going to take too long to get there, you hear what I'm saying?" Joe Cat's voice was pure urban New York. It was deep and rich and filled with the confidence of a Navy SEAL commander. "Ronnie is gonna get in touch with Kevin Laughton, a FInCOM— Federal Intelligence Commission—agent I trust...works out of D.C. He'll send someone out to Hatboro Creek— someone you can trust with that tape of yours."

Ronnie? Veronica. Of course. His wife.

"What I want you to do," Joe continued, "is go out to wherever Blue is being held and tell him about this noon assassination attempt. Do whatever you need to do, Lucy, to get him out of that prison."

Lucy took a deep breath. "You want me to tunnel him out of there?"

Joe laughed. He had a deep, husky laugh. "If you have to, yeah. Do whatever it takes. Just don't get Blue or yourself killed."

Before Joe hung up, he gave her his home phone number, the SEAL Team Ten headquarters number, and Kevin Laughton's, the FInCOM agent's, number. Just in case.

Lucy hung up the phone.

Do whatever it takes. Whatever it takes. Whatever.

She picked up the phone and dialed Sarah's number. She knew she was going to wake her friend up.

"'Lo?" Sarah answered sleepily.

"It's me," Lucy said. "How much money do you have in your savings account?"

Lucy worked quickly. She dug out the files for both her house and her business from her home office. She found the title for her truck. She gathered her savings-deposit passbooks and uncovered her checkbook from her dresser.

She searched the Charleston Yellow Pages, making phone call after phone call until she found exactly the right type of entrepreneur she needed. She gave him directions to Hatboro Creek and made him promise to arrive no later than 9:00 a.m., when the local bank opened.

She made a copy of the microcassette, using her telephone answering machine to play the miniature tape and holding the microcassette recorder above the speaker. The quality of the tape was going to stink, but she didn't care. As long as the words were faintly audible and the voices were identifiable. She stashed one of the tapes in the kitchen utensil drawer for safekeeping.

At 8:57 a.m. she climbed into Sarah's car and headed downtown.

Sarah was standing on the sidewalk in front of the bank. Lucy parked and got out of the car.

"I can't believe I let you talk me into this," Sarah said worriedly. "It's the thirty-thousand dollars Richard was intending to spend to modernize his office."

"You'll get it back," Lucy said, hoping she was telling her friend the truth. "I can't tell you how much I appreciate this. Your money pushes me over the top."

"I had no idea you had that much," Sarah said.

"It's mostly tied up in the business," Lucy said. "Look, before I forget, I hid a tape in my kitchen, in the utensil drawer. If anything happens to me—"

"Oh, God, don't say that."

"It's important," Lucy said. "On my bulletin board is a phone number of a federal agent named Kevin Laughton. Make sure he gets the tape."

"The tape from the utensil drawer." Sarah nodded. "Why the utensil drawer?"

"I was going to hide it in the toaster, but then I thought, what if someone comes in and wants some toast...."

Lucy looked up as a heavy man in a business suit and an incredibly obvious toupee approached them. It had to be Benjamin Robinson, the man she'd found in the Yellow Pages. It *had* to be.

"Ms. Tait?" the man said, looking questioningly from Sarah to Lucy.

Lucy held out her hand. "Mr. Robinson," she said. "I'm Lucy Tait. Shall we go into the bank and get down to business?"

A skinny man stopped near Blue in the prison courtyard during the morning exercise period. He lit a cigarette with hands that shook and stared up at the sky.

"You gonna be snuffed," he said.

It took a moment before Blue realized the man was talking to *him*. He looked away from the man, down at the ground at his uncomfortable sneakers, as the meaning of what he'd said sank in. Snuffed. Killed. "When?"

"Lunch," the man replied.

That soon. Blue felt the familiar surge of adrenaline as his body prepared for a fight. "How many?"

"Too many. Even if you fight back, they gonna get you. If you don't show up at lunch, they do you at dinner."

"How many?" Blue asked again. There was no such thing as too many. He just had to know in advance so he could plan, strategize against an attack.

"There's thirty of 'em, bubba. All hard timers."

Thirty. God. Not impossible, but not good odds, either.

"They gonna get you," the man said.

Thirty. This was gonna be a tough one. This guy was quite possibly right. "Why tell me about it, then?"

"I'm telling you because if it was me gonna die, I'd want to know." The man flicked ash from his cigarette, still not looking at Blue. "Write a will," he said. "Make peace with whichever God it is you believe in. Or get on line for the telephone—call your girl and tell her you love her." He started to walk away. "Tie up loose ends."

Get on line for the telephone. Lord, if only he could. But Blue didn't have telephone privileges yet. Not for another week. And according to the skinny inmate, Blue wasn't going to live that long.

Blue went inside the main building to the library.

"I'd like a pen and a piece of paper, please," Blue said to the burly inmate who was acting as librarian.

Silently the man laid both on the counter. Blue could see reflections of his imminent death in the silence of the man's eyes.

"Thanks," Blue told him, but the inmate said nothing, as if Blue were already dead. The pen was attached to the counter by a chain so no one could steal it and turn it into some kind of weapon. He stood there, lifted the pen and held it poised over the paper.

Damn. This was going to be harder to write than he'd thought.

He started it off easily enough: "Dear Lucy." But after that it got much harder.

He didn't have time for it to be hard. He didn't have time for it to come out perfectly. He knew what he wanted to say, so he just had to say it. He wrote, trying hard to print legibly.

I've had a lot of time to think over the past twenty-four hours, and every time I try to fit you into this puzzle of who killed Gerry, the picture comes out looking all wrong. Whenever I think of you going to the police station, intending to deliver information that would strengthen their case against me, I just can't believe it.

I've been thinking about Travis Southeby, about the way he stood up against me at the Grill, about the way he took such pleasure in telling me you had turned me in. At first I accused him of playing head games with me, and now I can't help but believe that he was indeed messing with my mind. I believed Tom Harper when he said you'd been to the police station, but what if he was lying, too? Or what if you'd been there, but for some other reason entirely?

I guess it all boils down to the fact that I don't want to believe them. I won't believe them. But I'm afraid it's too late. I'm afraid they already won.

It kills me I didn't see you when I had the chance. I'm not sure I'll have that chance again, because someone in here wants me dead—probably so that I won't be able to prove my innocence and open up the question of who really killed Gerry.

Maybe I'm a fool, and maybe you're involved with these murderers. But I don't want to believe that. I'm not going to believe that. If I'm going to die, I'd rather die loving you.

Blue took a deep breath, then plunged on.

I've never said these words to anyone ever in my life, let alone written them down, but somehow over the past few days, I fell in love with you, Yankee.

I thought you should know.

He started to sign the letter "Carter," but crossed it out and wrote in "Blue."

He folded the letter in thirds and pushed the pen back toward the librarian, who again said nothing. He asked for an envelope and a stamp, and the librarian pointed silently down the hall toward the tiny room that served as the mail drop-off and pick-up point.

While Blue was there, several guards came in. They rattled off a series of numbers. It took him a moment to realize they were ID numbers—*his* ID numbers. They were looking for him.

"You're wanted in the warden's office," they said as he dropped his letter into the mail slot.

Was it possible the warden had somehow found out about the death threat? Was he going to put Blue into solitary until the danger passed? It was a long walk to the warden's office near the front gate of the prison, and Blue had plenty of time to speculate.

But when the guard opened the office door and Blue walked inside, the warden's words surprised him.

"Your bail has been made," the man said. "Sign the paperwork, change your clothes and you're free to go."

His bail had been made. Half a million dollars. Who the hell had come up with half a million dollars just like that? And just in time, too.

The clock on the warden's wall read 11:10. In twenty minutes, the inmates would be lining up to go in for lunch. In twenty minutes thirty men would be looking for him, ready to snuff out his life. But he wouldn't be there. He wasn't going to be forced to fight with thirty-to-one odds. Relief flooded through him, hot and thick. He wasn't going to die today. At least not before lunch.

"Who posted bail?" he asked.

"Does it really matter?"

Blue shook his head. "No."

He quickly changed his clothes, strapping his belt back on. They hadn't found the knife hidden inside the buckle. That was good. Maybe his luck was starting to change.

The guards led him down the hallway to a locked gate. He went through it, then down another corridor toward another locked gate. He could see someone standing on the other side of the thick security wire. As he got closer, he realized exactly who was standing there, waiting for him.

Lucy. God, it was Lucy. His luck was definitely changing.

Her face was wary, as if she wasn't sure of her reception. She held his gaze, though, searching his eyes as the guard unlocked this final barrier.

And then he was free. He was outside the prison, in the visitors' waiting area.

"*You* paid my bail?" he asked. It wasn't what he really wanted to say to her, but it was better than just standing there, staring.

She nodded.

"Where the hell did you get half a million dollars?"

Lucy nervously moistened her lips and shrugged, giving him only a ghost of her regular smile. "Remember that computer software business I own?" she said. "Business has been extremely good lately."

"But you couldn't have had that much cash…."

She shook her head. "No, it's almost all tied up in the working capital. I used the business as collateral, along with some other things and some borrowed money, and…" She shrugged again. "I didn't have anything to do with your arrest, Blue," she said, her voice fast and low. "I mean, I was there at the station, getting my gun from my locker, and Bradley asked me a question, and I answered it as best as I could and all of a sudden Travis Southeby had a warrant for your arrest. I didn't…I wasn't…" There were tears in her eyes, but still she held his gaze, silently begging him to believe her.

"It's required by law that I escort you to the front gate," the guard told Blue.

He ignored the guard and took a step toward Lucy. "I know," he said.

She wiped at her tears with the heels of her hands, refusing to cry. "You do?"

"Yeah," he said. He wanted to pull her into his arms, but he was oddly nervous. He was in love with this woman. Somehow knowing that changed everything. He was afraid to touch her, afraid of giving himself away. Sure, he'd just written his deepest feelings in a letter, but there was no way he could say any of that aloud. "It took me a while, but I finally figured it out. Lucy, I'm sorry—"

"Come on, folks," the guard said impatiently. "Save the teary reunion for outside the gate."

Lucy turned to face the guard, her chin held high, her eyes blazing. "I just paid half a million dollars so this man could walk out of here with me—and we're going to walk out of here on our own good time, when *we* want to, and not one minute before. Thank you very much."

Blue felt himself smile for the first time in what seemed like centuries. "I think I'm ready to leave," he told her.

The guard escorted them to the door, and then they were out in the humid air and finally outside the gate.

Freedom.

"Was it awful?" Lucy asked quietly.

"It's over," Blue said.

Their eyes met, but only briefly, only for an instant, before Lucy looked down, and Blue knew with a deadly certainty that if he reached for her, she would pull away.

When he'd first seen her standing and waiting for him on the other side of that gate, when he'd realized that *she* was the one who'd paid his bail, he thought for a moment that it had to be proof that she loved him. What woman would risk everything she owned for a man she didn't love?

But then he remembered her friend Edgar. Lucy had only been friends with Edgar, yet she had sacrificed much to be with him in his last few months.

Her loyalty to her friends was clearly unswerving. But Blue didn't want to be only her friend any longer. He wanted more, God help him. He wanted more, but the fact that he'd lost his faith in her just might have destroyed whatever fragile love she was starting to feel for him.

Blue had to reach for her; he had to try. But before he could, Lucy started walking, heading toward the parking lot and her truck.

"Matt Parker's wife told me R. W. Fisher was paying Matt lots of money to say he saw you in the woods with Gerry," Lucy told him.

R. W. Fisher?

"She also said that some of the men in the police force were involved," she continued.

Blue knew that. He'd had a gut feeling about that right from day one.

"So I followed Fisher, and sure enough, he met with Travis Southeby and Frank Redfield," Lucy told him. "I have their conversation on tape. They're involved with some kind of money-laundering scheme set up by an organized-crime syndicate from New York. The way I figure it, the mob gives them money and they inflate the income of their businesses, take a cut high enough to pay the higher taxes and then some, and give the rest back. Gerry was involved up to some point. My guess is he went along with it for a while, using his construction business to get a lot of the mob's dirty money back into circulation. But he probably started feeling guilty and wanted out. When he made noise, they killed him. The mob sent some guy named Snake down to do the deed."

Blue was astonished. "Shoot, you've been busy."

"There's more," she said. The dust from the parking lot coated her boots, and she stopped to face Blue, wiping the dulled leather on the back of her pant legs. "Alpha Squad is back from their training exercises. I spoke to Joe Cat. He's on his way. In the meantime Veronica contacted somebody named Kevin Laughton over at FInCOM. It's just a matter of time until the FInCOM agents get out here."

Blue had to laugh. "You did all that *and* raised the money to pay my bail?"

Lucy nodded. She started walking again. Her truck was down at the end of a row of parked cars. "All we need to do now is find someplace safe to hide until the FInCOM agents arrive."

Blue stopped suddenly and grabbed Lucy's arm. "Someone is hiding behind your truck," he said in a low voice.

Lucy went for her gun, but she wasn't fast enough.

Travis Southeby stood up, aiming his gun directly at Blue. "Don't move an inch," he warned Lucy, "or I'll put a hole in him."

"Let him shoot me," Blue told her, his eyes never leaving Travis. "Then plug the son of a bitch between the eyes. I know you can do it. You told me you were a good shot."

"I'll kill him," Travis said. His voice was high, his hands shaking slightly, his florid face tense. "Slowly put your hands in the air."

Lucy did. "I can't risk it," she whispered to Blue.

Travis held his gun on Blue as he came toward them and quickly took Lucy's gun from under her jacket, from her shoulder holster.

"Damn," Travis said. "I couldn't believe it when the warden's assistant called and told me that Blue McCoy had made bail. Half a million dollars." He looked at Lucy, using the back of one hand to wipe his perspiring forehead. "What the hell were you doing working on the police force with that kind of money in your bank account?"

"What the hell are *you* doing on the police force with your kind of morals?" Lucy responded tightly.

Travis just handed Lucy a set of keys. "My car is right here, next to yours," he said. "Get in."

Blue took the keys from Lucy's hand. "I'll drive," he said. "She doesn't need to come along."

"I'm afraid she does," Travis said. He was being very careful to stay at least an arm's length away from Blue. He knew if he got close enough, Blue would try for him, regardless of the weapon Travis held. He aimed his gun at Blue's head. "Get in the car, or so help me God, I'll drop both of you right here and right now."

Lucy's heart was pounding. She knew that Blue didn't want to get into that car. She knew he wanted to stay right there, out in the open of the parking lot. She knew he was just waiting for the right opportunity to go for Travis. She knew if Blue had been the one carrying a gun, he would have jumped Travis when he got close enough. But Lucy couldn't ignore the fact that Travis's own gun was aimed steadily at Blue.

Blue had his thumbs hooked in his belt, one hand resting on his buckle. His eyes flicked to Lucy for half a second. "Do what he says," he told her softly. "Get in the car." He reached out, the car keys held flatly in the palm of his hand. "Please."

Whatever Blue was planning to do, he wasn't going to do it until Lucy was at least somewhat removed from the scene. Whatever he was planning to do, the fact remained that Travis had a gun and Blue didn't. If someone was going to get hurt or killed, it was likely to be Blue.

Lucy took the keys from him, letting her fingers linger in the warmth of his hand, well aware that this moment could be the last time she touched him.

And suddenly all of her doubts about exactly what their relationship was, all of her doubts about Jenny Lee, all of her fears that given the choice between the two of them Blue would choose Jenny, all of that ceased to matter. Nothing mattered but the way Lucy felt.

Blue looked at her again, just briefly, sending a silent message with his eyes. But the message that she wanted to give him in return, the words she wanted him to hear, were not ones she could trust to be conveyed through a single look.

"I love you," she breathed.

Blue looked back at her, his eyes betraying his surprise.

She turned and climbed into Travis's car.

Blue forced his eyes away from Lucy, back toward Travis and his gun. She loved him. Lucy *loved* him. She was his friend, but she also loved him.

Blue knew that if he could just make it past the next few minutes, he was going to have a real honest-to-God shot at living happily every after. Lucy loved him and he sure as hell loved her.

This was what Joe Cat and Veronica had found. This was why Cat had been nearly insane with worry when terrorists had hijacked the cruise ship Veronica had been on. Blue stared into the little black barrel of Travis's gun, silently willing the man to keep that gun aimed right at him. If he turned and aimed that thing at Lucy, Blue wouldn't be able to fight back. He wouldn't be able to risk it.

And he'd just about worked his knife free from his belt buckle....

"You get in now," Travis said to Blue, gesturing to the car with his head. "We're gonna go for a ride."

Blue didn't move. At least not his feet. "I don't think so," he said. "You're gonna have to shoot me. And then, when your gun is empty, I'm gonna walk over there and snap your neck the same way Gerry was killed. Don't worry—it doesn't hurt. I imagine the last thing you'll hear is your bone cracking. It's probably powerfully loud. But only for an instant."

Sweat was rolling off Travis now and his hands shook even harder. "I said, get in the car."

Inside the car, Lucy could see Blue, his hands still resting clearly in Travis's view, thumbs looped around his belt and...

Blue's belt. Blue was working to get his knife free. As Lucy watched in the rearview mirror, she saw Blue put his hands down at his sides, and she knew he'd somehow palmed the knife.

God, a knife against a gun. She had to do something to put the odds more in Blue's favor, and she had to do it now.

Blue moved toward the car, waiting for the perfect moment to strike. He had Travis shaken up. He just needed some kind of distraction and...

Lucy started Travis's car with a roar. Startled, Travis looked away from Blue.

It was only for a split second, but Blue didn't hesitate. He threw with unerring accuracy, and Travis fell with a scream, his gun bouncing on the dirt parking lot as he grabbed his wounded leg. Blue grabbed the gun, holding the barrel under Travis's chin as he took Lucy's gun from the man's pocket.

The knife was buried up to its hilt in Travis's thigh.

"You're still going to die," Travis hissed at Blue.

"I wouldn't pull that knife out if I were you," Blue told him. "At least not until you get to the hospital. I aimed for a major artery. If you pull that out yourself, you'll bleed to death in about two minutes."

Travis's pale face got even paler.

"Get in," Lucy said urgently to Blue. "Fisher's truck just pulled into the parking lot."

As if to punctuate her words, a shot rang out, and the rear windshield of Lucy's truck shattered.

"At least they have lousy aim," Blue said, throwing open the back door of Travis's car and climbing in behind Lucy.

Lucy pulled out of the parking lot with a squeal of tires as Blue climbed over the seat back into the front. She glanced at him. "I'm surprised you didn't kill Travis," she said.

"Are you kidding?" Blue said. "And miss seeing him stand trial for Gerry's murder?" He turned around, squinting to get a better view of the truck that was chasing them.

It was a monster truck, with big, oversize tires. It looked as if Fisher himself was driving. But someone else was next to him, riding shotgun. Literally.

"What if he bleeds to death?" Lucy asked about Travis.

"He won't," Blue said. "I was messing with his head when I told him I hit him in an artery. That was total bull. I was trying to immobilize him."

Another shot rang out, but as far as Blue could tell, it didn't hit Travis's car. Lucy pushed the car even faster, but the truck kept up. Easily.

Blue turned around, quickly scanning the interior of the car they were in. It was an upscale foreign car with a big engine, loaded with all the extra features. Travis even had a car phone built into the hump between the two front seats.

They were heading north on Philips Road. Lucy was taking the curves faster than she should and the tires squealed and moaned. Blue tried to visualize exactly where they were. Philips Road intersected with Route 17 not far from Northgate prison. And somewhere west off Route 17, between Philips Road and the turnoff to Hatboro Creek, was the local television station where Jenny Lee worked. Bingo. Blue picked up the car phone. He had a plan.

He glanced back at the truck just as the rear windshield shattered. The shooter had put a scope on his rifle. They were in trouble now.

"Faster," he said to Lucy. "And keep your head down."

"I can't do both," she said tightly.

"You have to," he said.

"Shouldn't you be shooting back at them?" Lucy asked.

Blue shook his head. "Handguns don't have the same range as a hunting rifle. It'd be a waste of bullets."

"Blue, I can't take this road any faster!" There was more than a touch of panic in her voice.

He put down the phone and drew Travis's gun instead, then braced his arms on the back of the seat. "Hit the brakes," he said to Lucy. "Now."

She looked at him in shock. "What...?"

He raised his voice. "Do it!"

She did. The car slowed, shuddering slightly, and the truck roared into range.

"Drive!" Blue shouted, emptying the magazine of the gun in rapid succession. He saw the truck's front windshield shatter, saw the telltale spray of red on the back windshield, and he knew someone had been hit.

If it was the driver, he hadn't been killed. As Blue watched, the truck pulled over to the side of the road and came to a stop. Lucy was watching, too, in the rearview mirror. "Keep going," Blue said to her. "As fast as you can."

"They stopped," she protested.

"That doesn't mean they can't start after us again," he said.

Several minutes passed in tense silence as Lucy drove as fast as she dared and Blue watched out the back for any sign of the truck. They were going up a small hill, and bits and pieces of the road behind could be seen in the valley below. He caught a glimpse of the monster truck, back on the road, still following them.

Lucy swore like a sailor when he told her. She glanced at the speedometer, pushing the car even faster, but otherwise didn't take her eyes off the road. "We're coming up on Route 17. Which way?"

"West."

Blue picked up the car phone again, dialing a number he obviously had memorized.

"Who are you calling?" Lucy asked.

"Jenny Lee."

Lucy felt herself grow very, very still. Jenny Lee. Blue was using the car phone to call Jenny Lee. She shouldn't have been surprised, but somehow, foolishly, she was. She was surprised and hurt. God, it was shocking how much it hurt. She'd anticipated this scenario. She'd been prepared for it. Or so she'd thought.

Somehow Lucy managed to keep on driving. Somehow she made the turnoff west onto Route 17. She had told Blue that she loved him, and he didn't even have the decency to wait until they were out of danger before he called Jenny. Maybe that was what hurt the most.

"Jenny Lee Beaumont, please," Blue told the receptionist, then waited while his call was connected.

Lucy was really able to open up out on the state road. She pushed Travis's car faster, listening to the rush of the tires on the road, trying not to listen to Blue talk to Jenny Lee. But it was hard not to overhear him.

"Remember when you came to the jail and I told you to be ready for me?" Blue said to Jenny. "Well, I'm on my way." There was a pause, then he said. "Ten minutes." Another pause. "Right." Then he hung up.

He turned to Lucy. "You know where the turnoff is to the television station?"

She nodded. She knew.

He looked at her closely. "You all right?"

Lucy nodded. "I'm fine." She glanced at him. He really didn't have a clue. He was gazing at her, concern in his eyes, puzzlement on his face. "Considering people who want to kill us are chasing us in a truck that can probably go a lot faster than this car," she added.

Blue turned around, looking out the broken rear window. "I winged one of them," he said.

"I thought you were supposed to be a sharpshooter," she said.

He turned to her again, and she could feel him studying her face. She held her jaw firmly, her mouth tightly, her eyes carefully on the road.

"I am," he finally said. "Travis's gun really sucks. I didn't have time to figure out which way it pulled. I didn't have time to compensate."

Blue turned around to watch out the rear window. Several more miles sped by with only the sound of the wind whistling across the broken window, breaking the silence.

"This is almost over," Blue finally said.

Lucy nodded. They were almost at the station. What he intended to do there, she didn't have a clue. She was afraid to ask. Maybe Blue planned to take Jenny Lee and escape in the television station's helicopter. After all, he was a Navy SEAL. He could fly a helicopter, no problem. Or maybe he intended to hole up in Jenny's office, using Lucy's gun to keep Fisher and whoever was with him in the truck—probably Frank Redfield—at bay until the authorities made the scene.

But maybe Blue wasn't talking about the danger they were in. Maybe he was talking about his relationship with Lucy. And it was true. It was almost over. If Blue was planning to be with Jenny from now on, there was no way his friendship with Lucy could continue on the way it had.

Blue swore, suddenly and loudly, and Lucy glanced up. The monster truck had reappeared in the rearview mirror. It was growing larger by the second, gaining on them.

Lucy could see the turnoff that led to the television station up ahead.

They weren't going to make it. Lucy could see the hazy sunlight glinting off the barrel of the hunting rifle as she glanced again in the rearview mirror.

"Get down!" Blue shouted, and she ducked. A shot rang out and Blue cursed.

Oh, my God. Blue was hit. The windshield had been sprayed with his blood. Somehow Blue wiped a clear swatch with his hand.

It was his arm. He'd been shot in the arm and he was bleeding.

"Blue," Lucy said. "Oh, God, Blue...."

Another shot rang out and the windshield broke, spider-webbing. Again Blue was there, kicking it out so that she could see.

"Your arm," she gasped, the force of the wind in her face taking her breath away.

"I'm fine," he said, his voice still soft and calm as he quickly ripped the tail off his shirt and tied it around his arm to stop the bleeding. "It's nothing. Just messy, that's all. Come on, Yankee. Here comes the turnoff. Don't slow— just take it."

Lucy pulled the wheel hard to the right and they skidded around the corner. It took a moment for their tires to get traction, but then they were off again, doing eighty down a road with a fifteen-mile-an-hour limit.

At the first speed bump they nearly launched into the air.

The truck was right behind them, and it bounced up and almost on top of them.

But then they were in the parking lot, heading toward the main building.

Lucy could see a small crowd standing out in front. It looked like a television crew, complete with at least two cameras and a whole bunch of technicians. What the heck…?

"Don't hit the brakes until we're almost past them," Blue told her. "Then just get down and stay down, do you understand?"

Yes. Lucy understood. Suddenly she understood.

She saw Jenny Lee Beaumont, dressed in pink as usual, standing in front of the crowd, a microphone in her hand, reporting live from the front of the television station.

Lucy understood. If R. W. Fisher and Frank Redfield were going to kill Blue and Lucy, they were going to have to do it on live television.

It was perfect. It was so perfect she had to laugh. Blue had no doubt set this plan up with Jenny Lee. He had no doubt figured that the time would come when the people who killed Gerry would try for him, too. But no one in his right mind would commit murder in front of an audience of two-hundred-thousand-plus viewers.

She hit the brakes hard and felt the car go into a skid and then finally stop. She didn't get down quickly enough, and Blue pulled her down, covering her with his body.

Lucy could hear shouting. She could hear the squeal of tires as the monster truck did a quick U-turn out of the parking lot. She heard the drumming of helicopters overhead as the FInCOM agents made the scene and took off after the monster truck. Then she heard the quiet sound of Blue's breathing and the pounding of her heart.

Blue shifted slightly so that most of his weight was off her. Lucy turned her head and found herself looking directly into his eyes.

"You all right?" he asked quietly.

She nodded. "Are you?"

He nodded, too. "My arm was just nicked," he said. "It's nothing to worry about."

Their legs were still intertwined. That felt too intimate, too wrong. Or maybe it felt too right.

She looked up to see Jenny Lee peering in the window at them.

"Whoopsie," Jenny said. "We'll get this interview a little bit later. Sorry. Didn't mean to interrupt, Carter."

Lucy sat up, hitting her head on the steering wheel. Blue helped her up and into the driver's seat.

"I'm okay," she said, rubbing her head. "I'm all right. You can go. I'm fine."

"Go," Blue repeated. "Go where?"

Lucy forced herself to smile. "Go to Jenny," she said. "It's all right." But then she caught herself. What was she saying? "No, it's not all right," she realized. "In fact, it stinks. In fact, you're a jerk, and I don't even know what I saw in you in the first place—"

"Lucy, what the hell...?"

"Go ahead," she said, glaring at him. "Go spend the rest of your life with Jenny Lee. I hope you like lace doilies and little pink flowers, because your house is going to be covered with them."

Blue was confused as hell. "Why would I want to spend the rest of my life with Jenny?"

"Because you childishly imagine you're in love with her."

Blue had to laugh. "Lucy, did you hit your head harder than I thought?"

"No."

She wasn't kidding. There were actually tears in her eyes. She was mad at him. She was *serious*. Blue stopped laughing. Where the hell had she gotten this idea? He ran his fingers through his hair, and when he spoke it was slowly and calmly. "I'm not in love with Jenny Lee."

"My point exactly," she said hotly. "You only imagine you are."

"No, I don't. I—"

"Yes, you do," Lucy insisted. "And you know what's going to happen if you marry her? After six months, she's going to bore you to tears."

"Lucy, I'm not—"

"That is if you don't suffocate underneath all those little pink flowers first."

"Why," Blue said as clearly and distinctly as he possibly could, "would I want to marry Jenny Beaumont when I'm in love with you?"

Lucy was silenced. The silence continued for several very long moments.

"Excuse me?" she finally said.

"You heard me the first time, Yankee," Blue said quietly, dangerously. "Don't make me say it twice."

"But I want you to say it twice," she said. And then she smiled.

Her eyes glistened with tears, but her smile was pure sunshine, pure joy. When she smiled at him that way, Blue could refuse her nothing.

"I love you," he said, touching the side of her face, losing himself in her eyes. Hell, that was easier to say than he'd thought possible. So he tried saying something that was even more difficult. "I think you should marry me, Lucy."

Lucy felt her smile fade. Marry. Blue. My God. She'd never dreamed... Well, actually she *had* dreamed. But she'd imagined they were just that. Dreams.

Blue made an attempt at humor. "You need me to say that one again, too?"

Lucy shook her head. "No." Her throat was dry and she swallowed. "No, I heard you."

She could see uncertainty in his eyes.

"What do you think?" he asked.

He honestly didn't know what her answer would be. Lucy cleared her throat. "You mean, move to California?" she asked, stalling for time. Did he know what he was asking? Was he just caught up in the emotion of the moment? How could she know for sure?

Blue nodded. "That's where Alpha Squad is stationed these days." He searched her eyes. "I've got an apartment outside Coronado. It's kinda small—we could get something bigger...."

Lucy didn't speak. She couldn't speak. He seemed to have given this some thought. He seemed lucid and certain.

Blue mistook her silence for hesitation. "I know being married to a SEAL isn't always fun," he said quietly. "I'd be gone a lot—too often. But I swear to you, while I'm away, I'll be true. Other wives might wonder or worry, but you'd never have to, Lucy. And when I'm home, I'll do my best to make up for all the time I'm away—"

Lucy interrupted. "Are you sure?" She couldn't stand it any longer. She had to ask.

"It's always hard when you've gotta leave on a mission, but Joe Cat and Veronica are making it work and—"

"No, I mean, are you sure you want to marry *me?*"

Blue laughed in surprise. "I guess you really didn't hear me the first time—or the second time, either. I love you."

He cupped her chin in his hand, leaned forward and kissed her. His mouth was warm and sweet, his lips as soft as she remembered.

"It wasn't love at first sight," he told her in his black velvet Southern voice, kissing her again. "It took longer than that. I can't tell you when I knew for certain. All I know is little by little, bit by bit, I realized I want you next to me, Lucy. I realized that I love you. I want you wearing my ring, taking my name, having my babies. I want you to be my friend and my lover for the rest of our lives. So please, marry me."

Lucy's heart was in her throat, so she opened her mouth and gave it to Blue. "Yes," she said.

Blue smiled and kissed her.

Blue sat down next to Lucy on the porch swing. "I spoke to Joe Cat," he told her. "I caught him before his plane left Kansas City. As long as I'm out of trouble, he's just going to turn around and head back home to Veronica."

Lucy leaned back against him, looking out at the deepening twilight. He smelled sweet and clean from his shower. He'd shaved, too, and she rubbed her own cheek against the smoothness of his face.

"One of the FInCOM agents stopped by while you were getting cleaned up," she told him. "Travis signed a full confession. Apparently he *was* there—along with Fisher and Frank Redfield—on the night Gerry died."

Blue nodded, just waiting for her to tell him more.

"According to Travis," Lucy continued, "Gerry was involved with some kind of money-laundering scheme. R. W. Fisher apparently knew some mob boss from New York who convinced him Hatboro Creek was the perfect sleepy little town to launder drug money. Fisher got Gerry into the deal, along with the Southeby brothers and Frank Redfield. Everything was moving along smoothly until Gerry started going to Jenny Lee's church. When Gerry got God, his conscience started bothering him, and he told Fisher and the others he wanted out of the deal.

"They threatened him and he was running scared, trying to figure out what to do. When you showed up, Fisher was afraid Gerry would go to you for help, so he told Gerry if he as much as *spoke* to you, they'd bring this hired gun from New York—a man named 'Snake'—to kill *you*. Instead, Snake killed Gerry."

Blue swore quietly.

"Travis said that Gerry *wasn't* drunk that night. He was sober. The drunkenness *was* just an act. Gerry was trying to make you leave town."

"He was trying to protect me," Blue said.

Lucy nodded. "Yeah. All those awful things he said to you weren't true. He cared about you—he didn't want you to be hurt."

"I could've helped him," Blue said.

"I know."

They sat in silence for a moment, just listening to the sound of the crickets whirring and chirping in the early evening.

"I told Joe Cat about you," Blue said.

She turned and looked at him. "Really? What did you say?"

"That I fell in love with a friend of mine. He seemed to understand." Blue leaned forward and kissed her. It was a slow, deep, lazy kiss that promised forever—a sweet, dizzying happiness for all time.

"I can't wait to meet him," Lucy said, settling back against Blue again, shifting so that her head was in his lap, so she was gazing up at him. He pushed the swing and they rocked gently. "Tell me more about him. Tell me about all the guys in Alpha Squad, and about California...."

Blue smiled down at her as he began to talk.

Smiling into Lucy's eyes was easy. Telling her that he loved her was easy, too. Asking her to marry him had been a breeze. Kissing her and making love to her were as easy and as natural as breathing. But sitting here on the porch swing, swaying gently as the evening descended upon them, Blue knew that talking to Lucy—his friend, his lover, soon to be his wife—was easiest of all.

Epilogue

Lucy stood in the back room of the naval-base chapel as Sarah adjusted her veil.

"I feel stupid," Lucy grumbled. "What is this thing hanging in front of my face? Is it supposed to hide me? Do I look *that* hideous? Why do I have to wear this anyway?"

"Because it's traditional," Sarah said calmly. Nora, her baby, now three months old, smiled happily at Lucy from the backpack Sarah wore. "You look beautiful, and you know it."

"It's not very traditional for the bride to be given away by her best friend and her godchild," Lucy commented.

Sarah gazed at her for a moment, then took out the pins that held the veil in place and tossed both pins and veil aside. "Fair enough," she said.

"I wish I were wearing my jeans," Lucy said wistfully.

Sarah shook her head. "Nope," she said. "Nice try, but I draw the line at the veil. No way am I letting you march down that aisle in blue jeans."

"I just feel so…not me," Lucy said. The dress was cut low, off her shoulders, with tiny cap sleeves, a tailored bodice and a long, full skirt, complete with a train.

"You look incredible," Sarah said. Nora gurgled and chewed on her mother's hair in agreement.

The music started, and Sarah took Lucy's arm. "Come on." Sarah smiled. "Wait till you see what's waiting for you at the other end of this church."

Self-consciously, Lucy let Sarah lead her out into the church. And then she stopped feeling self-conscious at all. Because standing there in the front of the church was Blue. Next to him stood the six other members of Alpha Squad. All seven men were wearing white dress uniforms and the effect was nearly blinding.

Lucy's gaze ran across their now-familiar faces. Joe Cat's smile was genuine and warm, but he couldn't keep himself from glancing across the chapel to smile at his wife, Ronnie. Lucy's first impression of Ronnie had been that she was an ice queen—until Lucy had walked into the Outback Bar to find the usually proper, English-accented woman cutting loose, dirty-dancing with her handsome husband.

And then there was Harvard. Daryl Becker. Along with his Ivy League education, Harvard possessed a first-class sense of humor. His shaved head gleamed almost as much as the diamond he wore in his left ear.

Cowboy, Wesley and Bob all grinned at Lucy. Cowboy winked. He was the youngest member of the squad and he did his best to live up to his reputation as a hothead.

Lucky O'Donlon was smiling, too—and oh, my God, standing next to him was none other than Frisco. There weren't seven men up there—there were *eight*. Alan Francisco was standing with the rest of Alpha Squad. Blue had taken Lucy to meet him at the rehab center several months ago, and Frisco had been in a wheelchair. It had been years since he was injured, and all the doctors had sworn he would never walk again. But today he was *standing*. He had a cane, but he was standing. Lucy looked around, but she didn't see any sign of a wheelchair. Had he actually *walked* to the front of the church?

And Lucky—Frisco's best friend and swim buddy—looked happier than she'd ever seen him. The two men were almost the exact same height and build. Lucky's hair was blond, while Frisco's was darker, but other than that, even their faces were similar enough that they might have been brothers.

Except Frisco couldn't hide the lines of pain around his eyes. He may have been standing, but it was hurting him to do so.

"Thank you so much for coming, Alan," Lucy said to him, emotion breaking her voice.

Frisco nodded. "I wouldn't have missed it for anything," he said.

And then, suddenly they reached the front of the church. Sarah kissed her on the cheek, and then Lucy was face-to-face with Blue.

Blue McCoy.

He looked incredible in his white dress uniform. Lucy hadn't seen him dressed up since Gerry's funeral, and before that at the party at the country club. Today, like that night, she was wearing a dress that made her feel peculiar, as if she were masquerading as someone else.

But Blue looked different, too. His shining blond hair was perfectly combed, every wave and curl in place. The rows and rows of medals he wore on his chest were overwhelming. His uniform was so clean, so starched and stiff and gleaming white. He gazed, unsmiling, into her eyes.

Who was this stranger, this sailor she was marrying? For one heart-stopping moment, Lucy wasn't sure she knew.

Then she looked down and caught sight of Blue's feet.

He wasn't wearing dress shoes like the rest of Alpha Squad. He was wearing his old, familiar leather sandals.

He was wearing his sandals, and she was wearing her cotton underwear. It was fancier than usual, but it was cotton. She'd insisted. They both had their hair combed differently, and both of them were dressed differently, but deep down inside they knew exactly what they were getting—exactly *who* they were going to spend the rest of their lives with.

Lucy smiled.

Blue smiled, too. And then he kissed the bride.